INTO THE NO ZONE

Also available
THE SIGN OF ONE

INTO THE NO ZONE

EUGENE LAMBERT

First published in Great Britain in 2017 by Electric Monkey,
an imprint of Egmont UK Limited
The Yellow Building, 1 Nicholas Road, London W11 4AN

Text copyright © 2017 Eugene Lambert

The moral rights of the author have been asserted

ISBN 978 1 4052 7736 5

59775/1

www.egmont.co.uk

Printed and bound in Great Britain by the CPI Group

For Jana

A NOTE FROM THE AUTHOR

If it's been a while since you read *The Sign of One* (volume one in this trilogy), here's a brief reminder of some of the main characters, terms and locations.

Colm	*Kyle's twin brother. Was raised as a Slayer.*
Dump world	*A world where humans exile criminals, refugees, etc.*
Gemini	*The ident resistance.*
Ident	*Identical twin. Considered evil on Wrath, because only one is pureblood and the other is a 'twist'.*
Ident camp	*Idents are held in secure camps until old enough to be tested.*
Kyle	*Teenage loner who grew up out in the Barrenlands. The narrator of this story.*
Nublood	*What ident 'twists' prefer to call themselves, as in nu-species.*
Peace Fair	*Annual ceremony, held near ident camps, where 'idents' are brutally tested and 'twists' winnowed from 'scabs'.*
Pureblood	*Someone who's 100 per cent human.*
Reapers	*Feral savages. Rumour has it they are cannibals.*
Saviour	*Despotic warlord who rules over Wrath. Father of Kyle and Colm.*
Scab	*Wrath slang for the pureblood twin, because after the Peace Fair they are branded to show they are no longer evil.*
Sky	*Gemini rebel, ident camp survivor and daring windjammer pilot. Kyle's friend and ally – sometimes.*
Slayers	*The Saviour's private army.*
Twist	*Wrath slang for a nublood twin, so-called because they are said to have 'twisted blood'. Faster, stronger and much quicker to heal than pureblood humans.*
Windjammers	*Crudely built ridge-running flying machines.*
Wrath	*The dump world where this story is set.*

PROLOGUE

It's her turn outside. After all the hours spent hiding in the dark and staying quiet, the cold drizzle that greets her is almost welcome. It'll be her first time at the lambing. Well . . . sort of.

Old Hicks takes them up the hill to the pens, her and a lad called Marat. Marat's sixteen, more than twice as old as she is, and won't waste time talking to a little girl. Fine by her, because talking is dangerous.

Talking can get you found out.

Tucked away in the gloom under the camo-netting, sheltered from the ever-shrieking wind, the girl finally gets to see the woollies close up. She's a bit disappointed. They're manky-looking and skinny, scraps of filthy wool still hanging off where they've been rough-sheared. Hicks flicks the beam of his shiner about and the girl sees sheep nursing a single newborn lamb each. But one ewe lies apart from the others, and seems restless. It gets up, bleats, paws at the straw-covered earth, then lies down again.

'That un's ready,' Hicks says, squinting at her.

The girl hesitates, unsure. 'Ready?'

'To drop. Don't just stand there gawping. Go see to it.'

Ready to drop. Oh yeah. She swallows and nods. Her sister's done the telling from her turn outside yesterday. Now it's up to her to do the remembering and play it so Hicks never guesses that today's little girl is not the same as yesterday's little girl.

So she scuttles around to the business end of the beast. Even though she knows what to expect, she still makes a face.

'You like that, huh?' Marat jeers.

See, it's messy back here. A little white head and two tiny black hooves poke out of an explosion of red skin. The girl doesn't know whether to laugh, cry or be sick. Marat sniggers at her.

She gives him the finger, while Hicks isn't looking.

Fortunately, the old ewe knows what she's about. The girl watches, bug-eyed, as the lamb slithers out and thumps wetly on to the straw. Only a little woolly thing, but the girl's amazed. It all goes exactly like her sister said it would. A new life, in front of her eyes. It's so beautiful.

Hicks is watching her. His slash of a mouth twists into a snarl.

'What you waitin' for?'

The girl takes a deep breath and swats the fussing ewe away. Gritting her teeth, she pulls at the stuff on the lamb's face. It's hot and slimy, but comes away easy enough. She makes sure the newborn's nostrils are clear of mucus, grabs a handful of straw and gives its face a quick tickle. The tiny creature – even littler than she is – sneezes. Its warm breath tickles her cheek back. 'It's breathing,' she calls out, excited.

Hicks grunts something at her, which she doesn't catch.

The worst bit is still to come. But her sister managed it, so she'll have to manage it too, so nobody suspects. That's the story of their two-pretending-to-be-one life. She lets the mother ewe back in to lick its newborn clean, fishes out her laser-knife and fires up its glowing green blade. Then, not waiting to think, she slices the cord close to the lamb's navel, dials up full heat and holds the fizzing green blade on to the bloody end until she smells flesh burning. The lamb kicks a bit, but it's not so bad. The bleeding stops. A dab of orange iodine from the pot and she's done. Her first lamb, and it looks fine, shaking less then she is. As she powers the blade down, the lamb lifts its head, wanting to suckle. She reckons it's a girl.

Hicks stomps over and gobs into the straw. 'Not a bad job.'

The girl's not listening; she's staring at the old ewe. It's lost interest in the lamb and is pawing at the ground again. Beside her, Hicks curses. The girl looks up, startled, to see him making the Sign of One. Marat comes over. One look and he makes it too – the sign against evil.

The girl's blood turns to ice. 'What's wrong?'

Hicks turns his back, lurches off to a corner of the pen and picks up some filthy old sacking. More cursing as he throws it at her.

'What's this for?' she says. Instantly realises this was a mistake.

'Same as yesterday,' Marat sneers. 'You forget already?'

'We're cursed,' Hicks growls, looking disgusted. 'Two blasted sets in two days. We'll be in the upper pens when you're done at the river. And don't lose the sack this time, you hear? They don't grow on trees.'

Finally, the girl understands. This ewe being restless again – it has a second lamb on the way. A twin lamb!

The sack. The river. She can't help shuddering.

One is good, two is evil. The words pound through her brain as Hicks shambles off swearing, pulling at what's left of his hair. Marat looks at the girl, his forehead knotted, like he's chewing on a bone inside his head. This makes the girl sweat. She does her dumber-than-dumb face and sketches the Sign of One. Not because she wants to: because she has to.

What was her fool of a sister thinking? Why didn't she warn her?

The ewe lies down, strains and bleats. The girl glimpses a second set of tiny hoofs start squeezing out into the world. And then the gate bangs shut against its stone gatepost, making the girl jump. She looks up and Hicks and Marat are gone. It's just her and the sheep now. She drops to her knees in the straw, shaking. The old ewe takes a break from straining to glare at her out of its dark-slot eye. She reaches out and runs her hand over its firstborn. The tiny wet thing butts her fingers with its snout, mistaking her for its mother. It cries out, desperate for milk.

How can this poor little thing be evil? the girl wonders.

Like everyone else out here she's half starved. Her pale face is pinched, her stomach swollen. She can't help thinking that this is two lambs for the price of one: two small bundles of wool and milk and mutton and hope – a blessing not a curse. She says this last phrase over and over again. It's word for word what her mother whispers to her and her twin sister every night at their going-to-bed time.

It's only the rest of the world that disagrees . . .

The old ewe tires and needs help. The girl pulls the second lamb out by its hooves, sorts its breathing like before and sees to the birth cord. Without thinking, she helps give the poor little doomed thing life. As the ewe starts licking and nudging it, she fights not to think about how she'll soon be sticking them both in the sack. Or how it will feel as the sack thrashes in the cold water. Most of all, she tries not to think about what will happen to her and her twin sister if they're ever found out. It won't just be a bag over their heads and a trip to the river. They won't get off so lightly.

The girl almost never cries. She has a quick cry now.

Stones crunch and rattle, dislodged by a boot. She looks around and Marat is back. He leans on the gate, chomping on a piece of bindgrass. Says nothing. Just stares at her. Real hard.

Does he see her tears in the gloom? She can't be sure.

Quickly, hating to do it, the girl stuffs the lambs into the sack. She shoves her way out and past Marat, shutting her ears to the ewe's frantic bleating. She runs down to the river, finds a quiet spot. Only she can't drown them, like her sister did. Instead, she takes a desperate chance. She hides them inside a dead tree, covering them with grass and leaves to keep them warm. She whispers to them that she'll come back when it's dark and sneak them home. Her mother will know what to do.

'You're a blessing not a curse,' she tells them.

But as she turns around, the girl sees Marat has followed her . . .

PART ONE
DIVIDE AND CONQUER

1
SO MUCH FOR BEING A HERO

I'm getting the hang of this being beaten to a pulp thing. They haul me to my feet. I shuffle forward in the fighting crouch I've been taught. And then our combat instructor, Stauffer, knocks all kinds of lumps out of me until I fall down again.

He's hammering me, laughing while he does it.

Plenty of other instructors and trainees are loving it too, watching the 'hero' of the Facility raid have his head kicked in.

Why not? If I were them, I'd hate me too.

It's Ballard's fault. He won't let me or my brother Colm fight for real, says we're too valuable to the Gemini cause to be risked. So while these guys we train with go off on hit-and-run raids, we sit tight here in our hidden base in the Deeps. That'd be enough to get us hated, but there are his speeches too. Rebel units from all over Wrath are flown out here to be rested, or for training. None of them escape Ballard's *we're-all-in-this-together-and-fighting-for-the-future-of-idents* speech. I get shoved in front of them, called a hero and made to tell my edited story – from finding out I was myself an ident and a nublood, through to how

I 'volunteered' to let myself be captured, knowing I'd be taken to the secret Slayer base known as the Facility; breaking out with my brother's help and activating the beacon buried in my arm so our rebel forces could destroy the base and rescue the hundreds of nublood kids enslaved there.

Ballard says my story inspires them. Says it's important.

Yeah, right. He should ask Stauffer if I inspire him. This was a regular empty-hand skills session until he'd picked on Colm even worse than usual, to wind me up. I can keep my temper when I'm taking the hits, but I lost it and called him out.

'Stay down, Kyle. Don't be stupid,' Colm hisses.

'I can take him,' I mumble.

I spit a gobful of red on to the dirt and groan. Something scrapes painfully inside me, like one of my ribs is bust. Above me, the bigmoon is already above the overhanging cliff, its crescent and rings bright in the darkening sky. Sky lizards circle in the last of the day's updraughts, their shrill whistling calls drifting down.

Even they sound like they're jeering.

'Hey, Kyle, we need to talk,' a familiar voice shouts.

I groan again as I see Sky elbowing her way through the watchers, breathing fast like she's run here. Only before I can say anything, I'm thrown back at Stauffer. Maybe I fight harder now *she's* here. Anyway, I nail him once – hard enough to pull a grunt out of him – before he knocks me back down again.

Sky squats beside me. 'You're the punchbag today?'

I shrug, so big-gob Colm answers for me, nodding towards the grinning Stauffer. 'Kyle challenged him.'

She scowls. 'Challenged your instructor? Smart move.'

Scowls are all I get from Sky these days. Not that we even see each other that often, now she's flying combat ops.

'Yeah, like you'd take his shit,' I growl.

'Make yourself useful,' Colm says, chucking her a wet cloth.

Sky dabs carelessly at my face. 'I've got news about my sister,' she says, all excited. 'I need to show you something.'

Around me, I hear the trainees muttering. Laughter too.

I grab the rag off her. 'I'm busy.'

'You swore you'd help me find Tarn. Remember?'

'How could I forget?'

I grit my teeth. Mistake. One's gone. I can wobble others with my tongue. Crap. Teeth take days to grow back.

'Hey, skinny girl,' Stauffer yells. 'After I'm done with your boyfriend here, how about you and me have some fun, huh?'

He makes it clear what kind of fun with hip thrusts.

Sky flicks him her middle finger.

'Quit messing,' she tells me. 'Finish him.'

My turn to scowl. 'Don't you think I'm trying?'

The look of scorn on Sky's face – bottle it and you could sell it as battery acid. 'You're being dumb, fighting like they trained you to. Arse-face is catching you because he sees you coming.'

'So how should I fight?'

'Like a Reaper,' she says. 'Dirty.'

I'm grabbed and thrown back at Stauffer. His mates want blood, not chat. He comes at me, gob hanging open, maybe wanting to finish me quick and show Sky what a big, tough man he is. Nearly does too, with me still thinking about Sky. Only he slips and misses, and I come to my senses. I duck and weave and throw jabs to get him to back up. I don't let him get close enough to hurt me.

'Come here, you little shite!' he snarls, starting to blow now.

Just as I begin to hope, I step back too far, straying across the rope on the ground that marks out our ring. Hands thrust me back at Stauffer, straight into his punch. He rattles my bones.

Down I go again, on to my knees.

And he's laughing at me again. They all are.

That's not what lights me up. These gommers can laugh all they like – what do I care? No. It's seeing Sky standing there, watching with her thin arms folded, contempt twisting her lips. Something rips inside me that isn't my cracked ribs. Before, I was fighting for Colm, and to wipe sneers off faces. Now I'm possessed.

I stagger back to my feet, spitting curses.

Stauffer stops his strutting and closes on me. I fake a half-hearted spin kick. He leans back, leaving his front foot planted. Careless. I pull out of the kick and stamp down hard, crunching the bones along the top of his foot. He screams and goes down, clutching at it. The fight's over there and then, but I treat him to a few kicks anyway as he rolls around in the dirt. Afters, we call this in the Barrenlands where I grew up. It sends a message. Mess with me again, Stauffer, and this is what you'll get.

'Cut that out!' Andersson, another combat instructor, shouts.

I glare at him, my chest heaving. 'Or what?'

Colm jumps between us. 'Take it easy, Kyle. You don't have to fight them all. Leave some for tomorrow, why don't you?'

He hangs his fist out. We bump stumps.

Even now I still cringe seeing my brother's finger gone. Took it off himself using a wood-chisel after Sky told him that's what was used on me. Says he did it to show he's Gemini now. Sky says it shows that Colm's even more of a gom than I am.

'C'mon, let's go!' Sky chucks my boots and shirt at me.

Andersson moans at us for clearing off before the training day is over, but Sky's a windjammer captain now and outranks him. She tells him to shut his face.

I give him a wink. I'll regret that later, but it feels good now.

Triumph wrestles with guilt. 'Dirty enough for you?'

It's a few minutes later. The pounding in my head has stopped and I feel less like tearing the throat out of anybody who so much as glances at me. A cold drizzle has started. It helps in a weird kind of way, cooling me down inside and out.

Sky shrugs and keeps walking. 'That loser had it coming.'

'I should've stayed down, like Colm said.'

My brother nods, bites his lip and looks away.

Sky blows air out of her mouth. 'What good would that do?'

I sigh, my ribs killing me, not needing another row about how I always take his side against hers. Which is crap anyway.

'Stauffer will heal, then he'll kill me.'

'He wouldn't dare.'

'Maybe we should tell Ballard what happened,' Colm says.

'I can't go running to Ballard the whole time.'

'Seriously,' Sky mutters.

We all shut up for a while as we trudge down the trail from the training grounds to the canyon floor. Scraps of golden evenshine strobe over us, sneaking through the camouflage netting that's hung overhead to hide us from any eyes in the sky. I clutch my hurting ribs, glare at Sky's back and think dark thoughts.

She glances back at me. 'What?'

I'm so startled, I blurt it out. 'When you hooked me up with Gemini, you swore we'd be among friends, all fighting together for the nublood cause. Hasn't worked out like that, has it?'

Sky snorts, her wet face glistening.

'Get real, Kyle. Nublood makes you faster and stronger, but it doesn't stop you being an arse like Stauffer.'

'Never said it did. It's just – *oof!*'

I trip. My ribs have another go at me, shutting me up.

Sky stomps off again, limping as fast as she can on her bad leg. Behind her back, Colm rolls his eyes at me. Not helpful. Ever since we were flown out here to the Deeps after the raid, this is how it's been. It's like they can't stand each other and I'm stuck in the middle, dodging glares and making excuses. I'm not saying it's his fault that things have cooled between me and Sky – that's more down to the way things have worked out – but he doesn't help.

'What's the rush?' I call out, not thinking.

She turns, her face one big snarl. 'WHAT DID YOU SAY?'

'Okay, okay,' I say, not wanting to get hit again. 'You've got news about Tarn. Can't you just tell us?'

'I figured you'd like to see!'

She takes a deep breath and looks away real quick.

Not quickly enough. I glimpse the bitter disappointment in her eyes and my guts twist themselves into knots. A winter ago, I swore I'd help her find her sister, Tarn. We bumped stumps on it. One way or another though it hasn't happened. There's always another mission for Sky to fly. I'm not allowed out of the Deeps. As excuses go it's a good one, but I feel I've let her down.

'Sky, I'm sorry. I –'

'What's *that* doing here?' Colm says, pointing.

I look. And my next heartbeat is a long time coming. On the landing field squats a matt-black Slayer windjammer.

'Relax,' Sky says. 'We forced it down a week or so ago. Took a while to get it launched again. I flew it in here today.'

'It's massive,' I say, taking in the bulk of it.

Sky's not listening. 'Hurry up. We'll hitch a ride out.'

Just then I hear the whoosh of a steam boiler. Seconds later I smell coal smoke. Gears grind and tracks clatter. Sky sets off at a stiff-legged run. Colm and I go after her, me clutching my side. As we emerge from the trail gloom I see a battered tractor chugging away from us. We chase after it, hang off the back.

Sky cheers up enough to nearly smile.

'Like hopping a windjammer!' she yells over the noise.

As we lumber across the field I check out the transport. Apart from some impact damage from a hard landing, and blast scars from the firefight that followed, this is one hell of a machine. It wasn't cobbled together from scrap in a back-of-beyond workshop. Our rebel jammers are rust buckets by comparison.

We drop off as the tow-tractor chugs around to the bow end. Sky has a word with some heavily armed guards. They nod, she waves at us, and we follow her inside the windjammer through a hatch high on its side, hauling ourselves up handholds set into the hull. Easily done any other day, but my ribs are killing me.

Colm offers a hand. I wave him away.

Techs are poking around inside. Sky ignores them and leads me through an internal hatch into the cargo bay. 'It's in here!'

'What happened to the crew?' I ask.

Sky shrugs. 'Killed or ran. What's it matter?'

Over to one side is a metal cage. The light from the few glowtubes in here doesn't reach, so she pulls out a shiner and thumbs it on. By its light I see the cage door gaping open. The lock's all melted as if someone's taken a plasma lance to it.

Sky clambers inside, squats down and shines the beam on to the hull at the back.

'Her tag,' she says, looking back at me, her green eyes shining.

2
TARN WAS HERE

All I see, after I clamber into the cage after her, is a bunch of scratches on the grey-painted metal of the hull.

'What am I looking at?'

'These!' Sky says, pointing.

Amazingly, it is the scratches she's mad keen to show me. There must be hundreds of them, scored and gouged into the metal. Most are old and tough to see clearly, as if they've been painted over. Others are fresher or deeper, still shiny. Sky points out one set in particular, tracing the lines with a shaking finger.

'Her tag,' she says again, biting her lip. 'Tarn was here.'

I lean in and squint, but still all I see is a bunch of random scratches. 'How can you know that?'

Sky's breathing catches and she stiffens.

'Look, I believe you,' I say quickly. 'I don't see it, that's all.'

She scowls at me. Again. 'A tag is your mark. Only you and your mates know it; that way it can't be traced back to you. In the camps we all tagged. The kick was to piss the guards off by tagging as many places as you could without getting caught.' She stares into space and shakes her head. 'Nobody tagged more than Tarn. My sister scratched her tags in places no one else dared.'

I can't help wondering if she's just seeing what she wants to see. No way I'm saying *that* though. Next thing I know, Sky's back on her feet and shoving past me out of the cage.

'There's something else,' she says.

I go to follow and my ribs take another shot, doubling me up.

'After that, can I go and get patched up?' I say.

Sky's hunting for something, flicking her shiner beam about and muttering to herself. I hear her snort.

'For a nublood, Kyle, you sure whine a lot.'

'Just because I heal fast doesn't make it hurt any less!'

There's a loud *clunk* sound outside and the windjammer lurches violently. I have to grab the bars of the cage to stay on my feet, which doesn't do my ribs any favours. Next thing, the floor sways and bumps under me. My guess is the tractor is hauling us away to a dispersal area in one of the Deeps' side canyons.

Sky finds what she's looking for. 'Gotcha!'

As I make it out of the cage, Colm catches my eye. He nods at Sky where she's messing with some device like a blaster crossed with a cleverbox. It makes a clicking sound. Looking satisfied, she aims it at the cage. The clicking swells to an angry howl.

'Hear that?' she says, like I'm deaf.

'Kill it, will you?' I say. 'My head's hurting enough as it is.'

She points the device away from the cage and it calms down.

'Look!' She shows me the screen on top of it.

'What's it show?' Colm says.

'Promethium-148,' I read, slowly. 'What's that then?'

One of the techs looks around. 'The old Earth name for

darkblende. Those kids you rescued from that Slayer Facility –
it's the stuff they had them mining. Lethal stuff, toxic and hot.
Pumps out loads of nasty gamma radiation.'

I scramble away from the cage triple-quick.

Tech guy sniggers. 'Relax. We're safe enough. The counter's
only showing raised rad levels. Nothing hard enough to burn us.'

I stare at him. He looks cool so I quit backing up.

And now I take in the eyeglasses, the tangle of headphones
around his neck, the flame-red hair. I know this smart-arse from
Bastion, the Gemini base hidden beneath the Blight shanty town.
He's the guy who picked up Rona's distress call.

'Hey, Ness, it's me, Kyle.'

'Oh yeah.' He peers at my face. 'What happened to you?'

I wipe my mouth. My hand comes away smeared with blood.

'Forget that,' Sky snaps, waving the counter-thing under my
nose. 'Darkblende gamma readings only show up inside the cage,
and nowhere else. So this cage held prisoners contaminated from
mining the stuff. Tarn's tag tells us she was one of them.' She
grabs my hand and squeezes it. 'This Slayer transport *has* to be
the one they shipped my sister out of the Facility in!'

I try to share her excitement, honestly I do. Only I'm hurting
and my head's still full of nasty thoughts from the fight.

'That's great.' I force a smile. 'But –'

'But *what*?' she says, real low.

'Look, I get it,' I say. 'This freighter here flew your sister out
of the Facility. So what? I don't want to piss on your fire, but
without the crew to ask we can't know where it took her.'

Sky turns her gaze on Ness. 'Tell Kyle what you told me.'

The tech's eyes go extra big behind his glasses. 'Hang on, Sky,

I only said I'd take a look. I've got lots of other work to —'

She sighs. 'Just tell him.'

Ness glances around, as if making sure his tech mates aren't listening. 'Okay, okay,' he whispers. 'So, like I said, I ran a scan on this jammer's nav-track and the crew didn't scrub its memory before our guys got to them. The data's scrambled, to level seven at least. It'll take some time, but I should be able to break it.'

We must be towed over a ditch or something because the floor leaps up under us. Ness staggers into me.

I push him away, harder than I need to. 'What'd he say?'

'He can hack into the transport's navigation system and track where it's been,' Sky explains. And Ness nods.

Colm, watchful and quiet up to now, mutters something under his breath that sounds to me like a disgusted: 'Great.'

Sky takes a deep breath and lets it out. Her green eyes drill into me. 'So we *can* find out where the Slayer bastards took Tarn. Then go bring her back, like we agreed.'

Even though I saw it coming, I still twitch. 'Just like that?'

I expect Sky to blow up at me. No. She just pulls her hand away and looks hurt. I've seen that expression a lot lately. Feeling guilty, I pick up the rad-counter from where she put it down.

Ness makes a grab for it. 'That's no toy.'

I fend him off, press the trigger and it starts ticking. Ness makes another lunge and knocks my hand. I end up accidentally aiming it at Sky. Only I must have the thing set wrong, because it howls so loudly I drop it. It hits the deck, squeals and cuts off.

Ness picks it up. 'Look what you've done. You've broken it!'

Sky gives me her best scowl. 'You're *such* a gom, Kyle.'

*

The Deeps are a maze of narrow canyons between sheer cliff walls. In this main canyon we now call home, the cliffs to the east overhang a rocky shelf, forming an immense natural amphitheatre. That's where all our tents and shacks are. The rocks below the shelf are riddled with caves and tunnels. These are too regular to be natural, but nobody knows who dug them out in the way-back-when before Wrath became a dump world and humans started arriving. Nobody cares much either. We just use them. Like this healer chamber I'm in now.

Shirt off, I'm sitting on an icy-cold metal table with my chest all strapped up. Rona's bandage is wound so tight around me that breathing is a battle. Just my luck that it was my foster-mother on duty. I figure she's strapped me extra-tight because she's so mad at me.

I hate this room's stink of soap, antiseptic and blood. It reminds me too much of the Facility lab where Slayer medics kept me prisoner, pumping my blood into my father, the Saviour.

Now she's stitching a gash above my eye.

'Kyle!' Rona scolds. 'Quit wriggling about, or I'll give you a mirror and you can stitch the damn thing yourself.'

'It hurts,' I say, staring at the curve of needle she's holding.

'Course it bloody hurts. Taking on a combat instructor . . . you're lucky he didn't kill you.' She frowns and leans in again. I feel the sting of the needle, a plucking at my forehead as she tugs the thread through. 'What were you thinking?'

'I lost my temper.'

'Your mind more like.'

'The guy was giving me a hard time,' Colm says.

'He doesn't know you're –?' Rona lets the question hang.

We never talk about Colm and me being the Saviour's sons. Apart from us, I think only Ballard knows. We leave that little detail out of the speeches he makes me give. Could be awkward, he says. Awkward? Colm reckons we'd be torn limb from limb.

It's a constant worry that we'll be found out.

'If he knew that, you'd be sewing me into a body bag,' I say.

Rona breathes out sharply, warming my ear with a tut. Six more stitches and she ties a knot and bites the end off. I brace myself to be bitched at – it isn't the first time she's had to fix me up.

'Oh, Kyle,' she says, sounding tired. 'I know it's tough with the grief you both get. But fighting will only make things worse.'

I squirm away, feeling all tight inside.

'Sometimes you have to fight. You don't understand.'

'I understand all right.' She hands me my blood-spattered shirt, and rubs her eyes. 'I'm just sick to death of fighting and war.'

'Ballard says we're winning,' Colm says.

'Don't *you* start! If we are winning, it doesn't feel like it. All us healers see are windjammers bringing us cargo bays piled high with wounded fighters to patch up. There's no end to it.'

She's not wrong; we've all seen them. It's six bigmoons now since the Facility raid and I guess it's like Murdo says – you go poking a stick into a wrathmite hole, don't be surprised when the bugs swarm out and bite you. The word reaching us out here in the Deeps is that Gemini's taking some serious heat. The Saviour's Slayer army has gone on the offensive, trying to wipe us out. The Blight is a smoking ruin and Bastion has been evacuated.

Rona sighs. 'So many die. Maybe they're the lucky ones.'

'You call dying lucky?' I say.

She looks through me. 'I had one nublood kid in here a week ago. Gut-shot. Screaming and bleeding all over the place. We fixed him up. He healed so quickly he was sent out again.'

'That's good, isn't it?' I say, confused.

'Is it? He was back yesterday. Blaster-burnt this time. What must it do to these kids' heads, being so badly wounded, patched up and sent back out to fight, or die? They're all so . . . young.'

Younger than me. Yeah, I know.

'You can't fight wars without taking losses.'

If Sky were here she'd be nodding, but Rona snorts as she swabs stuff on to my stitches.

'Oh, listen to you. Those losses have names, and mothers too. But I'm wasting my breath. You won't listen. The young think that dying only happens to other people.'

I duck away from her swabbing. Whatever she's putting on me stings like crazy. 'You're saying we shouldn't fight?'

She dredges up a sad smile. 'I'm not. Kyle, I'm a healer, not a fighter. Even when I was your age I couldn't kill, whatever the cause. That's why I served the way I did, looking after you.'

Before I can stop her, she messes up my hair.

That does it. I have to tell her.

'They hate me. Colm too. We train the same as they do, but while they go off to fight we sit on our hands, safe here. You should see the looks they give us – like we're cowards!'

I glance at my brother. He seems more interested in the floor.

'That's nonsense. You serve in other ways, that's all.'

I taste bile in the back of my throat.

'Yeah? Tell them that. Making stupid speeches for Ballard.

Him banging on about what a hero I am. Why can't we be fighters like the rest of them? Fighting Slayers would be easier.'

'Now you're being stupid.'

'At least we'd know who our enemies are.'

Rona clicks her tongue. 'Your work is important. So is Colm's. People here are scared and anxious. We've taken a hammering and Ballard needs you to remind people that we can win.'

She goes to help me into my shirt.

'I can manage.' I jump down from the examination table.

'Suit yourself.' Rona starts tidying away the bits and pieces of her healing trade. 'Do you want something for the pain?'

'No. I don't want anything. I'm done here.'

I struggle into my shirt, even the buttons wanting to fight me.

'How's Sky?' Rona says, watching.

'How should I know?'

My foster-mother's grey eyes meet mine. 'She was here not long ago, fired up about something. I told her where to find you.'

I hesitate, wondering if Sky's said anything to her. I bet she has. She's here loads – they get along big time. Rona never says it, but I know she wishes Sky and me would get back together again.

'Sky's got a lead on her sister,' I tell her reluctantly.

'That's great news!' Rona's face brightens. Only now she must notice my scowl. 'Don't you think?'

How can someone who's seen forty summers be so dumb?

'She wants me to help her rescue Tarn and bring her back,' I say.

'Ah. You did say you would.'

'Yeah, but I can't. Ballard would never allow it.'

'You've asked him?'

I scowl at her. 'There's no point.'

'Why not?' Rona says. 'If you find Tarn, there's a good chance you'll find the other missing nublood children too.'

'Hasn't Ballard got enough on his plate?' Colm says, as he sets off towards the exit tunnel. 'Like making sure Gemini survives.'

Rona sighs. 'I was just thinking of Sky, that's all.'

'All Sky thinks about is Tarn,' I say, unable to hold it in.

'You're wrong there,' Rona says, shaking her head, lips pursed. 'Think what Sky's been through. She doesn't shout about it, but she still cares for you. Take my word for it.'

'If you say so.' I go to follow my retreating brother.

'And I thought you cared for her,' she says.

I look back. 'I do. Or I try to. These days, it's . . . tough.'

'Try harder then. You two should squabble less and talk more. Sky was there for you when you needed her, remember? And she needs you, more than you know.'

'Are you coming or what?' Colm calls.

Rona smiles, but it's a troubled smile. Even I can see that.

'And please, no more fighting,' she says. 'I've enough to do without stitching you up. Another windjammer's on its way.'

She goes back to cleaning and tidying.

Colm is waiting for me where one of the shafts leads up towards the surface, leaning against the wooden ladder.

'What was that about Sky?'

'Nothing. Let's go find Squint, then feed the dragon.'

3
RUMOURS

These days of early firstgreen, with dayshine sticking around longer, warmth in the air and leaves uncurling on the trees, Squint is put to work in the hidden fields down-canyon. Alongside some half-starved fourhorns, our food growers have him hauling ploughs and wagons. We worry he'll pick up damage we can't fix, but don't get a say. Funny how it works. Nobody wanted the rusty metal and burnt-out electronic junk that Colm and I cobbled Squint together from. Sneered, they did. Yet soon as they saw him up and running, they stole him off us. Requisitioning, they called it.

For the cause. Everything for the cause.

When we find Squint he's done for the day, lashed to a ground-anchor while a man hoses mud off him. He sees us coming, whips his tail about and buzzes his head off.

'How'd he do?' I ask.

The man shuts off the water and shrugs. 'Not bad. Crashed on me once in the morning. Worked fine after it warmed up.'

'Do you need him tomorrow?'

'They don't plough themselves.' The man glances at the fields, stubble sticking up into the gloom under the camo-nets.

'Okay,' Colm says. 'We'll check him over.'

The man nods and hurries away. No thanks or nothing.

Soon as he's gone I pull a bone-carved tube from my pocket and blow gently into one end. It makes a hissing sound.

Squint's head lifts and his tail thrashes.

Colm grins. 'Do you *have* to?'

'I do.' I blow the whistle much harder now, three times.

Squint hurls himself towards us, ripping the ground-anchor right out of the ground as if it were fixed into butter. He very nearly knocks us both over with all his excited jumping up.

'Pleased to see us, huh?' I say, trying not to laugh because laughing hurts, even with my ribs strapped.

'Thought you'd dumped the jumping-up code,' Colm says.

He's laughing too now as he tries to fend Squint off.

'I stuck it back in again.'

'Why? You like being covered in mud?'

'It's fun, him making a fuss. Like having a dog.'

After a struggle I unclip Squint from the anchor trailing behind him. Squint calms down and drops into his ready-state crouch, hydraulics hissing. I pocket the whistle and watch Colm as he goes and screws the ground-anchor back into the dirt. Me, I'd leave it where it fell, but not him. Same skin, different thinking.

'Good little boy,' I tell Squint, scratching him behind his ears. Not real ears of course, just microphone mounts.

He hoots, sensing my touch.

'You *do* realise it's not alive,' Colm says. Like always.

It's been a tough day and I almost get cross with him, but catch myself. I think Colm's often too clever for his own good; he thinks I'm too hot-headed. Rona says we've only had six months' practice at being twins, unlike the other idents here who've had a lifetime, so we'll both still be working it out. Whatever. All I know is that looking and sounding the same is easy; putting up with the differences is harder. I'm trying to get better at that.

'Don't you listen to him, Squinty,' I say.

Squint beeps twice, which means 'I don't understand'. Work-bots only recognise verbals like *Lift, Forward, Drag* and *Drop* as standard, but we're working on that. His crude vox-box doesn't run to speech, only beeps, hoots and whistles. What we really need is to get our hands on one of those flash units out of a windjammer, the ones that warn the pilot if she's stalling or landing with the gear up. Splice one of these in and he *could* talk.

'What d'you think of his new leg? Not bad, huh?'

Colm hasn't seen Squint's new foreleg yet. This one's by far the best I've scavved yet, and a decent match to his other legs too.

'Where'd you get it?' He sounds impressed.

So he should be. The casings are hardly rusty at all, just some light pitting. The hydraulic lines look good too, no patches. Look real close, there are even some shiny bits on the pistons.

'Traded welding work for it with one of the steam-winch crew.'

'Maybe he'll walk straighter now.'

'He does,' I say, pleased. 'C'mon, let's go. It's getting dark.'

'Shouldn't we check him?'

'No. I'm beat. Anyway, there's nothing we can do about him

crashing. You'd crash too if you had two brains.'

See, no way could we scav a proper processor for Squint. Too rare. Too valuable. Instead we patched together two half-trashed boards nobody wanted. The least damaged one acts as master, passing stuff it can't do to the other board. Only sometimes they trip over each other, and that's when poor Squinty crashes.

Colm shrugs and we head off together. I click my fingers and Squint follows along, still dripping.

Night settles on the Deeps as we walk and dark shadows pour in to flood the canyon. We skirt round the big cavern at the bottom of the cliff where off-duty fighters hang out. You can trade rebel-minted creds in there for snacks, or – if you're dumb enough – for gut-rot liquor brewed from potatoes. In the smoky lantern light I see the place is heaving with people already.

'Big crowd,' I say. 'Wonder why?'

'Let's go find out.'

'Later maybe. We should feed the dragon first.'

Truth is – my head's still too dark to want company. And Stauffer might be in there on crutches, or some of his psycho mates. So we carry on to the kitchen tents, raid the bins and bag some fresh chicken guts, her favourite.

Halfway up the trail to where she's penned we stumble across a pack of youngsters playing the Peace Fair game. A bored-looking older boy has been roped in to act the Slayer and do the Cutting and Unwrapping. Two little girls, so spit-alike I bet their own mother can't tell them apart, are already wrapped. The 'twist' will have a cut drawn on her forearm under the bandage, the 'pure' won't. I played it when I was little, but it freaks me out after seeing the horror of the real thing. And they're not supposed to be playing it, not here in a rebel camp.

I can't help scowling. 'Can you believe *that*?'

Colm shrugs. 'They're just kids.'

The guessers turn their backs and the older boy swaps the two wrapped girls about. They squeal with fear and excitement. And now the guessers start clapping and chanting.

'One good, two evil! Cut them, bind them, unwrap them!'

The older boy sees us. He grins and shrugs as if to say, *This wasn't my idea*, puts a finger to his lips for the girls to stop squealing and calls to the rest that they can look again. As they turn, he pulls out the knife for the pretend Unwrapping and brandishes it.

'One good, one evil!' he hisses. 'Which is which?'

The kids shout their guesses, spit flying from their mouths.

I grab Colm's arm. 'I don't want to see this.'

'It's only a game,' he says, but lets me drag him away.

The stone-walled corral is built into the cliff's overhang. By the time we get there it's full night-dark, but just enough of the bigmoon has hauled itself above the western clifftops to throw some useful shine down. Colm hangs back, looking after Squint while I creep up to the gate and peer through it. A lump of darkness stirs at the back wall. I hear a hiss, a warning rattle of neck feathers, her chain scraping. We only call her a dragon for fun of course. Really she's a sky lizard. And not just any sky lizard – she's a queen. Twice the size of the males, ten times as vicious.

I'm waving the bag to give her the smell of the chicken guts when I hear footfalls behind me. I whip round, blade out.

'Thought I'd find you here,' Fleur says.

She's got a fake-scared face on. Behind her are some of her

deadhead mates, watching, swapping grins. That's what they call themselves, the kids we rescued from the Facility.

I clutch my side. 'What you doing, creeping up on us?'

'Heard you took a kicking,' Fleur says. 'Ouch. Look at you.'

I put the blade away and straighten up.

'You should see the other guy.'

'Hey, Fleur,' Colm says, and shifts his feet.

She smiles at him. 'Hey, Colm. How's it going?'

While they talk, I scan her face like I always do, looking for any hint of accusation or blame. But not a bit of it – just the same fair hair, freckles and sad expression as her ident sister, Fliss, the girl who sacrificed herself to lead away the Slayers hunting Sky and me near Drakensburg. Reassured, I open my mouth to mumble the same question I always mumble. Before I can get it out though she glances my way and shakes her head. Still no word on her sister, that tells me. Still missing, presumed to be dead. Yet here Fleur stands, looking pleased to see me.

Okay, so I played a part in rescuing her and her mates from the Facility, but still . . .

'They say you smashed Stauffer's foot,' she says. 'Lamed him.'

I shrug. 'Tosser had it coming. Anyway, he's nublood same as us, so he won't stay lame.'

'More's the pity,' Colm mutters.

'Think he'll come after you?' Fleur says.

'Wouldn't you?' I say, a little more edgy than I meant.

Time to change the subject.

'You here to help feed the dragon, Fleur?'

'No way. I've lost enough fingers already, thanks.' She grins, holds her fist out and bumps stumps with me and Colm.

'Wouldn't want to come between you and your lizard girlfriend.'

'Scared, huh?'

'Whatever. Look, hurry up. I've got big news to tell you.'

'Oh frag, not you too.'

The smell of rank breath hits me and I hear the snap of powerful jaws. I turn to see the huge, leathery bulk of the queen sky lizard facing me, her triangular head rammed against the bars of the gate, long snout poking through. Her four big compound eyes glitter in the moonshine as she watches us. Her sting-tail swishes dirt back and forth. They hack the stinger bit off every so often. I check to make sure it hasn't grown back, and it hasn't.

'Hungry, are you?' I whisper.

She jaw-snaps again and whistles. A milky-white membrane flicks across her lower eyes, fastened on the bag of offal. She's fed on live goats. I give her treats because I feel sorry for her.

'Hurry up,' Fleur says, wrinkling her nose.

Braced to fling myself away if she goes for me, I peel the bag of chicken offal open and hold it out. The lizard tilts her huge head, flares her snout-slits and sniffs, sucking air into her lungs with a sound like a blast furnace. Now she gapes, showing me row after row of razor-sharp fangs. Her crazy-long tongue flicks through the bars and explores the bag. By the time I quit flinching it's already coiled up back inside her mouth. She tail-thumps, her dark neck feathers lifting and spreading. In better light we'd see them go all sorts of colours. Holding my breath I lock eyes with her and push the bag through the bars.

'Chicken's your favourite, isn't it?'

Behind me, Fleur groans. 'Can't you just throw it?'

Whoof! The big lizard lunges and plucks the bag out of my

hand so quickly I hardly have time to twitch. I swallow. With my ribs hurting and strapped, no way would I have been fast enough to dodge if she'd gone for me. She could've had my arm off easy if she'd wanted to. That was dumb, no three ways about it.

'You're crazy, you know that?' Fleur says.

'It's not right, caging her like this,' I say, backing off, a bit shaken. There's lizard drool on my sleeve so I crouch to wipe it off in the dirt. I watch as the lizard wolfs the scraps down in one big gulp. Inside my head I see other cages, holding ident children. If that's so wrong, why isn't this?

Colm half smiles, half winces. His thinking smile. 'Maybe not, but let her go and they'd all go. We'd lose our cover.'

He's right, as always. Sky lizards and people don't mix. The local sky lizard colony would have cleared off as soon as we moved in, but with their queen trapped down here and her stink calling to them, the males stick around. When the occasional Slayer windjammer comes scouting, they see the sky lizards circling, and their droppings white-scarring the rocks, and look no further.

Cunning and necessary, I guess. Still can't say I like it.

Fleur huffs. 'You ready to listen now?'

In the moonshine her eyes look massive. Like Sky inside the Slayer transport, the girl can hardly stand still – she's so full to bursting with news. Behind me the massive lizard hisses and slams into the bars, hungry for some more chicken guts.

'Listen to what?' I say, distracted.

She grins. 'You ain't heard about the peace deal then?'

'The *what*?' I glance at Colm, but he looks as stunned as I do.

Fleur laps up our surprise, her grin even wider. Behind her, the deadheads nod and mutter among themselves.

'Seriously,' she says. 'That's the buzz going around – a peace deal's on the table. There's already a ceasefire. The Council's meeting to discuss it right now. Our hit-and-run raids must be hurting them more than we thought.'

Colm gets his voice working. 'How come we didn't hear about this?'

'It only happened a few hours ago, that's why. While Kyle was getting his ass kicked. It's all everyone is talking about.'

'What *happened* a few hours ago?' I say.

'An encrypted message came in. Soon as our comms guys unscrambled it, Ballard, Mendela and the other top people all shipped out on our fastest scout windjammer. One of the launch crew overheard them. They've been summoned to an emergency Gemini Council meeting to discuss a Slayer peace offer!'

Fleur sighs, long and hard. 'Seriously. The war is over.'

4
ARGUMENTS

A week goes by with no sign of Ballard and the other rebel leaders returning. I'm still struggling to get my head around what Fleur told us. Peace treaty? War over? It makes no sense, like taking a step and finding there's no floor to put your foot back down on. But something big is going on for sure. We've been ordered to 'cease offensive operations with immediate effect'.

Some say this proves the rumour. I don't know about that.

What I *do* know is it's weirdly quiet and tense in the Deeps. Rona reckons everybody's gone from yakking about peace deals to holding their breath. Weather's been odd too. Firstgreen usually brings strong easterlies, but for days the windsocks have hung limp. Only in the last few hours has the wind picked up again.

One good thing – at least Colm and I seem forgotten now.

I'm not complaining. See, I'm all healed, tooth regrown, strapping gone and ribs good again. And no wind means no windjammer flying, so I get to see more of Sky. She's sitting cross-legged on the end of my bunk right now, her back to me, honing the long-bladed hunting knife I gave her. The steady *rasp-rasp* of steel on stone drags a yawn out of me.

I breathe in and fill my nose with the sweet smell of the gun oil she uses. It makes a very welcome change from the usual stink of damp and sweaty bodies.

'How sharp d'you need it?' I say, stretching.

'Sharp,' Sky says. 'Needs a fine edge to cut through bone.'

By rights she shouldn't be in here. Deeps rules – one lot of sleeping tents for male fighters, another for women. No pairing-up allowed. War comes first, something like that. But rules and regulations slide off Sky like rain runs off a fourhorn's greasy back. She comes and goes as she pleases. I'm glad. Whenever she limps in here my heart starts thumping. Can't help it.

So far today we haven't argued. Not much anyway.

Sky inspects her blade, spits on the whetstone and goes again.

I go back to watching her vid. That's against regs too, shot by her co-pilot Kallio's helmet-cam on the last relief mission they flew to the Blight before our jammers were grounded. Jagged rocks flash close past the canopy. The early dawnshine picks out streaks of orange and yellow in cliffs that were grey a minute ago, green leaves clinging to stubby, wind-thrashed trees.

'Do you have to fly *so* bogging low?' I say, flinching.

Sky doesn't look up. 'The lower we scrape the ridges, the less likely we are to be picked up on the run-in.'

'That's crazy low though,' I say, wincing as I spot some grazing fourhorns looking *down* at her windjammer as it whines past. They look about as horrified as I do. And Sky's fast, but she's only pureblood fast. One mistake, she's chewing on rock. She banks round an outcrop, chucking the jammer about like it's a toy.

I'm pretty sure the right wing tip clips some branches.

She glances across at the camera – at Kallio – and grins. Which stings, seeing as I mainly get scowls.

Ahead, jinking about as it tracks the lower slopes of the ridge, I see the lead windjammer with their mission commander, Ekway, inside it. The dawnshine catches it as it banks left and tucks even closer to the rocks. I glimpse the Gemini symbol painted on the hull and under the stub-wings – a massive black handprint with the little finger painted blood-red. Twist-black-four we call it. I hold my left hand up and look at the stump where my little finger was, before the Answerman took it for his collection of grisly trophies, the price for his answers. It's healed clean – course it has – I'm nublood. Yet even now it shocks me, like it's a stranger's hand I'm looking at. Weird too how it still itches sometimes on damp mornings, as if thinking about growing back.

In my earbuds I hear Ekway's voice on Sky's tac-comm.

'Blight in five. Get ready for the drop.'

That drags my eyes back to the cleverbox screen, and a good view of Sky. Her hair, hacked off by Fliss when we were on the run together, is back to bleached-white dreads and nearly shoulder length now. Her cheekbones are daubed with the black paint jammer pilots wear; her jawbone works as she chews something. Her eyes, the dark green of deep water, flick about restlessly, checking instruments. I make out the teardrop inked under her left, in memory of Tarn. One twitch, they both die, yet she's obviously loving every second. I never get to see her like this on the ground, so alive. I reckon she just doesn't know what fear is.

I must mutter something because real Sky takes a break from her whetstone and glances back at me. 'Where are you at?'

'You're about to hit the Blight.'

A massive bang makes me jump and curse.

On-screen Sky swears too, and I see a sticky smear of blood and guts and yellow-gold feathers sliding up the canopy.

'Was that the bird?' she asks.

I nod. 'Scared the crap out of me.'

The view changes as Kallio unstraps and clambers back into the cargo hold to cut the crates loose on Sky's signal. His hand mashes a red button on the hull. The ramp drops down, opening up the back of the windjammer, and I can almost feel the wind slap and tug at him. A steep, rock-strewn slope blurs past, so close it seems he could reach out and burn his fingers on it. He looks down. Way below is the valley bottom, green and yellow fields streaming backwards. Labourers straighten and look up, gobs open, as they soar over. I hear a buzzing. A light by the open hatch starts flashing, red and urgent, counting down the thirty seconds to the drop.

Sky dives them down now until they're among the weeds, so low the downwash from their lifters kicks up a giant rooster tail of dust and earth behind the windjammer. Above the shriek of the wind I hear a crackling, tearing sound, and some bangs. Kallio's view jerks forward to the flight deck. The sky ahead is a wall of snapping flame and writhing smoke. Lethal blobs of green seem to drift lazily upwards to flash past, barely missing.

'They're shooting at you!' I exclaim, flinching just watching it.

Sky grunts. 'Yeah, Slayers have a bad habit of doing that. They've stuck guns all around the Blight. We took loads of ground fire.'

Something clatters the hull, knocking the windjammer's left wing down until Sky catches it and levels them. Kallio's view shifts to the open back again. And now they're hurtling low across the jumbled sprawl of shanty-town roofs that is the Blight. Or *was* – this isn't the same place I stumbled through on my way to see the Answerman. This filthy maze of shacks, plywood, corrugated iron and sun-bleached plastic looks like some giant, fire-breathing monster has stomped all over it. Everywhere fires blaze unchecked. Columns of ugly black smoke billow into the air. In some open places I glimpse corpses left lying where they fell.

Seconds later I spot the first barricades. Piles of rubbish and rubble, burnt-out wrecks of Slayer landcrawlers, anything the desperate Blight defenders can lay their hands on.

Poor Blight. So close to Prime, it's taken the biggest beating. We destroyed their precious Facility, so now the Slayers are taking their revenge by levelling the Blight and going after our rebel base underneath it, Bastion. Our besieged forces there are helping the Blighties fight, but are barely clinging on. Sky reckons three-quarters of the Blight is overrun or abandoned.

The drop light flicks from red to green. Kallio lets the crates go. One by one they rumble backwards to the open ramp and tumble out. Their drogue chutes snap and fill.

The view swings right.

I twitch big time as I see Prime itself, crouching there high on the hill above the Blight, like a gigantic, stone-walled toad. Within those walls, metal towers gleam like mercury, flinging the dawnshine back at Kallio's helmet-cam. It's *his* stronghold.

The Saviour. Warlord. Lawmaker. Despot. Ruler of Wrath.

Our enemy. And . . . my father.

So hard to believe, even now. So wrong. So unfair.

His fortress too – that was where they once dragged me and sucked my nublood out to pump into him, to heal his crippled, failing body. The memories reach inside me through my eyes, grasp my guts with ice-cold fingers and start to squeeze.

I've seen enough. I hit stop, yank the buds from my ears.

'Wow,' I say, fighting to keep my voice level. 'Blight's a mess.'

'Did tell you,' Sky says, without looking up.

With the sun on the canvas all day, it's still warm in the tent. She's peeled her jumpsuit top off and knotted it round her waist. I put the screen down and watch her sadly, the way her shoulder bones slide under her T-shirt with each stroke of the stone in her hand. Muscles stand out like cables in her skinny arms. A crescent of pale skin uncovers at the small of her back as she leans forward. Tempting. I could reach her with my toes and give her a tickle. Would do a while back, without thinking. Not now.

I've been shrugged off enough. It's no fun.

Anyway, we're not alone. Others are off duty and taking it easy too. Colm's on the upper bunk above us, reading something. I bet his ears are flapping.

Sky coughs. She's got another cold.

'This peace deal,' I say to her back. 'What do *you* think?'

Finally, she quits with the whetstone, holsters the knife and squirms around to face me. 'It's only a rumour.'

'What if it turns out to be true?'

'Even if it is, we both know it won't be worth squat. Slayers are snakes. The Saviour's the biggest snake of all. You don't make deals with snakes, you just stamp on their head.'

A man struggles inside through the tent flap. Sky darts a glance at him as he heads for his bunk, and looks disappointed.

'Still no word from Ness?' I ask her.

She shakes her head. 'Still working on it. He'll crack it soon.'

'And if he doesn't?'

'He'd better. For his own good.' She pats her knife.

I'm working on a scowl when she winks. *Not* funny though. Here we are, with what could be a miraculous peace breaking out. We could have a future, for the first time in our lives. But that doesn't interest Sky in the slightest. Course not.

Wood creaks above us. Colm's upside-down face appears.

'If this peace deal does come off,' he says, 'maybe we'd do a prisoner exchange. You could ask for your sister.'

Sky sneers. 'You think that's likely?'

Colm, his upside-down face reddening, shrugs at her.

'More likely than you rescuing her. And you're forgetting something, Sky. Right now there's a ceasefire. Screw that up by trying to bust your sister out of wherever she's being held and Ballard will skin you.'

'Any deal will just be a trick,' she snarls. 'Of all people, you should know that, what with being raised a *Slayer*.'

She stresses the last bit. Deliberate. Nasty.

Is this why Sky can't stand him? Rona said it was jealousy, me having Colm, her missing Tarn. I'd thought it was my brother saying that going after Tarn was dumb, that our cause comes first.

'Colm didn't choose that,' I say through my teeth.

She rocks back and holds her hands up. 'Okay, okay. All I'm saying is no way am I hanging about here, waiting on some peace treaty that might never happen. Soon as Ness comes up with the goods, I say we go looking for Tarn.' Her eyes find mine and drill into them. 'That was the deal. Remember?'

We go looking for Tarn. I roll the words around my mouth, not saying them aloud, just tasting them. They taste of ashes.

But I *did* make that deal. 'Sure.'

Colm lets out a disgusted sigh and rolls out of sight.

'You're always moaning about wanting to fight. Going after Tarn with me is your chance to see some action,' Sky says.

My face goes hot. 'I do want to fight, but –'

'Yeah, yeah,' she cuts in. 'Ballard says you're too valuable.'

'He is too valuable,' Colm says.

'I'm not,' I say. 'Sky's right. I stopped being valuable after I led Gemini to the Facility.' The truth is, Ballard and the rest of the rebel council are only worried I'll get myself captured. We're sure the Saviour was hurt bad in the raid. They don't want Slayers getting their hands on my nublood and healing him again.

Sky nods. Her eyes go narrow and sly.

'Ballard's not here to stop us, is he? What about it, Kyle?'

Before I can say anything Colm jumps down from his bunk. Never have I seen my brother look so fed up, which is saying something because he tends to the grim and serious.

'Don't be crazy,' he says, almost spitting.

Sky laughs her bitter laugh. 'What's your problem?'

He curses. 'You are. You think you can do what you fraggin' like, and to hell with everybody else.'

Her face, always so pale and bloodless, goes white. She hops off the bed and faces him, hand on the hilt of her knife.

'That what you think, huh, Slayer-boy?'

I scramble up and get between them. 'Don't call him that.'

She shoves me back a step. 'Tell your gom of a brother to shut it.'

But my brother isn't done arguing yet. 'Don't listen to her, Kyle. She'll get you killed, for nothing.'

Sky's lips twitch. 'Nothing? My sister's a nothing?'

She snatches up her cleverbox and stalks off.

I curse and close my eyes. When I open them again, Sky's long gone. Colm looks at me and slowly shakes his head.

'Don't,' I tell him, as his gob opens. 'Just don't, all right!'

5
THE FIREFIGHT

I love my new-found brother. I do. We share everything: we like the same stuff, make the same jokes and laugh at them. Sometimes I wonder how I ever got along without Colm.

Now though, I need a break from him slagging off Sky.

Not that he's all wrong, but I'm not in the mood to hear it. I slip away, leaving him chuntering away to himself on his bunk. Soon as I'm outside the tent I stand up straight and suck fresh evening air deep into my lungs. It calms me down. There's still hope, I tell myself. Maybe this peace deal *is* for real. And I like Colm's suggestion about trading prisoners. Getting Tarn back like that would beat sneaking off with Sky and defying Ballard.

A gust slaps the tent's canvas and blows my hair into my eyes. If it stays like this, Sky will be flying tomorrow. No, she won't. I remember our windjammers are grounded.

I hesitate, then go looking for her.

Two women she shares her tent with are outside it, smoking. They tell me Sky's not there. I glance doubtfully at the tent flap. The older one blows smoke in my face and smiles.

'She ain't. Honest. Take a look inside if you like.'

'Any idea where she is?'

They swap looks and shrugs.

'You guys had another bust-up?' the younger one asks.

'Something like that,' I mutter. And clear off, my face all hot.

I consider tracking Ness down to see if Sky's stropped off to have a nag at him, then get a better idea. I make my way back out through the gathering darkness to the canyon where the captured Slayer windjammer was hidden away. My hunch pays off. The rear loading ramp is down. A flicker of light shows. I peek inside. The light is from a shiner hung up on the bars of the cage. Sky is sitting inside, her back against the hull where Tarn scratched her tag. Her head is down, her arms wrapped round her knees.

She's so still. Is she asleep?

I do a cough to let her know I'm here. Good job too. Her head snaps up and a blaster appears in her hand.

'It's only me,' I tell her.

'Oh joy,' she mutters. But at least she puts the gun away.

I step inside. 'What are you doing?'

She glares at me. 'Thinking. Being with my sister.'

'Want me to go away?'

She hesitates. 'How'd you know I'd be here?'

'I didn't, not for sure. I just –'

The wail of the landing siren cuts me off, followed by some distant shouting and the chuff and clank of steam tractors.

'Sounds like we've got incoming,' Sky says.

'Bit late and dark, isn't it?' I say.

I hustle back to the ramp and stick my head out. The landing area is all lit up now by lines of brightly flaring oil-burners.

She limps over to join me on the ramp.

'They're back then,' she says.

I spot the small windjammer on final approach. Sky knows her jammers way better than I do, but even in the dark I can tell which one this is – the fast transport that flew Ballard and the other rebel leaders out of here a week ago. Air brakes already out, its lifters howl as they're throttled up to landing power. It dives towards the ground, flares late and touches down. The howl dies away. I hear the rumble of wheels pounding the hard-packed dirt.

'Nice landing,' I say.

Sky grunts. 'You reckon?'

The burners are doused, plunging the Deeps back into a smothering darkness. Sky shifts beside me.

'So what do you want?' she says.

I throw my hands up. 'I don't *want* anything.'

'Yeah, you do, Kyle. That's why you're here. You want me to let you off the hook for helping me find Tarn. Don't you?'

'No. You're wrong,' I lie, squirming.

'Am I?' She tilts her head to one side. 'So when Ness finally comes up with the goods you will help me?'

'What if we mess up the ceasefire, like Colm said?'

Sky shows me her teeth in a sneer. 'Oh, quit with the *Colm says this, Colm says that crap*, will you? That's all I boggin' get from you these days. Think for yourself.'

'I do think for myself. It's just . . . he talks a lot of sense.'

'Run back to him then. You've got your brother; you don't need me any more. I'll only get you killed, for nothing.'

'Oh, come on, Sky! It's not like that.'

'So what's it like? Tell me.'

I take a deep breath, then let it out. 'Maybe our cause *should* come before what we want. Like the people here who have children, but still choose to risk their lives fighting for Gemini. They're fighting for everybody's ident children, not just theirs.'

'Colm preach that at you, did he?'

'Just because you don't like him doesn't make him wrong.'

Sky folds her arms, looks away and says nothing.

'You were all for the cause yourself once, when you thought Tarn was dead. We need to build a world where purebloods and nubloods live together in peace, that's what *you* said.'

'What if I did?' she says over her shoulder.

'So what's changed?' I say. 'Look, can't we just talk about this instead of always arguing? Rona says the other missing nublood kids could be in the same place Tarn is. You should tell Ballard what you've found out. Maybe he'll authorise another raid to rescue them. That's got to stand a better chance than just us two.'

'Why didn't I think of that?' she says, all sneery.

I grit my teeth. 'Why not?'

She looks back, her face one big scowl. 'Because we're clinging on as it is. And now this fraggin' peace deal.' She coughs and turns away again. 'No way will he go for a raid.'

'You don't know that,' I say.

'I do,' she says, coughs and looks away again.

Meanwhile, out on the landing field the landed windjammer drops its ramp. A dozen or so passengers exit down it, led by Ballard, his silver hair unmistakable even at this distance. Armoured steam tractors roll forward to meet them with loads of fighters running ahead. These fan out to form a defensive cordon around the newcomers and escort them to their rides.

Weird. Why would our leaders need guarding out here?

Then I see why . . . and it sucks all the spit out of my mouth. Those guards aren't for Ballard, Mendela and the rest – they're for the tall figure in a matt-black cloak walking with them.

A Slayer. Here. In the Deeps.

'What the hell?' Sky says.

Spit leaks back into my mouth as I slowly get over the shock of it. And now, in spite of everything, I start to laugh.

'What's so funny?' she demands.

'Never thought I'd be glad to see a Slayer,' I say, grinning. 'But I am now. If Ballard's brought one here, that *has* to mean the peace deal is no rumour. Fleur got it right. The war's over, Sky!'

Sky glares at me as if I'm mad.

'Yeah?' she says. 'And fourhorns can fly.'

'Oh, come on. What else can it mean? Let's go and find out what's going on. Maybe they'll make an announcement.'

But Sky shakes her head again and frowns, looking more through me than at me. 'You go. I'll see you later.'

'You don't want to know what's up?'

'It's not that, I – look, I'll be along in a while. Okay?'

'Sure.' I hesitate, then figure I can't be forever biting my tongue with her. 'You never know, Sky, maybe Colm's right too and we'll end up swapping prisoners. Anything's possible. If this is a peace deal, it'll be our best chance of finding Tarn.'

'*Our* best chance?' Sky says, staring.

I shrug. 'Like you said, we bumped stumps on it.'

She smiles. A bit sad and pained-looking, but it's something.

I'm halfway back to the main base, striding out, hope buzzing away inside me as I wonder if Wrath is finally about to cut me my first-ever break. That's when I hear the blaster fire.

My heart sinks. I reckon some drooler has seen the Slayer, lost it and started shooting. Ahead of me the tractors judder to a halt. The escorting fighters crouch and level their pulse rifles.

More crackles of blaster fire. I see the flashes. And realise I'm wrong.

It's from way beyond the tractors – where all our tents are. Where I left Colm muttering into his bunk.

Now I hear the *tump-tump* of pulse rifles. Returning fire?

Peace deals and Slayers forgotten, I take off towards the flashes. The only weapon I've got is my hunting knife. No match for blasters, but it'll have to do. Luckily, by the time I've pounded my way there the firefight seems to be over. People are milling around, mostly half dressed like they've just rolled out of their bunks, pushing and shoving and craning to get a look at what's happened. Smoke curls up into the night, spark-filled, stinking. A few heavily armed fighters are shoving everybody back.

'Who was shooting?' I say, elbowing my way forward.

Nobody here seems to know, so I work my way through the crowd until I hear some guy mouthing off about what he saw.

'All three of 'em was wearing masks,' he's saying. 'Piled into that tent over there and started blasting. I was having a smoke when I seen 'em go in.' He shakes his head. 'Crazy, it was.'

'Where are the shooters now?' somebody calls out.

'All dead,' the man says. 'We got 'em. Not me, I didn't have no gun. One of the guys in the tent zapped two. The last one tried to do a runner. A buddy of mine took him out.'

More voices call out questions.

'Who were the shooters? How many of our guys were killed?'

But I'm past listening. Behind the line of fighters holding us back, I catch a glimpse of a tent in flames.

The tent that Colm and me bunk down in.

Panicking now, I shove my way to the front of the crowd.

'Let me through! My brother's in there!' I yell.

This cuts no ice with the hard-faced fighters keeping us all back.

'Take it easy, fella,' one growls.

'I need to see if my brother's okay,' I say through my teeth.

'What you *need* is to stay back,' he says.

'Okay, okay,' I say, do a big old sigh, and turn away for just long enough to make them think I'm heading away.

Turn, drop my shoulder and hurl myself through them.

Two go down. One staggers, shoots a hand out and grabs me. An elbow in the face sorts her. A second later I'm at the blazing tent. That's as far as I get though. The flames are too fierce and stop me in my tracks. If anybody's inside they're cooked.

'Colm!' I reel backwards.

Into hands that drag me away. My feet are kicked from under me and I'm pushed down, flat on my face. I struggle, despairing and mad as hell, but just get to eat more dirt.

I quit fighting and lie still. Wondering. Fearing.

Finally, after what feels like forever, I'm hauled back to my feet. I lash out, more to share my pain than trying to break free.

'Quit that!' Somebody slams a hard punch into my kidneys.

That kills. I hunch over.

'The brother?' a deep voice says behind me.

'Says he is.' They turn me around.

There – frowning at me – is the great man himself. Ballard.

Truth be told, I'm shocked. The same craggy face and close-cropped silver hair. The simple grey cloak of the Gemini Council worn over his combat fatigues. Only this Ballard is way more bent than I remember, impossibly older since I last saw him.

He signals to the men holding me. 'Go easy.'

I'm held less tightly now, do my best to straighten up.

'Kyle?' Ballard says, his face mournful. 'You're not hurt?'

'I'm all right,' I mumble, glancing around at what's left of the still-burning tent. 'Colm was in that tent there. Is he –?'

Can't ask it, in case I get the answer I dread.

I don't get a second chance. A quick whispered order from Ballard to his fighter escort and now I'm being hustled away.

'Wait, wait!' I call out. 'What about my brother?'

But Ballard's not listening. Flanked by his wary bodyguards he follows along slowly, his head down, as if deep in thought.

'Kyle!' Sky shouts. 'What's going on?'

I look over my shoulder and see her trying to push past the cordon to reach me, only to be shoved roughly back.

Her raging face is the last thing I see.

The guards put a bag over my head. Everything goes black.

6
STRINGS AND STINGS ATTACHED

After a forever of stumbling along blindly and being pushed, I'm stopped, turned and shoved backwards. Hinges squeal, metal clangs and bolts rasp home. Finally, the hood is pulled off. I squint around at a small rock-walled chamber. Table. Bench. Covered shit-pit in the corner. Closed metal door. Loads of guards.

'Why the bag over my head? What's going on?'

I'm wasting my breath. None of the guards will answer me; they just watch me out of their bored, tough-guy eyes like I'm some not-very-interesting bug. I give up asking, lie down on the bench and glower up at the rock ceiling, sick to my stomach.

Does this mean Colm is dead?

Time crawls by, slow and ugly. Wrath knows how long it is before the oil-starved hinges squeal again. The chamber door opens outwards and . . . Rona and Colm are shepherded inside.

Seeing me, Rona's hand flies to her mouth.

I jump up from the bench. Rona dashes across the room, throws her arms round me and hugs me so tight I can hardly breathe.

'Kyle! Oh, thanks be to goodness, we were so worried.'

I hug her back, while over her shoulder I gawp at Colm. He looks shaken, his face pulled tight. His left arm is in a sling.

'You're *alive*,' I blurt out.

He grimaces. 'Yeah. I think so.'

Rona lets go of me, dabs at her red-looking eyes and takes a quick healer look at me. 'You're not hurt, are you?'

'I'm fine,' I tell her. 'I – uh – wasn't there to get shot at.'

One of the guards who brought them in steps up, clears his throat and lays a gloved hand on her shoulder.

'You've seen the boy needs no healing,' he says. 'Let's go.'

I glare at him, but Rona shoots me a quick warning look. She reaches out and pulls Colm and me together. 'Listen to me,' she says, frowning, 'you're safe here at least. Do what they say and don't make any trouble. They won't let me stay with you, but I won't be far away. Everything will be all right. Okay?'

We each get another quick hug before she's taken away.

After the door slams shut behind her, the guards left inside shove us towards the bench along the wall. A minute ago I'd have shoved back to spite them. Now I can't be bothered. I'm more interested in hearing what my wounded brother has to say.

'What happened?' I ask him. 'A guy said three masked shooters burst into our tent and then opened up with blasters.'

Colm nurses his bandaged arm and nods.

'I was half asleep. The tent flap lifts and some guys barge inside. Next thing I know they're blasting the hell out of your bunk.'

I stare at him, appalled. 'So what did you do?'

'They shot up my bunk next.' A painful smile tugs at my

brother's lips. 'Only I'd got such a fright when the shooting started I'd already fallen off it. It was lights-out and dark inside. With all the blasting, maybe the shooters dazzled themselves. My pulse rifle was still up on my bunk, so I cleared off as fast as I could. They came after me, but by then our guys were shooting back.'

I can't help glancing at his bandaged arm. Rona's handiwork.

'I got lucky,' he says. 'Four of our mates were killed in the crossfire, more injured. It was a slaughterhouse.'

'Who did this?' I splutter. 'And why? I don't understand.'

'Me neither. But . . .' He takes a deep breath, sighs it out. 'My first thought was that Slayers had somehow tracked us down and sent in a suicide squad to take us out. For revenge, or to teach us a lesson, like even out here in the Deeps nobody's safe. Only before I was taken away, I got a good look at the shooters. They were Gemini fighters. I've seen them around. And before you ask, it wasn't Stauffer or any of his thug mates.'

Colm's words stomp about in my head, but make no sense.

'You're saying our own guys tried to kill us?'

He nods. 'And it was definitely us they were after. They came straight to our bunks. It was a hit. We were the target.'

'Why?' I say, dry-mouthed.

'I don't know. Lucky you weren't in your bunk, huh?'

'Too right.' I shiver. And now I finally remember that I've got my own big news to share. I tell Colm about how I saw the windjammer land and the black-clad passenger it unloaded.

'Ballard brought a Slayer *here*?' he says, rocking back and chewing his lip. 'Guess the peace deal must be on then.'

'Yeah, that's what I thought.'

'So when did the jammer land?'

I think back. 'Not long before the shooting started.'

Colm nods and pulls what I call his serious-thinking face.

Which sets me thinking too. 'Coincidence?'

'Could be,' he says, but really slow, like he doesn't believe it.

I glance at our guards. They're still all watching us, unblinking, unmoving, as if carved out of stone. I'd figured we'd been stuck in here for our protection. Now I'm starting to doubt. These guys are doing a great job of making me feel more like a prisoner.

'Wonder how long they'll keep us in here?' I say to Colm.

He sits on the bench, swings his feet up and stretches out. 'Who knows? We should get some rest.'

'Hey, what about me?'

But my brother's eyes are closed already, and he looks so destroyed I haven't the heart to make him shift.

I settle for the dirt floor. It's as uncomfortable as it looks.

Without windows in here it's only a guess, but based on how stiff I feel after hours of squirming around on hard-packed dirt, I reckon it's early morning when they come for us.

We each get a beaker of water and a biscuit to munch as we're marched along one rock-hewn corridor after another, minded by a dozen or so heavily armed guards. Finally, we're shoved into a room where Ballard is waiting, sitting behind a massive round table. His wire-framed glasses reflect the glowtubes so I can't see his eyes, but his lined face is one big frown. I'd hoped Rona would be there too. She isn't. The only friendly face belongs to Scallon, the senior healer woman who pulled that bolt out of me back in Bastion. She gets up, greets us and shows us to a couple of spare seats.

'Why are we here?' I whisper.

And wish I hadn't as her face falls.

'You'll see,' she says, and returns to her seat.

I glance around the room. Apart from Scallon and Ballard and some watchful guards, there are two other people here, both seated at the table. Like Ballard, they wear the long grey cloaks of Gemini Council members. The tall black woman is Mendela, Defence Commander of this Deeps outpost. The irritable-looking plump man with the savagely pockmarked face I've never seen before.

'So there they are,' fat guy says.

He inspects Colm and me, a look on his face like we're pieces of fruit to choose between and both of us seem rotten.

'Hard to believe,' Mendela says, 'it all hangs on *these* two boys.'

I swap glances with Colm. He looks worried too.

Ballard stands up, waving away a guard who leaps forward to try and help him. He takes his glasses off and rubs his eyes. He looks tired, like he didn't get much sleep last night either.

'Kyle, Colm,' he says, blinking at us. 'You must be wondering –'

Fat guy slams his hand on the table and interrupts angrily, chins wobbling. 'For Wrath's sake, Ballard, you're wasting time we haven't got. We have important things to discuss.'

Ballard stiffens. 'We do, Councillor Schroeder. But first I think we owe these boys an explanation.'

Schroeder glares at us and snorts, sending spit flying.

Well, I can do angry too. I jump up. 'What the hell's going on?'

I expect to be shouted at, but Commander Mendela smiles. Not Ballard though. He looks like he's in pain.

'Sit down, son,' Mendela says. 'We like defiant, but we've got something to tell you and you would do well to listen.'

I swallow and sit down again, feeling more than a bit stupid.

Ballard clears his throat. 'As Councillor Schroeder says, the Council has much to discuss, so I'll be brief.' He puts his glasses back on and his gaze settles on me. My head pounds and blood hisses in my ears like static. 'You boys will, I'm sure, have heard the rumours of a peace treaty between us and the Slayers.'

I nod, not trusting my voice. So does Colm.

'Well, the rumours are true,' Ballard continues. 'If Gemini ceases fighting and we withdraw our forces to the Barrenlands, in return the Saviour will grant us a sanctuary out there.'

'So tempting.' Mendela's voice is thick with sarcasm.

Ballard sighs. 'As you might expect, the peace offer comes with many strings attached. Ident children must still be handed over and held in camps. Instead of Peace Fairs, as soon as nubloods are identified they will be returned to us in our Barrenlands paradise.' He sighs deeply. 'However, the strongest of them will first be required to do two years' service down darkblende mines. After completing this, they too will be returned.'

'*If* they survive the two years,' Scallon says.

'Be quiet!' Schroeder snaps.

I shake my head, dazed, struggling to take this in. Two years down a darkblende mine is crap, but sanctuary sounds good.

'There is one other condition,' Ballard says.

Mendela pulls a grim face, as if she's chewing a mouthful of something sour. As for Scallon, she won't look me in the eye.

Colm and I say it as one. 'What *other* condition?'

Ballard winces, his watery eyes like grey pools in cracked

rock. 'The final condition is that we hand you both over.' He pauses, maybe to let this sink in. 'Unless we agree to all these conditions before the next doom moon, the peace offer will be withdrawn. The Saviour will order the mobilisation of a conscript army to fight alongside his Slayers. He says they won't rest until every nublood on Wrath is hunted down. Extermination, pure and simple.'

'The sting in the tail,' Mendela says, and sighs.

My head pounds like someone's taken a club to it. *So this is how it all ends,* I think dismally. *I should have fraggin' known.*

'And you'd do that? You'd hand us over?' I croak.

Ballard just looks at me, stony-faced.

'So that's why those fighters tried to kill us,' Colm says.

'Huh?' I glance at him. He's staring at Ballard.

Ballard nods. 'Details of the peace offer must somehow have reached here before we did. The Saviour wants you alive. The attempt on your lives was an act of sabotage by Gemini hardliners who wish to fight on regardless. With you dead, the peace deal is dead too. They will have known that my first act upon my return would be to place you in protective custody.'

I'm not sure I get all this, not fully, but one thing I *do* get: Colm and me, we're screwed. I lick my lips. 'What happens now?'

He pulls at his beard. 'That, Kyle, is for the Council to decide.'

'I'm glad to hear it.' Schroeder wobbles to his feet. 'Let's get this farce over with. Bring in the damn Slayer.' He clicks his fingers at the guards by another door at the far side of the chamber.

They scramble to unbolt it and swing it open.

In walks a woman dressed head to foot in Slayer matt-black.

I gasp. Beside me, Colm lets out a strangled-sounding moan. Because it's not every day you see a ghost. The last time I saw this woman was during the Facility raid, when Murdo Dern emptied his pulse rifle into her at point-blank range, almost cutting her in half. Yet here the High Slayer stands in her fancy black-leather uniform trimmed with fur, with her raven-dark hair and the cruel lines in her face no amount of powder can hide. A smile twists her full lips, and I see her obvious delight at our shock and confusion. Morana, High Slayer of the Barrenlands.

'No fraggin' way!' I howl, gulping air, sending my chair flying as I lurch to my feet again. 'You're dead. I saw you killed!'

'Only, as you see, I'm very much alive,' she says, sneering.

Ballard grits his teeth. 'You're here for a reason, Slayer, so get on with it. Take your look. Tell us if you're satisfied.'

She darts him a mocking glance. 'Who are you again?'

'You've one minute, and no longer.'

They swap glares, until she shrugs and turns from him to Colm and me. She steps around the table, coming closer.

'Don't be shy,' she says. 'Show me your handsome faces.'

I back up, but hit rock wall.

She glances at my brother and spots his heavily bandaged arm.

'This merchandise has been damaged.'

'A scratch,' Schroeder says quickly. 'Nothing more.'

Morana nods and her gaze slides across to me. 'So alike, yet I have the feeling you're the twist, Kyle. Am I right?'

I give myself a bit of a shake, conscious Ballard's watching me.

'I'm nublood,' I tell her. 'We call ourselves nublood.'

She shows me a mouthful of too-perfect teeth and laughs.

'Oh, do you now? How dull. I think "twist" has far more of a ring to it. Now come closer, Kyle, and let me see you.'

'Drop dead.' I stay where I am.

Mistake. She looks at Schroeder. He curses and signals. Two guards grab me and shove me forward. I struggle. Nothing doing. They're both nubloods and loads bigger than me.

'That's better.' Morana peels off a glove. Her body armour creaks as she reaches out and turns my face this way and that, studying me closely. Then she strokes my cheek, her fingers cold and lingering, exactly as she did that day back in the Barrenlands when she'd captured Sky and me.

'So tell me, Kyle, how does it feel to play such an important role in the future of your pitiful species?'

Her breath warms my face. I gauge the distance to her head to see if it's worth trying for a headbutt. But she's too far away and the guys holding on to me are too strong.

'That's enough,' Ballard calls out. 'Leave the boy alone.'

Morana gives me one last icy glare, then lets go. Pulling her glove back on, she turns and stalks back towards the open doorway and the waiting Gemini guards.

'Very well,' she announces, as cool as you like. 'I will report back to the Saviour that you do indeed have his beloved sons.'

Ballard says nothing, just looks grim as hell.

Schroeder's a different story – I reckon the man seems pleased.

Mendela hauls herself to her feet. 'Is she done here?'

'She is,' Ballard says. 'Take her away.'

'I'll see to it personally that our guest,' Mendela wrinkles her nose at Morana, 'is returned to the rendezvous point, with all the necessary safeguards so she can't find her way back uninvited.'

Ballard nods, and Morana is escorted away.

There's a long, ugly silence.

And I finally let out the breath I've been holding.

Our guards bring two new benches, one for Colm, another to replace the one I took out my rage and despair on.

'Smash these,' a guard warns, 'and you don't get more. Okay?'

I mutter at her that I won't.

'This is bullshit,' I say to Colm. 'Can you believe it?'

My brother's not said a word since we were dragged back here to our cell, just stared into space and shaken his head a lot. So I'm glad when he finally looks at me.

'It's a trap,' he says. 'A clever one too.'

But I've also done some thinking since I quit smashing stuff.

'I don't see it. The Slayers must be dreaming if they think we'll chuck our guns away and shuffle off to hold hands out in the Barrenlands. Once we're there, they'd have us trapped. No way will the Council go for it. They'd have to be crazy.'

Colm takes a deep breath and hisses it out.

'What?' I say, irritated.

He clutches at his hurt arm and winces. 'Kyle, this isn't about peace or sanctuary in the Barrenlands. It's about divide and conquer, setting brother against brother.'

I grind my teeth. 'Just for once, can you speak plainly?'

'Okay, okay. Look, I grew up a Slayer, so I know how they think. This peace offer's fake, I'm sure of it. The Saviour has no intention of letting Gemini have a sanctuary in the Barrenlands or anywhere else. He just dangles the thought. It's bait on a hook.'

'And when we bite he's got us trapped?'

'It's simpler than that, more cunning. They'll make sure every Gemini fighter knows what's supposedly on offer. Some will clutch at the straw. Who can blame them for wanting an end to a lifetime of fear and fighting? Others will want to fight on though, sod the cost. Before you know it, Gemini will split into pro-treaty and anti-treaty factions. We'll start fighting among ourselves.'

I stare at him, gob open, hairs standing up on the back of my neck. 'Surely the Council will see that too?'

He shrugs. 'Maybe. But can they stop it? It's happening already, here in the Deeps. That's why my arm's in this bloody sling. And why we're stuck in this hole being guarded.'

I twitch. 'So the hardliners can't have another pop at us?'

Colm nods and tries for a smile. 'You're not as thick as you look.'

We sit there silent for a while.

'Don't know about you,' I say eventually, 'but I could've died when that door opened and Morana walked in.'

'Seriously,' Colm says, 'I could've done without that.'

I hesitate, but it has to be said. 'Murdo killed her. I saw it.'

'You had just been shot. Maybe you —'

'Maybe nothing! Ask him if you don't believe me.'

'I do believe you. But we've got more to worry about than a High Slayer coming back to life. Maybe her body armour saved her. Who knows? What matters is Gemini risked bringing her to the Deeps so she could identify us. What's that tell you?'

'Ballard's not as smart as we thought?'

Colm glances at our guards and they seem not to be listening. 'Ballard's no fool. Everything he does, he does for a reason. I think it tells us that the Council will go for the peace deal. You heard the woman — she's here to check the merchandise, to make sure we're still alive and kicking, ready to be handed over.'

'You think too much,' I croak.

'Sometimes I wish I didn't,' he says, and grimaces.

Another long silence. In my head I play back Colm's words, trying to find holes in his thinking that hope might fit into.

Nothing doing. There are no holes.

'Okay, fine,' I whisper, straightening kinks out of my neck. 'I get it. We're screwed if we stay here. Either we'll be handed back to the Slayers, or we'll be lynched by hardliners.'

Colm frowns. '*If* we stay here? You say it like we've a choice.'

'We'll get word to Rona and Sky. They'll bust us out.'

He says nothing, but his face is my face — I see the doubt.

'You got a better idea?' I ask.

'I'm working on it,' he tells me. And then, 'No.'

7
THE COUNCIL DECIDES

I'm squeezing off a last few sit-ups when our guards let Rona in. She's the only visitor we're allowed while we rot here like rats in this stinking hole, waiting for Gemini's leadership to make their minds up about the peace treaty. Three days we've been stuck here, and it's doing my head in.

'Hey, Rona,' Colm says, and smiles.

To listen to him, you wouldn't think he's gone mad. I nod at Rona and wipe the worst of the sweat off with my shirt.

'Oh, Kyle, must you?' she says.

This is *so* Rona. I'm to be handed over to Slayers or killed by my own kind, and she's worried I won't have a clean shirt.

With a sigh, she unpacks her bag. Even though she was searched on the way in, our watching guards stiffen.

'Any news?' I ask her.

She shakes her head. 'I'll tell you when there is. Now hand over your bowls. No point letting this broth get cold.'

Colm fetches the food bowls while I pull my shirt back on.

'Maybe no news is good news,' she says.

'You reckon?' I glance at our scratches on the rock wall.

It's eighteen days to the next doom moon. We've been crossing them off. Just thinking about it makes me shiver. Most nights our smaller and faster-moving dogmoon chases the bigmoon around Wrath's sky. Four times a year however, roughly at the turn of the seasons, it climbs higher in the sky than the bigmoon. That's when we call it the doom moon, and everybody is all *oh no!* and moaning about how it brings bad luck and savage weather.

Rona calls it superstition and nonsense. I guess we'll see.

'Don't worry, the Council will do the right thing,' she says. She slops slimy-looking broth into our bowls from a flask.

'Right for who?' I say. 'What *is* this?'

Colm dives right in. Being a martyr must be hungry work.

'It's all I could get,' Rona snaps. 'With everybody too busy arguing, nothing's getting done, least of all cooking.'

'What happened to your face?' Colm asks her.

'It's nothing,' Rona says, but too quickly.

I look up and now I see the swelling under her left eye.

'Was that . . . because of us?'

'Eat your broth.'

I push my bowl away untouched. 'Was it?'

'When people are scared they can do stupid things. I'm being escorted here now. Don't worry. It won't happen again.'

'It's getting ugly then?' Colm says.

Rona hesitates. 'Worse than ugly.' She lowers her voice. 'That Schroeder is whipping things up, making pro-treaty speeches. There's been rioting. Four people died last night.'

'For the treaty, or against it?' I ask.

'Does it matter?' She pushes my bowl back at me.

Even though I feel sick inside I choke a few mouthfuls down, for her more than me. And it's not as bad as it looks. Then again, it's been a good while since I last ate a proper meal.

'How's your arm?' Rona asks Colm.

He holds his arm up in its sling. 'Getting there, I think.'

I snort, hearing this. 'He still can't hardly move it.'

Rona suggested getting some of my nublood into him so he'd heal quicker, but the guards won't let her bring healing gear in. It's a curse. If we do bust out, him having two arms would be good.

'Hey, Colm, tell Rona what you told me this morning.'

He scowls, and says nothing.

'I'll tell her then. He said that it's okay if we're handed over.'

'I did *not*! All I said was — if the Council could negotiate a realistic deal, something that might actually work, but still had to hand us over, who are we to say it's too high a price?'

'You believe this?' I say to Rona.

She looks pained. 'Your brother's entitled to his opinion.'

'You *agree* with him?'

I get huffed at. 'No, I don't.' She turns to face my brother. 'You're brave to say it, Colm, but sacrificing yourself will achieve nothing. No good will come of making deals with Slayers.'

'Like I said!' I kick out at the dirt floor.

Colm shrugs and gets on with emptying his bowl.

I shove mine away and ask the question I've been busting to ask. 'Did you talk to Sky?'

'I did. She . . . asked after you.'

'Frag that,' I whisper. 'Will she help us?'

Rona glances at the guards. They're stretching, not watching.

I pull at her arm. 'Rona?'

And see the pained expression on her face.

'Kyle, I'm sorry. Sky can't help. She's tried to see you, but they won't let her. I know it's tough, but there's no way we can get you out of here. You're too important and too well guarded.'

'So we rot here until they hand us over?'

Rona leans in, grabs my hand and won't let go.

'Don't give up hope, Kyle. Our leaders will see this peace offer for the sham it is. And I heard talk that it's a last throw of the dice for the Slayers — because they know they're losing the war. If we fight on, we'll beat them and have peace on *our* terms!'

'You believe that?' I whisper.

She breathes deeply and nods. 'I do.'

Only I've known her too long to be fooled. She's just saying this.

In the middle of that night, we get our first taste of the trouble brewing in the Deeps. A distant roaring and crackling sound from outside wakes us up, loud even through the armoured door. Seconds later I hear the heavy *crash* of our base-defence guns opening up. Our guards get all excited. We're dragged to the back of the cave. They take up defensive positions in front of us, kill the glowtubes and plunge the chamber into darkness.

Okay for them, they have night-see goggles. We're blind.

'What's going on?' I ask, but get no answer.

Then all goes quiet again. Not long after, our cell door opens and the glowtubes flicker back on. A tense-looking Gemini officer hurries inside and takes a long, hard stare at Colm and me.

'Both confirmed safe,' he says into his throat-mike.

Through the open door I hear lots of distant shouting outside. Also the faint huffs and clatters of a steam engine. Still nobody will tell us what's going on. Course not. The officer leaves, the door's bolted again, and we're left to crawl back on to our benches and try to get back to sleep, our heads full of wondering.

At dawn we get an unexpected visitor.

It's Ballard. Even more surprisingly, he orders our guards outside so he can have a word with us in private.

I get a very bad feeling, and I see Colm swallow hard too.

Ballard has us sit at the grubby, food-spattered table. He sits on a stool opposite and picks up the water jug. 'May I?'

I lick my lips and nod. 'Sure.'

'Please do,' Colm croaks.

Ballard fills a beaker with water and takes a few sips. I can't help noticing how his hands are trembling.

'I'm here,' he says gravely, 'to tell you the Council's decision.'

My breath scrapes in and out of me.

For what feels like the longest time he regards us both from under his bristling grey eyebrows. Then he scowls.

'I'm afraid they voted in favour of the Slayer peace treaty.'

Colm empties his lungs in a gasp.

Me, it's like someone starts bashing nails into my skull. I'm stunned, yet not surprised. No way was the Council ever going to back the two of us against possible salvation. I stagger to my feet, clutching at the table and knocking my stool over.

A guard appears at the open door and levels his pulse rifle.

Ballard lifts a hand. 'It's all right. The young man has had a shock, but he won't do anything foolish. Will you, Kyle?'

I look down the rifle's barrel and shake my head.

Ballard tells the guard to stand down and waits until he ducks outside again. 'There was nothing I could do,' he says, sounding as tired as he looks. 'For my part, I argued the decision was not the Council's to make, that all Gemini fighters should vote. Difficult perhaps, yet not impossible.' Grimacing, he levers himself up from his stool. 'Unfortunately my suggestion was rejected.'

Colm jumps up and runs to help him, despite his injured arm. I glare at him, then catch myself. None of this is *his* fault.

Ballard thanks him and starts pacing about.

'Do we get a last good meal?' I jeer.

He stops and looks at me. His face is lined and grim. Next thing I know, he straightens up and shakes his head.

'All my life, I've fought for what I believe in. I won't quit now on the say-so of fools. I've no intention of handing you over.'

'But you said –' I shut up.

Colm looks bug-eyed too, and it takes him a few tries to get his voice working. 'What about the peace deal?'

'To hell with it,' Ballard growls. 'And to hell with the Council too, and all their weak-kneed dithering. Had they treated this farce of a peace deal with the contempt that it deserved, perhaps the damage could have been contained. Now it's too late. All over Wrath, Gemini is tearing itself apart.'

'You'll let us go?' I say, relief like a geyser inside me.

Ballard frowns at me, more sad than angry. 'It's not that simple. I'm afraid you'll have to stay here a little longer.'

'Why?' I feel I've missed something.

'Let's just say that my situation is . . . *awkward* at the moment.'

Colm nods, like he follows this. Me, I'm lost. Before I can ask Ballard what he means, he unzips his jacket, pulls a leather holster from an inside pocket and places it on the table.

'This is yours, I believe?' He slides it towards me.

I pick the holster up. Inside it is the slug-thrower Rona gave me when I went on the run after finding out I was a nublood. A weapon from the Long Ago on Earth, it once belonged to the Saviour. Before she died, my birth mother nearly killed him with it.

'Where'd you get this?' I say, amazed.

'Our forces found it at the Facility. I'd planned to give it to you under more auspicious circumstances, but needs must. Take a look, Kyle. You'll see we've made some improvements.'

I pull the gun out. It's shiny and well oiled now, no rust anywhere. I flick it open. Two chambers are loaded. Not with proper bullets mind, more like modded blaster rounds.

'Thanks!' I blurt out.

Ballard sighs. 'You must both give me your word you won't use it on your guards. They're on your side.'

The steel grip is cold in my hand. And the chill spreads to the rest of me as I get why there's only two rounds. One for Colm, one for me. It's our way out, in case he and his loyal fighters can't protect us from those who would hand us over.

Feeling numb, I give my word. So does Colm.

Ballard solemnly bumps stumps with each of us and turns to go. At the door he hesitates. 'I'm very sorry it has come to this.'

You're sorry? But I say nothing.

'For now I remain in overall command of the Deeps, but those who are pro-treaty already openly call me traitor. Even among my allies many feel you two are – shall we say – a luxury we can no longer afford.' He frowns and stares at me. 'It's odd,

Kyle, I'm no dreamer, yet I've always had a sense that you were somehow the key to unlocking our future on Wrath. Only how can you do more than you have already?' He shakes his head. 'While I have it within my power, I will continue to protect you. I give you *my* word.'

With that, he steps through the doorway and is gone.

When Rona comes in later her face is drawn. I ask if she's heard about the Council's decision. She sighs and says she has.

'What's it like out in the Deeps?' Colm asks.

'Not good,' she tells us. 'Schroeder's followers were on their way here to seize you, but Ballard's fighters turned them away.'

'Was that the shooting we heard last night?' I ask.

She spills some of the soup she's pouring into my bowl. 'It's got a bit of meat in it this time. Eat up now, before it goes cold.'

I gaze at her, suspicious. 'Rona?'

Finally she meets my eye, looking so troubled I get a lump in my throat and wish I'd kept my mouth shut.

'It's Sky,' she says.

My heart goes bang. 'Is she all right? What's happened?'

'I'm sorry, Kyle. She's gone.'

'Gone? What do you mean gone?'

My foster-mother sighs. 'Last night a windjammer launched without clearance. The winch-launcher was hacked and remote-controlled. They tried to shoot it down. It got away.'

That heavy blaster fire last night . . .

I feel dizzy, like I've stood up too fast.

'No way! Sky wouldn't clear off without me –'

Words stick in my throat as the truth sucker-punches me.

Ness must have come up with the goods about her sister's location. And here's me, trapped and useless. A liability, that's all.

Colm doesn't look surprised, but clutches at straws for me.

'Are you sure it was Sky?'

Rona slumps down on to a stool. 'It was the *Never Again*, your mate Dern's ship. He has form for clearing off when the going gets tough, I hear. Only he was found later in a ditch, tied up and gagged, a lump on his head big as a lizard egg.'

I groan. 'Don't tell me. Sky did it?'

She nods and tucks away a stray lock of her greying hair. 'Dern says she poured a liquor bottle down his neck before clobbering him. He's mad as hell. Can't say I blame him.'

My spoon slips from my hand and clatters on the table.

'I don't believe this.'

I'd been sure that if push came to shove and Ballard couldn't protect us, Sky would get off her arse and rescue us.

Colm was right though. Sky *doesn't* care.

'I'm sorry,' Rona says, reaching for my hand.

But I'm too gutted and too fast . . . and I won't let her have it.

8
A CLOSE CALL

I toss and turn, tangled in my excuse for a blanket. Dark thoughts stomp around behind my closed eyes, keeping me awake. Can Ballard *really* save our necks? *Stomp*. Or was that just talk? *Stomp*. After all we've been through together, how could Sky run out on me like that? *Stomp. Stomp*. It's all I can do not to moan out loud. Colm's bench creaks as he turns over and I hear his fed-up-sounding sigh. Seems he can't sleep either.

I turn over again so my back is to the guards, pull the gun Ballard gave me out from where I'd stuffed it between my sleeping roll and the wall, feel the weight of it in my hand.

Stomp. Stomp. Stomp. I push *that* thought away. Hard.

Instead I try to picture Sky's blink-and-you-miss-it smile. But all I can see in my mind's eye is her scrunched-up angry face, scowling at me for not being mad keen to go looking for Tarn.

I curse her. And ache with missing her.

One of our guards stirs behind me. I hear her big yawn.

I put the gun back, squeeze my eyes shut, pretend to be asleep. And sleep, being sneaky, claims me when I least expect it to. Next thing I know, I'm on my back and Sky's astride me. She's dressed all weird and wild like a Reaper, beads and feathers and mud-plastered hair. Bare-armed, bare-legged, skirt rucked up on her thighs. She's rocking back and forth, crooning stuff in some weird language. Somehow I know I'm only dreaming, but don't fight it. With both hands, Sky starts smearing spirals of blue dye on to my bare chest. My hands are resting on her knees. Smooth knees, no scarring, no shrivelled skin from when her leg got crushed. I slide my hands slowly higher, expecting to get slapped. The dream-Sky growls deep in her throat and leans forward, her breasts brushing my chest. She kisses me like she means it. Like she used to.

Only to suddenly rear back up.

I stare in horror and disbelief. She's still mostly Sky, but the lower half of her face ripples and becomes the snout of a nightrunner showing me a maw full of sharp fangs.

Just as the creature lunges for my throat, I wake up again.

'What you playing at?' Colm mumbles.

Dazed, still shaking from my nightmare, I think I've kicked him.

'Shut it!' one of the guards hisses, finger to his lips.

Behind him, the other guards fan out silently. Pulse rifles levelled, they cover the armoured door. And I'm awake enough now to hear the thumps and bangs and shouting outside.

Colm jumps up. 'What's going on?'

I roll off my bench as the guard who shushed us hustles over.

'We've got company,' he says. Working quickly, he topples our heavy wooden benches on to their sides, piles one on top of the other and orders us both to take cover behind them.

'Stay down. And don't worry, we won't let them get you.'

The words are hardly out of his mouth before something strikes the door with a massive clang. The armour plating buckles inwards, its centre glowing an ugly red. Thick, foul-smelling smoke writhes inside through the badly cracked frame.

The guard curses and scuttles back to rejoin his mates.

'Hardliners?' Colm says.

I don't waste time answering and make a lunge for my old slug-thrower where it's fallen on the floor. Only two blaster rounds, but that's two more than having no weapon at all.

The door is struck again and comes crashing in like some giant has given it the boot, taking two of our guards with it. There's a deafening thump as it hits the floor. More acrid smoke billows in. Through this I glimpse armed figures shuffling inside.

Our guards open up, pouring lethal green pulses into the smoke. Some of the attackers drop, the rest scramble back outside and take cover behind the door frame. Sticking their rifles inside, not bothering to aim, they return fire. A red beam lashes over Colm and me and hits the cave wall right behind us. I duck down, expecting a shower of rock splinters. When they don't come I look up and see sparks crawling over the rock.

'Shocker beams!' Colm says. 'They want us alive.'

'Yeah? Wanting's one thing, and getting's another,' I say.

It's so weird. I spent the night shaking, but I'm not shaking now. I risk a look over our bench barricade and see the guard who stuck us here get hit. He staggers back, foaming and twitching, covered in sparks. Hits our bench. Goes down. Stays down.

I thrust the gun at Colm. 'Cover me!'

Before he can stop me, I throw myself over our barricade and make a dive for the downed man's pulse rifle. Angry red shocker beams buzz around me. Colm yells at me to come back. I ignore him, pick up the rifle, spray a few wild shots at our attackers and grab for the man's belt of spare mags. It takes several heart-stopping seconds to rip them free of his body before I scramble back.

Colm drags me down into cover. 'You're mad!'

I give him the ammo belt and squirm around until I'm kneeling facing the door. 'Just feed me fresh mags when I shout.'

An attacker leans in and fires a burst through the doorway.

I lash back with a burst of my own. The feel of the weapon thumping back into my shoulder is good. But the firefight gets fierce confusing after that. There's smoke everywhere, lit up by dazzling beams. A man screaming in his last agony.

My rifle locks open, so I duck back down. 'I'm out, I'm out.'

Colm fumbles a fresh pulse mag at me. I ditch the empty, slot the new one home and start firing again.

They throw smoke cans and rush us, twice. Both times we beat them back. But more of our fighters are hit. Squinting through the smoke I see only one of our guards is still standing. And she's been winged – her left arm hangs uselessly by her side.

I'm out again. Colm throws me the last mag on the belt.

And now there's loads more yelling outside. A volley of green pulse-rifle blasts, seemingly fired from outside, smacks into and around the mangled door frame. With a thin scream, one of our enemies staggers inside, only to be hit again and again. He pitches forward on to his face, his back leaking smoke.

Next thing I know our attackers quit shooting at us, forced to turn and face a savage counter-attack from their rear.

Colm grins at me, his face slick with sweat. 'About time!'

'Better late than never.' I grin back.

I pop my head up again to see better, just as our last guard left standing goes for payback. She dumps her rifle, grabs a grenade and pulls the pin with her teeth. Only as she swings her arm back to chuck it a stray pulse-rifle shot slams into her chest.

She screeches and flies backwards.

The grenade arcs through the smoky air, clatters off the bench. Without thinking – gom that I am – I catch it.

'Just because you're nublood and heal so fast, Kyle,' Rona says, grinding the words out through her teeth, 'that doesn't mean you have to keep getting yourself hurt!'

Fleur snorts. I squirm around and glare at her.

'What?' she says.

'Hold still,' Rona snaps.

She's using long-jawed pliers to dig iron and rock out of my scorched butt and lower back, and it hurts like crazy. I'd be howling and yelling, only I'm shamed enough already at Colm and Fleur watching me bent over a table with my trousers around my ankles. Beside my head is a metal dish. Each lump of rock Rona drops into it makes it rattle. Fragments of metal ring it like a bell.

It's nearly full, and not for the first time.

'How much more?' My jaw aches from gritting my teeth.

Rona swabs some stinging painsucker paste on to the latest hole she's dug into me. 'I'm nearly there.'

Exactly what she told me the last time, and the time before.

It was Fleur's lot who showed up to save us. The deadheads.

She says ever since details of the peace deal got around, they've been waiting to make their move. And they won't be thanked either, saying they owed me and now we're quits.

One bit of shiny among all the crap, I guess.

Crap like the casualties they took. Five dead, one still busy dying from a blaster shot to the chest. He's over on another table, his breathing horrible and liquid. Rona's done all she can.

More people dead because of me.

Ballard, who's been and gone already, said my quick thinking made their sacrifice worthwhile. Me, I wonder what the dead guys would say? And I got lucky, that's all. The lid had already been kicked off the shit-pit. My throw didn't miss and the pit was deep enough to swallow most of the grenade's blast. Okay, so I caught some shrapnel and I'm covered in filth — most of which isn't even mine — but I'm still alive. As for my brother, not a fraggin' mark on him. Seems I shielded him from harm . . . and the rest.

The deadheads don't owe me now. Reckon he does. Big time.

'Done,' Rona announces. She holds a twisted bit of iron up to the light, squints at it and clatters it into the dish.

With a groan of relief, I stand and haul my trousers up.

'Aw,' Fleur says, and laughs.

Worth a scowl, only I can't be bothered. I'm too busy hobbling around, making sure I can still walk. Seems I can. Colm hands me back my holstered pistol and I clip it on to my belt. Rona rinses her butcher tools under the tap. I watch blood and bits of me swirl around and around and disappear down the hole.

If only I could disappear that easily . . .

It's been quiet for a while, but now more vicious-sounding

gunfire lashes back and forth outside. I make out the crackle and snap of blaster fire, the heavy *tump-tump* of pulse rifles.

Rona sighs. 'More fighting and dying. Where does it end?'

Before he left us, Ballard said he was going to make one last appeal to the pro-treaty and hardliner factions. I can't help wondering now if the shooting is their answer to him.

My brother's over by the chamber's hatch, guarding it. He's ditched his sling so he can wield a pulse rifle. From his set face I can tell it's costing him pain. According to Fleur, her deadhead mates are covering the key ladders and trapdoors in the tunnel complex. Ballard couldn't spare any of his fighters.

'Wonder who's winning?' Fleur says.

'Who cares?' I say. 'If hardliners win, we're killed. If pro-treaty wins, we're handed over. Either way we're fragged. We need to get the hell out of here, and quick.'

'Oh, Kyle, please don't start that again,' Rona says. She takes a break from packing away her healing gear to scowl at me.

'This is our last chance,' I say, struggling to keep my voice level. 'While they're fighting among themselves, we slip away. We'd be doing Ballard a favour. He wouldn't have to defend us. But if we stay down here we'll end up caught like rats in a trap. Those kids who bust us out will have died for nothing.'

I dart a glance at Colm, and he nods reluctant agreement.

Rona chews her lip, says nothing. Fleur doesn't look chuffed either. 'Ballard ordered us to hold here till he got back.'

'What if he doesn't come back?'

She goes to answer, but Colm hisses a warning.

'I heard something!' He steps back and levels his rifle.

I'm hauling my pistol out when two big deadhead kids shove

Murdo Dern through the hatch and into the chamber. His hands are clasped behind his head, his jacket and jumpsuit are a mess, and his blaster holster flaps loose and empty at his hip.

Despite this he grins at us. 'Take it easy, guys, it's only me!'

Fleur jumps up. 'What's *he* doing here?'

'Caught him sneaking about outside,' one of the kids reports. 'Says he needs to talk to Kyle. Life or death, he says.'

The other kid hands a blaster to Fleur. Murdo's, I reckon.

Rona sniffs, very loudly.

'No need to be like that, I'm here to help,' he says, looking from Colm to me. 'And glad to see you're alive and kicking.' His face scrunches up. 'Wow. You stink!'

'Shit happens,' I say, my face burning.

Meanwhile, the deadhead who handed her the blaster whispers something to Fleur. She scowls. Not good news then.

'What's going on?' Rona says.

'Schroeder's pro-treaty lot seized the windjammers and the landing fields. An anti-treaty mob is on its way to take them back. Ballard and a few fighters loyal to him are stuck in the middle, trying to keep the peace. It's getting nasty.'

'Nasty?' Murdo snorts. 'The Deeps has had it.'

Fleur tells the two deadhead kids who brought him in that we'll take it from here. They clear off back to their posts in the tunnels.

'So, Murdo,' I say. 'You going to tell us, or what?'

His eyes narrow. 'Let's go somewhere quiet, Kyle. You and me.'

'No chance, Dern,' Rona says, shaking her head.

And she's right too. 'Quit messing,' I say. 'Just tell us.'

He loses the grin and rubs his stubble. 'I want to make a deal.'

Rona lets loose another disapproving sniff.

Murdo ignores her. 'I figure if anyone knows where that bitch Sky cleared off to in my *Never Again* it's you, Kyle.'

'How could he know?' Rona says.

'Maybe I do,' I say quickly. 'But why would I tell you?'

Murdo's grin stretches itself across his battered face again. 'You scratch my back, I'll scratch yours. I'll get you out of this mess and in return you'll help me track Sky down so that I can get my *Never Again* back.'

Hope thumps my head so hard I can hardly think. A way out.

'Sounds good to me,' I say, looking around.

'If you find Sky, what'll you do to her?' Fleur says.

Murdo blanks her. 'That's the deal, Kyle. Take it, or leave it.'

9
NEGOTIATIONS AND INTERROGATIONS

I don't get to say whether I'll take Murdo's deal or leave it because my brother butts in with a 'Hang on!' and a wary look.

It's catching. Rona and Fleur look sceptical too.

I throw my hands up. 'Why not?'

Colm looks past me to Murdo. 'How can you get anybody out? Without your jammer you're trapped here the same as us.'

It's like he slapped me. Why didn't I think of this?

Murdo doesn't blink though. 'I don't do trapped. A friend is on her way here to pick me up, and there's room for Kyle too.'

My guts flip-flop between despair and hope.

'Pick you up? How?' Colm says. 'The landing areas have been seized. If she puts down, no way they'll let her take off again.'

'You think I don't know that? There are loads of ways to skin a fourhorn. Forget your damn landing fields and quit with the dumb questions. Do we have a deal, Kyle, or don't we?'

And then everyone is staring at me.

I swallow. 'On one condition. You get us *all* out, not just me.'

Murdo pulls a face like he's swallowed something sour. He

glances quickly around the room, as if counting heads.

'Deal. But that's it,' he says grimly.

More gunfire bangs and crackles outside, even closer now.

Murdo hoists an eyebrow and pretends to listen. 'Hear that? It's let's-get-out-of-here time. Come on, Kyle, as soon as you tell me where Sky's headed we can all be on our way.'

'I don't think so,' Rona says, using her no-messing voice. 'Get us out first, Dern. When we're safe, Kyle will tell you.'

Murdo scowls. 'Don't trust me, huh?'

Rona curls her lip. 'I've been around too long.'

'It's a deal,' I say quickly. 'So what do we do now?'

Murdo spits on his hand. 'I want your word you can find Sky.'

'I can find her,' I say, and spit on mine.

We shake on it. As we do he pulls me close and shoves his face in mine. 'I'm taking a fierce chance, Kyle,' he hisses. 'Everybody and his mutt is after you now. Slayers, Gemini, you name it. If you're screwing with me, you'll wish that you'd stayed here.'

'Cuts both ways,' I say, tugging my hand free.

Murdo gives me one last narrow-eyed glare and fixes his grin back in place. 'Okay, here's the score. I'll go find a comm and tell my friend to expect more bodies. Meanwhile, you guys want to lose those Gemini uniforms and get back into rags like you wore when you first got here. She'll be here at sunrise. Meet me at the Brokeback trailhead an hour before that. And this is *crucial* – we travel light. If you're not wearing it, dump it.'

Rona glances at her overstuffed bag full of healing gear.

He shakes his head. 'Forget it.'

'Brokeback trailhead, hour before dawn,' I say. 'We'll be there.'

Murdo heads off, but looks back from the hatch.

'I'll have my blaster back too,' he says.

Fleur scowls and throws it to him. He holsters it and ducks outside. Colm goes and pushes the hatch closed behind him.

And now Rona turns on me, her eyes troubled.

'Do you *really* know where Sky's gone?'

I lick my lips. 'Sort of.'

She looks at me like I've grown horns or something.

Fleur laughs. 'This I've got to hear. You don't know, do you?'

I dart a look at Colm. He's frowning too, but doesn't look at me like I'm mad. I figure he's thinking what I'm thinking.

'We need to talk to a guy called Ness,' I say.

Quickly I explain how Sky had him hacking the nav-comm of the captured Slayer transport that once carried her sister.

Rona knew this. Fleur looks surprised.

She's smart though. 'You think Ness cracked it.'

'And told Sky. Now she finally knows where Tarn was taken, so she steals Murdo's *Never Again* and clears off after her.'

'Leaving us behind,' my brother mutters.

Rona sighs. I don't know why – he's just telling it like it is.

'Only problem is,' Fleur says, wincing at me, 'Ballard's orders were to keep you here until he's back.'

My head spins. She can't be serious, can she?

The dying deadhead kid on the table moans now, real pitiful. We all look around; it's impossible not to. Rona runs to check on him. When I look back, I see Fleur shaking her head.

'Frag my orders,' she says. 'I'll go. Where do I find this Ness?'

'What if she can't find him?' Colm asks, looking gloomy.

'She'll find him,' I say, pawing through some old clothes the deadheads brought us. We've all traded our Gemini uniforms for whatever fits best. I'm after a jacket now.

'What if he's been killed?'

I curse. 'Then we lie. I'll make something up.'

To be fair, it does seem ages since Fleur set off to find Ness. Long enough for me to have a long overdue scrub anyway. And with every minute that crawls by, the sounds of fighting outside get louder and closer. I try not to think about that. Instead I go to ask Rona for something for my stinging backside, only to see her pull a bloody sheet over the kid with the sucking chest wound.

'He's gone,' she says, like his dying is her fault.

I didn't even know the poor guy's name. How crap is that?

A good while later Fleur's back, shoving a lanky man before her.

'Ness!' I call out. 'Am I glad to see you.'

'And what about me?' Fleur says, smiling. Then she spots the sheet-covered body on the table and the smiles fades.

'Why've I been brought here?' Ness says, his voice up and down. Marks on his long face tell me he didn't come willingly.

'Relax,' I say. 'Nobody's going to hurt you.'

'*She* did,' he says, scowling at Fleur.

Fleur shrugs. 'The gommer gave me no choice. I found him snivelling under his bunk and he wouldn't come out.'

'I was *not* snivelling. I've got a cold, that's all.'

'Leave him be,' Rona says. 'As if there isn't enough fighting!'

Before anybody can stop her she leads him to an empty healing table, sits him down and starts treating his bruised face.

'Can't that wait?' I say, twitching.

'Won't be a minute.'

Except she is of course. And all we can do is grind our teeth.

'There. That's better.' She steps back at last.

Ness goes to hop down from the table, but I shove him back. 'You found out where the Slayers took Sky's sister, didn't you?'

He swallows hard, and nods.

'And you told Sky?' I hold my breath.

'You know what Sky's like – she made me tell her.'

I shoot the others a relieved told-you-so look.

'So tell *us* what you told Sky.'

Ness glares at me 'Why should I?'

The crash of an explosion shakes the chamber. A crackle of blaster fire answers it. My brother curses under his breath, real nasty too, and aims his pulse rifle at Ness's head.

'You've got five seconds!'

Ness looks horrified. He's not alone – I think we all do.

'Colm?' Rona says.

My brother's finger whitens on the trigger. 'Four.'

'You're no killer,' Ness says.

Colm sets his jaw. 'You sure about that?'

Ness glances at me. 'Is he *serious*?'

Out of the corner of my eye I see Rona's mouth hanging open. By now though I'm pretty sure what my twin is up to.

'He'll blow your head off, Ness,' I say. 'He's mean like that.'

'Two,' Colm hisses.

'What happened to three?' Ness protests.

'One!'

'All right, all right, I'll tell you!'

I shove Colm's rifle aside, just in case. 'Let's hear it.'

Ness takes a second to get his breath back. 'You won't like it.'

'Get on with it!'

'The Slayers flew Sky's sister to the No-Zone.'

And now it's his turn to be stared at like he's sprouted horns.

We've all heard of it, but only in fireside tales told by hungry wordweavers to earn a crust. It's make-believe to scare little children. A distant land crawling with Reapers and weird, bug-eyed monsters. Enter the No-Zone, you won't come out alive!

'There's no such place,' Colm says, and aims his rifle again.

Ness's eyes bulge behind his glasses.

'There must be. It's marked on the Slayer nav charts!'

The guy says it so fiercely, so desperately, I can tell he's not bullshitting. I push Colm's pulse rifle down again.

'Sky's headed to this No-Zone?'

Ness nods miserably. 'I guess. Where else?'

He mumbles something else that I don't catch because I'm too busy feeling hollow inside. Murdo will freak when we tell him Sky's headed someplace that doesn't exist. Bound to. But what kills me is being reminded how she ran out on us.

Ran out on *me*.

I'd forgive Sky most things. I'll never forgive her for this . . .

PART TWO
NO-ZONE

10
WAITING FOR MURDO

It feels good to be above ground, fresh air in my lungs. Stars spill across the sky above us, scattered in a band like glittering seeds. The old bigmoon is up and throws out enough shine so we can see where we're going. It's colder up here. My breath mists and dew turns the rocks slippery underfoot. Our route to Murdo's rendezvous will take us up past the sky lizard's corral. Rona's struggling to keep up so we take a breather below it, on the ledge where Colm and I saw the kids playing the Peace Fair game.

How long ago was that? Feels like forever.

Ness starts complaining again. Fleur shuts him up. We couldn't leave him behind to squeal about the No-Zone, so we're dragging him along. A pain, but Fleur said we'd have to waste him otherwise and Rona wasn't having that. Having Fleur along is good news anyway. I've seen her in combat training – she's tough and lethal. Brave too, like her sister. For a while there she *wasn't* coming, reluctant to run out on her deadhead friends, until Rona talked her round. I think they're both worried about

Murdo looking for revenge if he catches up with Sky.

Colm's glad about Fleur too. I reckon he fancies her.

I stuff my hands into my pockets to keep them warm, and feel something. I pull out Squint's whistle.

Poor old Squinty. I blow it. Who'll look after you now?

'Don't!' Colm hisses. 'You'll get us killed.'

'Relax. Only Squint can hear it.'

'And what if he comes running? He's not exactly quiet.'

'He won't.' But I throw the whistle away, knowing he's right.

We head off again, creeping along, and it hits me how thin the line is we're walking between life and death. Out there in the darkness, scared people will be peering through gunsights. Kick a stone, or cough, and they could hear us. I breathe shallow and watch where I'm putting my boots. Another vicious firefight breaks out on the canyon floor below, lighting up the sky with brilliant red and green flashes. A heavy pulse cannon opens up in squirt mode, the *tump-tump-tump* so loud I can feel it. We crouch down until the shooting stops and the valley falls quiet again.

'We'd better keep moving,' I say.

As we climb past the stone-walled corral, the giant lizard stirs. There's a steam-piston-like whoosh as she sniffs us. Not long after, Colm steps off the trail and squeezes through a crack in the rock face. After a clamber over broken rock at the bottom, this leads to a gulley and a half-seen trail that winds even higher.

'This is it,' he whispers.

Behind me, rocks rattle underfoot. When I look round I see Ness making a break for it back the way we came.

I curse and scramble after him.

No need. A figure steps out in front of Ness. He goes to shove past, there's a scuffle and he goes down. By the time I get there he's flat on his back, clutching himself and groaning.

Rona stands over him. 'Oh dear, hope I haven't hurt him.'

'Nice one,' I say, gaping.

A smile, a pat of my shoulder and she steps round me. Colm arrives. Together, we haul Ness back to the trailhead.

Fleur stalks over. 'Ness is a liability.'

'I know,' I say, and warn him that if he pulls that stunt again we'll look the other way and let Fleur do what she likes to him. Then I take Colm aside. 'You *were* bluffing back there, weren't you? You wouldn't really have killed him, would you?'

He's slow answering. 'Probably not.'

'Only probably?' I stare at him.

'Like Sky said, I am Slayer born and bred,' he whispers.

Ness struggles up. Fleur shoves him back down with her boot.

'Let me go, guys,' he says. 'I won't squeal.'

'We can't take that chance,' I say. 'Anyway, you're safer with us. We'll get you out of here, away from the fighting.'

'Safer?' he says, still clutching himself. 'Being around you and your brother doesn't strike me as safe. Everybody's after you.'

'Yeah? Tell us something we don't know,' Colm says.

'Guys, I don't blame you for running. I would too. I just don't want to be caught in the crossfire.'

Fleur curses. 'I still say we waste him.'

'On the other hand,' Ness says quickly, 'I've always wanted to see more of Wrath. I promise I won't run again. Okay?'

'That's enough, Fleur,' Rona snaps.

'What's keeping Dern?' Colm says. 'He should be here by now.'

I look where he's looking. Dawn's creeping up on us. Across the valley, dayshine is already licking at the tallest of the mountains east of the Deeps, the peak they call High Rigg.

'Colm, are you sure this is the Brokeback trailhead?'

He nods. 'I've hiked here.'

'What if Murdo doesn't show?' Ness asks.

'He will,' I say, trying to sound more confident than I feel. I scramble up on to a rock outcrop and watch the trail below us.

Only nothing moves. Where the hell is the guy?

To keep my worries from crowding me, I get Fleur to lend me a blade and start scratching my name into the soft rock. I'm on Y when Colm clambers up beside me.

'What you doing?' he asks.

'Leaving something behind. Want me to carve yours too?'

He forces a smile. 'Can you spell it?'

'Ha ha.' I finish my name and carve C-O-L-M, trying not to think about a tree with K-Y-L-E carved next to S-K-Y. After I'm done I scan the trail below, trying to pull Murdo's shape from the gloom. Nothing doing. He's still nowhere to be seen.

'I know we got grief from some people here,' Colm says, 'but the Deeps was the first place I ever felt I belonged. Stupid, huh?'

I sigh. 'I'd thought we were safe at least.'

'You think Dern will show?'

I roll on my side. Nod. 'Yeah, I know he will.'

'How can you be sure?'

'There he is.' I point out Murdo, beckoning from above us.

As we scramble up to Murdo, I lose track of Ness for one second. That's all it takes. Every fool and his dog know the trails around the Deeps are wired with trips. He blunders into one.

A *thud*, a *whoosh* and a *crackle* like the world's on fire.

The flare blossoms into a small sun over our heads and then drifts down under its parachute, its smoke trail pointing an accusing finger. We all go to ground, but Ness stands there gawping. I haul him down into a thicket of stink-grass.

We land on Fleur.

'That settles it!' A blaster appears in her fist.

'It was an accident,' Ness howls.

I use all my speed to snatch the weapon away from her.

'Don't! You'll give our position away.'

'Like he hasn't already?'

The wind up here is pushing the flare away from us fast and already its light is starting to dim. We wait until it fizzles out completely and gloom settles back over us.

'Move,' I say, pulling Ness up.

Murdo comes running down to us. 'Which genius tripped that?'

I shove Ness forward. 'This gommer here did.'

Murdo curses, shoves past and peers down into the canyon through small darklight binoculars. He curses again, real nasty.

I look too and see light beams stabbing about. 'What the–?'

He thrusts the bins at me. 'Look.'

Through them I see fighters sprinting up the still heavily shadowed trail, shiners strapped to their pulse rifles.

'Oh crap! They're coming after us.'

'Who is?' Fleur says.

I scowl. 'Does it matter?'

Murdo glances at the sun on High Rigg then grabs his bins

back. 'Not good. We need more time. Twenty minutes at least.'

'Those guys will be here in ten,' I say.

Fleur unslings her pulse rifle. 'I'll slow them down for you.'

She heads off back the way we came. Only I'm hauling enough guilt around already and there's no way I'll let her sacrifice herself for me like her sister did. And I've got a better idea.

'Hang on!' I call after her. 'I'm coming too.'

This goes down badly with Rona and Murdo. Both yell their heads off at me to stay, but there's no time to explain.

I get in Colm's face. 'We'll be back. Make sure Murdo waits!'

'What are you up to?' he asks, his face all confused.

'Tell you later.'

I scramble after Fleur.

When I catch up, she rolls her eyes. 'Go back. I can do this.'

'Shut up and listen.'

I tell her my big idea. She likes it. We pound downwards together, squeeze through the crack on to the lower trail. Not long after, we're back at the ledge under the overhang. At the back looms the stone-built corral with the queen sky lizard inside.

'How do we do this?' Fleur asks.

'You got a shiner?'

'Think so. Yeah.' She produces a tube and hands it over.

From inside the corral comes a hiss and a clatter of chains. We run over towards the iron-barred gate. To save my night-seeing, I thumb the shiner to red before powering it up. A risk, but only a small one as the ledge should hide its dim light from the fighters below. Beyond the bars the lizard's eyes throw the red back, four pools of liquid fire. She rattles her neck feathers.

'It's only me, Kyle,' I whisper.

Fleur tuts in disgust. 'Leave it out.'

The she-lizard doesn't like this and hisses very loudly.

'Don't rile her,' I tell Fleur.

'You said you wanted her mad.'

'Yeah, but not while I'm standing here.'

I butt Fleur's blaster up against the gate's crude lock, throw a rag over it so no blaster flash will betray us, squeeze the trigger and keep it squeezed. Heat stings my hand until the lock gives. Before it can cool and weld itself shut again, I kick it free. Inside the corral the unimpressed sky lizard spits and tail-thumps.

Fleur elbows me. 'Um, maybe I should've asked this before, but now the gate's unbolted, what's to stop her coming after us?'

'She's chained. I'll need to blast them.'

'Oh.' She looks relieved. 'Right, I'll go keep a lookout on the trail up here. Where will you be?'

'Back of the corral.'

Fleur clears off. Glad for the shiner's dim light, I scuttle round behind the corral to find the hole the chain end comes out of and the ring to which it's shackled. When I do I suck my teeth. Both the chain and the ring are thicker than I remember.

I dial the blaster to maximum power. Will it be enough?

Next thing I know, Fleur is back, fumbling her way round the wall towards me. I quickly kill the shiner.

'They're here!' she whispers.

The mighty sky lizard hisses and rattles her neck feathers, then the chain tugs savagely as she must hurl herself at the unbolted gate. I hear boots scuffing stone and startled curses.

A woman's voice shuts them up.

'Keep it down. It's only that dumb sky lizard.'

I take a breath, jam the blaster's muzzle against the chain and keep the trigger pressed, wincing as blaster spatter hits my hand.

'Back there!' somebody yells. Boots scrunch closer.

Just when I think I can't take the pain any more the chain lets go. It immediately lashes inside and I hear the gate bang open. In all the time I've fed her I've never heard the sky lizard's full roar. I do now, together with shouts, screams and tearing sounds. Somebody gets off a few pulse-rifle shots. I see the green flashes and hear the thumps.

They cut off. The sounds of slaughter continue.

'Let's go, let's go!' Fleur pulls me after her.

I'm half blinded by blaster flare and glad about it because the little I see as we creep away is sickening enough. The giant lizard is hunkered down, snout deep in torn flesh, busy feeding.

By the time we regain the ridge at the top of the trail, dawn is well and truly here. We stop to catch our breath.

I hand Fleur's blaster back.

'Them or us,' she says, and shrugs.

I'm not sure I buy it though. She looks as sick as I feel.

It's brighter up here, and I see the trail splits to head either north or south along the ridge. I'm wondering which way the others went when I spot the arrow made from pebbles.

'Look, they went south.'

'Yeah, I've seen it,' Fleur says, 'but take a look behind you!'

I turn, just in time to duck as the rust-streaked hull of a windjammer whistles past low over our heads. An open loading ramp hangs down at the back and some sort of hook trails after it, bouncing about madly at the end of a long cable.

Our ride out of here. Got to be.

'Hang on, where will it land?' Fleur says.

'It *can't* land. Not up here. Anyway, its gear's not down.'

We chase after it. After we crest a small rise, wondering turns to fearing. Half a klick ahead I see Rona, Colm and Ness. They're standing with their backs to us. Above their heads a rope is stretched between two of the hardy, wind-twisted trees that cling to these heights. More ropes rise up from each of them to meet it. We stop and stare. It looks like a hanging.

'What the hell?' I say.

Murdo stands off to one side, arms spread, as if signalling to the windjammer, which now turns and dives down towards him. Its trailing hook snags the rope between the trees.

And Rona, Colm and Ness . . . are snatched up into the air!

11
AN UNCERTAIN WELCOME

The windjammer pulls up before hurtling past over us, Rona, Colm and Ness dangling in a line behind it. I hear a thin scream – Rona's I think. As the machine climbs away steeply they look like bits of rag fluttering in the wind. But as I watch I see they're closer to the open hatch at the back now. They're being hauled inside.

Murdo shouts something and beckons for us to join him.

Fleur shoves me to get me going.

Soon as Murdo sees we're on our way he quits waving and gets busy laying out more ropes. By the time we reach him he's already slung another tough-looking line between the trees and is busily tying off the rope ends with what look like slip knots.

'If Rona and Colm are hurt –' I say angrily.

He turns around, the same old annoying grin on his face.

'Relax. They're fine. Bruised and maybe some grey hairs, that's all. How else did you think we'd get out of here? In the smuggling trade we call it skyhooking. Lets us pick up cargoes from places we can't land. If Sky were here, she'd tell you all about it.' This last bit comes with a sly wink.

He picks up bundles of rope already tied into a few loops and hands them to us. 'Your harnesses. I'll help you into them.'

He's already wearing one, I see that now.

'I can do it myself,' Fleur says.

Murdo shrugs. 'It's your neck, kid.'

Me, I'm not proud. 'Okay, show me what to do.'

He helps me climb into my harness, gathers it into a bunch at the front and clips it all together with a snap shackle.

Fleur watches, and struggles into hers.

Lines hang down from the rope strung horizontally between the trees, the loops spliced into their ends clipped to our harnesses already. Each line is quite a bit longer than its neighbour.

'So what do we do?' I ask, my voice cracking.

As if I wasn't scared enough already, I hear shouting from back the way we came. We've been seen. Murdo pulls out a small hand-held comm unit and growls something into it. All I catch is the word *now*! Pulse-rifle shots *tzziip* past over our heads. I throw myself flat. Fleur unslings her pulse rifle and returns fire.

I'm wishing I had a rifle too when there's this sudden loud whining sound and a shadow flickers across us. I'm yanked off my feet and dragged along the ground, fierce fast. A boulder comes rushing up. I roll frantically left, barely missing being brained. My relief is short-lived – something heavy pounces and wraps its cold legs round me, crushing my ribs. Next thing I know I'm in mid-air, the ridge falling away below my kicking feet.

Whatever's got hold of me, I can't breathe. My seeing fades . . .

*

I groan. Seems the thing to do given how banged-up I feel. I take a deep breath and force my eyes open.

'Hell of a ride, huh?' Murdo says, grinning down at me.

Rona's face joins his. 'Are you okay, Kyle?'

'I'll live,' I croak.

While Murdo undoes my harness, I check myself out. My jacket and trousers are torn and scuffed. My whole body hurts. But nothing feels broken and I've still got my fair share of skin so I reckon I've got off lightly. Thankful, I sit up. I'm at the back of a windjammer's cargo hold, otherwise filled by crates and rusty machinery. Colm, Fleur and Ness are crouched with a powerful-looking winch that has to be what hauled us aboard.

Colm gives me a fist pump. 'We *made* it!'

Only now do I get that we've left the Deeps behind. And even though I don't know where we're headed, or what happens next, I feel such huge relief. It's like I could float up off the deck.

Rona smiles. 'We're not safe yet, but it's a start.'

Even Ness has a bit of a smile for me.

I hear a beep and something butts my back. I glance around and can't believe my eyes as I see Squint squatting there. A few fresh dents and scratches, but he looks all right.

'Squinty!' I shout, delighted. 'Where did you come from?'

He launches himself and knocks me flat again, stands over me twitching and shaking. Luckily I know what this signals and roll away from under him. He gives a last beep that tails off, before his legs buckle and he slams belly down on to the deck.

'That junk yours, is it?' Murdo asks.

I pick myself up slowly. 'Mine and Colm's.'

He scowls, clearly unimpressed. 'We're lucky the rope took

its extra weight. That thing could've easily got us all killed.'

'We think that's why you passed out,' Rona says to me. 'Squint was hanging off you, so you couldn't breathe.'

'What's it doing now?' Murdo says. 'Playing dead?'

Squint's just having one of his deadlock fits, but I figure I'll explain later. See, I'm too busy staring at the tall woman who's just ducked into the front of the cargo bay from the flight deck. Before she closes the hatch behind her I glimpse a man's head and shoulders at the windjammer's controls.

At the sound of the hatch shutting Murdo spins round, holds his arms out to her and shows her all his teeth in a smile.

'Gant! Good to see you. It's been too long.'

She scowls at him. 'Yeah? Not long enough if you ask me.'

The woman wears an ancient leather jacket over an oil-stained grey jumpsuit. Her hair is long and dyed blue. Getting on in years, she's still striking enough to attract looks. An old scar carves down through her ruined left eye socket. In place of the eye is some sort of polished red gemstone. A bloodstone, I think.

Rona stands up and faces her. 'Thanks for picking us up.'

Gant nods at her, then her gaze slides back to Murdo. She stares at him in a way I wouldn't fancy being stared at.

'You know, Dern, I've got better things to do than haul my ass hundreds of klicks out this way to save your worthless neck.'

'I'll make it worth your while,' Murdo says quickly.

'You'd better.' And now she turns that stare on the rest of us. 'Listen up, you lot. This is my windjammer so my rules apply. You don't touch anything. If I give you an order, you jump to it. Stick to these two rules, we'll get along.'

'Sounds fair,' Rona says.

'Glad to hear it,' Gant says, glancing at me for the first time. Her one good eye flicks from me to Colm, and goes wide.

'Are you out of your fraggin' mind?' she spits at Murdo.

He just shrugs. 'I had no choice.'

'No choice? Just some friends, you said. You lying bastard. Everywhere I go I see these kids' faces on wanted posters, with a massive reward. If word gets out I'm carrying them I'm a dead woman. And you *knew* this, yet still had me pick them up.'

'Word *won't* get out,' Murdo says. 'I can explain.'

A blaster appears in Gant's hand. She aims it at Murdo's head.

'Oh sure,' she says. 'Like always.'

Murdo winces, then rattles through telling her how Sky stole his *Never Again* and how it's just cruel bad luck that we're the only people on Wrath who know where she's headed. While Gant's watching him doing the telling, I drop my hand slowly into my parka pocket and take hold of my old slug-thrower.

If she wastes him, I'm guessing we're next.

'Look, I was *desperate*,' Murdo says. 'What else could I do? The Deeps is a bloodbath. I'd no other way of getting myself out. And you'd have done the same, don't tell me you wouldn't.'

They glare at each other for what feels like the longest time.

That's when I finally notice it — Gant's a leftie, so holds her blaster left-handed. And that hand, like mine and Colm's and Fleur's . . . is missing its little finger.

Shocked, I blurt out. 'You're one of us. An ident!'

Gant turns her fierce gaze on me. 'So what?'

'So doesn't that *mean* anything to you?' Rona says sharply.

'Yeah,' Murdo says. 'C'mon, Gant. Be reasonable.'

She pulls a face like she's heard all this before, but slowly lowers the blaster. Murdo lets his breath out and relaxes. Big mistake. The woman lashes out at him, snake-fast, smashes him hard across the face with the hilt of the blaster.

'That *reasonable* enough?' she snarls.

Fair play to Murdo – after a bit of a stagger back from the blow, he sorts himself out and stays on his feet, clutching his jaw.

'I guess I had that coming,' he mutters, grimacing.

Gant's blaster disappears back to wherever it came from and she turns and stalks back towards the flight deck.

I breathe a quiet sigh of relief.

'Gant, we're sorry we've mixed you up in this mess of ours,' Rona calls after her. 'We didn't mean to.'

The woman glances back. 'Yet you have, haven't you?'

She ducks through the hatch and slams it after her. I hear the snick of catches sliding home. Murdo lowers himself gingerly to sit cross-legged on the deck, still clutching his jaw.

'Your girlfriend seems nice,' Fleur says.

He shows her his middle finger. 'She's not big on surprises, that's all. But Gant and me, we go way back. She'll get over it.'

'You think so?' Rona says, her face saying *because I don't.*

'Now what do we do?' Colm says.

'We hang tight,' Murdo growls. 'If I were you, I'd hold on to something in case she tries to dump us out the back.'

This sounds like good advice as the deck shifts and bumps under us. I scramble to catch hold of some netting around the nearest crate. The others do likewise, grabbing on to whatever's closest.

Another bump, making us jump again.

'Is Gant doing that?' Ness says.

'Feels more like some turbulence,' Murdo says.

Maybe. I'm not taking any chances and wedge myself in tighter. The bumping gets fiercer and we all trade worried looks.

'At least we're out of the Deeps,' I say.

Me and my big mouth! Something slams into the outside of the hull. The windjammer staggers under the impact and rolls steeply left wing down. I end up hanging off my crate, the others all tangled together in a heap on the down side of the hold. Slowly the transport rights itself. More loud bangs. The windjammer rocks wildly with each hit. We're thrown from side to side. And now I hear terrifying scraping, scratching and tearing sounds.

Whatever's out there, it seems set on ripping its way inside!

12
DEAL'S A DEAL

Murdo's the first to pick himself up. He fights his way to a ladder on the forward bulkhead, and scrambles up it to where flickering dayshine streams in through some sort of clear plastic observation dome sticking up from the windjammer's hull.

'Sky lizards!' he shouts. 'Frag it, they're swarming us!'

The flight-deck hatch bangs and Gant lurches into the hold clutching a pulse rifle. 'How many?'

Murdo slides down the ladder, lands next to her.

'Looks to me like the whole lizard colony's attacking us.'

Another impact sends us all stumbling about. Somehow I end up at the foot of the ladder, so I figure I'll see for myself what's going on outside. I haul myself up until my head's in the dome. What I see sucks a groan of disbelief and horror out of me. A dozen or so of the smaller male sky lizards are clinging to the top of our windjammer's hull, tearing at the metal plates with their taloned feet. Above us, the sky is thick with hundreds more.

'They can't get through the hull, can they?' I shout down.

Murdo draws his blaster and does something to its muzzle. 'Don't need to. Their weight'll drag us down.'

He aims the blaster above his head.

'Hey, what the frag are you doing?' Gant yells at him.

'Needs must,' Murdo sneers.

He squeezes off a narrow-beamed blast that punches a hole through the sheet metal of the hull. Outside, I see a sky lizard let go and tumble off backwards into our slipstream.

'You got one!' I yell, all excited.

Only for three more to swoop down and take its place. And I've been spotted. Wings folded, gaping and showing their fangs, lizards scrabble along the curved hull towards me.

Murdo blasts again, but misses.

Something snaps inside my head. A fake peace deal, Sky runs out on me and now these lizards are screwing up our escape. I rage at the unfairness of it all and pound my fists on the dome.

And . . . the lizards stop. They back off. They cower away.

Gobsmacked, I quit my pounding and gawp as the lizards spread their wings and fling themselves off, screeching as they go. With all their weight gone so suddenly, our windjammer leaps higher in the air. I'm nearly thrown from the ladder.

'What just happened?' Murdo shouts.

I look down at anxious faces looking up. Takes me a second to find my voice. 'They've cleared off.'

'What? All of them?'

'Every single fraggin' one,' I say hoarsely.

Murdo laughs. So does Gant. Next thing, they're all hugging and bumping fists while I hang off the ladder, still shaking.

I take one last look outside. And that's when I hear an ear-splitting shriek and glimpse the queen sky lizard's vast body hurtling at us.

'No, no!' I scream at her. 'Look, it's me, Kyle!'

Hours later, they're still giving me crap about what happened.

'The lizard whisperer,' Murdo says, smirking.

They all reckon the queen only broke off her attack because we happened to fly past some invisible line in the sky that marks the limit of her colony's territory. I know better. She saw or heard me, and some part of her tiny lizard brain recognised me as the human who'd fed her and freed her. While others threw stones and prodded her with sharp sticks, I was never cruel. That's what saved us, I'm sure of it.

It's like Rona says – do right, and you'll get the reward.

'Give him a break,' she groans.

Windjamming isn't agreeing with her. She looks like death.

Gant looks down from on top of a crate, where she's checking the patches are holding. Between them, she and Murdo shot quite a few holes in the hull while I was ranting and raging.

'I think it's sweet,' she says, with a wink for me. 'A great big she-lizard like that chasing after the kid just to save him.'

'You chased after *me* once,' Murdo says.

'Funny,' she says. 'I remember it the other way around.'

I wouldn't say the woman's chilled out completely, but at least she's not waving blasters about. Dayshine streams through the dome and it's warm in here now the holes are patched. Squint's back online. Ness is taking a peek at his boards to see if he can sort him. We're high, there's loads of reliable lift, the Deeps are over two hundred klicks behind us and nobody's on our tail. The hold stinks a bit of hot oil and rusty metal, and that's good too. It reminds me of my Barrenlands childhood, spent around machines.

I close my eyes and wish that I could curl up here forever.

When I open them again, Murdo is splashing milky-looking liquor into a beaker. He found the bottle leaking in a small crate that broke open during the lizard attack and persuaded Gant it'd be a sin to waste it. They've been knocking loads back.

'Get that down you,' he says, thrusting the beaker at me.

Behind his back I see Rona's pursed lips. I knock it back in one, cough as it burns and laugh too loud.

'What's so funny?' Gant asks.

I look up into her gleaming gemstone eye.

'Nothing. Except the whole of Wrath is after me, and Rona's more worried I'll get drunk and make a gom of myself.'

Gant looks at Rona, then back at me. 'She cares, that's why.'

I can't help glancing at the stump on her left hand. She sees me looking and her smile fades. Before I can say anything she's back off to the flight deck. And no sooner does the hatch close behind her than Murdo is beside me, refilling my beaker.

'So, Kyle,' he says, all matey. 'Where's Sky's headed?'

Behind him Ness opens his gob, but Colm jabs an elbow to shut him up. Rona shakes her head at me, like I was born yesterday.

'When we're safe,' I say. 'That was the deal.'

'What d'you call this?' he says, throwing his hands up. 'Our deal was I get you out of the Deeps. I've done that. Haven't I?'

'How about you tell us where Gant's taking us?' Rona says.

'Sure. When you've told me what *I* want to know.'

And suddenly I can't be bothered with all this arguing. Like the man said, he's delivered. We're free of the Deeps.

'Sky's heading for the No-Zone,' I say.

Silence. Out of the corner of my eye I see Rona and Colm scowling at me. Well, tough. I've done the right thing.

Murdo grinds his teeth. 'You think that's funny, do you?'

'Tell him, Ness,' I say.

Ness twitches so hard he bangs his head on the winch.

'It's true.' Rubbing his head, he fills Murdo in on the captured Slayer transport, Tarn's tagging and hacking the nav-comm to find out that its destination was the No-Zone.

Murdo looks stunned. 'That's impossible.'

'I don't make mistakes,' Ness says, all sniffy. 'And I'll tell you something else – it was no one-off trip. The logs showed that transport made regular monthly runs to the No-Zone.'

We all look at him wide-eyed.

'You never told us that,' Colm says.

Ness blinks at us. 'You never asked. You just grabbed me.'

I'm watching Murdo. He's shaking his head.

'Ness says the No-Zone does exist,' I say. 'It's on Slayer charts.'

'Oh, it exists all right,' Murdo snarls. 'I've seen it – from a distance. Because that's as close as you can get. You can't fly there in a windjammer. It's a bunch of jagged mountains sticking up in the middle of a boggy, Reaper-infested flatland, with no ridges to run to get you over there. That's why we don't bother marking it on *our* chart. That's why it's called the No-Zone. You're wrong. And our deal's off!'

He might as well have kicked me in the head.

'I can prove it!' Ness says. 'I made copies of the transport's nav-logs, one for Sky and one for me.' He produces a cleverbox and has a quick play with it. 'Gotcha. Check it out.'

Murdo snatches it from him. He takes a long, hard look at its screen before stomping off to the ramp end of the hold.

The rest of us swap anxious glances.

Rona shakes her head. 'You shouldn't have told him. Not yet.'

'We made a deal,' I say.

But I keep an eye on Murdo, and my pistol close to hand.

Other than Ness, who clearly prefers his own company, we all huddle closer. I notice Colm's beaker is still full of liquor. He's hardly touched the stuff. I grab it and drink it for him.

He frowns. 'If Ness is right, there must be more to this No-Zone place than Murdo thinks. Why else would a Slayer windjammer fly nublood prisoners there, halfway across Wrath?'

I gasp, and it's not just the liquor. I've had an inspiration.

'Another secret Facility!' I say, all excited.

'That'd be my guess,' Colm says.

Fleur looks thoughtful. 'And that'll be why you rescued less of us than expected when you destroyed our Facility. Maybe the missing kids are working other mines out in the No-Zone?'

We talk about it for a while, but nobody comes up with any better suggestion than mine. Then, for some reason best known to itself, my arse decides to start the healing itch like crazy, reminding me Rona was digging chunks of iron and rock out of it not too many hours ago. I have to stand up and prowl about.

Ness goes back to messing with Squint.

Murdo studies the cleverbox, his back to the ramp. Once I could almost swear I saw him smiling.

A sign that our deal might still be on? I can only hope . . .

13
BLAST FROM THE PAST

Long into the afternoon, Gant flies us along ridges that track roughly south-east. Murdo's head stays stuck in Ness's cleverbox and he won't tell us where we're headed, no matter how many times we ask. There's bog all to do, so we curl up on some old packing blankets. I don't mean to sleep, but wake up some time later with a shiver. With everything that's happened, I'd almost forgotten how the dead Morana woman showed up in the Deeps. I sit up, meaning to tell Murdo. After all, he killed her.

Before I can, Fleur nudges me.

'Something's different,' she says, peering up at the dome.

I look too, and she's not wrong. I'd got used to seeing clouds and blue sky through the plastic, now a sheer ridge towers above us. The wind noise is louder too. We're flying faster.

'Murdo, what's going on?'

Amazingly, he stirs himself and looks up from the cleverbox. 'Relax. Gant's taking us lower. We must be close to my perch.'

'Your *what*?' Fleur says.

'Perch,' I say. 'Secret landing field.'

Smugglers like Murdo can't land their windjammers at proper Slayer-patrolled way stations if they're carrying shady cargo. Instead, according to Sky, they operate from hidden little scraps of flatland clinging to the low ridges, many of them barely long enough for a skilled pilot to bang a jammer down on.

Colm heads up the dome ladder. I follow him.

Below us the flight-deck hatch bangs open and Gant sticks her head out. 'Your perch, Murdo. You'd better fly the landing.'

He hustles forward and ducks through the hatch.

'Do *you* see any place to land?' I say, worried.

'A bird would struggle to land here,' Colm says. 'This is mad.'

Everything ahead looks too steep or too rocky. Yet even as I think this we pitch into a steep dive. Air brakes bang open.

Tree-smothered slope rushes up.

At the last possible second, Murdo hauls back. Hard. We stagger over a belt of trees in a nose-high mushing stall and slam down on a half-glimpsed grassy ledge. Colm and I go flying and land on a crate. By the time we've picked ourselves up, Murdo's already out of the cockpit and opening the rear loading ramp. Fresh air floods in, bringing with it the shrieks of startled birds. We all follow him outside and look about. All there is to see is some swaying bunch-grass, trees and rocks. No buildings. No steam winch.

Colm asks how we launch out of here again.

'You'll see,' Murdo tells him, and disappears off somewhere.

I'm checking out the windjammer's landing gear, which seems miraculously intact, when Gant walks down the ramp.

'Quit your gawping,' she calls to us. 'We've work to do!'

For the next hour she has us slaving to camouflage the

windjammer. First we drag a net over it to break up its outline, then we chop leafy branches and arrange them to cover it. Ness moans. I'm happy enough doing the work. After so long stuck in that cave back in the Deeps, it feels good to work up a sweat. And we finally get to meet Gant's co-pilot. He's been doing stuff on the flight deck, but comes out now and helps us finish off the camouflage. Gant tells us his name is Yonny. Small, dark and wiry, he looks friendly, but say what you like to him and all he does is grunt back. I'm fed up of this until Rona spots the poor man's got no tongue.

Murdo reappears. Grinning, he tells us Yonny once told somebody something he wasn't supposed to.

'Gant found out, took a knife and –'

'Don't listen to him,' Gant says, coming over. 'The creep tells everybody that old lie. Yonny lost his tongue way before I hired him. Suits me though – most men talk too much.'

'So what now?' Rona says.

Gant raises her eyebrows at Murdo, making her scar squirm.

He hesitates, then says: 'We'll stay the night here. Tomorrow Gant leaves us. After that it's down to you guys.'

'What's down to us?' I say, confused.

'Whether you stay here or come with me to the No-Zone.'

We all glare at him, horrified.

Gant narrows her eyes. 'The . . . No-Zone?'

'Long story. I'll tell you later,' Murdo says, and walks away.

'You do that,' Gant says. She sees our shocked and angry faces. 'What did I tell you about men and their big mouths?'

Murdo's wading through the waist-high bunch-grass, heading for the back of the ledge. I jerk my head at Colm and we go after him. He reaches a sheer bit of cliff face covered in slimy green and purple vegetation. Me, I wouldn't touch the stuff, but he steps to one side and somehow disappears behind it. We're swapping looks when there's a whining sound. Amazingly, the vegetation starts winching itself up the cliff face, gathering itself as it rises like the window blinds Rona fixed up for our cabin back in Freshwater. A gaping cave is revealed. Inside, its bulk filling the space, stub-wings folded upright, is another windjammer. And not just any old ridge-running transport – I'd know this one anywhere.

'No way,' I croak. 'That's Sky's old jammer. *Rockpolisher*.'

I remember another deal now, one Sky made with Murdo when we were on the run at Haggletown. Full salvage on her abandoned windjammer against him flying us to Bastion.

One thing seems sure – Murdo got the best of that bargain.

Me, I'd like a poke around the *Rockpolisher*. Rona says we should check the ledge out while there's dayshine.

'What's to check?' I mutter.

She gives me a look like I'm being dumb. So does Colm. And now I get it – Rona wants away from Gant and Murdo.

'I mean,' I say, too loudly, 'yeah, why not?'

Colm fetches Fleur and the four of us wander off. Unfortunately Ness spots us and insists on tagging along, ignoring our scowls.

Half an hour later we've seen all there is to see, which isn't much. Under the trees we flew in over I find animal runs and improvise some snares using bark-fibre and bent over saplings. Rona tries to help, but it's been a while for her and she just gets in the way. Colm, Fleur and Ness haven't a clue. The noise they make stomping about and crunching twigs! It's boggin' obvious none of them has any outdoor survival skills. If it comes to living off the land and fending for ourselves, it's not looking good.

Finally Ness gets bored and clears off, leaving us alone. We're already out of sight of Gant's jammer, so we just hunker down.

'What do we do now?' Rona says.

Nobody answers her. We all trade gloomy looks.

Which goes to show I'm not the only one done with feeling relieved at escaping the Deeps. We've got no safe place to run to that I can think of. Our only allies – if you can call them that – are smugglers and mercs. And now we have to choose between hiding out on this scrap of land, or chasing after Sky in some mad attempt to get Murdo's windjammer back for him.

Thinking about it is like a knife ripping into my guts.

'What about this place?' Rona says.

'What about it?' I say, sharper than I meant to.

'It's tucked away, and we'd have the cave for shelter. There's a dribble of a waterfall, so water wouldn't be a problem. And I've seen some herbs and edible plants. Kyle, you could teach Colm and Fleur how to trap and hunt. I say we hide out here.' She glances at me, obviously hoping I'll support her. But I'm not so sure. I pretend to look around, as if considering it.

Colm frowns. 'We hide? For how long? The rest of our lives?'

'You got a better idea?' I jeer.

'Kyle!' Rona snaps. Then to Colm: 'What do you suggest?'

My brother shrugs and shakes his head. There's a long, uncomfortable silence after that. In the end, Rona gives me such a mute look of appeal that I have to say something. Anything.

'Maybe Gemini won't go under completely?'

Colm snorts. 'The pro-treaty guys will do the deal with the Slayers. They'll get military help, so they'll win. Gemini's dead.'

'What if we're not found by the doom moon?' I say.

'Yeah,' Fleur says. 'The deal's off then.'

'It won't be,' Colm says, shaking his head again. 'The Slayers will come up with a compromise. Idents doing an extra year down the mines, something like that. By the doom moon everybody will be gut-sick with infighting and slaughter. They'll do any deal.'

'My deadheads will *never* deal!' Fleur says.

'Then they'll –'

I catch my brother's eye and he leaves it unsaid.

'Okay, forget Gemini,' I say. 'If the Saviour's badly wounded, how long can he last without my blood to heal him? A few weeks or months maybe? It won't be forever. After he's dead, whoever succeeds him maybe won't care about us any more. Why should they? Then we can crawl out from whatever rock we've been hiding under and go live someplace nobody knows us.'

Fleur mutters something like: 'Loads of ifs and maybes.'

I turn on her. 'What's your call then?'

She smiles, real grim. 'There's four of us, only one of Murdo. We stick a gun to his head and make him fly us wherever we want in the *Rockpolisher*. And that way he can't go after Sky.'

I see from Rona's frown that she doesn't like the sound of this.

'Okay, but where would you make him fly us to?' I ask.

Fleur has no answer to that. And now there's a crashing-through-bushes sound from the direction of Gant's windjammer.

Yonny appears out of the gathering gloom and beckons until we follow him back there. As we climb the ramp into the hold I'm greeted by smells that chase away all thoughts of hopeless tomorrows and sets my stomach rumbling. Turns out Murdo's handy at rustling up hot meals as well as piloting.

By the time we're done stuffing our faces it's full dark outside. A cloudless night, the temperature plummets. With the ramp still down it's cold even in here and our breath starts misting.

Night creatures are stirring too now. I hear a particularly nasty-sounding snuffling and grunting. Ness, who'd got up to stretch his legs on the ramp, comes scuttling back inside.

'Did you hear that? What is it?'

'Go out and take a look,' Fleur says, straight-faced.

'Ha ha.' Ness clambers past us to get as far forward as he can.

'Whatever it is, it won't come in,' Rona says.

Squint comes and butts up to me. Thing is, his chassis is freezing cold. I give his ears a quick fondle, shove him away and burrow under my packing blankets. Gant flicks a switch and the ramp lifts and closes. She and Yonny head forward to the flight deck.

Murdo perches on a crate, tugs his collar up and does a big shiver. 'Brrr! Cold, isn't it? So you guys made your minds up yet about tomorrow? Staying here, or coming with me?'

'We're still deciding,' Rona says.

He pulls out an evil-looking clasp knife and starts digging dirt out from under his nails. 'Fine. It's your call. I can't force you to come along, although I could sure use the backup. Tell you what, I'll make you a new deal. Help me get my jammer back and I swear I'll do whatever it takes to find you guys someplace safe afterwards, even if it means flying you halfway across Wrath.'

'You've got Sky's jammer,' Rona says. 'Fly us in that.'

The merc's lip almost curls itself off his face.

'Before I salvaged the *Rockpolisher* a scavver gang stripped her. She flies, but only just. Anyway, I can't waste the time. Every second I'm not after it, my *Never Again*'s getting further away.'

'It's only a machine,' Rona says. 'I'm talking about saving lives.'

Murdo jumps down from the crate and glowers at her.

'You don't get it, do you? Without that machine, I'm a nobody, back crawling about in the muck and filth again. Do you goms have *any* idea what it took to get the *Never Again* and make her what she is? I've begged, stolen, lied, cheated and killed for her. She's go-fast and can land anywhere. She's modded and tricked out with gear you can't imagine . . . and she's MINE!'

He shoves past Rona, hits the button to lower the ramp.

'I'm out of here tomorrow. Gant too. If you want to come with me, just say so. If you stay here, well, there's no food stashed, but there's shelter and water and it's firstgreen so it'll get warmer. Even so, I give you three weeks. You'll starve, or go mad and kill each other, or the wildlife will have you.' He looks at each of us in turn, me the longest. 'Your call.'

With that he steps down the ramp and into the darkness.

Ness dashes after him. 'Hey, Murdo, wait for me!'

Colm gets up. For one astonished second I think he's leaving too, but he just closes the ramp again. We all hunker back down under the few blankets we have. Nobody says very much.

Another life-or-death choice to make. And there was me thinking growing up out in the Barrenlands was tough. I'd cut my arm off to return to those days.

    A while later I catch Colm staring at me.

    'What do you think?' he asks.

    'Don't know,' I say. 'I'll sleep on it.'

    It's a lie. I've already made my decision. I'm just not saying.

14
DECISION AND SACRIFICE

With so many grim thoughts slamming around in my head, no way do I think I'll get any sleep. Yet somehow I do, only to wake up with my mouth tasting like something's died in it. I roll over and see the rear hatch gaping open. It's a dark, drizzly start to a new day outside. Grey slabs of cloud hide the ridgetops above us.

With a start I realise I'm alone in here. And someone's heaped extra blankets over me. Rona, I bet. Babying me.

I'm putting my boots on when I hear a loud metallic grinding. Cursing, praying I'm not too late, I race outside. And breathe again. The noise comes from the *Rockpolisher* as it slowly inches its way out of Murdo's cave. Rona, Colm and Fleur are standing watching it, their backs to me, hoods up against the rain.

A leafy branch just misses my head.

I squint up into the drizzle to see Yonny grinning down from on top of the windjammer's hull. He gestures for me to climb up and give him a hand stripping the camouflage off.

'Yeah, in a minute,' I say, and hustle over to join the others.

When I get there the *Rockpolisher* has cleared the cave. It's pulling itself along using a cable secured to a rock at the far side of the ledge. The grinding sound must be from an internal winch. I nudge Colm to let him know I'm here.

He looks around and nods. 'I was about to come get you.'

Rona notices I'm here. 'Hey, sleepy.'

One look at her face is all it takes. I was mad to think she'd left me sleeping so I'd miss Murdo's take-off. She wouldn't.

'Hey.' I pull my hood up, feeling guilty.

The windjammer's teardrop canopy is open. Murdo stands in the front of the cockpit, peering down over the nose at the cable. I can't help shivering. The last time I saw a man standing there it was Sky's co-pilot, Chane, and he was dying. I can still hear his screams, see the blood spew from his mouth.

'Where's Squint?' I ask Colm, giving myself a shake.

He shrugs. 'Don't know. He'll turn up.'

We put Squint in guard mode last night and stuck him outside. By now however his AI should have him hurtling towards us, wagging his tail and getting in everybody's way. Weird.

Murdo shouts for help. He has us shift the far end of the cable to one rock after another so the *Rockpolisher* can slowly haul itself along the landing area. Gant and Yonny are doing the same with their machine. Soon both the jammers are lined up beside each other, facing the huge drop below the ledge.

'O-kay, and now what?' Colm says.

I'm wondering too. They can't winch themselves into the air. My stomach rumbles. 'I'll check the snares.'

'No need,' Fleur says. 'I took care of it while you were snoring. Two were sprung, only by the time I got there something bigger had helped itself. Nothing but bloody fur and bones left.'

I say nothing. It's not what you'd call a great omen.

Meanwhile, Murdo and Yonny pull a section of massively thick and hairy rope from where it lay hidden in the bunch-grass. They hook Gant's cable to a big eye-loop in the middle of it and then step back. Murdo twirls a finger in the air. Inside Gant's windjammer the winch whines again, hauling the big rope back towards it. Yonny takes over the signalling, and Murdo hurries back to us.

'You guys coming with me, or rotting here?'

'We're staying,' Rona says.

I feel like a traitor as I shake my head. 'No, we're not. Sorry, Rona, but Murdo's right. We can't stay here.'

Rona's face goes pinched and shocked. I guess I've never contradicted her like this before, not in front of others.

Colm piles in. 'I agree with Kyle.'

Fleur just shrugs. 'You know what I think we should do.'

The rain starts to lash down heavier now as Murdo turns and grins at Rona. 'You should listen to Kyle,' he says.

She snaps at him, demanding he give us some time alone.

'Fine,' he says. 'Don't be long. Dayshine's wasting.'

He hurries away, back to Gant's jammer. While we wait for him to be out of earshot I glance nervously at Rona. And flinch as I see how old and tired my foster-mother looks. She sighs, takes me by my arms and stares up into my face.

'Please, Kyle,' she says, her eyes glassy with tears. 'Half my life I've spent keeping you safe. Ever since I saw you as a baby, all I wanted was to give you a life. We've managed before, we'll manage here. Tearing off to this No-Zone place is madness.'

I pull away gently, having to blink away my own tears.

'Not as mad as staying here. You heard those night creatures snuffling about. Without a jammer to shut ourselves away in they'll look at us as prey. Even if they don't gobble us we'll starve. I doubt I could feed myself up here, let alone four of us.'

'We can't trust Murdo,' Rona says fiercely.

'So *don't* trust him. Go with him and we can keep an eye on him. Make sure he's not tempted by that reward on our heads.'

'And what about Sky?' Fleur says.

Rona stiffens visibly. 'I'm not responsible for Sky.'

'If Murdo catches up with Sky he'll kill her,' Fleur protests.

'Stop, stop! That's enough!'

We all look around crossly, but Murdo's shout was aimed at Gant in her cockpit. She powers down the winch inside her windjammer and the grinding sound tails off. The rope's been stretched out into a long V-shape with the jammer's nose hooked on to the point. Each end is secured at the cliff edge. Whatever it's made from, it's elastic and quivers under the strain.

'It's a bloody catapult,' Colm says.

I'm wondering what stops the windjammer being fired over the cliff, then I spot the cable out the back of it, attached to a ground-anchor. Moments later, Gant and Yonny appear on the open loading ramp. Each drags a thin wooden crate behind them.

Rona tugs my sleeve. 'About Sky. There's something –'

Only whatever she's going to tell me I don't get to hear as Murdo stomps over to us. The rain plasters his long blond hair to his head, but hasn't washed away his grin.

'Time's up,' he says. 'Who's coming with me?'

Rona takes a deep breath, before sighing it out. Somehow, she dredges up a smile. 'We *all* are. I'll be needing a bucket.'

I give her a big hug, not caring who sees.

Gant joins us now, her blue-dyed hair whipping about her head. She dumps her crate and holds up a spinning wind meter.

'Twenty, gusting thirty,' she announces. 'We're good to go.'

At her nod, Yonny crowbars open one of the crates they've hauled over. I see pulse carbines, spare magazines, blasters, flares and grenades nestling among straw.

'You're *giving* me these?' Murdo says, sounding shocked.

'No way,' Gant says. 'These are for your friends. From what you told me they'll be needing all the firepower they can get.'

Yonny fits the lid back on the crate and hammers it closed. I watch, gobsmacked. One carbine alone would fetch more creds than I'd earn in years of fixing mech stuff.

'Thanks, but we don't need these,' Rona says.

'Yeah, we do,' I say quickly. Colm and Fleur echo me.

Gant turns her mean, one-eyed gaze on us. 'Don't go telling anyone now. I don't want people saying I've gone soft.'

Takes me a while to get she's kidding.

I swallow hard and force a grin. 'Not soft. Reasonable.'

She sticks her left fist out and we bump stumps and fists, like we're all mates now. Murdo even gets a quick hug.

'Your turn to save my ass next,' she calls back to him over her shoulder as she and Yonny head back to their windjammer. They disappear up the loading ramp and it closes behind them.

The rain eases as we stand there, watching and wondering. Murdo warns us to stand back and gives Gant a thumbs up. The windjammer's lift-cells spool up and the undercarriage's hydraulic rams extend as weight comes off them.

Murdo drops to one knee and jerks his hand forward.

There's a loud *twang* behind the jammer. It lurches forward and starts to pick up speed. Too slowly? Halfway to the cliff, I'm sure I could run faster. The whine of the lift-cells rises to a shriek. Still the windjammer sticks to the ground.

Horrified, I watch through my fingers as it plunges over the edge and out of sight.

The shriek cuts off. I cringe inside, waiting for the crash.

Murdo makes for the cliff edge. We run after him and stare down.

'There!' Fleur shouts, and points. Way below us, so small it looks like a toy, Gant's windjammer pulls out of a steep dive and banks left to tuck in against the slope. Its shadow flickers over scrubby trees clinging to the slope as it heads away to the north.

It must hit lift because I see it climb higher.

'Show's over,' Murdo tells us. 'Give me a hand.'

Legs braced and leaning back, he's tugging the elastic rope back up from where it's hanging down over the cliff edge.

Colm and I run to help.

Again I look for Squint, but he's nowhere to be seen.

Ten minutes of hauling and winching later the *Rockpolisher* is hooked on, all set to go. Murdo stands up in its open cockpit and yells down at us to get aboard if we're coming.

'Have you got Squint in there?' I shout.

'Your pet's with Ness. Move it. We ain't got all day.'

We're barely aboard when the ramp lifts and starts closing behind us. And now, finally, I see Squint in a corner of the hold.

I call out to him. 'So this is where you've been hiding!'

He doesn't move, not even a twitch.

I figure he's just suffered another processor deadlock until I see some of his body panels are missing and wires are sticking out of him. Up close it's worse. Squint's eyes are dull and there's a big, empty hole where his power-stacks once slotted.

'Ness!' I yell, furious, incredulous. 'What've you *done*?'

'We, ah, needed a few bits.'

I spot the tech watching me from the hatch to the flight deck.

'You scavved his fraggin' stacks,' I snarl.

Murdo shoves past Ness and gets between us.

'Relax! We need the extra juice to jump-start the lifters. Don't worry, you'll get them back when we're done with them.' His glance flicks from me to the others. 'Right, you all saw Gant's launch, so if you don't want your necks snapped I suggest you get busy strapping yourselves in.' He points out jump seats bolted to the cargo-bay walls. 'Soon as I pull that pin, we're gone.'

With that, he ducks back through the hatch.

I swallow my rage. 'Okay, guys, pick a seat. Make it quick.'

The hold's glowtubes dim as Murdo fires up the *Rockpolisher*'s lift-cells. It takes five tries before they stay spun up.

'I hope this thing can fly,' Colm says, as he straps himself in.

'We'll soon find out,' I say, helping Rona.

Next thing I know, the deck lurches under me and we're moving. I dive for the nearest jump-seat and grab for the straps. Too late. The lift-cells scream and the windjammer's nose drops. I'm flung out of the seat. My back bangs into metal and I find myself pinned to the roof of the hold, weightless and helpless, looking down.

The others gawp up at me, wide-eyed.

For a second it's fun. I laugh at their stunned faces. Until Murdo hauls his controls back and lifts us out of our nosedive.

Suddenly I'm heavy again. I fall back down on to the deck.

Me being me . . . I land on my head. I'm not laughing now.

15
TEMPTATIONS, FRIGHTS AND NEWS

We didn't get far that first day of flying, barely a hundred klicks, before something went wrong with the *Rockpolisher* and Murdo had to bang us down sharpish on another of his smuggler perches. Three days later and he's freaking out because we're still marooned here, with him and Ness struggling to fix the problem. The rest of us are less fussed. Rona says we need the break, to take a breath and feel the sun on our faces and live another day. She says we've earned it, although I don't see how.

This perch is a flattish summit crouched down in the shadows of taller, sharper peaks. Fleur and me are off checking my snares, but finding each is as empty this morning as when we set them.

Frustratingly, loads of dirthoppers share this lump of rock with us. Big-eared, plump, plenty of meat on their bones. But they're smart little critters. Too smart for us anyway. Not one will stick its furry little neck into a noose. Instead they mock us from a safe distance with their hoots and whistles. Try to get close, they dive down holes. Fleur lost her temper earlier and blasted one. Great shot, only it was like killing a mouse with a sledgehammer. No meat left to chew on, just charred fur. I'm not *that* hungry. Yet.

The next trap is also empty – loads more hoots and whistles. I kick at it. 'I say we forget it.'

Fleur says nothing, busy squinting over my head at something. I look too. The sun dazzles me, but I make out a black shape in the sky. And go cold. It's flying right over us.

'Get down!' I shout.

We throw ourselves flat. I've hardly hit the dirt before I see my mistake and curse. What I took for a Slayer windjammer is just a few sky lizards flapping north. A big female leads. The smaller males follow in a loose spearhead formation. Hell, I can hear them calling to each other now as they flap on out of sight.

Fleur laughs, her breath warm on my skin. Which is when I realise we're clinging on to each other.

This gets awkward fast. I let go. A beat later, Fleur lets go too. Rolling away I gaze up at the empty sky, my heart pounding. Beside me Fleur sighs. She props herself on her elbow so she can look down at me, sad-eyed and serious.

'Kyle, we need to talk.'

'What about?' I say cautiously, watching as she hooks a stray blonde hair out from where it's caught in her mouth.

'Sky. You still love her, don't you?'

'What's *that* matter now?' I mumble, confused and embarrassed.

I go to sit up. She stops me, using her nublood strength.

'Colm says you do.'

'Been talking about me behind my back?'

Fleur doesn't blink. 'Listen, if we catch up with Sky, it could get ugly fast. Murdo is out for revenge. We just need to know which way you'll jump if things get rough.'

'We?' I suck in a lungful of air, let it out slow.

'Come on, Kyle, it won't kill you. Do you love her, yes or no?'

'I don't know. Maybe. She makes it tough.'

Fleur slow-nods. 'I get that.'

'My big mouth of a brother tell you anything else?'

'He doesn't understand what you see in her. Course that's just because he doesn't know the real Sky, not like we do.'

And only now, because there's no limit to how dumb I can be, does it hit me that Fleur – being Fliss's sister – will have grown up in the same Ravenhole ident camp as Sky. I've known Sky for just over half a year; Fleur's known the girl most of her life.

Stupid maybe, but I feel a stab of jealousy.

'Was it the *real* Sky that ran out on me?' I say, bitterly. 'Oh, don't worry, I won't stand by and let Murdo hurt her. I couldn't.'

She nods. 'Good. Neither could I.'

With a grim smile she lets me get up. We're brushing leaves and twigs off ourselves when Colm comes running up.

'Hey, did you see the liz–?' he calls out.

And shuts up, his face a picture of surprise and suspicion. I mean, it's not like Fleur and me are pulling clothes back on or anything, but it must look bad, like we've been fooling around. Serves him right, I reckon, for shooting his gob off behind my back.

'We saw them,' I say. 'Bloody things scared the hell out of us.'

'Where've you been?' he says, his glare flicking back and forth between us. 'I've been calling for ages.'

'Wasting time checking empty snares,' Fleur tells him.

He gives us a *yeah*, *right* look.

'So what's up?' I say quickly. 'Why the panic?'

Colm tells us through his teeth that Murdo and Ness have got the *Rockpolisher* going. Murdo wants us back so he can launch.

'You seriously didn't hear me shouting?' he says.

'Too busy,' I say, pushing past him.

Back at the windjammer, Rona's already strapped into a jump seat and clutching her bucket. Murdo beckons impatiently from the hatch to the flight deck. 'One of you guys, give me a hand.'

I beat Colm to him, but soon wish I hadn't. A minute later, I'm hanging in my straps in the co-pilot seat, mouth dry, watching as rock shoots up to meet us. Only at the last second does Murdo ease his control column back and pulls us out of our dive. I'm pressed into my seat. Next he flings us hard left, hugging the steep slope. As he throttles the lifters back to cruise power I let out the breath I've been holding.

'Do we *have* to fly this close?'

'You call this close?' Murdo laughs and does something. Rocks and trees lunge nearer, whipping past in a terrifying blur.

I say nothing else, rigid with fear.

He winks, slides us back out a few metres, then has me follow what he's doing by loosely holding my co-pilot set of controls. Not long after, we hit our first solid lump of ridge lift. It's as if someone kicks me in the seat of my pants and the windjammer seems to leap higher. Lift-callers quit their *bong-bong* moaning and start chirping, sounding happier. Murdo works us steadily higher, pulling back to slow down in lift, pushing forward to speed up through sink, talking me through every move he makes on the controls.

He stops climbing just shy of the ridgetop. 'You take her now.'

'Do what?' I say, bulging my eyes at him.

But Murdo won't take no for an answer. He says if he can take breaks we can fly further in a day, and catch Sky quicker.

'Follow the ridge,' he tells me. 'If lift knocks a wing up, push it back down. Stay this tight to the hard stuff. Got it?'

'Are you out of your boggin' mind?'

He doesn't answer, and folds his arms across his chest.

More days slide by and we settle into a routine. Each morning, weather allowing, we set out to reach the nearest smuggler perch that'll take us closer to the No-Zone. They're not programmed into the *Rockpolisher*'s nav-comm; Murdo has them all in his head. Once we reach it, either we land or – if the ridge lift's still good – we try for the next perch en route, knowing we can double back. Once we nearly come unstuck because our target perch is a bust. Somebody, Slayers probably, has littered the landing area with undercarriage-wrecking boulders. Murdo sees it late, aborts the landing. We end up low and it costs us another day as we have to divert.

With Fleur, Colm and me helping on some of the easier ridges we fly further and for longer, dawn to dusk. This last landing had us sucking our teeth, peering down into a gloom-filled valley to spot the perch he's sure is there, but can't see. I spotted it in the end, and I'm still shaking from watching our final approach into the inky darkness.

The landing was brutal. Rona's no softie and she screamed.

By now our food is getting short. We're into old emergency

rations, hard tack that tastes like sawdust. No way can we risk stopping at a regular way station for supplies.

Being hungry beats being dead, I tell my growling guts.

The shortest route from the Deeps to the No-Zone would've taken us through Slayer heartlands, past Prime and the Blight. Unwilling to risk this, Murdo has chosen a more looping track, a big swing out east. Says Sky must've done the same. I'm less sure. For Tarn, Sky is crazy enough to risk anything.

Three more days' flying and Murdo says we'll be looking at the No-Zone. He's in a nasty mood, having counted on catching up with Sky before then. By my reckon it'll also be close to the doom moon and the Saviour's cruel deadline. Each night now we see the little dog climb ever higher, chasing after our bigger moon.

Nobody talks about the peace treaty. What's there to say?

After we've camouflaged the *Rockpolisher* and choked down some hard tack, Murdo lets us light a small fire. We huddle round it, as the flames leap, dance and spit. I'm glad for its warmth, but get a lump in my throat at the smell of woodsmoke. It reminds me of other fires, when I was a nobody back in the Barrenlands.

I wish I could be that nobody again.

Tearing my eyes from the flames I gaze up into the blue-black night sky. Countless stars wink down at me, uncaring. Each is another sun, I know that much. One – I don't know which – is Sol, where all us humans came from. That's if I *am* human.

Colm sees me looking. 'Beautiful night, huh?'

We're talking again. I can never stay mad at him for long.

'When I was little,' I say, 'I'd spend hours looking up at the stars when I should've been asleep. My favourite wordweaver stories were of worlds where humans lived in glittering towers as tall as our mountains. Everybody was well fed and happy. There was never any fighting. You think there *are* worlds like that?'

'Why not? They can't all be dump worlds.'

'What about worlds where idents are a blessing, not a curse?' I say, repeating what Rona once said.

'All of them. It's just a shame that we can't get there.'

I hear the yearning in my brother's voice and feel it too, an ache inside me. We came from the stars, but there's no way back. Wrath is locked down. We're stuck here for good. Or evil.

'What's *that*?' Fleur says, firelight flaring off her cheekbones.

I hear a low rumble away to the south-west. Gunfire?

'Thunder,' Murdo says, his head wreathed in smoke from the bitter-smelling weed he's puffing on.

Another rumble and I figure he's right. A storm, that's all.

I'm throwing fresh wood on the fire when Ness stumbles down the ramp and announces he's picked up the Saviour's feed – the propaganda broadcast that plays around the clock on screens in Prime and other larger settlements.

The fire is forgotten. We pile back inside the hold and crowd round Ness's cleverbox.

The screen shows a grainy image of a Slayer woman's bleak face, her gob open, paused mid-word. Ness taps the screen and her slash of a mouth starts working again.

'. . . main news again. After months of heavy fighting, our heroic coalition forces have secured the insurgent stronghold known as the Blight. Commander Kessel, in charge of the assault, reports all resistance has been crushed and thousands of prisoners taken. Executions are ongoing. Demolition operations will follow, to wipe this nest of evil off the face of Wrath once and for all.'

She pauses. Her face gives way to a picture of devastation.

Hollow-eyed men, women and children shuffle towards the camera, clad only in rags, hands held above their heads. Behind them I see smouldering barricades and crushed shacks. An armoured Slayer landcrawler sits to one side, exhaust stacks belching smoke, its blasters trained on the shuffling survivors. And now the view cuts to a shot from a windjammer flying overhead.

It is the Blight. Flattened. Burning.

'What's she mean, *coalition* forces?' I ask, but get shushed.

The camera cuts back to the rebel prisoners. A woman, obviously badly wounded, limps out of line. One wrong step, that's all. A Slayer steps up and wastes her. There's not one of us watching who doesn't jump. Even Murdo curses. I think I'm going to be sick. But we keep watching. It's impossible not to. The camera shifts to show dazed-looking rebels, coughing and choking, staggering out of a smoky tunnel entrance to surrender. They're pounced on by Slayers, who beat them before dragging them away.

'Stop!' Fleur shouts. 'Ness, go back a bit and freeze it.' She jabs a finger at the screen. 'They're not all Slayers.'

I'm hardly able to believe what I'm looking at. She's right.

'Those guards –' I croak.

'Gemini,' Colm gasps. 'Pro-treaty.'

Among the Slayer ranks there are men and women wearing Gemini combat fatigues under matt-black body armour.

'Traitors!' Fleur spits. 'How *could* they?'

'See their sleeves,' Colm says.

The traitors have torn their Gemini shoulder insignia off and wear the Slayer death's head in its place. I go to swallow. Can't. The Saviour's plan must be working. Pro-treaty Gemini rebels throwing their lot in with the Saviour and his Slayer army, turning against their anti-treaty brothers and sisters. Ness restarts the feed and we get to watch more beatings. One of the ex-Gemini fighters is getting stuck into the prisoners as savagely as any Slayer would.

Then it hits me . . . I know the guy's cruel face.

'That's our combat instructor. Stauffer!'

Colm leans closer. 'The one you fought? It is too.'

But now Slayer woman's back, talking from a little box in the top left. A wanted poster fills the rest of the screen.

Rona's hand flies to her mouth. She shakes her head.

Fleur curses. 'It's you guys!'

I'm the face on the left. Battered. Bruised. Blood wriggling out of one nostril, left eye swollen closed. I'm glowering at the picture-taker, like I want to kill him. Colm's face is on the right, head back, dull-eyed, sneering. Or maybe they're both me. Whatever. Somebody's messed with the pictures, to make us look meaner and more vicious. More like monsters.

Everybody starts talking at once. I hiss at them to shut up. Slayer woman's off again.

'Coalition forces continue the hunt for these two ruthless ident assassins who seriously injured our Benevolent Saviour earlier this year. Both narrowly avoided capture after the surrender of their wilderness hideout . . .' The image switches briefly to show us an unmistakable shot of the Deeps, and then returns to our wanted poster. 'It is likely they are being sheltered by ident diehards in a cynical attempt to sabotage the historic peace accord between humans and twists. Loyal citizens of Wrath, if you have *any* information that might lead to the capture of these fugitives, you must report what you know to the authorities. The penalty –'

Whatever she says next we don't get to hear. The picture breaks up, dissolving into a snowstorm of spitting static. Ness fiddles with the cleverbox, but he can't get it going again.

'Signal's weak. Storm's killing it.'

A louder and closer rumble of thunder suggests he's right.

Maybe it's the thunder, or the rain lashing the hull, or the thoughts crashing around in my head at what I saw on the Saviour's feed. Either way, it takes an age of writhing about beneath my moth-eaten blanket before I finally fall asleep. Only to find myself tearing through darkness so thick it smothers me, branches lashing at my face and a pack of nightrunners snapping at my heels.

I wake up with a start, blanket gone, sweating and shivering.

Rona's shaking me, very gently. 'You okay?'

'Just a bad dream,' I whisper.

No point telling her the truth. Which is how terrifying it is to wake up from one nightmare to find I'm stuck in another.

What can she say to make *that* better? Nothing.

She pulls my blanket back over me. 'When you were little, I'd cuddle you and promise that tomorrow's another day; that things wouldn't look so bad in the dayshine. You'd settle down again.'

'You're *not* going to cuddle me?' I say, like I'm worried.

Rona half smiles. 'I'm too tired; you're too old. And no amount of dayshine can fix what's going on. But –'

'At least we still have each other,' I say, before she can.

'We do. Now try to get some rest. Another long day tomorrow.' She kisses my forehead and heads back to her blanket.

Later on, the storm blows on by to batter the next valley downwind. The rain eases, until the loudest sound is snoring. I'm still tossing and turning. It's like my head's a windjammer and Sky keeps on sneaking aboard. She's good at that, nobody better. I picture her cold and alone, curled up in Murdo's *Never Again*. Or under a bush, already on the ground in the No-Zone.

I curse her for running out on me.

I pray that wherever she is she's all right.

And fall asleep wondering if I ever sneak inside Sky's head . . .

16
SO CLOSE, BUT SO FAR

The next day, Murdo is forced to perch us early. Ahead the weather is closing in again. Dark clouds with bulging, rain-full bellies are clamping themselves down on the ridges. Way too risky, even for him.

The sky lizards stream on past us though, not bothered. The further north we fly, the more of them we're seeing. Mainly they flap along high above us, but sometimes they drop down to soar the ridges like we do. Hundreds. Thousands. Too many to count even if I were good at numbers, which I ain't. So far we've managed to stay clear of them, and they've paid us no mind.

'Where d'you think they're headed?' Fleur says.

'Who cares?' Rona says, doling out the hated hard tack. 'As long as they leave us alone. That's all I ask.'

'Have you ever seen so many?' I ask Murdo.

'Half a day's flying we've lost,' he moans, not interested.

Lost maybe, not wasted. With loads of dayshine left, Colm and I go for a walk to stretch our legs and find some ruts torn through the hard-packed dirt. Ruts our jammer didn't make.

We call Murdo.

One look and he's rubbing his hands together.

'That's my *Never Again* all right!'

We're all like, 'How can you be sure?'

But where the ruts end he finds marks where the jammer's outriggers planted themselves, and a clear impression of a welded repair he'd once made. That settles it.

'How far ahead is she?' Ness asks.

I spot a twig beside a rut and peer at its snapped-off end. Dark brown. Bone dry. 'A week, give or take,' I tell them.

Murdo straightens up, looking sour.

'That bitch is crazy. My *Never Again*'s a fast ship, but even so. She must've cut straight through the Slayer heartlands.'

'Sky was never short of nerve,' Rona says.

'Nerve's one thing, sense another,' he growls. 'Let's just hope she didn't pick up any Slayer pursuit on her way through.'

All the rest of that day I wonder how she's managed it. We've been hitting the ridges hard in her old windjammer, taking risks and stretching each day's flying. On easier runs Colm, Fleur and me have spelled Murdo on the controls, so he can grab some rest. Sky must've done all the flying herself. No breaks for her. And the last time I saw her she wasn't even feeling very well.

'She's tough as they come,' Fleur says, when I mention this.

'Single-minded anyway,' Colm says, glancing at me.

Rona's at our crate table, putting together a new medbag from the contents of her pockets and some herbs she's found and picked on our way here. 'I just hope Sky's okay.'

'She'll be in the No-Zone by now,' I say. 'Wonder what it's like.'

Murdo's holed up in the cockpit, boozing. But he must be listening because now he shambles into the cargo bay, eyes bloodshot, his face one big scowl. 'No need to wonder,' he slurs, leering around at us. 'Pressure's climbing. Weather's set to clear. Day after tomorrow you'll be seeing it for yourselves.'

'I've got a question,' Colm says.

'Ask it quick then. I've got drinking to do.'

'Let's say Sky made it to the No-Zone. How'll you find her?'

Murdo taps his nose, second try. 'I've got tricks up my sleeve. If my *Never Again*'s there, I'll find her. Don't you worry.'

'What about Sky?' Fleur calls out as usual.

Murdo sways on his feet. 'She stole more than my coat . . .'

With that he ducks through the hatch and slams it after him. But we know what he meant. Wrath justice is brutal. Catch a man stealing your coat, law says you can skin him alive.

Rona and I swap worried looks.

'Hard to see how this can end happy,' Fleur says, biting her lip.

Colm mutters something under his breath.

'What?' I snap, without meaning to.

'This is Wrath,' he says louder. 'There are no happy endings.'

A hairy landing on the smallest perch yet, and a long pre-dawn trudge back up into the hills above to find a pass, through which Murdo says we'll see the No-Zone. Colm and I go with him. Fleur and the rest stay to guard the *Rockpolisher*. By the time Murdo finally calls a halt, the new dawn is pinking the peaks to our west.

'There,' he says, bent over, wheezing.

Through the promised gap the dawnshine lights up an isolated group of mountains further to the north, islands of rock thrusting skywards out of a vast, mist-swamped sea of jungle. I take a closer look through my pulse rifle's scope. At full zoom I make out distinct peaks, jagged snow-capped spikes.

'How far?' I ask Murdo.

He's got his breath back. 'Fifty klicks, give or take.'

I flip the scope to night-see and check out the dimly lit jungle. My skin crawls. So does the ground. Bright green in the scope, the mist looks almost alive as it slinks through dense undergrowth, swirled along by some breeze. And towering above the jungle are the biggest trees I've ever seen! The tallest must reach up hundreds of metres into the sky. One's trunk is so wide I wonder if a hundred people all holding hands could reach round it.

'That jungle looks ugly,' Colm says.

'Maybe it looks better in dayshine?' I say doubtfully.

Murdo spits. 'Only if you're a bug, a snake or a Reaper. It's nothing but swamp and slime and nasties. The vegetation's so thick it's impossible to hack through, and there's no lift above it, not even on a sunny day. This really is the arse end of nowhere.'

As the day brightens, I look at the No-Zone again. And grunt as I spot what seems like a sheer wall of rock between us and the bigger peaks beyond. Stare as hard as I like, I see no way through.

I point it out to Colm, but he's already seen it.

'Looks impenetrable,' he says to Murdo.

'It can't be,' Murdo says. 'If Slayer transports can fly into the interior, so can we. We've just got to find their way in.'

'How do we even get over there, with no ridge to soar?'

I've been wondering that too. Even with our lift-cells at max power, in still air our windjammer is always sinking, about a metre a second. We've flown this far by ridge-running, sticking close to mountain slopes facing into-wind, using the updraughts to lift us and keep us airborne. That won't work here, with flat jungle between us and the No-Zone. The flight out there will be a straight glide and – if Murdo's right – there's little or no hope of lift from thermals because it's swampy and wet.

It looks impossible.

'We'll get there,' he says. 'Now shut up and keep an eye out. I've got stuff to do, and don't want to get eaten doing it.'

He produces a cleverbox and a coil of wire from his pack. One end of the wire plugs into the box. The other he ties to a stone and tosses up into a nearby tree, looping it over a branch. While he's doing this, Colm and I squat down either side of him, sweeping the surrounding rocks for threats. I catch yellow animal eyes watching us, but only small ones. Nothing too worrying.

'Right,' Murdo says. 'Let's get a fix on my *Never Again*.'

Colm and I forget our guard duties – this is way too interesting.

He taps the screen. The cleverbox chirps.

'Gotcha! She's okay.'

My heart skips a beat. 'Sky?'

Murdo laughs. 'My *Never Again*. Diagnostics mostly in the green. Systems up and running. Good strong fix. Take a look.'

He flips the cleverbox around. I see a chart, a red triangle flashing in the middle. Must be his precious *Never Again*. It's surrounded by contours, pulled in tight. Mountainous terrain.

The red dot's not moving. Sky must have landed.

I swallow hard. 'Inside the No-Zone?'

'Yup.' Murdo zooms out with a flick of his fingers.

The contoured area on the chart shrinks to a small island among a sea of swamp symbols, the red triangle still winking at the centre. Another tap and a red line runs from the windjammer triangle to become a twitching arrowhead at the edge of the screen.

I look the way it points and see the distant No-Zone.

Sky's somewhere there. Alive. Probably.

'Why didn't you do this before?' Colm asks him.

'You have to be this close. A hundred klicks is about the limit to activate the tracker, less with rock in the way.'

'Nobody else can pick up the signal?'

'They'd need some serious kit. It channel-hops.'

I ask him to zoom in again. When he does, I point out a large blank area in the middle of the screen.

'How come it isn't showing any contours there?'

Murdo laughs. 'We're lucky to have any at all. This is the No-Zone.' He sleeps the cleverbox and stuffs it back into his pack.

By the time we've slogged our way back down to the *Rockpolisher* the sun is high in the sky. Rona's pacing about on the ramp. She calls out we're incoming. Fleur and Ness come running out.

'Get a fix?' the tech calls to Murdo.

'A solid one.' Murdo chucks his cleverbox to him. 'Stick the coordinates in the nav-comm.'

'On it.' Ness scuttles back inside.

'Who'd like a bit of breakfast?' Rona says.

'Forget it,' Murdo snaps. 'I want the lot of you back on board, strapped in and ready for launch. Move yourselves.'

'What's the rush? The No-Zone's not going anywhere.'

She's talking to air. Murdo's already gone, pulling himself up the hull to the open cockpit.

A second later, I hear the *thunk-thunk* of relays engaging. The *Rockpolisher*'s old lift-cells whine as they spin up.

'No-Zone then,' I shrug at Rona. 'Hungry or not.'

'Looks like it,' she says, and sighs.

What I should do now is hug her and tell her I love her, in case things go wrong. But I don't. The others are all watching.

'Inside!' Murdo bellows down at us. 'You guys deaf, or what?'

17
AN UNPLEASANT SURPRISE

A minute or so later and we've launched and are climbing back up in weak ridge lift. Fleur's in the co-pilot seat; I'm in the jump seat behind her. We'll do none of the flying, but Murdo knows as well as we do that our nublood eyes see further. He growls at us to keep our eyes peeled for sunny into-wind rock.

'And if you see birds or lizards slope-soaring tell me. We need every scrap of altitude before we set off, so we reach the No-Zone with enough height to do some scouting around.'

'Yeah, yeah,' I say. He's told us this twice already.

For the next hour, Murdo chases updraughts and works us slowly higher and higher. The best lift always hides tight in to the rock faces so that's where he flies us. So close sometimes I half expect to see our wing tip strike sparks from the rock. I cling to my jump seat with sweaty palms. Even Fleur is wide-eyed.

Then the day starts warming up.

'Now we're talking,' Murdo mutters, as he hooks a monster updraught boiling off a huge slab of dayshine-heated rock. Our lift-sensors go crazy bleeping. Quick as a flash, he cranks us into a steeply banked turn to stay in it. We ride this gift all the way up until we clear the summit of the ridge. Even then it keeps on pumping, taking us higher. After so long skulking along the low ridges it's a weird feeling to look down at the world spread out beneath us. I feel exposed, like I've been stripped naked.

Colm sticks his head through the hatch.

'Wow! That's some view.'

From the hold behind him, I hear Rona retching into her bucket. I ask him how she's doing. He tells me she's coping.

Luckily Murdo flies more gently now – big, lazy figures of eight, light touches on the controls to keep us climbing in the core of the updraughts where the lift is strongest. The ridgetop drops further away below us, and the air gets noticeably colder.

'That No-Zone looks weird,' Fleur says.

From up here we can see over the nearer ridges, all the way north to where the No-Zone's mountains stick up tall and unexpectedly from the emerald plain surrounding them. Even in the dayshine there's something so gloomy and forbidding about them that it sucks all the spit from my mouth. I swear I can see some dark red stains on some of the slopes, like dried blood.

'They're just mountains, that's all,' Colm says.

'On their own though,' I say. 'Like they were dropped there.'

Murdo uses every last bit of his piloting skills to climb us as high as he can. The altimeter on his panel clicks through fifteen hundred metres, the highest we've been. But even I can see the numbers slowing down. The lift-sensors sound less chirpy too.

He curses. 'Come on, lift, don't you run out on me now!'

It does. We top out just shy of two thousand.

'This high enough?' I ask.

'It'll have to be; it's all we're getting.'

Without another word Murdo turns our nose north towards the distant No-Zone. We leave the ridges behind and coast out over the plain of jungle. His fingers dance across his panel and the whine of the lift-cells climbs in pitch to a shrill scream. Full emergency power to stretch our glide to the max. . .

Holding my breath won't keep us in the air. I still can't help doing it. Ever since we left the ridges behind, the lift-sensors have done nothing but moan. Sink is *everywhere*, like Murdo said it would be. He jinks us left and right of track, only it's as if the swamps and swirling mists below are reaching up to drag us down.

Murdo says nothing. Doesn't have to. With every minute that goes by I see his jaw working harder at whatever he's chewing.

Ahead of us the No-Zone's mountains creep ever closer and loom bigger. But they're also sliding steadily up the canopy. We're undershooting. At this rate we'll be down in the mist before we get there, even with both the *Rockpolisher*'s worn-out old lifters running at full chat. How much longer can they stick that? I'm sure I smell burning, like they're starting to cook. And I don't fancy our chances if we end up in the swamp.

Colm leans past me to look at the panel in front of Fleur. I look too. On it is a chart display. The green dot that's us is pretty much halfway to the mountains – our point of no return.

'Maybe we should turn back and try again later,' he says.

'We turn back when I say so!' Murdo growls. 'Shut the hell up and let me get on with flying. I know what I'm doing.'

That why you're sweating like a hog, I want to say, but don't.

A few moments later it's too late. We're past halfway now.

Committed. No going back to the ridge we left.

'How are we doing?'

A pale-looking Rona joins Colm, peering through the hatch from the hold. She gives my shoulder a quick squeeze.

I don't have the heart to tell her. 'We're, uh, getting there.'

'Look!' Fleur shouts, pointing. 'Dragons. See 'em?'

'So what?' I snap. She'd made me jump.

'So, you big gom,' she says, slapping at me, 'they're circling!'

She's right too. A few klicks out in front of us and off to our left, more sky lizards flap towards the No-Zone. But a few are stretching their leathery wings out and turning lazy circles.

Murdo doesn't hesitate – he cranks us around towards them.

'What if they attack us again?' Rona says.

'We'll take that chance,' Murdo says. 'They're in lift.'

I grab Rona's hand. 'Get back to your jump seat. Strap in.'

She nods and staggers back into the hold with Colm helping her. As we get closer I see the sky lizards are circling over a small clearing in the jungle. Only a flatlander would call it a hill, yet it manages to stick up like a dome above the writhing mist. None of those massive trees grow there, or else they've been cleared. All I see is dark earth and some round things that could be . . .

'That's a village down there!' Fleur yells.

'*Was* a village,' I say from a dry mouth. The round things were once crude huts. Now they're ruins with holes gaping in them, blackened and still smouldering from where they've been burnt down. Telltale smoke curls up into the air. Bodies are littered outside them. Two sky lizards have landed and are squabbling over one, ripping the corpse apart.

Murdo flies us in above the still-circling lizards, which pay us no attention as we bank into a turn. And they *are* in lift! Nothing massive, but at least the lift-sensors quit their moaning.

We get a too-good view of the carnage.

'Are those dead guys Reapers?' Fleur says, looking down.

'Looks like it,' I say. 'Wonder what happened?'

'Who cares?' Murdo says. 'They're dying's done us a favour.'

Using all his skill he screws us higher. He's also able to throttle back our overheated lifters and cut them a break. The whole time it seems the wind's drifting us closer to the No-Zone.

'Sorted,' Murdo says through his teeth.

Lucky, I think.

As the lift tops out, he heads us on our way again.

Fleur and me bump fists, and when Colm reappears we laugh and bump him too. A bit of altitude makes us all brave again.

Which just shows how stupid we are, because even with Murdo banging us back to full emergency power we're soon low again and back to sweating and swapping anxious glances. We make it to the No-Zone, but so low that Murdo has to jink us round one of the big trees. The sheer rock wall that guards its interior rears up above us. Problem is – it's lined up the wrong way for ridge-running, being *along* the wind not *across* it, so there's no chance of updraughts.

Another thirty seconds and we'll slam into it.

'Now what?' I ask, fighting to keep my voice level.

'We go through it,' Murdo says.

'I hate to tell you this, Murdo,' Colm says, 'but that's rock.'

'Fleur?' Murdo says.

She's head down over Ness's cleverbox, staring at its screen.

'You're left of track,' she says now, as cool as you like. 'Drift right a bit. More. Bit more. Yeah, that's good.'

Good? How? We're still heading for solid rock.

My heart slams inside me. I cringe back from the canopy, like that'll save me if we smash into the cliff. Until finally I spot something. Directly ahead the rock face is smooth and dark grey, the only feature a long thin crack running down and right. But that's only an illusion. To the right of the crack the rock is darker, like the different shades of blue sky either side of a rainbow. That, and the water spilling out of the bottom of the crack, is what give it away. It's *not* a crack – it's an edge.

'Got it! Murdo, aim just left of that crack.'

I lean forward between him and Fleur, and point and point and point. The rock to the left isn't lighter; it's further away. What I'm looking at is a hidden fold in the rock.

'What do you see?' he snarls.

But it's too late and I don't have the words. 'Trust me!'

Murdo curses and banks us hard left.

And I'm right. As we fly past the 'crack' it opens up behind us, revealing a steep-walled, shadow-filled gully, a boulder-strewn torrent glinting at the bottom. It looks as if the main rock face has fallen forward leaving a narrow cleft behind. There's no time for punching the air though. No sooner do we see it than we're slap bang into the clutching hand of yet more sink. We lurch lower. Murdo curses, stands the *Rockpolisher* on its right wing and jams us into the gully. Rock walls blur past on either side, a handful of metres away. The gully twists and turns. Murdo has to keep flicking us left and right so we don't rip our wings off.

Several times I think we're dead meat. And then I'm sure.

Fleur screams. 'Right! Go right!'

Ahead I'd swear the ravine ends in a rock wall. Only it's fooling with us again and swerves hard right instead. Murdo grunts, banks us right wing down and hauls back on the controls so hard my chin is forced on to my chest and my seeing greys out. We make the turn. How? I don't know.

Somebody cheers, a ragged cry of relief. Could've been me.

The gully walls open out and the ground seems to fall away beneath us, giving us a welcome load of height back.

Murdo lets out a low whistle. 'Tell you what – I wouldn't want to be the first guy to run this route.'

'You'd have to be mad,' Fleur says, laughing.

'What's that?' I say, peering ahead through the canopy.

Coming up fast, couple of klicks to run, a slender, natural stone bridge arches across the ravine. We're way too low to clear it.

'No sweat,' Murdo says. 'There's room to fly under it.'

'No there *isn't*.' With my far-seeing nublood eyes I see what he can't yet – chains hanging down under the bridge.

A deadly windjammer trap, and we're flying straight into it!

18
ROCKPOLISHER DOWN

Murdo sees the wrecking chains and curses.

'We have to go back!' I shout.

Even as I say it I know it's impossible. The gully's still far too narrow to fly a three-sixty, no matter how steeply banked.

'Can't!' Murdo snaps, which settles it.

He pulls the windjammer's nose up and slows us down until we're mushing along on the ragged edge of a stall, alarms shrieking. He's buying us a precious few seconds, but that's all. I peer desperately at the now clearly visible chains, searching for a break in them.

There isn't one. And every second they get closer.

'There!' Fleur yells and points. 'Rockslide.'

Murdo shoves the controls forward and we pitch into a dive.

'I see it!' I shout, frantic with hope. 'It's made a gap.'

Under the left side of the arch, a fresh-looking rockslide has taken a bite out of the rockface of the gully, leaving an overhang behind. Between this and the first of the wrecking chains there might just be enough room to squeeze our jammer through.

Murdo yells at us to strap in tight.

I turn to shout at Colm to get back to his jump seat in the hold, but he's already gone. Now Murdo stuffs our nose down even steeper. The wind goes from whistling past our canopy to shrieking. I hold my breath, barely able to watch as he spears us down towards the gap in the rock caused by the slide.

Which gets bigger and bigger and . . . is not big enough.

Murdo fills the cockpit with more curses. At the last possible instant he rolls us hard right.

I throw my hands up to protect my face. There's a massive bang and a fierce scraping, like we're a knife being sharpened on a grindstone. Through my fingers I see dark rock flash past.

Sparks flare. Metal screeches.

The *Rockpolisher* staggers and yaws sideways.

Then – somehow – we're through. One of our stub-wings is bent and torn, but we're still flying. Murdo rolls us level again and sends us leaping skywards, trading speed to gain height. Not before I glimpse windjammer wreckage strewn over the gully floor. All my relief drains away, like a hole has been torn in my guts. Was that wreckage the mangled remains of Murdo's *Never Again*? I pray it wasn't. Nobody, not even Sky, could hope to survive such a smash.

Fleur glances back at me, eyes shining. ' Close call, huh?'

I'm too gutted to answer.

In front of me Murdo is wrestling with his controls. The panel in front of him lights up all red. Alarms go off, loud and insistent. With an oath and a swipe of his hand he silences them.

I look past him and see how low we are, despite his climb.

Next thing I know, dazzling dayshine spears into the flight

deck as we finally escape the gully's clutches. A milky-green lake glitters beneath us, foothills climbing from either side. Directly ahead I see the inner mountains of the No-Zone reaching for the sky. A few klicks away a jungle-smothered ridge rears skywards. It faces into-wind. Can we reach it though?

As soon as I think this, our lifters stutter. New alarms sound.

'Not now!' Murdo roars, slamming his fist on the panel.

The plastic cracks, and the lifters quit their stuttering and pick up again. The heavily damaged *Rockpolisher* staggers on. Somehow we make it across the lake to the ridge where Murdo latches on to some updraughts and manages a climb, before taking us deeper into the No-Zone. But there's only so much that hoping and holding my breath can do. With a bass *thud* the portside lifter quits on us. Straight away we go left wing down and start to sink. Only a smart turn by Murdo saves us from slamming into the ridge.

'We're on fire back here!' Colm shouts from the hold.

I loosen my straps and take a look through the open hatch. Thick, oily smoke twists itself up through the deck plates. And I can smell it now too, choking and acrid.

Murdo levels our wings. It doesn't help. We're still sinking like a stone. 'Brace!' he yells. 'We're going down.'

Off to our left there's open ground. I tap his shoulder and point.

He shakes his head. 'No good. If we land out there, the next Slayer transport to come this way is bound to spot us.'

Instead he cranks us hard right towards a col on this ridge we're running that's shaped like a fourhorn's riding saddle. We just barely scrape over it, only to find ourselves looking down in horror at a mess of jumbled-up rocks. The one thing that's flat down there is winding, milky-green and wet.

'The river,' Murdo spits. 'It's all we've got. Hang on!'

He stuffs our nose down and bangs open the air brakes. From the hold I hear Rona's scream. Even Fleur pulls a grim face. The smoke from the fried lifter is in the cockpit now, curling round my feet as Murdo lines us up on the river.

Just a few rocks left to clear . . .

Thud! Thud! Thud! Our last lifter chews itself up.

We flop down out of the air the same way a shot bird does. I don't even have time to curse. We hit the rocks so hard I bang my jaw on my chest. The canopy shatters into a thousand shards in front of me and I'm flung sideways as the wing on my side digs into the river. An explosion of dark water erupts upwards as it carves a deep furrow and turns us around before being torn off.

After that it's just impressions. Dark. Light. Dark again. Metal screeching. Floating. Crashing down again. Icy water lashing my face. One last impossibly violent smash.

I cringe in my jump seat, stunned, waiting for pain to hit, listening to the angry hiss of hot metal turning water to steam, watching filthy brown river water foam back off the remains of the canopy. A bit of broken windjammer falls off outside and makes a splash. My hoarse breathing is the loudest noise after that, until some startled birds arrive overhead, cackling loudly.

Fleur, looking like a drowned rat, a bloody gash across her forehead, twists around to look at me. 'You okay?'

'Think so,' I say. And tell her she's had a bang on the head.

She feels it and shrugs. 'Scratch. I'll live.'

Murdo starts unstrapping himself, shaking his head and

muttering. He's wet too, but as far as I can see he isn't hurt.

'Call that a landing?' Fleur says, trying for a smile.

He struggles up and scowls at her. 'I can only fly what's under me. This changes nothing. Just means we'll have to do a bit of walking to find my *Never Again*, that's all.'

I stare at him in disbelief. 'What? You didn't see it then?'

'Didn't see what?' he snaps.

'Your *Never Again*. Spread all over that gully we flew through.' With poor Sky's body rotting inside it.

Murdo shrugs. 'That wreck? Yeah, I saw it all right. Wasn't my *Never Again*. Been there years judging by the state of it.'

My breath explodes out of me like a bomb going off. Shaking with relief, I start fumbling to unstrap myself. Next thing I know, Colm's by my side, pulling me out of my seat.

'Your mother,' he says, all wide-eyed. 'She's hurt.'

It's a shambles back in the hold. Stuff is thrown everywhere. Wires hang down, flicking about and sparking. The force of the crash has broken the windjammer's back. Dayshine spills inside through massive cracks in the hull and the ramp at the back, which has fallen wide open. And now I see Rona stretched out flat on her back on the deck, moaning and kicking her legs.

Ness, his back to me, is on his knees beside her.

I rush around to the other side of her and squat down. 'Mum! It's me, Kyle. Can you hear me?'

Her eyelids flicker, but she doesn't respond. A dribble of spit leaks from a corner of her mouth. I see some blood in her hair.

'What should we do?' Colm says, kneeling beside me.

Horrified, head pounding, I glare at him. 'What happened?'

He grimaces. 'It was rough when we hit. Stuff flying everywhere. I found her here. Either she didn't buckle up right or her straps tore loose. She must've been thrown about pretty bad.'

'Will she be okay?' Ness says.

I say nothing. Rona groans, squirms and kicks out again. I lean over and feel her pulse banging away in her throat. Good. There's nothing wrong with that anyway.

I call her name a few times. Still no response.

'What's with the kicking?' Colm asks.

'Who knows? She's the healer, not me.' I feel so helpless.

Colm nods, then surprises me by reaching out and brushing a lock of Rona's hair away from where it's fallen into her eye.

Seeing him being so caring gets me going again.

'She's probably just knocked out,' I tell him. 'If she can move her legs, that's good. Means her back can't be broke. Only I can't wake her up. We'll just have to wait until she comes to by herself.'

'We need to get the hell out of here. Now.'

I turn around to see Murdo and Fleur frowning down at us.

'He's got a point,' Fleur says, biting her lip. 'What if somebody saw us crash? We should make ourselves scarce.'

'You mean Reapers?' Ness says, and swallows hard.

'Or Slayers,' Murdo says, and gestures at the broken hull. 'We've no idea who or what is wandering about out there.'

'We can't move her,' I protest. 'I don't know how hurt she is.'

Murdo looks at me real ugly, one hand on his holstered blaster. Only before anything bad can happen, Rona's grey eyes flutter open. She lifts her head off the deck and looks at us, her face pulled tight with pain. 'Are we in the No-Zone?'

I forget about Murdo. 'We are. We had a hard landing.'

She winces. 'Feels like I banged my head.'

'Does anything else hurt?'

She gives a short laugh. 'Better to ask me what *doesn't* hurt.'

'Can you walk?' Murdo asks her. 'We can't stay here.'

Rona sighs. 'I can try. Help me up, Kyle.'

But even with Colm and me helping her, she can't manage it.

'It's okay, I'll fix you a litter,' I say.

Blinking back tears I glare at Murdo, daring him to say anything. He gives me a hard look, then shrugs like *fine, but make it quick* and stomps off outside.

Ness goes to follow. I haul him back and tell him to help my brother with getting Squint going again.

Colm gives me an uncertain look. 'Squint?'

'Look, just do it. If we're going any distance, we'll need him.'

'How can I help?' Fleur says.

'Stay here,' I say. 'Look after Rona.'

'Stop fussing. I'll be fine,' Rona says, squeezing the words out. 'Fleur, go and help Kyle.' Eyes closed, she waves us away.

As we head outside I see how the *Rockpolisher* has rammed itself tail first into the bank of the river. A bit of luck, as it lets us scramble ashore without having to swim for it.

Safely on the bank I look back and shiver, remembering V-shaped ripples as hungry leatherheads came for Sky and me in another river. But no ripples here. Just tranquil water sliding on by, as if we didn't exist.

'That's one seriously messed-up windjammer,' Fleur says.

Understatement. The old *Rockpolisher*'s spine is broken behind the flight deck so the nose droops one way and the tail the other. The rusty hull plates are torn and plastered in thick grey river mud.

'Good job Sky can't see this,' I say.

I spot Murdo now, waist-deep in the river, crowbarring one of the outer hatches open to get at the camo-nets.

Fleur points out some scrubby-looking trees. 'Will they do?'

I squint. 'The younger ones should. Let's go see.'

Turns out they're nearly ideal. I hack and trim some tall saplings into two long litter poles. Two lighter branches will serve as cross-braces. We drag them back to the crash site.

'I'll need your jacket, Fleur.'

'What for?' she says.

'You'll see.' I pull my parka off, button it up and turn it inside-out, leaving the sleeves inside. Reluctantly she hands hers over, faking a shiver even though it's not cold. Whatever. I do the same with hers, before sliding the two long poles through the sleeves so the two jackets form a soft bed for the litter. The last thing to do is to lash and cross-brace them into an A-frame, about the width of Squint's back at the narrow end, wider at the other end. It's a good job I can do it without hardly any thinking because my head's full of worrying about how badly Rona's hurt.

'You've done this before,' Fleur says, watching.

'It's how we used to drag sick people in from outlying farms in the Barrenlands using a fourhorn. You strap the pointy end on the fourhorn's back and the wide end drags across the ground.'

'Shame we don't have a fourhorn.'

'We've got better than that.'

I head back inside the wreck, leaving Fleur to finish off the bindings. First thing I see is Rona propped up against a crate, smothered in blankets and looking a lot better. She sees me and manages a smile. The second thing I see is Squint. He's still lying in a heap with Colm and Ness both gawping into him.

They both look around as I stomp inside.

Ness shakes his head. Colm gives his lip a big old chew.

'What's the problem?' I ask, worried.

Ness climbs stiffly back to his feet and shrugs. 'It's strange. His power-stacks are back in, yet we can't get him to boot.'

I take a look. Everything seems like it's been wired okay.

'No power for days,' Colm says. 'Maybe . . .'

He leaves it hanging, but I know what he's thinking. Squint's built from scavved tech scrap way older than we are. Without power for so long, his memory might be trashed.

'Try him again,' I say.

'I'm sorry, Kyle. I think he's had it.'

'Just do it,' I snarl at them. 'We *need* Squint.'

Colm sighs, flips up the flap on the back of the bot's neck and hits the start-up button. The power-stacks beep to show they're live. Squint's eyes flicker through the first stages of booting. Each of his four legs twitches in turn, their hydraulic rams hissing.

But that's as far as boot-up gets. Squint's eyes go dark again.

I shove Colm aside and try myself. Twice. Same deal.

My brother throws his hands up. 'Like I told you, he's had it.'

And that does it – frustration explodes inside me. Next thing, I'm raging at Squint and kicking him. Get a few solid ones in too, before Fleur and Colm drag me off him. They hold me until I'm done struggling, then step back and watch me, all wary and awkward as I pant and shake and glare, daring them to say something.

Something nudges my leg. A plaintive beep.

And when I turn around there's Squint back on his feet behind me, eyes bright again and tail thrashing wildly. He looks weird with half his casing off and still a little bit wobbly on his legs.

'Squinty!' I sob with shame and relief.

Another beep and he jumps up, nearly knocking me over.

Ness laughs nervously. 'Right. So *that's* how you boot him up.'

19
BITERS AND REAPERS

Our first night inside the No-Zone we camp a dozen klicks north of our emergency landing. By climbing back to higher and less jungle-choked ground we've made good time considering, although not fast enough for Murdo. Squint dragging the litter has worked out well and Rona's never complained, not once. Our 'camp' is a hole burrowed among the roots of one of those sky-reaching trees. Whatever creature dug it is long gone – we hope – leaving a pile of chewed-up old bones and a musky stink behind. It's slamming down with rain outside, but I've rigged a cover from camo-net and piled cut brush on top to keep the worst of the wet out.

With the slow pace we're going at, according to Ness's cleverbox we're three days' hike from Murdo's *Never Again*. No sign of Reapers yet. Them being sneaky, I don't take that to mean too much.

'Will this rain ever stop?' I say, peering outside.

Colm looks up from bathing his hands in rainwater. 'It's doing us a favour. Nobody will be out in this, not even Reapers.'

'Yeah, well, let's hope so,' I say. And wince, seeing how shredded and blistered his hands are. When the ground got bumpy, we took turns carrying the low end of Rona's litter to give her a break. He did his fair share, despite not having my nublood strength. It must've hurt like hell.

'Want me to look at those?' Rona slurs.

We all look round to where she's been sleeping, back propped up against the tree root. Her eyes look sunk into her head.

Colm tells her he's okay. 'Go back to sleep now.'

'Feeling any better?' I ask her.

Rona gives me a weak smile. 'Will you kick me if I say no?'

I blush, deserving that. 'Can I get you anything?'

She closes her eyes. 'No thanks. I'm good.'

I know she's far from good – I also know better than to argue. Earlier I found some painkiller herbs and brewed them. She kept them down. That's helped, but it's made her dopy too. She reckons she's broken a rib or three, that's all. I just hope she's right.

'Tell me something,' Colm says, frowning at Murdo who's sitting and picking his teeth. 'You're so sure your windjammer is out there somewhere and hasn't crashed, so how did Sky make it past those wrecking chains when we couldn't?'

That gets everyone's attention.

Murdo pulls his finger out of his gob. 'Who cares?'

'It doesn't worry you?' Colm persists. 'Those chains are still there, blocking our way out even if we find your windjammer.'

My heart sinks. Frag it, I hadn't thought of that.

'Worrying never got me anywhere,' Murdo says. His sly grin is back now. 'The Slayer transports must be equipped to remote-control the chains and hoist them out of their way. Sky couldn't do that, could she? I figure she got lucky and stumbled across a different route in here. When we find her, we can ask her.'

'What if we don't find her?' Colm asks.

'That'd be a shame.' Murdo's grin turns wolfish. 'But not the end of the world. Relax. I'll find us a way out.'

Leaving Sky trapped in the No-Zone. He's got it all figured.

'Hey, how about a fire?' Ness says. 'I'm freezing.'

Murdo looks at me like *what do you reckon?* I'm not surprised. None of these guys have a clue what they're doing in this backcountry. Murdo's like Sky – a fish out of water without a windjammer under him. Fleur swapped her ident camp for the Deeps and I've never seen her so wide-eyed and jumpy. Colm tries, but he grew up in a palace. As for Ness . . . well, if it's not tech stuff, the guy's beyond useless. Rona's too hurt to be any help. Until we get to the *Never Again*, it's all down to me.

'Bad idea,' I say. 'We don't want anyone smelling our smoke.'

Anyone, as in Reapers.

Ness scowls and waves a dead man's finger at me. 'No way can I eat this muck raw. It needs cooking.'

I scavved these on the way here. Finger-shaped, white and swollen, they're the larvae of something even nastier looking.

'You'll have to go hungry then,' I tell him.

I glance at Rona, sure she'll smile at hearing me repeat something she's said to me a thousand times, but she's asleep.

Colm chokes one down and I'm impressed. Murdo starts one, only to spit it out. Fleur and Ness say they'd rather starve. Even with loads of practice, I quit at three. Outside our refuge the rain slashes down in one last, extra-vicious downpour before fading away to drizzle. The rich and loamy smell of damp worm-chewed soil fills my nostrils. Everywhere is dripping water. Above that the night noises of the surrounding forest can be heard again. Branches creak in the breeze. Wind-stirred leaves are like a thousand paws scurrying past. I hear distant croaks and grunts and hoots – the No-Zone's wildlife going about its business.

'Sounds fierce creepy, don't it?' Fleur says, hugging herself.

'If it goes quiet you should worry,' I tell her.

I stand up from my seat on Gant's weapons crates and stretch. Along with pulling Rona's litter, Squint hauled both crates here on his back. I scramble outside to check on him and have a pee. Squint's fine and pleased to see me. Through a gap in the rushing clouds I see the crescent bigmoon with its shadow-cut rings riding high. The much smaller dogmoon is lower, but catching up every night. I'm buttoning up when somebody struggles out to join me. The noise they make could wake the dead.

'Kyle, it's me, Murdo. Where are you?'

'Over here,' I whisper.

He blunders over. 'Think she'll be okay? Rona, I mean.'

I tell him I hope so and turn to head back.

Murdo grabs my arm. 'She's a good woman.'

'You think I don't know that?'

'Course you do. I just wonder whether we're doing her more harm than good dragging her along like this.'

His face is in shadow. I can still guess where this is going.

'You've got a better idea?'

He shrugs. 'Rona could rest up here, with Fleur or Colm to look after her. That way we'd make it to the *Never Again* a day earlier. Ness and me could get started on prepping her for self-launch out of here, while you run back and fetch —'

'No way,' I say. 'We stick together. That's the deal.'

'Listen, kid. My jammer is our only way out of this fraggin' No-Zone. If we don't get there fast, Sky could clear off again. Or some Reapers could find it and gut it. Without it we're screwed.'

'I can't help that. We're moving as fast as we can.'

'It's not fast enough,' he growls.

A twig snaps. I reach for my gun, but it's only my brother.

'What's going on?' he says.

I tell him what Murdo just suggested.

Colm spits, something I've never seen him do. 'If you were hurt, Dern, Rona wouldn't leave you behind. No matter what.'

Murdo curses. 'All I'm saying is . . . oh, forget it!'

He shoves past us and stalks back to the shelter. I wait until I hear him fumble his way inside before I let out a groan.

'Great. That's all I fraggin' need.'

'Tell him you won't do it,' Colm says. 'He won't go on ahead without you. He needs you to find the *Never Again*.'

'He's got Ness's cleverbox.'

In the dim moonshine, my brother looks grim. 'He has to sleep sometime. If we got our hands on it, we could smash it.'

Got to admit, I'm more than a little shocked.

'I don't know,' I say. 'No. Hopefully it won't come to that.'

It's a long, dragging night, like so many before. Me, Colm and Fleur take turns on watch, listening out for sounds that don't belong. Murdo doesn't offer, just curls up in his bag and snores his head off. Ness we don't ask. If I'm not on watch I'm looking after Rona. I dribble water into her mouth when she asks for it, and soothe her one time when she wakes and cries out.

Eventually, after what seems like forever, a new dawn sends its soft light slinking and winking inside our refuge, past the ragged edges of the netting. I crawl over to Rona and check on her. She's awake already and smiles, seeing me coming. But I can't say I like the look of her face. Her skin's pulled tight and seems waxy.

'Ready for another fun day in the No-Zone?'

She grimaces. 'Can't wait. Maybe I could walk a bit today.'

Sadly, that's never going to happen. Even with Colm and me helping her, she can't stand, let alone walk.

'Too bad I'm not nublood,' she says, trembling after the effort.

I say nothing, but I've thought this myself a thousand times. If she was, she'd be well on her way to healing already. Or if she was my birth mother we could get some of my nublood into her and heal her like I once healed Colm.

Ifs and buts – as much use as a blunt knife.

Colm nudges me.

I follow his look and see Murdo pulling his pack on. My mouth goes dry. 'Are you going on ahead of us?'

He gives me a stony-faced look, and shakes his head. 'Nah. Best if we all stick together. But let's get going.'

'Thanks, Murdo.' I dart a relieved look at my brother.

It's a slog fighting our way deeper into the No-Zone and the biters don't help. Last night's rain must've stirred them up, plus it's a hot day for firstgreen and I've led us lower to cross a river-valley. Down here bugs fill the air with their buzzing, eager for our blood. Their orange bodies are thumb-sized, and when they bite it's like being stabbed. We're all sweating like pigs and wearing everything we've got to keep them off. I have everyone plaster their face and hands with river mud and that helps, but by the time we drag ourselves back to high ground everybody's had enough.

At least up here there aren't so many biters.

'Let's take a break,' I say as we stumble across a clearing.

The others collapse, like I've cut some invisible strings holding them up. I check on Rona and get a weak thumbs up.

Fleur gives her head a big old scratch. 'This place is supposed to be crawling with Reapers as well as bugs. Where are they?'

I've been wondering that myself, but now I look up.

And start.

'Closer than you think,' I say, pointing.

High above us, hanging upside down from tree branches, are a dozen or so rope-tied bodies. Each body is wrapped in the tattered remains of a fabric shroud daubed with swirling blue symbols. Through a tear in one shroud I see rib bones.

Everybody's back on their feet now, except Rona and me.

'That some sort of warning?' Murdo asks.

I shake my head because I've seen stuff like this back in the Barrenlands. 'It's what Reapers do with their dead.'

'I thought they ate them,' Ness says, gulping like a fish.

'Yeah, well, now you know.' Below the bodies hang dozens of lidded clay pots, swinging in the breeze. Curious, I get up and lift the lids of the lowest ones for a look. And wish I hadn't.

Each pot contains two little skeletons.

'What's in them?' Fleur asks

'The bodies of infants.'

'There's so many of them,' Colm says, grim-faced.

Seeing the long-dead Reapers puts strength back into tired legs. We clear off and cover a good few klicks before Murdo suggests stopping again. Only by then I've an itch between my shoulder blades that's no bug-bite. Hints of movement behind us tug at the corner of my eyes. Fleur is glancing back too. Soon as we're hunkered down I tell them I think we're being followed.

Murdo narrows his eyes at me. 'Reapers?'

'Not Slayers anyway, I'd see them. It could be an animal.'

I look over at Fleur. She just shrugs.

'What do we do?' Ness says.

And yet again they all stare at me expectantly.

I tell them to carry on ahead to the next crest and wait for me there. 'I'll hang back here to see if we are being followed.'

Colm shakes his head. 'I'll stay too.'

'No. It's probably nothing, but best to be sure.'

'And if there *are* Reapers?'

I try for a smile. 'If you hear me shooting, then come running.'

20
AMBUSH

A few minutes later I'm kicking myself for refusing Colm's offer. It's tough to be brave when your only company is fear. I'm lying belly down in some stink-grass, downwind of the small clearing we stopped in. My heart thumps as I look along my rifle. Green slanting dayshine plays across the bare earth, making shadows dance. It's quiet, only some buzzing and a whisper of wind.

With a *tzzziiip*, a snapper-beetle lands on my carbine's muzzle. It turns a few circles, looks at me from black shiny eyes, snaps its wings back inside its armoured body and . . . just sits there.

Female I reckon, from the rainbow colours.

I blow softly to shift her. No chance. She's quite happy there, and I daren't blow harder or louder. I have a think for a second, then break off a long stalk of stink-grass to poke her with.

Tzzziiip! She sees the writing on the wall and buzzes off.

That's when I see the young Reaper woman.

She's standing in the middle of the clearing, gazing my way. Her face is painted white with a black smear of soot or something across her eyes. Dark hair is long and mud-plastered, bare arms and legs covered in swirling blue patterns. A slender throwing spear is in her left hand; more stick up from a sling worn on her back.

The breeze fetches me the stink of her filth and sweat. Sweat stings my eyes and my breathing goes ragged.

She knows I'm here. What the hell's she waiting for?

I throw myself aside, just in time.

A spear meant for my back slams into the ground. Big hands on it lead up to a snarling Reaper face. He goes to yank it back out, but it's gone deep and fights him. That saves me.

I swing my carbine around and pull the trigger. The shot staggers him, but somehow he stays on his feet. And now his spear comes free. With a roar he lunges at me again. I squeeze the trigger again, keep it squeezed, walk the green pulses up his heavily tattooed chest.

That sorts him. This time he goes down and stays down.

Breathlessly I scramble up, only to need all my nublood speed to duck a spear thrown by the Reaper woman.

Cursing, I shift aim towards her. Only she's seriously fast. A second spear is already on its way and hisses by my face, stinging my ear. My snap shot misses. And now she takes off running, staying low and weaving to make me miss again. Just before she reaches the cover of some trees I finally clip her. She cries out and stumbles, but keeps going.

'Finish her, Kyle!'

'Don't let her get away!'

Murdo and Colm are running back down from the crest.

I run after her and plunge into the gloom under the trees. Careless. For a second I'm blind. She jumps out at me and I'm very nearly split in two by her spear thrust. In knocking it aside, my rifle and her spear go flying. She makes a grab for another spear. I drop my shoulder, charge and knock her down. Good job I roll away fast though because she nearly guts me with a knife before struggling back to her feet. I pull my hunting knife. We circle round our blades, feinting and slashing, each looking for an opening. Her left shoulder's all seared flesh and that arm hangs limp. How she stands, let alone fights, I don't know. But she does. And despite being badly hurt she's way better at blade-fighting than I am.

Fine. I step back, haul my slug-thrower out and aim it left-handed between her hate-filled blue eyes. Shame to waste one of my only two bullets, but better than getting cut or killed. Only now some stray dayshine catches her paint-daubed face. She's younger than I thought. A girl, roughly my age. And she's shaking.

I tell her to drop the knife. She does too.

'Why couldn't you leave us alone?' I say, sort of pleading.

She scowls and mumbles through her teeth. 'These are our spirit-lands. Whoever you are, you've no right being here.'

I hear Colm yell my name. Reaper girl's blade is still close so I make my glance quick. Through the trees I see him and Murdo standing over the dead guy and peering about, looking for me.

'Over here,' I call. 'I've got her. She's hurt.'

Their heads jerk my way.

'So waste her and come back,' Murdo calls. 'Hurry up!'

I grit my teeth. It's ugly, but he's right – if this Reaper girl's dead she can't tell tales. She'd kill me if things were the other way around, and maybe eat me. My trigger finger twitches.

Her head drops. It's like she flicks a despairing glance down at her belly. I'm healer raised, so when I glimpse a hint of bulge where the rest of the girl is muscle I get what it means.

No fraggin' way. No, no, no.

I hear boots thumping ground. It's Colm, running to help me. What would *he* do? I don't know.

I pull the trigger. The gun barks and kicks back. And it's not like I miss her – I just blast into the ground deliberately.

Reaper girl's eyes go wide and confused.

Putting a finger to my lips I pick up my rifle. Then turn and walk away, praying my reward isn't a spear in the back.

It isn't. Not yet anyway.

As I emerge from the trees and back into welcome dayshine, Colm is standing a few metres away. 'You'd no choice,' he says, as long-faced as I've seen him.

I push past. 'Let's go.'

He runs after me. 'You okay?'

'Fine. Leave me be. I don't want to talk about it.'

We walk side by side, back to where Murdo crouches over what's left of the other dead Reaper. My pulse-carbine hits have torn him to shreds. Bile rises in my throat.

Murdo glances up and grins. 'Good job. Was it just the two?'

I nod. 'Guess so. I didn't see any others.'

'You took care of the hurt one?'

'Blew her head off. That good enough for you?'

Murdo grunts his satisfaction, straightens up and shows us a mess of blood-matted fur hanging on a cord. I flinch until I figure out what I'm looking at. Six freshly killed rockhoppers. And they're big fat ones too. They'll make good eating.

'Where'd they come from?'

Murdo nods down at the dead Reaper. 'His loss, our gain.'

That night we don't get so lucky with finding shelter and end up hunkering down under some trees below the ridge line. We stay high, figuring it's safer, but it's windswept and soon gets bitterly cold. Still, at least there are no bugs and we can scrape the mud off our faces. We eat well too. Murdo produces a fancy little pot with a self-heating bottom so we can cook without a fire. I gut and prepare the rockhoppers and we crowd the pot, watching and sniffing and licking our lips, like a pack of animals around a kill. It takes a cruel long time, but never has meat tasted so good. We sit about in the moonshine, chewing and sighing, our stomachs confused and growling, hot grease dribbling down our chins.

'A few scraps,and you'd think we're saved,' Colm says.

Feeling guilty, I pull him aside so the others can't hear my whisper. 'Listen, I only pretended to kill that wounded Reaper girl. I know I should have, but I couldn't. I'm sorry.'

He sighs. 'Let's hope we all don't end up sorry.'

What can I say? Nothing.

And now he surprises me by smiling. 'Can't kill a Reaper in cold blood. Not much of a monster, are you.'

I pick at the scab on my ear. 'You think that's funny?'

'No. It's sad.' He sighs. 'It's so easy to convince people twists are monsters. The Saviour blames you for any bad stuff that happens, and shows everyone some poor nublood who's been tortured half to death until he's mad and looks a monster. People end up believing, then hating and fearing you because you *are* different. Soon there's no way back. How do you prove you're not evil? Smile and hand out sweets? Sparing that Reaper, when you had every reason not to, proves you're not evil. Only nobody saw, did they? And even if they did, they'd think you did it just to fool them.'

I shush Colm, worried the others will hear.

He stands, pulse rifle in hand. 'Maybe if we'd won the war we could have been merciful afterwards, shown people nubloods aren't the monsters they feared. We'd be in charge, doing all the shouting. Hang on long enough and people would forget.'

My turn to snort. 'But we lost the war.'

'Yeah. There is that.'

We look up through the trees at the night sky. The yellow dogmoon, with its two big craters like eyes, is almost at its fullest and not so far below the bigger, blue-tinted crescent moon. Can't be that much longer now before it's the doom moon.

In their shared glow he smiles at me. 'I'll take first watch.'

'Fine. I'll do the next.'

He nods and clambers up on to the ridge above us.

'I'm glad you didn't kill the Reaper.' It's Rona, her voice creaky. She's been so quiet I'd forgotten she's lying right behind me.

I squirm around to face her. 'We'd be safer if I had.'

She sniffs. 'There's been enough killing.'

'Sky would've killed her.'

'You're not Sky.'

My head fills with sour thoughts. 'If it weren't for her we wouldn't be here now and you wouldn't be hurt.'

'Don't, Kyle. You can't think like that.'

I see now that she's hardly touched the meat I gave her. 'You've got to eat. Isn't that what you were always telling me?'

'I'm not hungry. You have it.'

And no matter what I say, she won't eat it. In the end I give it to Ness. Apart from Colm on lookout, everyone settles down for another long and nerve-wracking night. It's quiet enough up here, but down below in the jungle-smothered valley bottom some kind of bitter struggle kicks off. A bird screeches. Something lets out a series of loud grunts. I can hear vegetation thrashing.

'Glad we're up here,' I whisper to Rona.

A corner of her sleep bag is loose. I go to tuck it in, and jump as her cold and bony hand shoots out to grip my wrist.

'Kyle, before I . . . there's something I've got to tell you.'

I take her hand in mine and try to squeeze some warmth back into it. 'You should rest now. Tell me later.'

She shakes her head. 'It's about Sky. You mustn't blame her.'

I almost laugh out loud. 'Why not? She ran out on us, remember? All that girl cares about is that sister of hers.'

Rona reaches up and strokes my face. 'Believe me, Kyle, you're wrong. Sky *does* care for you.'

I twitch. 'Strange way of showing it.'

Her hand slumps back down and her eyes close, like she can't keep them open. But her lips are still moving so I lean closer.

'I told her to go,' she mumbles. 'She didn't want to.'

Gobsmacked, I rock back. 'You did *what*?'

But all I hear now are her shallow breaths, rattling in and out.

21
EYES THAT SEE NOTHING

I'm on lookout at dawn, so it's Colm who finds Rona and comes and tells me, tears in his eyes. I run back down to find her stiff and cold and gone from her body, her grey eyes open, but staring up at nothing, her face smoothed out and young again.

Murdo brushes her eyes closed.

'She's done suffering, Kyle,' he says, his voice rough.

He stands up and herds the others away so I can be alone with my mother. I drop to my knees beside her. I stare and stare.

How long before I feel a hand on my shoulder? Don't know. It's Colm. He says nothing. I hear him anyway and see the broken look on his face that's the match of mine. And it's as if the world stutters and starts turning again. The birds still sing their heads off at the dawn. My heart still beats and my right ear itches where the spear nicked it. And now I hear sobbing behind me. Wouldn't have thought it, but it's Fleur. Ness stands there with her, wringing his long-fingered hands. Murdo's busy packing his gear.

'She hated slowing us down,' I tell Colm.

So many better things I could say, only that's all I can think of.

He swallows, his face jumping. 'Kyle, I'm so sorry.'

Murdo blocks the dawnshine, pack in hand, his face set.

'Wrath rest and keep your poor mother, Kyle, but those Reapers you killed will be missed. Others are bound to come looking for them. We need to keep moving.'

Colm turns and glares at him. 'And what about Rona? Do we just dump her here? That what you're saying?'

Murdo gives me a look like *tell him to back off*.

I have to drag myself to my feet, get between them. I should be the one raging, but I can't. I'm too numb, too full of loss.

'It's not his fault,' I tell my brother.

Each word feels like lead on my tongue. My voice is weird too, buzzing in my head. Colm's shaking he's so mad, but he listens to me, takes a deep breath and nods at Murdo.

And now it starts raining. The soft rain that Rona likes. Liked.

Colm's jaw clenches. 'Fine. We bury Rona, then we go.'

'No,' I say, stirring myself. 'It's too rocky. We'll take her with us. Bury her later, somewhere safe. A place she'd like.'

Somewhere she won't be dug up by animals or Reapers.

Murdo doesn't like it, not wanting to be slowed down again. A big argument kicks off, which I haven't got the stomach to listen to. I shut it out and watch the rain landing on Rona's face. A trick of the dawnshine makes it look as if she's smiling.

One last gift from a lifetime of gifts.

'We'll take care of Rona,' Fleur says. She leads me back up to the lookout point, sits me down. 'You okay to keep watch?'

Colm fetches me, not long later. They've strapped Rona's body into the litter, still inside her sleep bag. Somebody's brushed the tangles out of her hair and washed the mud from her face.

Tears sting my eyes. Somehow I hold them back.

It isn't easy. Ness has picked some firstgreen flowers. He hands them out. One by one, we take our turns, tucking them round Rona. Murdo goes first, and I go last. My hand shakes, and I'm hardly able to breathe as I tuck the flower into her hair and take a last look at my mother. I kiss her cheek for the last time. Step back, cold and numb and lost. Colm leans past, zips the sleep bag up to cover her face.

I can't watch and have to look away.

'She always loved the rain on her face,' I tell him.

'I know, but better to remember her alive,' he says.

I'm not listening. See, it's hit me that Rona will have known she was dying and kept that knowing to herself. One last secret to spare and protect me. The story of my fraggin' life.

I wish she *had* told me. At least then I could've said goodbye.

All that day, I carry the pole ends of the litter instead of letting them drag along behind Squint. My arms are almost ripped out of their sockets. Colm offers to help a few times, only I won't let him, glad for the pain. See, the pain stops me thinking. The others take turns trying to talk to me, lifting their voices to sound all bright, the way you hear children talking to their pet dog.

I don't answer them. In the end they leave me alone.

The only thinking I can't get out of is the navving. Not the big-picture-head-north stuff – the sun tells us our heading – but the little stuff, like will it be faster to go round that tangle of trees ahead or fight our way through it? I grit my teeth and point, and plod along in my private hell, my back, shoulders and arms screaming.

We walk all day, and most of the next day too.

Finally we stop. Ness peers from his cleverbox into yet another jungle-choked valley.

'I reckon the *Never Again*'s down there.'

And they all stare at me again.

I flinch, feeling drained and useless, like I'm coming down with swamp pox. I have to suck a few lungfuls of air inside me and give myself a shake. Ness offers me a peek at the cleverbox. I wave him away though. I can still picture the squeezed-together contours and this valley matches, as clear as fresh water.

'He's right,' I tell them, my voice rusty. I point out a huge rock that looks something like a fourhorn's snout. 'There's a side valley behind there. That's where the beacon is. Or was anyway.'

Sky too, with a bit of luck.

Somewhere deep inside me a bit of glad wriggles around. Only then I remember we wouldn't be here if it weren't for her.

And poor Rona would probably still be alive . . .

The *Never Again* is right where I said she'd be. Fleur's on point and spots it as we pick our way downslope. It's tucked under the shelter of some trees on the valley floor, the dark hull covered in the same camo-netting we used on the *Rockpolisher*. Well done too – if we weren't looking, we'd walk right by without knowing. I expect Murdo to take off running towards it. But no, he goes cautious and has us all crouch down and watch for ages.

In the end, Fleur catches my eye and stands up.

'Wait here,' she tells Murdo.

She makes for the jammer and I scramble after her. If Sky's still inside we'd better get to her first, before he does.

When I catch up with Fleur she glances at me and nods. Nothing moves and it's awful quiet. Before we step out from the shadows between the trees, I unsling my pulse carbine and check the mag is seated securely and the safety's off. I glance back the way we've come, but wherever the rest are hiding I can't see them.

'How d'you want to do this?' Fleur whispers.

Licking my lips, I call out, 'Sky! Are you there? It's me, Kyle.'

We wait, holding our breath. All I can hear are insects buzzing and a distant screeching as a bird maybe calls to its mate.

I call again. Still no answer.

Sweat slides down my face. Something's wrong with the windjammer I see now. Under the draped camo the hull sits left wing down as if the undercarriage has collapsed that side. And it hasn't been winched here into cover; this is where it's ended up after landing just short of hitting these trees. Behind the machine I can see the small and flattish patch of relatively open ground Sky set down in, alongside a slow running river. It's covered in waist-high, rubbery-looking shrubs, with bits of lighter brown that could be snapped branches, but I can't pick out an obvious trail of destruction from the landing run. Either the shrubs have bounced back up on their own or Sky's been covering her tracks.

I grit my teeth and step out into the dayshine.

Nobody shouts, spears or shoots me.

'Nice move, Kyle,' Fleur jeers, stepping out too. 'Real stealthy.'

We duck under the netting, find the switch that drops the rear loading ramp and push it. Nothing doing. It's locked. I bang on it with my rifle's stock. Still nothing. We head forward, past the mud-splattered and buckled undercarriage legs. Fleur clambers up on to the hull for a peer through the canopy.

'Nobody's home,' she says, jumping back down.

My head's so mixed up I don't know if I feel disappointed or relieved. Slinging my rifle I head back up to fetch the others. Ten minutes later Murdo hot-wires the loading ramp to drop it. He clambers inside, jaw set, leading with his blaster. Only it's like we thought: Sky's not there. Neither is the key thing she stole to disable the jammer's security. It's hard to tell which Murdo is more pissed off about, he does so much cursing and hull-kicking.

Staying well out of his way I take a look around. The jammer's cramped sleeping compartment is a mess, which isn't like Sky.

And it stinks too. Colm wrinkles his nose. 'Buzzweed?'

I say nothing, but I'm sure he's right. Only what would Sky be doing chewing such filthy, head-wrecking crap?

Fleur has a root around. 'Look!'

And she holds up Sky's powered leg brace that lets her walk about on her destroyed leg without needing a crutch.

I gawp, imagining all kinds of horrible.

'Why leave it here?' Colm asks.

'Maybe she didn't mean to,' Fleur says. And her grimace tells me what she's thinking – that Sky didn't leave the *Never Again* under her own steam, but was carried away by Reapers.

I run back outside and cast around for tracks or signs of a struggle. No way would Sky let herself be taken without a fight.

Colm and Fleur follow and watch me.

'Find anything?' he asks.

I'm shaking my head at him when I spot the tracks and crouch down. They're faint after all the rain we've had, but definitely lead away from the windjammer. A single bootprint take turns with small holes dug by a heavily leaned-on stick.

Sky! I take a deep breath, and slowly sigh it out of me.

'She walked out of here by herself,' I tell them.

Fleur looks as relieved as I am. 'But why leave her brace behind?'

'Maybe it's bust.'

'Think you can track her?'

Colm, sitting on the end of the ramp, answers for me. 'Don't need to. We know where she's going.'

And he's right, of course. As boggin' always. Bust leg brace or not, Sky will have one thing on her mind: finding her sister. She'll head for where the Slayer transport landed.

I picture her shouldering her pack and limping on her way.

'Why'd she put down here?' Fleur asks.

'Well, she can't land where the Slayers transports put down. This must be the closest alternative she could find,' Colm says.

'Check it out!' Ness calls.

He's on the ramp, waving something. I go and snatch it off him. It's a picture of me, torn from an old wanted poster.

'Where'd you get that?' I croak.

'Flight deck. So cute it was. Stuck above the control panel.'

I scowl and tuck it away.

Murdo stomps out on to the ramp, a face on him like thunder.

'How bad is it?' Colm asks, looking worried.

Fleur joins us. 'Yeah, are we flying out or walking?'

'It's worse than I thought,' he growls. 'A cracked landing leg, shock-loaded lifters that'll have to be stripped. It'd be three days' work at least, *if* we had a crane and a crew of techs. We don't!'

His anger feeds mine. 'Can you fix it or can't you?'

Murdo goes to snark back at me, but must see I'm spoiling to rip heads off. 'I can fix it. Won't be quick though.'

'How long?' Colm says.

He considers. 'Two weeks. Depends.'

Mine isn't the only face to fall. Two weeks might as well be forever if this No-Zone *is* crawling with Reapers.

Rubbing his stubble, Murdo bangs on about building A-frames and levers, jury-rigging this and that, blah bloody blah.

Colm pulls me away. 'C'mon, let's go find a place for Rona.'

And he's so good. I walk the feet off him hunting for where to lay Rona in the ground, change my mind a dozen times, yet he never once sighs or mutters. Anyway, in the end I give up looking for the perfect place and settle on a tree-shaded bit of slope looking down on the *Never Again*. When the leaves drop with the winter, there'll be a view of the river winding away beyond it. Rona was always one for stopping to admire the view.

Colm fetches a rusty old digging pick and a shovel.

'Which do you want?'

I take the pick and fight back tears.

We get stuck into the digging. I break the ground, and Colm shovels it up and out. Being around healing I've dug my fair share of burying holes. And I won't lie – I always knew the day would come when I'd end up digging one for Rona.

Only not like this. Not so soon.

See, that's hope for you. Sneaky. Blinkers you from dread, so you can keep going. Sky mocks it, says it's only for losers. I think that's harsh. Hope's hard-wired, like Squint's firmware.

I take over the shovelling from Colm. A grave hole has to

be deep enough to stand up in. The ground's hard here and it's back-breaking work, but between us we get it dug. Then we collect rocks, big as we can manage, and pile them ready.

Colm trudges off to fetch the others.

They're a while coming and I'm glad; means I get my goodbyes said before they arrive. Murdo stays away, too busy. Fleur asks if I want to say something. I shake my head. There's no ceremony, just a rough hole dug in the ground and a bunch of people, tired and scared, doing something they wish they didn't have to do. And it gets worse. Bodies are fierce heavy things. As we struggle to lower Rona's sleep-bag-wrapped body into the hole we drop her, and the *thud* my foster-mother makes when she hits the bottom is awful. I have to climb in and sort her out, so she's lying straight.

Climbing back out is the hardest thing I've ever done.

They take turns throwing fistfuls of soil on to her and muttering the usual *Wrath rest her and keep her* crap.

I throw last, but say nothing.

Rona's dead, not resting. And Wrath can go frag itself.

But then I remember Sky's picture of me. I chuck it in too. The scrap of paper drifts down like a flutterfly and lands facing up at me. It's the only precious thing I have to give.

'We'll finish up,' Fleur says.

She hugs me like a sister, and Colm hugs me like a brother.

Ness leads me back to the *Never Again*, and it's a good job he does because I kind of fold inside then and my eyes sting and give up on seeing. He goes inside, but I sit out on the ramp and clamp my arms round my knees. Squint nuzzles into me until I give in and pull him close. From back up the hill I hear the rattle of the stones we gathered being thrown in to form a layer to stop animals getting at Rona. After that, the hiss and thump as they shovel soil in. I close my eyes, but see dirt hitting Rona's face, so open them again and gaze up at the darkening sky until my eyes water.

A star appears, a lonely white dot. I wonder where Sky is.

Hearing distant whistling I look north and see sky lizards circling, wings outstretched. It's beautiful. An aerial dance.

Yeah, right. What am I thinking?

As I watch, the highest lizard suddenly folds its wings and drops on to the lizard below it. Locked in a terrible embrace, falling like a stone, they tear and claw and screech at each other. One lets go and flaps away. The other, wings trailing uselessly, plummets down on to the rocks below.

Other lizards quit soaring and swoop down after it.

That's Wrath for you. Fighting, dying and little fraggin' else.

22

NO SMOKE WITHOUT FIRE

Even the Barrenlands would sometimes take a break from bleak and ugly. You'd get the odd morning lit so lovely that Rona would tip me out of my bed, yelling and complaining, to see it.

Like a cruel joke, this is such a morning.

Dawnshine spears in from the west, low and fierce. The grass shimmers under a heavy overnight dew, and the forest is alive with the dripping of water as it falls from firstgreen leaves. The air smells so rich and fresh it pulls a sob out of me. If only Rona were alive to enjoy it. But she isn't, and I have to deal with that. Digging my nails into the palm of my hand, I step off the ramp.

Fleur's on watch, cross-legged on top of the camouflaged hull of the *Never Again*, a ratty old blanket around her shoulders. Her head hangs down though. Dozing I reckon.

Holding my breath I glance back into the cargo bay. Colm's still asleep. Murdo and Ness are out of sight on the flight deck, where they've spent the night working to backdoor the jammer's security and regain control.

I start to walk away, but don't get far. A throat being cleared stops me. I turn around and Fleur is frowning down at me.

'Sneaking off somewhere?'

'Thought I'd do some hunting,' I lie.

She's no fool. 'Always go hunting with a backpack, do you?'

I grit my teeth. 'Okay. I'm . . . going after Sky.'

'Thought you might,' she says with a knowing smile. Shrugging her blanket off she stands up and stamps on the hull three times. Seconds later a sleepy-eyed Colm stumbles out on to the ramp, clutching a rifle. Right behind is Murdo, blaster in hand.

I figure they were expecting Reapers.

'What's going on?' Murdo says.

Colm fixes me with the same knowing look Fleur did.

Fleur jumps down, landing beside them. 'I caught him sneaking off after Sky, just like Colm said he would.'

I scowl at my brother first, and then at Murdo.

'Why shouldn't I? You don't need me to fix your jammer.'

Amazingly, Murdo looks more thoughtful than angry. Not a look that suits him. 'Planning on coming back, were you?'

I grit my teeth, keep my mouth shut.

Murdo looks scornful. Then he rubs his bloodshot eyes and tells me how, not long before dawn, he and Ness finally backdoored the windjammer's systems. 'The first thing we did was check the f-log. Guess what? Sky flew into the No-Zone using exactly the same route we did.'

'But what about the chains?' Fleur asks.

'She got past them somehow,' Ness says, joining us.

'How? We couldn't.'

'Look, it doesn't matter how,' Murdo snaps. 'Those chains aren't our problem now that we're *inside* the No-Zone. They're just to stop intruders like us, who will always arrive low on the way in. We'd never fly down into that gully on our way out because we'd be far too low to make it across the swamps and back to the ridges we came from. But seeing Sky's log got me thinking. I checked the return flight logs from the Slayer transport that brought Sky's sister here. Their way out is exactly what we did on the way over here. They launch, work themselves as high as possible in ridge lift until they can clear that high rock wall. Once you're *that* high, you can glide back easy. And that's our way out too. We fly over, not through.'

I stand there, trying to get my head around this. I'd had a desperate idea that if I somehow found Sky and brought her back I could do a deal with Murdo. In return for him not harming her, she gets us past the chains and out of the No-Zone.

That's stuffed now, isn't it? He doesn't need her help.

'So what?' I say. 'I'm still going. You can't stop me.'

'I'm *not* stopping you,' Murdo says. 'You want Sky. Well, I want something too. We've only got one set of self-launch rockets. That means we get one shot at getting out of here. If I miss a climb, then we're back on the ground again, trapped here for good. And to get high enough we'll have to soar the same ridges the Slayer transports use. Some are close to where they've landed. The logs show the flights, but you've seen the charts — they're blank there. You'd be heading that way. You could check out the ridges. See if the Slayers have lookout posts on them, or blaster cannon. We don't want to get up there and run into any more nasty surprises, do we?'

It's as if a fierce wind I've been leaning into suddenly quits blowing. I stumble forward into understanding.

'You *want* me to go looking for Sky?'

Murdo sighs heavily. 'Not exactly. But you will anyway, and your eyes could improve my chances of getting out of here.'

'If I bring her back, you won't harm her?'

He gives me his word that he won't – whatever *that's* worth.

Only now do I realise my brother's slipped away. I'm peering about, worried and wondering, when he pads down the ramp from inside the *Never Again*, a pack slung over his shoulder.

'I'm coming too,' he says, all grim-faced.

Didn't think I'd ever smile again, but I smile now. Sadly maybe, but it's a start. I shove my fist out. 'You better keep up.'

We bump stumps, and avoid looking each other in the eye.

Last thing I do before we set off is check on Rona's resting place. Colm and Fleur have done a good job, planting it with long grasses so that when they've had some rain and stood up again, you'd never know she's down there in the cold ground.

Which chokes me right up.

Murdo looks almost sorry to see us go. Almost. He gives me a hand-drawn plan of the Slayer transport's return flight route, marked up with his best guesses at ridges and wind directions. I give it to Colm, who claims to understand it. Fleur climbs with us for the first few klicks. To see us safely on our way, she says. She's got her usual brave deadhead face on. I'm not fooled.

When we climb high enough that jungle gives way to something more like forest, she's soon at it again.

'I want to come too!'

Colm shoots me a hopeful look, but I shake my head and tell her she's the best person to keep an eye on Murdo and Ness and make sure they don't clear off without us.

'And we'll be back before you know it,' I say.

In the end, cursing and unhappy, she agrees to stay behind.

We say our farewells on the steep hillside, the *Never Again* out of sight in the valley below, the river glittering in the dayshine.

'You better come back,' she says, 'or I'll kill you.'

At first Sky's tracks are clear, especially her dragging leg. Higher up though the ground becomes more rocky and barren. Tracking becomes slow-going. We soon decide to forget it in favour of taking the most direct route to where the Slayer transport landed.

'You think she's there already?' Colm asks.

I nod. 'Should be. She's had eight days to get there.'

That's according to the *Never Again*'s f-log. Knowing Sky, she'll have set off not long after landing. Unless the terrain's completely impassable it can't take us more than three days. If she *isn't* there yet it'll be because she's lying dead somewhere.

We climb some more until I glance back and see Colm sweating and gritting his teeth. He swears he's fine, an obvious lie. I get him to set the pace from now on. Truth is, rushing through Reaper country is stupid. Best to step slow and be wary. And the terrain *is* getting harder.

We haul ourselves up on to one ridge to see another chasm yawning before us, which we have no choice but to drop down into and climb back out of. It's a brutal and lung-busting slog. Climb, look in dismay, descend, climb again . . . and repeat. Every klick forward costs us at least five klicks of hard up and down.

It gobbles hours and energy and Colm's legs.

By the time the sun's low he's wobbling. I'd hoped to push on overnight if there was moonshine, but he's had it, so we hunker down between some boulders and shelter from a bitter wind.

'Bet you wish you'd stayed with Murdo,' I say.

'No way,' he says, teeth chattering.

'How d'you feel?'

'I'm f-fine. Just a little b-bit cold, that's all.'

But what can I do? We're stuck here. Going back isn't an option. We make it through the night by huddling up back to back and set off again as soon as it's light enough to see our way, desperate to pump some blood around our numb bodies. Mist greets us, but this soon burns away. The sun is just short of midday when we climb out of one valley and peer down into the next. And there it is ahead and below us – the ridge that will lead us to Sky, winding its knife-edge way north into the heart of the No-Zone. It kind of had to be there for the Slayer transport to soar along. Still, it's one hell of a relief to see it at last.

'Not bad cover too,' I say, 'if we stay below the treeline.'

The ridgetop is scrubby and open, just a few hardy, wind-bent trees sticking up from it. Its left flank is thick with trees from not far below the summit. The right flank is steeper, vertical in some places, and looks impassable. Clouds hide the far end. I want to mark it on Murdo's chart, but can't. Colm's lost it. He says he was sure I had it and goes to stand up from where we're crouched among some jumbled boulders. I curse and yank him back down.

'Wait. Let me take a look first.'

Through my rifle's scope I scan the ridge.

'See anything?' Colm asks, sounding cross at being grabbed.

'Hang on.' It seems quiet enough, although Reapers won't be jumping up and down. I look again, checking the tree-smothered lower slopes. And see grey-blue curling up. 'Smoke!'

'Where? Are you sure?'

'Left side of the ridge, in the distance. See the taller trees?'

'Oh yeah,' he says, dry as you like. As if the smoke is interesting, but that's all. 'Reaper fires, I suppose. So what do we do?'

I take another look, give my lip a good chew.

'It's like those chains again. If Sky got past, so can we.'

'Who says she *got* past here?'

I scowl at him. 'Shut up. Let's get going. At least now we know where the Reaper camp is; that's something.'

We check our rifles are loaded and locked, and I lead off.

Leaving the cover of the boulders we hike down on to the left side of the ridge and into the welcome gloom and shade of the wooded slope. Almost immediately we hit a trail, boring its way like a tunnel through the closely packed trees and giant ferns.

'Wildlife didn't make this,' Colm whispers.

I shake my head. 'Reapers.'

The soil underfoot is hard-packed, hardly a weed in sight it's so well used. I shiver, thinking how many countless feet must have tramped along it to sink it this shin-deep.

Colm steps on to it. 'Think it leads to that smoke we saw?'

'Bound to,' I tell him.

Even so, it's tempting. It'd be faster and easier going on the trail, with less chance of being heard. But it's risky. It could be guarded, or we could just run into Reapers using it. In the end we decide a better bet is to climb up on to the ridge and wait for the sun to go down before trying our luck at creeping past on top.

Up there though we get another fright.

Colm's a pace ahead. He curses and jumps back into me.

'Watch out!' I shove him away.

'What the frag is *that* about?' Colm gasps.

And now I see what my brother saw. I step back too.

Dead guys hanging upside down from one of the few wind-bent trees, swinging slightly in the breeze. All seven are tied to face the way we'd have come had we followed the ridgetop. Their eyes are gone, long sticks poke out of the empty sockets. Something's been done to them so leathery-looking skin still hangs off their bones instead of rotting. Their throats are cut and each wears a bright-red necklace of beads to mimic blood. And what I first took to be guts and stuff, all tumbled out, turns out to be pink-painted pieces of wood threaded on a string.

Hung on and around them are loads of weird-looking symbols made from twigs and plaited grass. Loads of Xs.

Colm looks ready to puke. 'Another Reaper burial?'

I shake my head. 'A warning. Turn back, or end up like this.'

23
MYSTERIOUS LIGHTS

In the black dark we leave our hideout and set off past the vague shapes hanging from the tree, giving them loads of room. We've a steady breeze to guide us; as long as I keep the chill of it on my left cheek we won't go wrong. It's nervy creeping along though, a drop to our right and Reapers so close. At least we're downwind of them, so even if they have dogs we should be okay.

But soon we have a problem.

Whether it's my nublood, or years wandering around an unlit Barrenlands, my seeing in the dark seems way better than Colm's. He stumbles into things and starts to lag behind. Doesn't say nothing, but I can tell he's struggling. Worried I'll lose him or he'll walk off the cliff, I figure I have to do something.

'Give me your hand,' I whisper.

'Why?' he whispers back. 'You scared?'

I discover I can still laugh, although I have to choke it back. Next thing, his hand feels for mine. We set off again, holding hands, and I hear him softly chuckling.

'If Sky could see us now,' he whispers.

Fact is though we're moving faster and a lot quieter.

A while later, when I judge we're well past where I saw the Reaper smoke, I tell Colm we'd best take a break.

'Shouldn't we keep going?' he says.

'We will. I just want to make sure we're not being followed.'

I squat, do the old hunter trick of breathing shallow through my open gob, and listen out for unusual sounds.

Nothing. That I can hear anyway. I breathe deep again.

'Happy?' he whispers.

Hardly. But I tell him it sounds like we're in the clear.

The dogmoon shows itself through a tear in the high cloud. Colm offers me his canteen. I'm not thirsty, but I take a swig anyway and thank him for it. Rona would approve.

'They're more human than I'd expected,' Colm whispers.

'Who are?' I ask, confused.

'Reapers. Those two we ran into.'

'Course Reapers are human. What did you think?'

He shifts beside me. 'We were told they were some early illegal settlers from way back when, before Wrath became this dump world. That they'd regressed or mutated or something like that, become half-men who lived more like animals.'

'They live like animals all right, but they're as human —'

I catch myself. As human . . . *as I am*? And how human is that? Even now I still wonder sometimes.

Colm asks me what's wrong.

I sigh up at the dogmoon. 'That Reaper girl I shot.'

'What about her?'

'Chop her hair, give her a good scrub to get rid of all the paint and the stink, and you'd never know she was a Reaper. With my kind it's not so easy. We can't wash being twists away.'

He shrugs. 'A wash wouldn't be wasted on you though.'

'Have you smelt *yourself* recently?' I say.

He laughs quietly in the darkness, sticks his fist out and we bump stumps.

For the rest of that night, only stopping occasionally to make sure nobody's on our tail, we put a good few klicks between us and where we saw the Reaper fire smoke. Other than startling some roosting birds and scaring ourselves half to death by bumping into a few wild fourhorns, our march deeper into the No-Zone is just a cold and hard slog. We're both glad when a hint of dawnshine finally appears out to the west.

Colm stops, as if to admire it.

'C'mon, we need to find cover,' I say, pulling at him.

He won't be pulled. 'Wait. I saw something!'

In the moonshine I look ahead of us. Our ridge has curved to the north-east for the last few klicks, crawling its way round the spreading flanks of two peaks that rise up like giant fangs.

'What?' I can't see anything unusual.

'A light. Between those peaks. It's gone now, but I *did* see it.'

And now I see it too. A white light winks on in the gloom between the twin peaks. About three seconds later the light winks off. Another twenty and it winks on again.

'Some kind of signal?' I say.

The words are hardly out of my gob before I hear a faint whine above the ever-present sigh of the wind. Lift-cells!

I grab Colm and use all my strength to tow him towards some nearby rocks. We barely make it into cover before a half-seen windjammer slides past low overhead.

'A Slayer transport!' he says, like I'm blind. 'Think they saw us?'

'Doubt it. Even if they did, they'd figure we're Reapers.'

We lift our heads up cautiously, but boulders block our view. I see a rocky outcrop above us and lead Colm in a steep, heart-in-mouth scramble up it. We throw ourselves down on its flattish summit and peer into the darkness. After a while I spot the transport again as it banks and turns away from the ridge.

Colm grunts. 'It's making for that light.'

I start to wonder if the light maybe marks some pass between the twin peaks. Reaching for my slung carbine I take a look through its scope, which flicks into night-see mode. Yup, there is a pass all right. I zoom in. The Slayer transport appears to leap towards me. I watch its wheels drop down and lock into place.

'See that, Colm? They've stuck their undercarriage down.'

Beside me, he peers through his own scope.

'Landing then. Can you see where?'

'Nuh-uh. We'd need to be loads further along this ridge. Back in your Saviour's palace days, you seriously never heard any chat about a secret Slayer base out here in this No-Zone?'

'I already told you I didn—'

I lunge and clamp my hand over his mouth to shut him up.

It's the stink of unwashed bodies that first warns me. Then the sound of scuffling feet. I let go of Colm, put a warning finger to my lips and jerk my head towards the way we climbed up here.

Colm nods and mouths, 'Reapers?'

I nod back. We flatten ourselves on the rock.

A few thumping heartbeats later I hear voices. And let out the breath I've held. Had they spotted us, the Reapers would be stalking not talking. I figure they're probably just out hunting. Cautiously I crawl to the edge of the outcrop for a look down, and see a dozen or so moonlit figures clamber up on to the ridgetop below. But they don't stop there — they head straight for our rock refuge.

I duck down again, stiff with horror.

'Think they saw the Slayer windjammer?' Colm whispers.

'Who cares? They're on their way up here!'

Rocks clatter not far below us, but as I'm readying my rifle a loud chanting starts up and the sounds of climbing stop. Colm shoots me a mystified look. I haven't got time for that. Instead I look over my shoulder for an escape route. And that's when I see what's up here with us — loads of piled stone cairns and clever little stick-animals. The nearest is about the size of my foot, made from twigs woven into the shape of a fourhorn, a stone in its belly to give it weight. The ledge is littered with the things. Fourhorns, goats, rodents and birds. Even a few sky lizards. Offerings for a good hunt, I bet.

I nudge Colm. He looks around, and starts.

Just then the Reaper chanting cuts off. There's a long silence, the kind that claws at your nerves. And now I hear bare feet slapping rock again. One or more Reapers are on their way up!

'Time to go,' I hiss at Colm.

We scuttle towards the far side of the outcrop, staying low. It's slow-going though. Tumble a cairn down or crunch one of the dried-up stick animals and they'll be on to us. And we're not going to make it in time. I drag Colm down behind the biggest cairn. A heartbeat later and Reapers are on the ledge with us. So close that their stink is overpowering. I hear them muttering and then a soft scratching sound of wood on stone, which I'm guessing is them placing their latest stick-animal offering on the ledge.

I'm hoping they'll leave now, when I hear another low whine. This gets louder, until another half-seen Slayer windjammer streaks past overhead. As this one goes by it lets out a deafening roar in its wake. A shower of sparks sprays from its underbelly. These light up and turn into sheets of dripping liquid fire.

What the hell? They're firing flares!

So much for cowering in the darkness. Everything on the outcrop is lit up by a blinding white light. Reaper voices cry out. And one of us knocks the cairn we're hiding behind. The pile of stones, all so carefully balanced, comes crashing down.

In the flare-light I see three Reaper kids.

They see us too and scarper before we can get a shot off, ducking back down the way they came and shouting to their mates. Cursing, we jump up and make a run for it, trampling animal figures. The flares are fizzling out as we reach the far end of the outcrop, but before they die completely I see the drop waiting for us.

Twenty metres or so of sheer rock. Impossible to climb down.

The dark closes in again and we spend a little bit too long staring into nothing. Next thing I know, Colm topples into me. I just manage to stop him taking us both over the edge. His knees give way and I'm the only thing holding him up.

I figure he's fainted, or something like that.

'Colm! Don't do this. Wake up!'

I lower him down and my night-seeing comes back enough to make out that his eyes have rolled back. His breathing's rough.

But while I'm gawping at him, I'm not watching my back. Something stings the side of my neck. Automatically I reach up . . . and my hand comes back holding a small wooden dart, fuzzy white stuff at the tail, sharp tip covered with sticky stuff that could be red. A heartbeat later and my head starts spinning. The darkness thickens. It bulges and sways and sloshes around as if oil were inside my eyes.

A dozen or so Reapers creep towards us across the rock, keeping us covered the whole time with their bows and blowpipes. I let go of Colm, stagger up, turn to face them.

When I try to raise my rifle, it's too heavy.

My legs buckle the same as Colm's did. I end up slumped on my knees beside him. I drop my rifle or it's taken off me. I smell tar and hear steel rasp on flint. A bark torch flares into life and its orange flame gives the gloom a shove back, dazzling me.

'Let's see what we got,' a voice says.

The torch swoops towards my head. Burning tar fragments drip across my face, stinging me.

'No fraggin' way!' one spits.

'Them's twains!' cries another, or something like that.

'See the faces on 'em, as like as like!'

Hisses. Curses. The flickering flame retreats. Half-seen figures scatter behind it, as if I've pulled a flamer on them.

I wish. Whatever I've been stung with, all I can do is watch.

In the dancing yellow fireshine I glimpse their crude leather-bound leggings and furs tied tight against the cold. Bright eyes peer at me out of slashes of black across white-painted faces. Their hair is mud-plastered, long and full of feathers and twigs.

They're just kids, stick-thin, bare-chinned.

The Reapers slowly edge back towards us, led by the kid with the bark torch. He looks the oldest. Even so I doubt he's seen his sixteenth year. 'They ain't clan, that's for sure,' he mutters.

The kid next to him reaches down, twitchy and ready to run. He fingers the cloth of my jacket. 'Shadow-walkers?'

I manage a blink and he snatches his hand back fast.

'Twains? Shadow-walkers?' torch-kid spits. 'Don't be a fool.'

'So what we do with 'em?' a girl says.

'Slit 'em,' a little one says, slashing a nasty-looking blade at me.

'Ear to ear,' another agrees. 'They'll bring bad luck.'

Torch-kid shakes his head, sending his dreads flying. 'Nah. I say we bring 'em back to Bossmomma. They'll make good offer.'

'Yeah. Yeah. Bring 'em for the offer.'

'They're fat 'n' heavy. No way am I carrying 'em.'

I quit listening, feeling strength leaking back into my muscles. And the kid holding my pulse rifle is not so far. Only now the boy who'd waved his knife at me crouches down beside me.

'You twains bleed red, do ya?' he whispers.

Next thing, he grins and pokes the blade's tip into my cheek. Hard enough to make me flinch and pull my head away.

His gob falls open. 'Hey,' he yelps, 'this twain's still kicking!'

I launch myself at him. He flails with his knife, but I yank it out of his hand and shove him away. Before the other Reapers react I'm up and staggering towards the kid with my rifle.

But staggering is all I can manage. I reel towards them like a hundred-year-old drunk, my body still full of their poison. The Reaper kids get over their surprise and jump back, staying clear of my clumsy swipes with the knife. They hoot and jeer at me.

Tears of frustration sting my eyes. My last chance and I blew it. Or maybe not. I turn back towards Colm. Better a clean death by my hand than taken alive by Reapers. It's what we used to say to each other in the Barrenlands.

But saying's one thing, doing another. If his eyes were closed, then maybe. Now they bulge open.

'Drop your blade, twain,' torch-boy yells at me.

I glance down at the knife in my bloody hand . . . and grunt with shock. I see the nick in the blade near the hilt no amount of honing could ever remove, and the wire-bound leather grip with the fancy S carved into it, which took me so many fraggin' hours to do.

No three ways about it – it's Sky's. Or was.

I'm still staring at it, slack-gobbed, when the Reapers rush me.

24
IN THE REAPER CAMP

My head is banging like crazy, so when I open my eyes I struggle to make sense of what I'm looking at. Dirt and sky have traded places and swing violently from side to side.

Finally I get it. My hands and knees are bound and I'm slung upside down under a pole, like a freshly killed animal. Two Reaper kids shoulder each pole end and are carrying me along a path through tangled trees. One has my rifle. The other has my pack, with my old pistol inside it.

Where's Colm? I manage a sneaky, slit-eyed look behind me. My brother's not there. Maybe he's up ahead then?

I hope so, but I don't look in case I get bashed again.

It's raining, heavy and relentless. The ground slopes up to our left so we're headed back the way we came. I shut my eyes again and dark thoughts pounce. Sky wouldn't hand over her knife; some Reaper must've prised it from her cold, dead fingers. Mostly though I just dread what's going to happen to us.

It's a long while before I open my eyes again, after I'm dumped on to cold and wet ground. My right hand, cut grabbing the blade off that kid, itches like hell as it heals. The rest of me feels like death warmed up, and my head is pounding. Or is it? No, the pounding is in my ears. It sounds like drums, or wooden pots being bashed together some distance away. I listen harder and hear cheers and laughter. But even as this awareness crawls through my sore head, the drumming and cheering fades away, replaced by shouting.

Looking through one of my captor's legs I see the low sun sliding feeble spears of light between big trees clinging to a slope, lighting up their green and yellow foliage, but leaving the trunks dark. It's stopped raining and an evening mist rises up from the soaked forest floor like it was breathing. I roll my head the other way and see we're on the outskirts of some sort of camp.

A mob of full-grown Reapers heads towards us.

I look around and see Colm dumped behind me. His face is turned away, but his chest rises and falls. Not dead. Yet.

'Twains, you says? Let me see 'em.'

A leathery-skinned warrior, his half-naked body covered with the usual swirling blue patterns, shoves his way through the Reaper kids who brought us here. He sees me flinch, bares rotting teeth at me and hoists me up to my knees. Other warriors grab Colm and drag him over, his feet scraping the hard-packed dirt. They kneel us beside each other.

My brother's head hangs down.

'You okay, Colm?' I whisper, but don't get an answer. What I *do* get is backhanded across the face by the Reaper holding me.

'Talk when yer told, not before!'

I grit my teeth and try not to look as scared as I feel.

Another Reaper grabs our hair, wrenching our heads up and

back. For the second time I hear curses and lungs emptying. The mob even shrinks back a few steps. Some filthy little Reaper children squeal their fear loudly, clutching their mother's legs.

One Reaper woman cries out. 'Them is twains all right!'

'What have we done to land this evil on us?' another moans.

I brace for fingers making the Sign of One. Doesn't happen. But I see the fear and loathing in their eyes as they peer at us – and that's horribly familiar. Being with Gemini these last few months, among idents, I'd nearly managed to forget how detested we are. *Twains* must be Reaper-talk for idents. I scan the gawping faces, searching for two the same. None. All singletons so far as I can see.

There's a big commotion at the back of the crowd.

'Shift your arses, Bossmomma's here!'

The Reapers around us glance back, then most scramble aside to get out of the way of another group heading our way.

My throat closes on me – this lot are not like any Reapers I've ever come across. At their head is a large, ferocious-looking woman with broad shoulders on her a man would die for. Half her face is hidden behind a bleached fragment of fourhorn skull, her right eye peering out at me through its one gaping eye socket. The rest of her brutal-looking face is powdered white, a thick slash of black from ear to ear. Her dreads are waist-length and still dark, if shot through with plenty of grey too. The drawstring leggings she wears are as crudely woven as anything anybody else is wearing, but her green-dyed wool cloak is of much finer quality. Dozens of cords are slung around her thick neck, dangling beads and teeth and small animal skulls over her big, sagging breasts. Her bare arms, still muscled, but well on their way to fat, are covered from wrist to shoulder with hammered-metal armlets, cuffs and bracelets.

Four massive Reaper warriors flank her. Shaven-headed, thickly bearded, their brutal, tanned-leather faces are notched and scarred and covered with crude blue stick-and-ink tattoos.

'What's all this noise?' scary leader-woman grumbles.

But now she sees Colm and me, and stops in her tracks so fast you'd think I'd gone and blasted her. She gapes her mouth in a big silent hiss, her eyes bulging all white and nasty.

She glares left and right, suspicious.

'What gom brought the likes of these here?' she thunders.

There's a long, scared pause. Eyes flick about and fingers point. One of the kids who caught us stumbles forward. It's torch-boy, and his face paint can't hide his nervousness.

'We found 'em on the north edge, Bossmomma,' he croaks.

I almost feel sorry for him.

'Did you now?' she says, real low.

He swallows. 'Spying they was, on the no-go place. And carrying too. Look here, see!' He holds up my pulse rifle to show her. 'We brought them for you. They'll make good offer.'

'Yeah,' another kid says. 'Brought 'em for the offer.'

The boss woman flares her nostrils, like she's sniffing their words. Behind her, heads nod. I hear the word 'offer' going around. Can't say I like the sound of that.

Bossmomma takes a long, hard-eyed stare at Colm and me. From the look on the exposed half of her face, it's as if she's wondering which of us has the most meat on our bones.

'Why did you come here, twains?' she says at last.

I've no idea what to say so keep my gob shut.

The big men flanking her don't like this. As one they flex their slabs of muscles and step forward. Bossmomma halts them with a raised hand. She leans so close now I can smell her stinking breath as she fingers my threadbare old jacket.

'You're bare-faced and not of the clan. So . . . who are ya?'

I'd swallow if I could, but my mouth's too dry.

'What does it matter?' I mutter. 'You'll kill us whatever I say.'

The woman scowls, her mouth like a slot cut in stone.

'Maybe. But there's dying fast and easy, or there's dying slow and nasty. I'll ask you one last time. Who are you, twain? And how do you come to be wandering our spirit lands?'

I'm still wondering what to say when Colm finally raises his head.

'We don't mean your clan any harm. There's a war going on beyond your spirit lands. We're just trying to stay alive. We came here to hide and to look for a lost friend, that's all.'

The big woman grunts. She paces back and forth, gazes at us with a strange look on her painted face that could be anything, but might be puzzled or even pained. She shakes her head.

Suddenly there's a banging and a rattling.

'What curse is this?' a man cries out.

The Reaper mob turns as one to look as a tall man wearing a large, hook-nosed wooden mask shoves his way to the front, helped by two shorter and likewise-masked companions. The rattle comes from a weird-looking skull the tall man is shaking, the banging from his mates' hand-drums. All three newcomers look well fed and are dressed unlike the other Reaper men, who like to show off their swirling blue tattoos and go almost naked except for scraps of cloth covering their bits. These guys are so well wrapped up you'd think it was still midwinter. Each wears a filthy yak fur over their rags. Their wooden masks are painted differently too – black with four thin white stripes running downwards, two either side of the hook nose, smeared from under the eyeholes downwards. Long, glossy black wing feathers are twined into their dreads. The tallest guy wears a headdress that's basically a large black bird, wings half outstretched, cruel beak gaping wide. The thing's obviously long dead, stiff and more than a bit tatty.

To me it looks mad, but I'm guessing this shouts to these Reapers that he's a big deal and not to be messed with.

The only person who doesn't look awed is Bossmomma. She keeps her grey eyes fastened on Colm and me, but stiffens visibly and mutters something that could be a curse. I see some head shakes and hear a few grumbles among the crowd. And catch a phrase repeated. *Shadow-walker. Shadow-walker.*

The two drummer Reapers stop short and squat down, muting their drums. But the tall one, he keeps on coming, shaking his skull-rattle thing, eyes glittering behind the mask. He stalks past Bossmomma as if she weren't there and fixes his glare on us. Then, as if he sees us for the first time, he lets out a piercing howl and staggers, throwing his free hand up, fingers spread wide.

Scares the crap out of me, he does. I let out a yelp.

'Twains! Doomspawn!' this guy moans. Spit froths out of the mask's gob hole and he capers about like he's gone crazy. 'It's a sign, I tell you. Shadows speak and shadows warn. The fireworms will be upon us unless we offer 'em up quick!'

He darts forward, rattles the skull in our faces and dances back. Behind him, his two lookalikes pound their drums, wailing and moaning. Some in the crowd pick it up and moan too.

'Shut it, the lot of ya!' Bossmomma yells, turning and glaring.

I watch as she and the masked weirdo with the bird headdress swap words. It's all too fast and thick to follow exactly, and goes on for a good few minutes of angry back and forth. One thing's for sure – there's hate in it. I hear that clear enough. Way I figure it, birdman wants to spill our doomspawn guts right here and now, and the Reaper boss woman's not having it.

Why? Don't know. But hope's a fierce thing – I'm with her.

And, luckily, she gets the last snarl.

'My clan, so my say goes,' she growls, waving a meaty fist under the birdman's hook nose. 'You'll get 'em for your lizard offer, but only after I say so! Till then, priest man, creep back to your shades and do your shadow-magic. Rattle your skull bones and bang your luck-drums. Keep the doom off us.'

Birdman hisses at her, but says nothing.

'Take 'em and stick 'em with the others,' Bossmomma says.

As we're dragged through the camp, I can't help gawping my head off. It's just so wrong, what I'm seeing. All my life I've heard Reapers are like animals, hunter-gatherers who know no better than to curl up under bushes when it got dark.

Yeah, right. Seems nobody told *these* Reapers.

Stumps stick up here and there, where trees have been felled to make room for their camp. Nestled among the middle branches of the surviving trees are tree houses, their walls built from sun-baked mud and grass-thatched roofs. Crude ladders lead up to small round entrance holes. Some are closed off by wickerwork shields; others gape open like dark mouths.

My gawping earns me a smack round the head.

We're hauled below one such tree house set apart from the others. It's seen better days. The walls are badly cracked and much of the thatch has gone missing. Flies buzz around. A stomach-turning stench hangs in the air. The trunk of the supporting tree is covered in deep scratches and the ground around is torn up.

I'm not left wondering why for long.

Metal rattles. A mangy-looking nightrunner appears from the shade behind the tree, howls and races towards us.

Only to be brought up short by a chain around its neck.

Colm and I both flinch, and our Reaper guards have a belly laugh. Three head off round the tree, staying clear of the torn-up ground that marks the nightrunner's reach. On their signal, another taunts it with a haunch of meat. It lunges and snaps, snarling and sending thick drool flying. Immediately the three Reapers rush in and take hold of the far end of the chain, which goes through a hole bored in the tree trunk and out the other side. Working together, they start pulling the nightrunner back towards the tree. What the creature should do is turn and go for them, but its teeth are bigger than its brain. It keeps snapping at the meat.

A minute later it's hard up against the tree trunk.

While the three Reapers hold it there, others heave a ladder up to the open hole in the tree house. Colm and I are picked up, thrown over shoulders, carried up and bundled inside. Bound hand and foot, there's nothing we can do. I bang my already banging head on the floor, and Colm lands on top of me. By the time he rolls off and I squirm around to stick my head out of the entrance hole, the ladder's long gone. The Reapers are lighting a circle of braziers around the tree and the nightrunner's loose again, prowling about at the end of its chain. As soon as it sees my head sticking out it comes tearing back, leaps up on its hind legs to claw frantically at the trunk, snapping and snarling.

Colm wriggles his way over, peers down and grimaces.

'I don't think it likes us,' I say.

'Ouch!' he says, recoiling as if struck.

Something whacks me in the cheek too. I hear shrill cheers.

Now I spot the Reaper kids whirling slingshots. We both have to wriggle quickly into cover either side of the entrance hole as a hailstorm of slung stones comes whipping inside.

A few more volleys of stones and jeers and they quit.

Gingerly I feel my cut cheek. My hand comes away smeared with blood. Colm's cut over his right eye.

'You should've stayed put with the others,' I say miserably.

Colm frowns a warning at me and jerks his head.

We're not alone. Huddled in the shadows against the far wall are a handful of Reapers. Did they hear me? I hope not, for Murdo's sake. And worryingly, they don't seem to be tied up like we are. Not good. If it comes to a fight we're screwed.

One Reaper slumps apart from the others, watching us.

'You're – kidding – me,' she slurs, scowling.

I can't breathe. *That* voice and scowl. *Those* dark green eyes . . .

25
LOOK WHO'S HERE

Back in the short but baking-hot Barrenlands summers we'd get these vicious whirlwinds. I got caught in one once, playing the fool and chasing after it. It spun back at me and picked me up. Then it tried to turn me inside out and scour my skin off before spitting me out, black and blue and stunned. That's about how I feel now as I take in her clay-daubed face; her skin-and-bone arms covered in writhing blue Reaper marks; the matted dreads, more grey than white now, all plastered with mud, leaves and twigs.

'Sky!' I say, my voice climbing. 'I was sure you were dead!'

'Not yet,' she says, and coughs up an ugly little laugh.

Colm mutters something. I ignore him. Seeing Sky slumped there, my first thought is to go to her. Would've done too, were I not bound hand and foot. And now a memory shoves between us, the sight of poor Rona's eyes staring at nothing.

'You ran out on us,' I say, choking on the remembering.

Sky stiffens. She paws at her eyes with the back of her hand, smearing the black face paint. 'I had no choice. The Deeps were falling apart.' Her voice is weird, sort of slides along.

'You busted yourself out,' I say. 'You could've busted us out.'

'Oh sure. Simple as that,' she slurs.

'You could've tried,' Colm says.

Sky's head sways on her shoulders. 'Who says I didn't? You don't understand. Ballard had you guys wrapped up tight.'

'We understand all right,' I say, sourly.

She goes to say something, but groans instead.

Colm nudges me. The other Reaper prisoners are watching us.

'What are *you* staring at?' I snarl at them.

Big men, some of them, yet they shrink from me like I'm poison. When I look back at Sky she's wiping blood from her mouth.

'Are you okay?' I ask her, despite myself.

She wipes her hand on a rag-clad leg already well smeared with blood. 'Just took a bit of a kicking,' she says. 'That's all.'

My rage leaks away, leaving me sick and empty.

A heavy silence stretches out between us until Colm whispers to me that we might want to have a go at untying ourselves. I glance again at the Reaper prisoners. They still look cowed by us being twins, but how long will that last?

For the next few minutes we work at each other's bindings. Thing is, we're tied with thin leather cord and picking at the knots gets us stone-cold nowhere. I lose my temper and try to wrench my wrists apart using my nublood strength. All I manage is to sink cord deeper into my skin.

'Hang on,' Colm says. 'I've got an idea.'

He scrabbles about on the straw-covered floor for a few seconds before he finds what he's looking for and shows me. It's one of the sharp little flints those Reaper kids slung at us earlier.

Duh. Why didn't I think of that?

I glance at Sky. She nods, and then her head lolls down.

I find my own stone. A good few minutes of fiddly sawing and Colm and I free our legs and rub some life back into them. Our wrist bindings we have to do for each other. He slices me as much as the cord, but I'm not complaining.

As soon as we're both free I haul myself to my feet and stretch the worst aches out. By now it's dark outside. The fires are still blazing and some of their light reaches up and spills in through the entrance hole. Some moonshine strays in too through the gaping holes in the thatch.

I take a deep breath. 'So, Sky, how'd you end up here?'

She doesn't answer, and crumples sideways.

Before I know what I'm doing, I'm kneeling by her side. She's lying on the floor in an awkward-looking heap. I settle her more comfortably, laying her on her back and scooping some of the filthy straw together to cushion her head.

Her eyelids flutter and she groans, but she's out cold.

Colm comes over. 'What's wrong with her?'

This close I see how awful Sky looks. It's not warm in here, yet she's dripping with sweat. I give her a quick look-over, best I can without stripping her rags off, and can't see any serious wounds or bleeding. But she's been in a scrap, that's for sure. Her face and arms are covered in scrapes and bruises and her lower lip has a nasty-looking split. She's groaning and squirming.

'Looks like she's got a fever.'

If I had my pack . . . but that's been taken. I've nothing to give her. Or do I? The nearest Reaper is chewing on something that bulges his cheek out and stains his broken teeth green.

I scramble up. 'Hey, you! What you eating?'

The Reaper looks at me warily, scowls and spits a big gob of juice so it barely misses my foot.

'What's it to you, twain?' he sneers.

Fine. I don't need to be told. I can smell its sickly stink. Kwai-nut. Filthy stuff, only scroungers can't be choosers.

'Got any more?' I ask.

'No,' he says, glancing at his Reaper mates. 'Tough, huh.'

'I'll take the one you've got then. Spit it out.'

He levers himself to his feet. And now he's up I see he'd make three of me easy. 'Why don't you come and get it,' he says.

'Uh, Kyle, are you sure about this?' Colm says.

'Spit it out,' I say again. 'I need it.'

'Drop dead,' the man rumbles, swaying slightly.

Sure. There's him, the big Reaper warrior, and there's me, just some snarling twain kid. No contest, he must think. But I'm nublood. And with a head fogged on kwai juice he's slow.

I step up and punch him as hard as I can.

He slams backwards into the dried-mud wall, thumping it so hard dust flies up all around him. Then he sort of pours himself down it into a boneless heap on the floor. As his mates scramble even further away, I prise his gob open and pull out the slobber-covered kwai-nut, while Colm watches all wide-eyed.

'What did you do *that* for?' he says.

I drop the nut and stamp on it. The well-chewed green husk splits open. I pick it up and tear it apart. Inside the nut's heart are the creamy-looking seeds I'm after. 'For these,' I say, wiping green crap off my fingers. 'Fetch me some water, will you?'

There's a bucket full of scummy-looking water in one corner, with a long-handled dipper sticking up. Colm nods and scuttles over to it. Meanwhile, I kneel and haul Sky up so she's sitting the way she was, her back against the wall.

As I'm doing this, her eyes suddenly flicker open again.

'Don't tell me you came after me,' she mutters.

'Where does it hurt?' I say.

'How long have you got?' She tries for her tough-girl smile, only it's more of a grimace. 'You sound like Rona.'

I say nothing, but I guess she sees the pain on my face.

'Kyle? What's wrong?'

'Nothing.' I show her the seeds. 'Now quit talking and get these down you. You've got a bad fever. These will help.'

She grits her blood-framed teeth. 'I don't need more drugs.'

'Trust me, you do. Why suffer?'

Colm arrives, dipper in hand, only it's broken and dribbling water. 'Here. Quick, drink some before it's all gone.'

And I know he can't stand Sky, but you'd never tell from the way he holds it gently up to her battered mouth. Sky takes a few eager gulps and sinks back against the wall.

'Okay, give me your poison.'

She takes three seeds from me and pops them into her mouth.

'Try not to chew,' I warn her. 'They taste –'

Too late. She bites down and pulls a disgusted face. 'Ugh.'

Colm fetches her more water. After some determined chewing and head-jerking, Sky manages to choke the seeds down. I shrug my jacket off and lay it over her. She shakes her head and tries to stop me, but a kitten has more strength.

'Quit fussing,' she sighs and squeezes her eyes shut.

'What's this *offer* thing, Sky?' Colm asks.

I tug him away. 'Later. Let's see about getting out of here.'

But I'm dreaming. No wonder the Reapers didn't bother hog-tying us so we couldn't get loose. It's a leg-busting drop to the ground below, and our starving nightrunner friend is still prowling around, ready to tear us apart. By each brazier stands a spear-carrying Reaper warrior. We're going nowhere. And I'm seen peering out. I have to pull my head back in quick as another volley of stones hisses our way. They miss, but I hear the Reaper kids' delighted laughter. And that's not all. The drumming and chanting has started up again in the main Reaper camp.

'They're celebrating our capture,' I say.

Colm forces a smile. 'Seems rude that we're not invited.'

'We're screwed, aren't we?'

'Looks like it,' he says, and frowns.

Not the answer I wanted. My fault though. Dumb question.

Sky stirs beside me on the floor. Since taking the kwai, she slept through the whole of the night and much of this next day. We're over by the entrance hole, as dry a place as any in the tree house because it's lashing down rain again outside and there's some thatch left this side. I keep expecting Bossmomma's warriors to come and drag us off to their mysterious 'offer', but they don't. And nobody bothers to bring us food either.

Sky sits up slowly, as if waiting for the fever to hit again.

'What was that crap you gave me?'

'Kwai-nut seeds.' I tell her how I think Rona used to use them as part of her recipe for her painsucker pastes.

'You *think* she used them?'

'How's your fever?'

She takes a breath and nods. 'Better, I guess.'

A gust shivers the thatch and drives a squall of rain through the entrance. Outside I hear an ugly crunching sound. I risk a look, and the nightrunner is chomping on something.

Colm takes a look down too. 'What's that it's got?'

'A thigh bone.'

'Human?'

'I'd say so.' My stomach must be less disgusted than I am; it rumbles, reminding me just how long it is since I last ate.

Sky goes to get up. 'I need a drink.'

'I'll get it,' I say, and for once she doesn't argue.

Colm wadded kwai-nut flesh into the crack in the dipper, so it doesn't leak. I fill it and hand it to Sky. She mutters a tired thanks, and sucks the water down. Funny, I think, how kwai-nuts are harsh and nasty outside, but so good on the inside.

I used to think that about her.

'Go easy,' I tell her. 'Or you'll make yourself sick.'

Sky finishes drinking anyway, like I knew she would. Then sighs. 'So was it Ness who squealed where I was headed?'

I take the dipper back and glance around at the Reaper prisoners, still huddled as far away from us as they can get. As long as we keep our voices to whispers, they won't hear.

'Yup, but he took some persuading.'

'You didn't hurt him?'

Colm almost chokes. 'What do *you* care?'

'Oh right. I forgot. All I care about is my sister, isn't it?'

'We didn't hurt him,' I say quickly.

There's a long, awkward silence. Above us the faint bigmoon

breaks free from the rushing storm clouds. It's near full.

When I look down, Sky is staring at me.

'Where's Rona? Is she all right?'

I swallow and have to look away. 'Rona's dead.'

It's the first time I've said it out loud, and it's more painful than being shot. It makes her being gone all the more real.

Sky looks as stricken as she's ever going to.

'What happened?'

I can't tell her. I'll cry if I do, and I won't have that.

Colm does me a favour and tells the dismal story for me, starting with the hardliners attacking our cell. When he gets to Gant skyhooking us out of the Deeps, she stops him.

'Gant? You know he once tried to steal her jewel eye?'

We both stare at her. 'What?'

'Never mind,' she says. 'Guess she's forgiven him. What then? You told Murdo where I was headed and she flew him all the way out here so he can get his *Never Again* back?'

'And to wring your neck,' I say.

Sky shrugs. 'That's Murdo for you. No sense of humour.'

'Gant didn't fly us here,' Colm says. He fills her in on how Murdo had stashed her old *Rockpolisher*, then skips to us flying into the wrecking chains, the crash and Rona being injured.

His voice catches. 'She must've been hurt worse than we thought. The day after was when we lost her.'

'She didn't let on how bad she was,' I say, my voice all over the place. 'Didn't want to slow us down.'

Sky shifts. 'She was a good woman, and a true friend.'

I say nothing. Couldn't even if I wanted to.

Now Colm tells her about the Slayer transports we saw and

the beacon light they followed into the inner No-Zone.

Sky sits up and leans forward. 'Did you see them land?'

'We couldn't, not from where we were.' Colm rubs his still-swollen neck. 'Then the Reapers caught us. You know the rest.'

There's another long silence after that. The sun disappears behind a solid bank of clouds. At some point the rain stops slamming down so fiercely. I find myself listening intently to the hiss of the wind and the gurgling of water running from unseen leaves, the patter as it hits the ground. Distant thunder rumbles softly as it heads away. I lose myself for a while in these familiar sounds of nature at play. Here we are, I think, hating and fighting and dying, sure we're all that matters. The wild world doesn't care though. It'll still be here when we're long gone.

Wrath knows why, but there's comfort in that thought.

26
SKY TELLS HER STORY

Colm clears his throat, hauls me back to the savage here and now.

'So, Sky, how'd you get past the chains?'

'I didn't see any chains,' she says.

'Under the bridge. You flew in the same way we did.'

'I did. Just like you described – tight turn round a crack in the rock face, then along a narrow canyon. It was night, mind you, but when I dived under that arch there were no chains.'

'You flew in at *night*?' I say, gobsmacked.

Sky shrugs. 'Didn't mean to. I was closing in on the No-Zone and looking for my last perch when I spotted a big fat Slayer transport ahead of me. I got a wriggle on and caught it up. Stuck to its tail all the way in. The goms had no idea I was there.'

'Murdo reckons the transports remote-control the chains, wind them up so they can fly through,' Colm says. 'You got lucky.'

'I got smart, you mean.'

'Then what?' I say.

'Things went all sour on me.' She pauses and presses a hand

to her chest. 'You got any more of those seeds?'

'Only two. That's all there were.'

'I'll wait then. So anyway, there I am in the dark with Murdo's night-see goggles on, my canopy tucked a handful of metres under the Slayer windjammer's rear loading ramp, when they fire off a bunch of flares! Can you believe that?'

Colm and I swap glances.

'D'you think they'd spotted you?' I ask.

'Nuh-uh. They never altered course or turned their blaster turrets on me. And it wasn't just flares – the transport starts pumping out this incredibly loud screaming sound too. Like a swarm of those sky lizards on heat, it was.'

Colm looks at her sideways.

'Go to hell,' Sky hisses. 'I was there. I know what I heard.'

'I'm not saying you didn't,' he says.

I wave at Colm to shut up. 'Okay, okay. What then?'

'Yeah, well, I screwed up. I'd found Murdo's buzzweed stash and had been chewing it to keep going and for . . . anyway, I was whacked and buzzed and not thinking straight. Like a gom, I watch the flares wriggling on their way down. Next thing, boom! They light the fraggin' sky up. Almost burnt my eyes out of their sockets. Overloaded the goggles. I had to tear them off.'

'So now you're flying blind?' I say, horrified.

'That why you crashed beside the river?' Colm asks.

'I *didn't* crash,' she says icily. 'I landed. While I was blinded I had to turn away from the ridge, so I lost the lift. By the time I could see a little, the Slayer transport was long gone and I was low and scraping rock. I couldn't get the goggles going again, so when I saw the river glinting under me I figured it was that or nothing.'

'And what's with your Reaper look?' I ask.

'What do you think? Everyone said this No-Zone place was thick with Reapers. It seemed like a good idea to blend in.'

'You've an eye for it, for sure,' Colm says.

Sky hesitates. 'There was a time I ran with Reapers. So what?'

I knew this. She'd told me, back when we were close. It was after she'd got out of the ident camp. It was that or starve.

'You left your leg brace behind,' I say.

She shifts, as if uncomfortable. 'Had to, didn't I? Reapers would never buy me having tech like that. Anyway, I soon ran into a hunting party. One second I'm slogging along on my own; the next I'm on my back, a spear at my neck. They look at my marks and my face not being painted, and know I'm an outsider. Thought I was dead for sure. They smacked me about, wanted to know what I'm doing here. I spun them some crap about running away from a tribe outside the No-Zone. Most still wanted to slit my throat, especially after seeing my bad leg. In the end one said he'd take me for his slave. That's what happened. I turned it on like I was all grateful; he and his mates dragged me back here to this camp.'

Pathetic? Grateful? I can't picture it.

Sky groans. 'Only then I went and killed him, didn't I?'

'You killed him?' I say, startled. 'What for?'

Her face creases in disgust and the answer is a while coming.

'I'm his slave,' she says at last. 'Gommer thinks he'll do what he likes with me. One night he reels in mad drunk, starts pawing at me. Says he'll have me himself first, then throw me to his mates for a go. I took his blade and stuck him like the pig he was.' She sighs. 'I'd been planning on making a run for it anyway;

now I had to. But I didn't get far. They caught me and slung me in here.'

'And then we turn up.'

'Yeah,' she says. 'That I *did* not see coming.'

'The kids that caught us,' Colm says, 'they kept on about us making good offer – as twains. What's all that about?'

'You don't want to know.'

'Just tell us,' I say.

'Look, there's lots of weird going on here. You know sky lizards come here during firstgreen, to mate? No? Well, they do. And these Reapers seem terrified of them. The fools call them fire-breathers, like they can shoot fire down out of their mouths.'

'Fire-breathers?' I say. 'You're kidding? They've got big fangs and bad tempers, but that's about it.'

'Not according to the tribe's shadow-walker,' Sky says.

I shiver, remembering. 'The masked nutter with the skull rattle?'

She nods. 'He's their shaman. The warriors mostly can't stand the guy; the rest fear him big time. He says sacrifices are the only way to keep the fire-breathers off the tribe's back.'

'So the offer's a . . . sacrifice?'

'I'd say so, from what I've heard.'

Colm sinks back against the wall. 'Oh great. We're to be fed to sky lizards? That's what you're telling us?'

Sky sets her teeth. 'I did tell you not to ask.'

I feel gut-sick. So this is how it ends – we get to die like goats, with our throats slit and thrown to sky lizards as an offer.

'You know what else is weird here?' Sky says. 'These Reapers are fatter than they ought to be. Way too well fed. And there are no idents. No kids, and none grown either. I asked one of the other slaves. Their shadow-walker says that idents are evil.'

'Why's that weird?' I mutter. 'It's the same all over Wrath.'

Sky shifts, her bones clicking.

'It isn't. The Reapers I ran with lived outside the Saviour's law. They didn't care if you were ident, pure or twist.'

I study her face. 'Are you serious?'

'Duh. Why d'you think I ran with them? But this white-face lot, they're different. Their shadow-walker makes them take any ident newborns and dump them in the forest to die. He says they're an offence against the spirit land, that otherwise they'd bring famine and misery and ruin down on the whole tribe.'

My mouth goes dry as I remember the two tiny skeletons inside those clay pots we found. 'Yeah, we found some.'

I tell Sky about them, and even she shivers visibly.

'Did the Reapers you ran with have a shaman?' Colm asks her.

'They didn't. Why?'

But he just shrugs and looks thoughtful.

The rain's stopped completely by now, and the wind's dwindled from a howl to a mutter. The chanting, drumming and pot-walloping starts up again in the main Reaper camp.

'Sky, what do you suppose they're celebrating? Our capture?'

She shakes her head. 'Hekki's safe return.'

'Who?' Colm and I say together.

'Bossmomma's daughter. She'd gone off hunting, hadn't come back and couldn't be found. Then the night before last, she showed up again, alone, without her bodyguard. They figured she killed him in a temper and taken her sweet time coming home to face her mother.'

Colm and I swap horrified looks. I can't help groaning.

'What?' Sky says. 'Tell me.'

So I lick my lips and tell her. Most of it anyway.

She shakes her head all the way through my telling, then snorts. 'All the Reapers in this fraggin' No-Zone and you run into the Bossmomma's daughter and leave her for dead.'

'They jumped me. It was self-defence.'

'Did she get a good look at you?'

I sigh. 'We fought. She'll know me all right.'

'You should've killed her.'

'Couldn't. Not in cold blood. The girl was already wounded and had no weapon. She was . . . no threat.'

And early with child – but I leave that out. Don't know why.

I peer down from the entrance hole at the nightrunner. It's not moving, asleep maybe. 'We need to get out of here.'

'Oh yeah. How?' Sky says.

'The nightrunner's right below us. I could drop on it, use it to break my fall. Maybe kill it, or slow it down. And you guys –'

I shut up, knowing I'm talking crap. We're screwed.

A while later something fumbles at my hand, making me start. But it's only Sky reaching out to me, her fingers like icy claws.

'Kyle, I'm sorry about Rona,' she says hoarsely.

Only I'm not ready for her sympathy and pull my hand away.

Shouts now. Chain-rattling. I glance outside and the big Reapers who brought us here are back and securing the nightrunner. Not long after, their ladder thumps into place outside.

They're coming for us. I stand, and take a shuddering breath.

27
THE JUDGING

All the Reaper prisoners, Sky included, are lashed to wooden posts along one edge of an open space. Colm and me get poles on the far side, opposite them. Four fires arranged in a square burn brightly in the middle. Looks like the whole of the white-face Reaper clan is gathered here, partying hard, stamping their feet, cheering dancers writhing between the fires, splashing golden-looking liquor into horn cups and knocking it back. Thick-armed warriors pound sticks on to animal skins stretched taut on circular frames, filling the night with a fast, rhythmic booming that ebbs and flows, but is never less than fierce. I try not to let it get to me, but it beats its way into my head and my blood, and has me baring my teeth.

I strain against the ropes binding me. That's hopeless too.

The partying goes on for hours, until it falls dark again. From time to time the masked Reaper shaman stalks forward to lob an armful of leaves on to each fire in turn. Sparks fly. Thick orange smoke curls up into the air. Its bitter stink, when it reaches me, stings my eyes and buzzes my head. No Reapers come near Colm and me, but I see plenty of fearful glances flicked our way.

To our right, raised up high on a rough wooden platform, Bossmomma's bulk fills a throne that's built from bones. It's a warm night for firstgreen, little or no pinch from the cold even after the day of rain. Even so she's draped herself in thick furs. Ignoring the fussing of Reaper warriors who attend her, she gazes at us, unblinking, her pouchy eyes glittering in the fireshine.

Beside her a smaller throne is empty. Her daughter's maybe?

Colm stirs. 'Sky's not wrong, they are *fat*.'

'So they're fat,' I say. 'Hunting must be good here. I just wish that woman would stop staring. Those eyes of hers, it feels like she's pulling my skin off.' My voice shames me by cracking.

Suddenly the drummers quit thumping. The dancers, sweat streaming down their bare chests, land their last leaps between the fires and crouch. The Reaper crowd shuts up.

Silence licks its lips and rushes back, fearful and menacing.

Bossmomma hauls herself to her feet. She beckons off to one side. Cheers erupt as a figure emerges from the crowd, leaps lightly on to the platform to take her place at her mother's side.

It's the Reaper girl I fought. I stare, and she stares back.

'Time for the judging!' Bossmomma bellows.

A branch crackles and pops loudly in one of the fires, shooting out a shower of red sparks. The shadow-walker man rattles his skull-on-a-pole thing, eyes gleaming behind his mask, and points a quivering finger. I tear my eyes away from the girl and watch as one of the other prisoners is untied from his pole. He's thrust roughly forward into the square formed by the fires, and held. It's the big Reaper I took the kwai-nut from. The young dancers rise up and prowl round him, poking and pawing, mocking him until the shadow-walker hisses at them, and they draw back.

'Who speaks against this man?' Bossmomma calls out.

A knot of Reapers surge forward. Fury twists their painted faces. They gesture and shout something about a back-stabbing.

The big man lifts his head and spits at them. Gets belted for it too, by one of his Reaper guards.

'Any speak for him?' Bossmomma calls out. 'No? Offer him then.' He's hauled away, kicking and cursing.

I glance back at the Reaper girl. She's sitting down now, as is Bossmomma. Hekki. The light from the flames leaps about on her face and I can't be sure if she's still staring at me or not.

The next prisoner judged is a grim-faced woman. She's greeted by a storm of howls. A stealer of food, which seems lower than a back-stabber in Reaper reckoning. Bossmomma again calls for someone to speak for her. An old man yells that the woman's accusers are liars, but his voice is one against many. He's shouted down.

'Offer!' Bossmomma calls out. 'Good for nothing else.'

On the so-called judging goes. Not one prisoner is spared from the offer. Soon it's just Sky, Colm and me left.

The shadow-walker raises his hand, points at Sky.

I know I should say something, but my tongue is suddenly too big for my mouth. Even if I had the words, they're trapped.

Reapers cut her loose and shove her forward.

With her bad leg and nothing to lean on, she takes one hopping step forward, stumbles and falls. She gets no sympathy from the Reaper mob; they whistle and jeer.

I glance at Colm, to see him looking as sick as I feel.

Sky struggles up. Too slowly. The Reapers who cut her free pick her up, drag her to the judging area and hold her.

'Who says what against the cripple girl?' Bossmomma calls out.

A Reaper warrior shoves forward, his meaty slab of a face one big snarl. 'This slave bitch killed my brother!'

Sky curls her lip and sneers defiance. If I'd forgotten what I loved about her, I remember now. For the first time since the judging started, Bossmomma sits up straight on her throne of bones and looks interested.

'Did you kill this man's brother?'

Sky shrugs. Only you don't shrug at the Bossmomma. One of the Reapers holding Sky yanks her head back by her dreads.

'Bossmomma asks, you answer her!'

'I killed him!' she yells. 'And I'd kill him again if I had to.'

I cringe, fearing the mob will tear Sky apart. Sure enough, threats and yells do get flung at her. However, to my surprise I also see plenty of nods and mutters, mainly among the watching Reaper women, many of them warriors themselves. I swear I even hear a few harsh barks of laughter.

Sky's accuser howls and lunges for Sky, a knife in his fist.

'Hey, stop him!' I shout, before I can think.

Too late – he's on her. But Sky levers herself off the guys holding her and plants the boot on her good leg viciously in his face. He staggers back. Reapers come running and haul him away, spitting and raging. She's messed his face up good and proper.

'Yeah!' I yell, delighted. I can't help it.

The crowd go even crazier, hooting and whooping. Blood spilt, a warrior humbled, what's not to like? Only now I see it's not only the Reaper girl who's staring at me, the shadow-walker is too. I shut my stupid get-me-killed gob.

The crowd also quiets as Bossmomma rises from her seat.

She climbs down from the platform and lumbers towards Sky. On her way, she picks up the blade Sky's attacker must have dropped. She sways, maybe a bit the worse for the jugs of liquor I've seen her knocking back, before holding the blade up so everyone can see it in her hand. Hard to be sure – so many lumps and lines on the half of her face I can see – but she looks amused.

'You're an outlander?' she says to Sky.

Sky, her chest heaving, nods.

'And a slave?'

'It was that or die.'

Bossmomma tests the blade's edge. 'So tell me, outlander, how did you kill my warrior, who took you as his slave?'

Sky goes to answer her, but the shadow-walker gives his skull bone a big rattle and interrupts.

'What does that matter? She admits she killed him.'

Bossmomma scowls at him. 'You've already got plenty of offer.' Then to Sky: 'How?'

'We fought. I took his knife off him.'

'Liar! The bitch slit Toram's throat while he was sleeping,' his brother roars from where he's still being held.

'You're the liar!' Sky fires back.

Bossmomma grunts. 'A warrior who loses his weapon deserves to die. This slave girl says she took your brother's blade. You call her liar. We weren't there so we can't know. I say if a blade started this, let another tell truth. Fight to settle it. Kill her and you avenge your brother. But if she kills you . . . then she walks.'

The shadow-walker throws his hands up and acts disgusted.

Not the watching Reapers – they love it.

'That's my judging, be done with it,' Bossmomma slurs. She signals and the Reapers holding the brother let him go.

He flexes his muscles, stalks forward to glower down at Sky.

'Fine by me. I'll cut her up good.'

'You think so?' Sky says, teeth gritted.

This is when it hits me – I'm about to see her die.

I watch helplessly as a Reaper uses his spear to draw a line in the ground from fire to fire, outlining a square. Meanwhile, somewhere in the crowd, I hear a goat squeal. An old crone shuffles forward not long after, carrying a blood-filled bowl. Chanting, she dips her hand and anoints Sky's face with a bloody red handprint. She goes to do the same for the big Reaper. He shoves her aside and does his own, then smears more across his chest and arms.

There's a scuffle. A one-legged Reaper leaning on a crude crutch has it taken away by a female warrior. She throws it to Sky.

'Here you go, girl. That's fairer.'

Her opponent objects, but boos and hisses drown him out.

Sky tucks the rag-padded crutch under her arm and the Reapers holding her can let go. She limps to the right side of the square formed by the fires. The brother stalks to the left side.

'What chance has she got?' Colm mutters.

'A little bit more now anyway,' I say, my throat aching. Knowing that Sky would prefer to die fighting is cold consolation.

The drummers start up again. Matching their rhythmic thump, the shadow-walker paces forward with swooping steps into the middle of the fires until he's halfway between Sky and her opponent, and facing Bossmomma. Once there he glares back and forth at each fighter, before letting out a loud trilling wail and launching into a weird kind of leaping and stamping dance, with loads of skull-rattling thrown in. What with this and the relentless drumming, the masked shaman soon has all the watching Reapers whipped up into a frenzy of cheering and howling.

The drums quit. The shadow-walker lands his last leap. He crouches and thumps a hand to the ground.

Freezes like that until the crowd goes silent.

Satisfied, he takes his hand away and stands. I see the knife left sticking up, its blade buried in the dirt up to the hilt.

'One knife, one life, one death!'

He dances back out of the way with the same swooping steps.

28
BLADE SPEAKS, FIRE LIES

The Reaper warrior throws himself forward, diving for the knife. So does Sky, but he's got two powerful legs to her one and his fist closes round the handle. Sky's nobody's fool though – she's seen this coming. Even as the man rips the blade free she reverses her crutch and sweeps it round with both hands. The crosspiece clouts his head with a meaty-sounding *thwack*!

For one heart-in-gob moment I dare to hope.

The Reaper reels, arms flailing. But his skull must be as thick as a fourhorn's and he stays on his feet. Keeps hold of the knife too. When Sky goes for another spiteful swing he blocks it. Sky has to throw herself backwards to yank the stick away from him. She staggers back and nearly goes down.

The watching Reapers cheer.

Bossmomma's out of her chair. So is her daughter.

The man feels his torn ear. Seeing his hand come back dripping blood he bares brown teeth at Sky in a savage grin.

Sky, crutch under her arm again, backs off. Don't blame her. Only thing is she's got nowhere to go.

The Reaper sees this. His grin becomes a sneer. He draws himself up to his full height and does that *see-how-tough-I-am* thing I hate, leaning his head to one side then the other, making the bones in his thick neck crack, standing his shoulder muscles up.

'You're dead,' he growls, folding himself into a knife-fighter's crouch. Empty hand reaching, blade hand close behind to deliver the killing stab, he shuffles towards her.

The watching Reapers swap looks and mutters.

Like when I fought Stauffer, Sky backs up too far. A cry goes up and eager hands shove her forward again. The warrior lunges, but she ducks his grabbing hand, pivots round her stick and kicks him viciously in the ribs with her good leg. He staggers back before slashing at her wildly. She's already out of reach.

They circle each other warily.

'Your brother cried like a baby as he was dying,' she sneers.

He snarls, lowers his head and rushes her.

Mistake. Again Sky pivots round her stick to make him miss, helping him on his way with an elbow to his kidney. He clutches his back and very nearly stumbles into one of the fires.

The Reaper mob goes berserk, roaring and cheering.

Again and again he rushes Sky. Each time she slips away and stays out of reach. Gets another kick in too, and a savage stick-jab in his back. I'm blown away at how fast and agile she is on her one good leg, the crutch a strength not a weakness. Even so I can see the end coming. This guy's a bull, strong enough to keep this up all night. And Sky's starting to breathe real heavy.

The Reaper closes on her again. This time Sky's a shade too slow. His blade catches her side and spills blood.

She crutches herself away, hissing defiance, but stumbles. And lands on the crutch, breaks it in half with a sharp crack.

My next breath won't come.

'Got you!' the Reaper bellows. He drags her to her feet, one-handed, as if she were made from feathers.

'Yeah?' Sky shows him her teeth in a grim smile.

And drives the splintered and broken end of her crutch into his belly as hard as she can. The big Reaper lets out a loud grunt and sort of folds himself round it. Staggers back a step, gob open and dribbling blood. Crumples face first down on to the dirt, which only serves to drive the crude weapon even deeper into him. He tries to get up. Fails. Then he's still.

The Reaper crowd goes even crazier. Me too. I yell and yell until I'm hoarse. And so does Colm.

Sky grabs the knife and brandishes it. 'Blade's spoken! I walk.'

This doesn't go down too well with dead guy's kin. A few spit threats and step towards her, but other Reapers are quick to block them. It seems a fair fight is sacred.

'Blade has spoken,' Bossmomma booms out.

All eyes turn to the Reaper leader standing and glowering down at Sky. She clears her throat and there's a sudden hush. I wait for a 'but' that never comes.

Instead the woman gives Sky a look of grudging respect, then raises her head and glares around at the spellbound mob. 'You all saw the slave girl win the fight. I say she's no longer a slave, that she's a warrior now. Does anybody say different?'

I see teeth gritted and hear some mutters. That's about it.

Sky nods grim-faced thanks to Bossmomma, wipes the blade on her leggings and tucks it into her belt. As she does this she darts a glance at me. In the fireshine, I see her frown.

Or do I? A blink later and she's hobbling away. Without her brace, or a crutch to lean on, it's painful to watch. Obviously she can put hardly any weight on the remains of her left leg.

Bossmomma must see this too. She clicks her thick fingers and a warrior attendant grabs his spear from where it's stuck into the ground, runs and offers it.

Sky gives her a curt nod of thanks and takes it. Leaning on its shaft she sets off again. The gathered Reapers step aside to let her limp past. Some, mostly women but by no means all, smile and pat her shoulder as she limps by.

Numb, mouth dry, I watch her go. And try to be glad. There's no point us all dying . . .

Only now the shadow-walker shouts: 'Stop!'

Sky freezes. So does my heart as he makes this big show of peering back and forth between Sky and us.

'What?' Bossmomma says crossly, arms folded.

'Shadows see all!' he cries out. 'And here they see lies.'

He jumps up on to the platform and whispers to her. Only to get severely scowled at, as if maybe Bossmomma isn't the greatest believer in what shadows see. The shaman doesn't give up though and keeps on at her with his whispers.

Bossmomma sucks in a deep breath and shrugs.

'All right, all right, I hear you.'

She steps to the edge of the platform. As the shaman did, she looks across at Colm and me, then down at Sky.

I swear that if a hair dropped into the dirt, I'd hear it.

'Our shadow-walker says you know these twains, that you keep their evil company,' she says to Sky, low and slow, jerking her head towards where we're still tied to stakes. *'Do you?'*

I start. My legs come close to buckling.

Reaper heads swing to stare. Eyes narrow with suspicion.

Cringing inside, I do my best stony face. It's a hard struggle when Sky glances at me with those green eyes of hers. I see pain in them – I'm sure I do.

But when she looks back at Bossmomma she's sneering.

'We shared your cage, that's all,' she says, and spits. 'I don't know them. I ain't never seen a twain before.'

'She lies!' the shadow-walker rages, stamping his foot. 'See the way they looked at each other! Both twains shouted for her to win the fight. You heard them. They *know* each other.'

I have to do something. And quickly too.

'You're wrong,' I shout, loud as I can. 'Your shadows lie!'

This does the trick, way better than I could have hoped. A heartbeat later all Reaper eyes are fixed on me not Sky.

At first Colm gives me a wondering look. Then he nods.

'And you're wrong about us too!' he shouts. 'We're twins, that's all. Just two brothers who look alike. That doesn't make us evil.'

'Don't listen to them!' the shadow-walker roars.

Too late. Our shouts have already crashed into the crowd. High on the smoke and liquor, his Reaper supporters stagger forward to bay at us, their white-daubed faces working furiously as they howl that we *are* evil. There are plenty of others though who don't howl, and trade uncertain glances. I even hear voices raised in protest, shouting we don't look evil.

Bossmomma grabs a spear and pounds it on the platform. The shadow-walker plunges towards us, but struggles, some

Reapers slow to get out of his way.

Colm says something. I miss it – too busy looking for Sky, not finding her . . . and trying to be glad.

In the confusion she's slipped away like I hoped she would.

One tiny spark of relief, which soon flickers out as the shadow-walker finally manages to shove himself between us and the howling Reapers. He faces them, yak-fur cloak whirling behind him, and thrusts an arm high into the air. Something flies from his hand. There's a flash and a deafening *bang* that has me pulling my neck down into my shoulders. Hundreds of bright little stars blossom above us, then drift down, crackling as they fall, winking out as they hit the dirt.

The Reapers quit yelling and let out a big mob groan. Blobs of after-light mess with my seeing, but I glimpse their gobs hanging open in obvious shock and awe.

'Hear me!' the shaman yells into the silence that follows. 'I walk with shadows. I know what's truth and what's lies. I tell you these twains are monsters and they will bring down evil upon us.'

'We hear you,' some Reapers chant back.

Others shift and scowl. Bossmomma, warriors at her back, strong-arms her way through the crowd towards him.

'We're *not* –' I start to shout.

Somebody clobbers me from behind. I twist my head around and see one of the shaman's masked cronies. He flashes a thin blade, then tugs his sleeve down to hide it.

His mate steps behind Colm. Got it. Shut up or else . . .

'While these twains live,' the shadow-walker shouts, 'they offend those who dwell in the shadows! I hear their anger, and it is fierce. You see how they send their fire-breather pets to gather on the high ridges. Soon I fear they will unleash them, to lay waste to our spirit lands.' He pauses to let his words sink in.

His supporters shout 'No!' and 'Save us!'

As Bossmomma stumps up beside him the shadow-walker spreads his arms in mock welcome. 'Then I say we do as we have always done. We must offer them, before it is too late.'

The Reaper leader glares at him, red-eyed, swaying visibly.

'Too late, my big fat arse! For years we've offered up our twain newborns to the forest because you say they'll grow up monsters and bring misery upon us. Yet when I look at these near full-grown twains, I see no monsters! Do your shadows lie?'

Howls and yells erupt from the watching Reapers again, even louder, most echoing their leader's question. And nobody shouts it louder than Bossmomma's daughter, on her feet too now.

The shaman draws himself up, his freakish bird headdress making him appear taller than Bossmomma. 'You see no monsters because these are the bane of Wrath, devils in human form, and show you false faces. Be glad you can't see their real face.'

He rattles his skull bones at her, but she backhands them away.

Colm and I trade wide-eyed looks.

Bane of Wrath. Devils in human form, he called us.

That's Slayer-talk! We hear it all the time on the Saviour's broadcasts. Only that's not something they'll be getting out here.

Meanwhile, Bossmomma and the shadow-walker guy go mask to mask with each other. Wrath knows what would have happened, but suddenly there's a shriek, jerking everyone's head around. In the jumping firelight I glimpse the terrified screamer – a young Reaper girl. She clutches her mouth with one hand.

With the other, she points out something behind me.

'Fire-breathers,' she screeches.

'They're coming to burn us!' somebody else wails.

More screams now. The Reaper mob huddles in on itself, a hundred fearful throats letting out a low moan. I strain to look back over my shoulder. High on the ridge above us, gouts of red, orange and yellow fire are tearing the darkness to shreds. Blasts of light explode, before drifting down. And now I hear a loud roar. The Reapers scatter. Many throw themselves down on the dirt. Still tied to my post, all I can do is watch as a vast, half-seen shape swoops down out of the night, spewing fire and light and roars. It screams past low overhead, wind-blast plucking at my hair, then climbs away, trailing columns of fire in its wake.

It's good, but it's no flesh-and-bone, fire-breathing lizard.

I've seen flares, and windjammers self-launching using rockets, so I'm not fooled. Behind all the fire-for-show, I glimpse the matt-black hull of a Slayer windjammer as its rockets lift it back up on to the high ridge, before flickering out. Then darkness rushes back in and grabs at my blinded eyes. The windjammer slides silently away in updraughts that must still be up there.

And its work is done – the Reapers are terrified.

Moaning their heads off they begin to pick themselves up. The shadow-walker and Bossmomma are quickly back at each other's throats, arguing about us being offered. In the end she throws her hands up and stalks off, flanked by her daughter.

'Guess we're for the offer then,' I whisper.

'You think?' Colm says.

I look for Sky again, but there's still no sign of her. Good.

One of the Reaper tree houses has caught fire. Smoke twists

up lazily from its thatched roof and I can smell its acrid stink even from here. There's lots of yelling and running around below it. One Reaper, braver than the rest, throws a ladder up and rescues some squealing infants from inside. I'm glad for that too. I've seen enough dying to last me.

Reapers fight to save the tree hut by slinging up hooks tied to ropes, trying to drag the smouldering thatch off.

I choke, drowning in despair for myself and Colm.

For a foolish few seconds back there I'd convinced myself that Bossmomma would protect us. Fat chance. The woman was just off her head and spoiling for a fight. I should've known.

We're screwed. There's nobody to throw hooks and save us.

29
THE PLACE OF THE OFFER

All that night they leave Colm and me tied to the posts, the shadow-walker's cronies for company. These club us if we try to talk, and laugh when we can't help pissing ourselves. And when the sun finally rises, we know it's our last dawn.

There's no waking up to find it's all been a bad dream.

Before we know it we're being hauled up a mountain trail, part of a procession making for the place where we're to be offered. At its head, Bossmomma rides on her bone chair, long wooden shafts stuck through it, carried by six lucky warriors. The rest of us do our own walking. Like all the prisoners, I'm shoved along by a Reaper guard using a long pole. There's a rope noose on the end and around my neck. Drag my feet and I'm poked in the back of the neck. Keep dragging, she pulls the noose tight and chokes me. I soon get tired of that and stride out.

At first I'd hoped to talk to Colm. Now I'm glad I can't. I could shout, but we'd only end up being choked for it.

Anyway, what's the point? What would I say? How you feeling, Colm? Scared shitless? Oh yeah, me too.

As the sun winds its way relentlessly up towards middle-day I listen to the *thump-thump* of my heart, and treasure the cold nip of the mountain air as it hisses in and out of my lungs. I pull the trail-stinks into my nose: the sweet smell of sap rising as trees unroll new leaves; the rich, damp muskiness of old leaves as I crush them underfoot, and savour them too. I delight in the nublood strength in my legs, and feast my hungry eyes for one last time.

There's plenty to feast them on. The recent rain has scrubbed the air crystal clear. From up here on the high trail, as it snakes its steep way up and around the flank of the mountain, the view reaches to forever. The sky is a delicate shimmering blue, a few fair-weather clouds floating about in it. Even the rock faces above us seem to sparkle in the dayshine. It's gob-dropping gorgeous and my eyes ache from staring. A beautiful day to die.

Without thinking, I stop walking.

Not smart. I'm cursed, shoved to my knees and choked back into the real world by the Reaper warrior holding my rope.

'Tell you to stop, twain, did I?'

I bulge my eyes at her in pathetic apology.

On we go, up to where the peaks scrape the sky and the waiting sky lizards wheel in lazy circles, trading whistling cries. *Hurry! We're hungry, bring us our twain meat!*

Colm looks back from ahead of me, his mouth pulled down.

I nod to show I'm okay, and squeeze a smile out. It's fake. Dark thoughts prowl around inside my head. Loads of questions haunt me too, that I'll never have answered now. Like how did High Slayer Morana come back to life? How come that shadow-walker spouted Slayer sayings? And the windjammer's fly-by, flares popping, making out that it's a flying fire-breather? Why?

As we plod ever higher I wonder if Colm has any of it figured out. Or if he blames me for leading him here.

I sigh, knowing I should never have let him come with me.

The sun is well on its way down, shadows slinking from their hiding places, when I smell the stomach-heaving stench of death. Then the trail turns a corner and widens out to become a flat shelf of rock the size of two *Never Again*s side by side. In the middle stands a long-dead ironwood tree, blackened and scorched, its still-mighty branches twisting and reaching high up into the air like the burnt limbs of some weird creature. All around it, clinging grimly on to the rock even in death, are its massive roots.

Suspended from it by hooks, swinging in the wind like grisly fruit, are a few torn-apart bits of several Reaper bodies. One still has his head and a trailing length of yellow spine. The rest are little more than scraps – a tattooed arm, bound hands still hooked on at the end of a rope. They've been here a while too, judging by the lack of flies. Bones are strewn all over the ledge, the marrow crunched out of them. No three ways about it – this is the place of the offer.

It stops me in my tracks until I'm poked in the back of my neck. I stumble on again, numb, my legs feeling like lead.

The procession halts where trail meets ledge, but us prisoners are shoved past and out on to it. The shadow-walker's two assistants hustle forward and get stuck into the grisly work of cutting down the remains of the last offers. I have to look away fast then.

Either that or puke my squirming guts up.

The edge is close enough that I can see the drop below. It calls to me, tempts me. I doubt the Reaper warrior holding my rope could stop me if I went for it. Maybe I could even take her with me. Serve the bitch right for choking me so hard. Only I make the mistake of darting a look across at Colm. He meets my look, his chin goes up and somehow he manages a trembling smile.

And that's that. Whatever happens, no matter how awful our end is, I can't leave him to face it on his own.

I smile back at him, hoping I look less scared than I feel.

There are harsh words and scuffles as Reapers jostle for the best spot to watch us being offered. I'm grabbed and carried forward until I'm under the tree. They dangle an iron hook in front of my nose. When my wrists were bound this morning they tied a fancy knot that left a loop sticking up. I see why now.

'Hook yourself on,' a Reaper orders.

Oh sure. I tell him, in detail, what to do with himself.

So what if I get choked again? It's worth it. Two Reapers force my arms up and hook me on. Others haul on the other end of the rope. The hook yanks my arms up until my toes barely touch the ground. The noose is taken away and I'm left hanging there, rope chewing into my wrists, desperately trying to stretch my toes down and take a bit of weight off my arms.

Colm's strung up facing me, the other offers all around.

Slave Reapers throw down large bundles of sticks they've lugged up here and start building fires. The shadow-walker's assistants prowl the ledge, sing-songing and banging their drums. The great man himself paces about, rattling his skull thing at us, evil-smelling grey smoke pouring out of it. He chants a dirge at us, stuff about spirit worlds and omens and crap like that.

But like hell will I do my last listening to this.

I close my ears and eyes and fight to picture Rona's face from happier days, when she was alive. It's hard, much easier to keep seeing her dead face, grey and waxy and still. Or the dirt hitting that sleep bag we wrapped her in, when we throw our handfuls.

Despairing, I open my eyes again.

They light the fires now, which crackle and smoke as they catch. And I see that they're not just for show. High above, sky lizard eyes have spotted us. I hear them cry out to each other. One quits his lazy circling and dives steeply down for a closer look. In a storm of leathery wing-flapping he settles himself on a rocky outcrop a hundred or so metres above us, to glare down at our ledge out of his big red eyes, hissing and beak-snapping. He's not alone long. More of his lizard mates follow him down and perch near him. I reckon the Reaper spears and the fires are all that's stopping them from hurling themselves at us for daring to enter their domain.

'They look good and hungry!' somebody yells.

I can't argue, and shudder. They do.

'Enough pissing about. Let's do this,' Bossmomma orders.

The shadow-walker bows real low, but I'd bet anything he's sneering behind his mask. He holds his arms up to the perched lizards. A knife glints in his right hand.

'Demons of the sky,' he calls out. 'Take these, our humble offers of flesh. Be sated, and rain down no more fire upon us.'

The sky lizards hiss, unimpressed.

Appeal made, he drops his arms and turns back to us. I swear his masked gaze settles on Colm and me. Instead he chooses the big guy I fought for the kwai-nut to be the first victim. One assistant kneels and grabs the prisoner's legs to stop him kicking. The other hauls the man's head back by the hair. He doesn't struggle.

The shadow-walker steps in front of him.

Kwai-nut guy isn't as out of it as he looks. With a curse he jerks his head forward and spits in the shaman's masked face. I somehow doubt he cares that he loses a fistful of hair doing it.

Nasty, but I can't help cheering. I hear some muffled laughs among the watchers too.

The shadow-walker doesn't even bother wiping the spit off his mask. Slow and casual, muttering his shaman stuff, he reaches up and pulls the man's head towards him. The Reaper resists, neck muscles bunching and straining. Then suddenly he sighs and all the fight goes out of him. His head bends forward. Next thing, I see them leaning into each other, almost like lovers.

'Sky demons, take this offer,' the shadow-walker calls.

His right arm goes back. And then thrusts savagely forward.

He drives the blade deep into the man's heart and gives it a big ripping twist. The big guy shudders and sags into him. I've seen plenty of ugly, but that's just so cold.

The shadow-walker holds the guy up until he's done twitching. Only then does he yank the blade out and step away. The dead guy, wrists still hooked on above him, slumps forward to dangle there all boneless, head hanging, chest slick with his blood.

The rope creaks as he swings, ever so slightly.

I force myself to keep looking, as if *yeah, and so what?*

The shaman works his way through the Reaper prisoners, sending each off to the long forever the same way, leaving them dangling and dripping blood. As each dies, the watchers send up a cheer. They're not the only ones getting excited. A loud swishing sound jerks my head up. The perched sky lizards see and smell the bloodletting. It sets them off into a frenzy of wing-beating and beak-snapping. More flap down to join them.

'At least Rona was spared this,' I whisper to Colm.

He's looking over his shoulder and mustn't hear me. When he finally looks back at me, his eyes are shiny. 'Have you seen?'

'Seen *what*?' I say, and look too.

The hairs on the back of my neck stand up. Both moons are faint against the deep blue of the sky, but the much smaller dogmoon has finally risen above the beautifully ringed bigmoon.

The doom moon. Peace deal busted then.

Good! I feel a sour kind of satisfaction. Until I remember the Blight is scorched dirt and the Deeps has surrendered. Are there any Gemini hardliners still out there left to see it and fight on?

The shadow-walker turns towards Colm and me now, the only prisoners not yet offered.

He shows us his long bloody knife.

My insides turn to iced water. I swing myself to face the watching Bossmomma, scrabbling my toes in the dirt to stay turned around.

'He says twins are monsters, but he's *wrong*!' I yell. 'Half wrong anyway, and I can prove it. Just let me show you.'

'No, Kyle,' Colm shouts. 'Please don't do this!'

I wince a sorry at him, and suck a breath in to finish shouting that I'm the only monster here; that I can prove it by healing impossibly faster than him; that my brother is innocent.

Only breathing in is as far as I get.

From behind, the shadow-walker lays a hand on my shoulder. I feel a scratch on my neck. And gag. It's as if invisible fingers clutch my throat. I'm helpless, like when the Reaper kids darted me.

'What was the twain saying?' Bossmomma calls.

I can hardly breathe, let alone answer.

'Nothing worth hearing,' the shadow-walker bellows back, striding between us. 'The rantings and ravings of evil.'

Bossmomma scowls, but leaves it at that.

The shadow-walker shoves his masked face close to mine, so close I see the red threads in his eyes, smell his rank breath.

'Nice try, twist,' he whispers.

I figure he'll offer me there and then. He doesn't.

Instead, he turns his back on me and steps up to Colm. *Inside my head, I start to howl.* He reaches up. *And scream.* Gathers my unresisting brother to him. *Scream some more.* He bows his head and moans: 'Sky demons, take this offer.'

No! Please!

His knife-arm thrusts forward.

Over the man's shoulder I see Colm's eyes widen. Then dull. The shadow-walker steps aside, lets my dying brother slump forward as red spreads across his chest.

All I can do is stare, dazed and disbelieving.

My legs are grabbed from behind, my head yanked back. The shadow-walker makes a big show of wiping blood off the knife on to Colm's jacket, and then steps in front of me. Puts his hand round my neck and pulls my head forward. 'Sky demons . . .'

I should be afraid, but I'm not.

Wrath has taken everything from me already: Sky, Rona and

Colm. Now it somehow robs me of my fear.

'Take this offer!' He drives his knife into me.

It feels more like a punch than being stabbed. And now comes a tearing pain in my side. I feel blood spurt, hot and wet.

All my strength leaks out of me. My seeing fades to black.

PART THREE
SHOWDOWN

30
RESURRECTION

A heavy dew blankets the long grass around me with countless tiny beads of light. Bugwebs lie scattered everywhere, their cunning art revealed as sparkling and glistening chains.

Only that can't be right. I'm dead. Offered, stabbed and left hanging to be gobbled up by hungry sky lizards.

I hear a gasping sound, then realise it's me making it. And if I'm seeing and breathing . . .

Hardly daring to believe I'm still alive, I look down to where I was stabbed. And grunt as I see the bandage wound round my waist, a big red and yellow stain at its centre. I move, feel the sting of a wound pulling apart, but mainly the itch of healing. I've been stabbed all right, but haven't been gobbled by any lizard. Neither am I hanging from a tree, waiting to be eaten alive. I'm lying on my side on sloping ground, chill grass pressing into my cheek, my wrists still bound. It feels like early morning. Just out of reach beside me, my brother lies flat on his face. He's not moving.

'Colm, can you hear me?' I say.

My throat's so dry it comes out as a croak.

'We've got a mover,' a man's voice announces.

'Relax, I've got him covered,' another man answers. 'About time too. Must be fierce strong the stuff he shoots into them, to keep a twist knocked out for so long.'

'You think *he's* the twist?'

'Woke first didn't he? Hey! You're the twist, aren't you?'

Next thing I know, I'm kicked in the back.

I'm stiff as hell, but roll on to my front and push myself painfully up on to my knees. My ankles are still tied together, so no point trying to stand up. I look around.

And get a fierce shock.

I was expecting to see Reapers. Instead, all three of these guys have black and brown and green-daubed faces, wear full combat gear and carry pulse rifles. For one desperate second I manage to make them Gemini fighters come to save us – until I see the matt-black body armour under their camo.

'Slayers!' I spit in disgust.

Two of them are sitting with their backs against a tree, taking it easy, legs stretched out, water bottles and food to hand. A third is on his feet and covering me with his pulse rifle.

'No need to be like that,' he jeers.

My head is pounding and my throat feels like I've had acid poured down it. I reach up to feel the back of my neck and find a big lump there, the size of a turkey-lizard's egg.

The Slayer steps nearer to me. 'Which of you is the twist?'

I glance at Colm. He's bandaged too and has a matching lump on his neck. Still out of it, although at least he's breathing.

'Don't get too close,' warns one of the others.

The Slayer backs off, scowling. 'Hey, I asked you a question.'

But after all I've been through today, I'm done with being scared.

'You know what?' I say. 'I forget.'

A vein stands out on his neck. 'Well, you'd better –'

'Leave it!' snaps one of the others, hauling himself to his feet now. 'We'll know soon enough. By the time we make it to the landing zone the twist will have healed. The scab won't. Okay?'

All three shoulder their packs, getting ready to move out again. At the snap of the leader's fingers, half a dozen Reapers also rise noiselessly from where they've been huddled, so quietly I hadn't spotted them. These are slaves, not warriors. I see it in their dull eyes, bent backs and heads held low. I see something else too that makes me flinch – a metal collar around each skinny neck. I swallow hard, remembering an identical device around my neck, the blistering pain it dealt if I didn't do what I was told.

The Reapers shuffle over, slide a long pole through the ropes binding Colm's hands and feet and lift him up so he's dangling underneath. They come for me next.

I shove the nearest one away. 'I'll walk.'

Six of them, one of me, and still bound hand and foot. It's not long before I'm swinging upside down under the pole.

The sun is as high as it'll get when we stop again. Some time ago we slipped inside a narrow, steep-walled gorge and we've followed it deeper ever since, worming our way deeper into the heart of the No-Zone. Colm's awake now and talking through gritted teeth, plainly feeling as crap as I was, although he won't admit it.

Me, I'm itching so bad with healing I could scream.

Between us we figure out what happened. The shadow-walker clearly zapped us both, using some kind of pricker in his left hand before he stabbed us. And our stabs weren't in the heart to kill, just so we'd bleed. With him standing in the way and us all bloody and slumped, we'll have looked as offered as the rest of them.

Colm sighs. 'It was cleverly done.'

'Yeah, but *why*?' I say.

'So that we could be handed over to these guys.'

Some distant yellow-throated screechers start up with their haunting calls. I've been fiddling with a twig, and snap it now.

I lick my lips. 'Do you think they know who we are?'

The Saviour's sons. Wrath's most wanted.

'Who knows? They haven't said anything.' My brother shrugs. 'But too-fat Reapers who fear idents; windjammers popping flares to look like fire-breathing sky lizards. This No-Zone's not just weird like Sky said – it's one big Slayer set-up.'

He winces and presses a hand to his bandaged side.

'Are you okay?' I ask, worried.

'Could've done without being stabbed.'

'Beats being killed.'

'Hope so.' He forces a smile. 'Do you hear what I'm saying though? This No-Zone's crawling with Reapers, like in all the stories, only they're controlled by Slayers. And there'll be a reason – another secret Facility out here or something. The Reapers are to scare intruders away, or catch them like they caught us. Even makes me wonder if Slayers spread the stories in the first place.'

But we're talking too much and too loud.

'Hey!' one of the Slayers shouts. 'Shut your ident gobs, or I'll come over there and shut them for you!'

We stop talking. I do some thinking of my own.

'That shadow-walker called me a twist just before he stuck his knife in me,' I whisper, when it's safe. 'Not twain. Twist.'

Colm glances around at the slaves, and nods.

'Figures. He's how the Reapers are being run. As their shaman and protector from the fire-breathers, he has a big say. He tricks them into doing whatever his Slayer bosses want. And the beauty of it is the Reapers have no idea they're being had.'

I breathe deep, taking all this in.

Then groan, as I realise I know all about set-ups like this.

'What's the matter?' Colm says, peering at me.

'I'm such a gom,' I tell him.

'Yeah? I could've told you that.'

'Shut up. Listen, remember that Peace Fair I told you about, where all this shit started? That was a set-up too. After the Cutting and Unwrapping, the Slayers faked executing the nublood kids so that when they spirited them away nobody would come looking. Well, guess what? That's what happened to us at the offer!'

Colm frowns, like, *You just figured that out?*

'You knew?' I say.

'Sorry. I didn't ask to be raised a Slayer, but it means I've seen how they operate. Peace Fairs, and peace deals. I had my doubts about the whole offer thing. Why haul us all the way up a mountain to sacrifice us? It seemed so . . . complicated.'

Good job I'm not standing, I'd fall down.

'You knew he wasn't going to kill us and didn't tell me?'

'I wasn't sure. It was just a guess.'

I bulge my eyes at him. 'Well, next time, tell me!'

Our Slayer guards are getting ready to move out again. I give my bound wrists a test, only this isn't some lousy Reaper cord – it's synthetic and might as well be steel. But as I do, a stick snaps, and not far away neither. The Slayers hear it. One trains his rifle on us, a warning finger to his lips. His buddies take up firing positions, aiming towards where the noise came from.

'Reapers?' one whispers.

Another pulls out a cleverbox and checks its screen. 'Nah. Nearest trace is seven klicks away.'

And now the twig-snapper is revealed. A jump-lizard sticks its head out of a bush, sees us, turns tail and scarpers.

Which is a shame. I'd hoped we were about to be rescued.

They rebind us so we're hobbled, a short cord between our ankles so we can shuffle along. A pain in the arse, but better than being carried. The day grinds on, a step at a time. We climb mainly, occasionally catching glimpses of a cleft in the rock above.

'We're close,' Colm whispers at last.

I nod, hot and sweaty on the outside, cold inside. I figured the same myself. It's the stiffer way the Slayers are carrying themselves now. And they've upped the pace, really pressing on.

But who or what are we close to?

Finally we make it up to the cleft in the rock. Waiting there, sheltered from the wind, is another small group of Slayers.

The bad feeling I've had for the last few minutes . . . it delivers.

This new lot of Slayers don't bother with camo. Neither does the woman at their centre. The only one not wearing a helmet, raven-black hair spills down over her shoulders. Her matt-black leather uniform is trimmed with shimmering nightrunner fur.

High Slayer Morana. Looking good for someone who's dead.

The Slayers who brought Colm and me here kick our legs from under us and force us both to kneel.

'The Reaper prisoners you wanted, Commandant,' the Slayer officer announces. 'Idents. And they match your description.'

She nods, her pale eyes glittering. 'So I see.'

I look past her. The cleft opens out into a wider ravine. Sitting back there, ramp down, is a small fast-looking windjammer.

'Any problems?' Morana asks. 'You weren't seen, or followed?'

The officer shakes his head. 'We watched our backs the whole way here. There was never a Reaper within five klicks of us. As far as our tame savages know, the prisoners are lizard meat.'

She grants the man a thin-lipped smile.

'You've done very well, Captain. We'll take them from here.'

The man salutes. The Slayers holding us let go.

'Oh,' Morana says. 'There's one last thing. Your reward.'

The officer swaps grins with his Slayer mates. Only when he looks back at her his grin is wiped away fast because she's aiming a snub-nosed blaster at his head.

'What the hell?' he growls. His last words.

She fires. The man staggers backwards, half his head gone. Before his body hits the ground his two mates are dead too, cut down by Morana's Slayers with short bursts of rapid-fire. The Reaper slaves turn to run. They're all slaughtered too. A Slayer goes around and finishes off anybody who's still twitching.

Colm and I stare in horror.

'What?' Morana says, unblinking. 'They'd seen your faces.'

'But – they were Slayers,' I croak.

She shrugs and smirks at us, a black-gloved hand toying with a bloodstone gleaming on a chain around her neck. I can't bring myself to look her in the eye, so I look at that instead.

I'm sure I've seen it before. But where?

Morana sees what I'm looking at. Her smile widens.

'Ah yes. Do you know, it took me a whole day to persuade your scab smuggler friend to give you up? An impressively stubborn woman, even if her loyalty was . . . misplaced.'

I start. Oh no. The red gem – it's Gant's fake eyeball.

She tucks it out of sight.

'But now to business. Which is the evil twist and which the traitor son? Let me see if I can tell you apart.'

She studies us, then jabs the blaster's muzzle at Colm.

'You're Kyle, the twist. Yes?'

'Don't tell her,' I call out, without thinking.

Colm glances across at me, grits his teeth and says nothing.

Morana loses the smile. She takes a deep breath and hisses it out, sounding annoyed. At her nod, one of her Slayers slings his weapon. He yanks Colm's left sleeve up, and holds up my brother's forearm so she sees the scars. All Slayers are obliged to cut themselves once a year to show loyalty and prove they're pureblood by healing slow. As the Saviour's son, Colm had to do it once a month.

Morana nods coldly. 'The traitor then.'

The man checks my arm now. I've no scars, just freckles.

'And the twist. The monster.'

'If I'm a monster,' I snarl at her, 'what are you?'

I get my head bashed for that, and a rifle muzzle jabs hard into the back of my neck, reminding me I'm only one squeeze of several trigger fingers away from having my head blown off too.

'So indignant,' Morana says, all smiles again. 'It's almost funny, your belief that you're human.' She holsters her blaster and lifts up her left hand. Slowly, elaborately, making sure I'm watching, she peels its close-fitting black glove off. 'But since you ask . . .'

How my eyes stay in my head I don't know. Because the hand she reveals is missing its little finger.

'You're an ident!' I gasp.

'The hell I am!' she snaps, eyes blazing. 'I'm a real twin.'

That shuts my gob for me. Of course! I should've guessed this. Reals are those unfortunates where both twins are pureblood. Looking like any other idents, they're thrown in the camps too. When both keep failing to heal fast after years of Cuttings and Unwrappings at Peace Fairs, they eventually end up being released as scabs. Thing is, I've heard 'reals' can be twenty or more by then, with scars halfway up their arm. Nightmare.

'You're Morana's sister?' I croak.

'Was,' she says, and holds her arms out, as if showing herself off. 'Now, as you see, I'm High Slayer Morana, resurrected.'

'I don't get it,' I blurt out. 'All those years suffering in the camps, why side with the Saviour? It was *him* who put you through that.'

She bares her too-perfect teeth at me.

'We did suffer. Grievously. But the camps are *your* fault. Without twists, there would be no need for them. The only twins would be real twins, like my sister and me. We'd be appreciated, thought of as special, even celebrated as nature's gift.' Her voice becomes shrill. 'You twists corrupted all that; made us something to be feared and loathed.' She takes a breath.

'Or have you forgotten your Wrath history?'

'History?' I sneer. 'Slayer propaganda, you mean.'

'Be quiet!' She slaps my face.

The rifle in the back of my neck means I can't duck. I've had worse though. I grin at her, all mocking, like Sky would.

Next thing I know, she's aiming her blaster right at my face.

I lose the grin. Surely she won't blast me, not if she wants to haul me and my healing nublood back to the Saviour and reap the reward that brings. Beside me, Colm curses and struggles to stand up, only for his Slayer guard to shove him back down.

'We know she switched places with Morana,' he mutters.

So what? I look from him back to her. She arches her eyebrows at me over the scorched muzzle of the blaster.

'Your brother got the brains, didn't he, Kyle? It was the same with Morana; she got more than her fair share, which is why she rose so much more swiftly up the Slayer ranks than I did. Until her untimely death, that is. Fortunately for me, there are those at the highest level of the Slayer Council to whom her death was an inconvenience. Eager for continuity, they made sure I was on the first windjammer that flew into the destroyed Facility. All I had to do was wear one of my sister's old uniforms, knock myself about a bit and stage my miraculous appearance. You should have heard the cheers of the rescue crews as they saw Morana staggering across the snow towards them, the sole survivor. It was touching.'

Gom that I am, only now do I get it. My blood turns to ice. Behind me I hear bugs buzzing on dead Slayers and Reapers.

'Why didn't you leave us for the lizards?' Colm says.

The woman's lip curls into a vicious smile.

'Take some fool's word that you're both dead? I don't think so. It's better this way. More personal, don't you think?'

'We won't talk,' I say desperately. 'Even if we did, nobody would believe us. You don't need to kill us.'

'Oh, but I do. There's my little subterfuge, of course. It might prove awkward if I were found out. And there's our beloved Saviour to consider. Did you know that your father was mortally wounded during his escape from your assault on the Facility? Even now his life hangs by a thread. His doctors all agree he could die any day and your twist blood is his last chance.'

I gape at her. 'But if you kill –'

'With you dead, he will die too,' she says, talking over me. 'And who better to succeed him than High Slayer Morana?'

31
REUNION

Her finger tightens on the blaster's trigger, only for a burly Slayer to hiss a warning. 'Commandant! Hold your fire.'

The woman's eyes bulge with fury. 'I give the orders.'

The Slayer's face is mostly hidden by his visor, but I see his nervous swallow. 'Commandant, we've got company. Reapers. A blaster shot will give our position away.'

He holds a cleverbox out to her, its grey casing smeared with blood. A cluster of green telltales flash on its screen.

Morana – or whatever her name is – lowers the blaster. 'And?'

The Slayer points at the screen. 'These dots are – *unghh*!'

Blood spews from the man's open mouth. He staggers forward and reaches for her. She just shoves him away. He collapses face first to the ground and I see the white-feathered arrow that's found the gap between his helmet and back armour.

I'm gob open and gawping at him when pulse rifles open fire, their loud *tump-tumps* sending a thousand echoes crashing and booming round the ravine we're in. Sounds like an army's assaulting us. The Slayer minding Colm is hit and collapses on top of him. The one behind me cries out and clutches at his leg. Morana's sister crouches and tries to spot the attackers. Only then she must have a better idea and swings her blaster back at me.

Finally I get my gob closed and throw myself flat.

Her blaster roars and a fierce heat singes my back as the energy bolt crackles past, barely missing me. My wounded Slayer guard isn't so lucky. As I hit the dirt I hear his agonised scream.

If my legs weren't hobbled I'd go for a lunge at the woman. But they are. I grab a handful of dirt instead and roll over. She glares down at me over her blaster, its muzzle still glowing red hot from the shot that missed. Her lips pull back from her teeth in a fierce snarl that nightrunners would flinch from.

'Heal this, twist!' she shrieks.

With all my strength and speed I hurl the dirt into her livid eyes. She cries out and staggers back, blinded. The blaster roars. Again her shot goes wide. Before she can get another one off I'm up, and throw myself at her. My wrists are still bound, but I manage to grab her gun hand and force it back until bones splinter. She grunts with pain and drops the blaster. I try for a chokehold now, but she claws at my eyes with her undamaged hand. Half blinded, I plant a desperate elbow in her ribs. Bad mistake. Her Slayer body armour protects her; pain spikes up my arm and numbs it.

She kicks my legs from under me and I'm on my back again.

For a split second we swap glares. I figure she'll dive for the blaster. Wrong. As I struggle to my feet, she takes off running back towards the Slayer windjammer. Okay, if she doesn't want the blaster, I'll have it. All around me pulse rifles still thump angrily as I snatch it up. To my left, Reapers rush a Slayer trooper. He nails one, but the others pile into him and pull him down.

Left-handed, shaking, I take awkward aim at the woman's retreating back. And see the real Morana at my mercy in the wreck of a Slayer windjammer, with me not able to take the shot.

Only I'm not that kid any more.

I stop shaking and squeeze the trigger.

Nothing. No blast. No kickback into my hand. I shake the blaster like somehow this'll fix it. But the fraggin' thing stays dead. She races up the windjammer's ramp and disappears inside. Two Slayers follow her in and the ramp lifts behind them. Even before it's fully closed I hear the shrill whine of lift-cells being spun up at full emergency power. Grass around the matt-black windjammer shivers, as if restless. And Colm knocks me on my arse.

'Watch out, Kyle!' he yells. 'They're –'

The rest of his warning is lost in an ear-splitting roar as the Slayer windjammer fires self-launch rockets and takes off, showering us in rocks and stones and soil. By the time I can look again it's high in the air and heading away. But as the booster rockets flare out all smoky I see green flashes as pulse-rifle rounds thump into it. Something flies off one of the lift-cell pods. It lurches wing down, trailing more smoke, and plunges lower out of sight.

I go to struggle up for a better look, but Colm holds me down. Good thinking. Slayers have been left behind and a vicious firefight is still going on. Be a shame to get my head blown off now.

One look at the blaster and I see the mag's loose from being dropped. I curse my fraggin' luck and slam it home. The blaster buzzes into my hand as it powers itself up.

Just in time too. A wounded Slayer reels towards us.

He sees us and goes to shoot. I beat him to it, blasting him in the chest and dropping him to his knees. Blast him again then, twice, more for spite than anything else.

'Let's hide in that long grass,' Colm says, and sets off crawling.

I follow. That's when I see Gant's false eye lying in the dirt and a puddle of broken necklace. I must have torn it off Morana's sister without realising. I scoop it up, tuck it away in my jacket pocket and sigh. Yet another person dead because of me.

By the time we make it into cover the shooting stops. My heart's the loudest thing now. Or maybe it's my brother's hoarse breathing as he lies beside me.

'We can't stay here,' I whisper. 'We'll be found.'

Only even as I squirm around to start crawling away from where the gunfire came from, it's already too late.

'You there, in the grass, come out with your hands showing empty and we won't hurt you,' a Reaper girl's voice calls to us.

Colm narrows his eyes at me. 'You believe that?'

I take a deep breath, wondering too. But that voice . . .

'What choice have we got?' I say.

I toss the blaster away. He watches wide-eyed as I struggle to a crouch, then raise my bound hands above my head.

'We're coming out!' I yell as I stand up. 'Don't shoot!'

And I don't get shot, or an arrow in the throat. A good sign.

Colm struggles up too. Facing us is a pack of mean-looking Reapers. The girl out front has a pulse rifle and holds it like she knows how to use it. Her wounded shoulder is hidden under the rag of a top she's wearing, as is her belly. Her face, and the rest of her well-muscled and tattooed body, are as I remember. Hekki. Bossmomma's daughter. The girl I should've killed, but didn't.

'You!' I say, even though I knew it would be.

'Me,' she agrees.

We stand there and trade stares while relief slugs it out with confusion inside my head. Did she just repay my favour of sparing her, behind her mother's back? Is *that* what just happened?

Colm clears his throat. 'Thanks . . . for saving us.'

'Yeah, thanks,' I say. So lame.

The Reaper girl shrugs. 'Don't thank me. Thank your friend.'

Her blue eyes flick past me. I snap my head around . . . and there's Sky limping towards us. Crutch under one arm, pulse rifle slung muzzle down over her shoulder. Her thin face is still smeared with Reaper paint. Sweat has made the black run.

It's as if the ground lurches under me. I feel all light-headed.

'What are *you* doing here?' I say. Stupidly.

'Saving your ass again,' she says, and treats me to that beautiful blink-and-you-miss-it smile of hers. 'Somebody has to.'

She limps closer and I see how worn out she looks. We're close enough now that I could easily reach out and pull her closer. Would she want that though?

I settle for staring.

'What?' Sky says, looking all defiant. 'Did you think I'd clear off after my sister and leave you to die?'

'Wouldn't be the first time,' I say, but chuck in a smile.

'Yeah, well, we all make mistakes.'

I show her my bound wrists. 'Any chance of being untied?'

'I guess I could.'

She reaches for a knife. Hesitates. Next thing I know, she's ducked underneath my outstretched hands, wrapped me in a fierce embrace and buried her painted face deep in my neck. I drop my bound hands around her and squeeze her back as fiercely. Dimly, I feel her stick hit the ground. Neither of us speak. Holding each other says it all.

How long do we cling to each other? Not long enough. Sky bumps her forehead into my chest and pulls away. I lift my arms and let her go, reluctantly.

Reaper girl picks up Sky's crutch and hands it back to her, before cutting Colm and me loose with a blade of her own.

'Kyle, Colm,' Sky says. 'This is Hekki, Bossmomma's oldest daughter. Hekki, this ugly one is Kyle. His brother's Colm.'

We trade looks and wary nods.

As I rub some feeling back into my numb wrists, I look around. Reapers are busy tending to a dozen or so fallen warriors, many of whom won't be getting back up. A moment later a Reaper folds one man's bloodied hand round the hilt of a knife, mutters something, and drives the blade into his chest to end his suffering.

A mercy. Even so I wish I could unsee it.

'We should go,' Hekki says, 'before the flying thing comes back. It's a long trail back and we'll be losing the dayshine soon.'

'Long trail back to *where*?' Colm and I say together.

Hekki darts a look at Sky. And suddenly I'm wondering what deal Sky cut with her, to save our necks.

'She'll take you back to their camp,' Sky says.

'So we can be offered again?' Colm says, frowning.

'You'll be safe there now,' she says. 'Things have changed.'

'Sounds like you're not coming with us,' I say, suspicious now.

'I'll catch you guys up. I've dragged my arse halfway round Wrath to be here, and we're only a few klicks from where the Slayer transport that flew my sister in landed. From the far end of this ravine I should be able to see it. I'm taking a look.'

'This isn't what we agreed,' Hekki growls.

Until now, Hekki's Reapers have been scavving Slayer weapons, looking to their wounded or watching us. Hearing their leader's anger they close in now, fingering their weapons.

'Great, just great,' I mutter to myself.

'I'm with Sky,' Colm says. 'We're here. We need to know.'

I stare at him, gobsmacked.

'Are you mad?' I say. 'The windjammer that got away, they'll be on the comm already, screaming for backup. This place will soon be swarming with Slayers. Anybody think of that, huh?'

'Hekki,' Sky says, teeth gritted. 'This is what I've been telling you about. Secrets and lies. Let's see what these Slayers are up to. We can have a look and be gone before they get here.'

Wrath knows why, but the Reaper girl looks at me now.

'If I cut you, how fast would you heal?' she asks.

'Why?' I say, confused.

'Don't be a gom,' Sky hisses. 'Just tell her.'

I shrug. 'Depends on the cut. Three days, maybe less.'

'And it would leave no scar?'

'No.' I'm guessing Sky's told her what my nublood can do.

Hekki shifts, an uncertain look on her face for the first time. 'And why did you not kill me, Kyle? You could have, easily.'

'I couldn't. Not in cold blood. And –'

I leave the rest unsaid, and flick a glance down at her belly.

She sees this, and starts. A few seconds later she lets out what sounds like a relieved breath and nods to Sky. 'Let's go then. But your friends will stay here with my warriors.'

'No way,' Colm says, frowning. 'Whatever's at the end of that ravine, we want to see it too. Don't we, Kyle?'

I roll my eyes at him, horrified.

'No, I don't,' I say, my voice shrill. 'I fraggin' don't.'

'Yeah, you do.' Sky grabs me and sets off, towing me after her.

32
RUINS

'Okay, okay, quit dragging me. I'm coming,' I say. Not that I want to, but I can't just let her and Colm go without me.

Sky glances back and lets go. 'Thanks.'

I'm shocked. Didn't think she knew that word. And the look on her face too – it's like her tough-girl mask slips a bit and I glimpse the uncertainty and desperation hiding behind it. That's when I get how massive this moment is for Sky – her chance at last to see where Tarn is being held.

'We're just going to take a look,' I say to her. 'That's all?'

Sky's mask snaps back into a scowl. 'For now. We can't do anything until we know what we're dealing with.'

Hekki leads the three of us along the ravine at a near jog. Despite looking done in, Sky somehow keeps up, crutching herself along on her good leg, her thin face set and determined.

I'd offer to carry her piggyback only I know I'd get snarled at.

'Why's Hekki's helping us?' I whisper to her. 'Okay, I spared her, but I shot her first and killed her friend. And how come you guys showed up back there to save us?'

'It's a – long story,' Sky says, in between harsh breaths.

'Tell it quick then.'

She throws me a quick glare, but nods.

'The Reaper you killed was only Hekki's thralle, a slave bodyguard, and you sparing her is all that matters. After I'd cleared off from the judging, I was feeling low about leaving you guys behind . . . again. Thought it'd be a good idea to snag a jug of that venomberry liquor the Reapers were all guzzling. Next thing I know, it's morning, my head's banging and I'm being sick all over Hekki. Turns out she's looked for me the whole night, since the judging. She drags me back to her tree house and makes me drink some harsh stuff. Sobers me up.

'See, she knows I'd lied about not knowing you and Colm. All her life she's been told twains are evil, but she wants to hear what I say. Not like she's just curious, she's almost pleading. The girl cares. As if it's life and death.

'So I tell her what Wrath's like outside the No-Zone. The Saviour and his Slayer army; idents kept in camps; how one twin is pureblood and the other nublood; the Peace Fairs and fake executions. I tell her nubloods aren't evil, just faster, stronger, quicker to heal. She listens with her eyes bugging out. I mean, can you imagine?'

'What did she say to all that?' Colm asks.

'Not much. Asked me which of you is the nublood. I told her.'

'Did you tell her it was me who spared her?' I ask.

Sky rolls her eyes at me. 'Course I did. Told her all about you. Like how you can be a bit of a gom, but no way are you evil.'

'Oh, thanks,' I say, pulling a face.

Either Sky doesn't see, or she pretends not to.

'Remember when we were on the run and my leg brace was bust? We couldn't stand the sight of each other back then and you were knackered. Yet you still spent the whole night fixing it for me. Well, I told Hekki about that – how it was the first kind thing anybody had done for me in ages and meant so much.'

'Then I asked her why she's so desperate to hear twains aren't evil. Should've seen her face – like she's swallowed a stinger-bug. But in the end she tells me that she's going to have a baby. Her first. And she's shitting herself she'll have twains and have to hand them over.'

'You tell Hekki *you're* an ident?' Colm asks.

'Had to.' Sky shows us her left hand, missing its little finger. 'Anyway, you know what I think? Nothing I said convinced her twains aren't evil – it was you sparing her, Kyle, with nothing to gain and everything to lose. And now Hekki's fierce keen I tell her mother what I've told her. Only with it taking her so long to find me, and all our talking, Bossmomma's somewhere up the mountain, taking you guys to their offer place. So Hekki gathers her Reaper mates and we go tearing up after you. I'm slowing her down though with my bad leg, so she leaves me with her warriors and runs on ahead. Even so she's not fast enough. She meets Bossmomma and the rest coming back down. She hears you're already dead.'

'But we weren't,' I protest, only to get scowled at.

'Yeah, I know that *now*. Only when I caught up with her, Hekki told me Bossmomma had seen you offered. We all figured you'd been gobbled by some stinking sky lizard.'

'They don't stink,' I mutter, under my breath.

'What did Bossmomma think of your story?' Colm asks.

'She sits there under an awning they've set up, stony-faced at first, staring at me like one of those no-blink lizards. I'm gutted about you guys and sure I'm wasting my breath. Then suddenly she jumps up and goes crazy, cursing and screaming that her clan's been killing their twain newborns for nothing all these years. And doing it on *her* say-so as Reaper leader. She's tough, but that's a kick in the head for anybody. You should've seen her raging.'

'So she believed you then, that idents aren't evil?' I say.

'Wouldn't be here otherwise, would I?' Sky says.

'Why *are* you here?' Colm says. 'You'd been told we were lizard meat. And what about that shadow-walker guy? Where was he while you were spilling your guts to Bossmomma?'

Sky snorts. 'That creep saved you.'

'*What!?*' I say, picturing his weird wooden mask, the stuffed bird above it, those black feathers twisted into his dreads.

'He'd been kept outside by Bossmomma's warriors,' Sky says. 'Hangs about, rattling his skull bones and peering in, obviously busting to know what's going on. Well, he gets his wish. They drag him in now and Hekki tells him what I've told them.'

'Bet he didn't like that,' Colm says.

'We figure he's working for the Slayers,' I say.

Sky shoots us an almost impressed look. 'Course the guy denies everything. He moans at Bossmomma that I'm a twain-friend so bound to tell lies and stir up trouble. Shuts her up, and has me worried. Then he goes and rattles his skull bones right in my face. Shouldn't have done that. I grab a knife off a Reaper and go for him. Figure I'll carve you guys some revenge. Only when I stick the blade in his guts, it won't go home. They pull me off him. But it doesn't matter, because in the struggle I rip the guy's mask and headdress off. And guess what? His fake Reaper dreads come with it, leaving a regulation, short-clipped Slayer haircut behind. We're all so stunned we just stand there and gawp at him. Which nearly gets us killed. The creep knows his cover's blown and pulls a blaster.'

'No way!'

'Yeah. Only luckily for us, Hekki's nearly as snake-fast as you are, Kyle. She takes it off him before he can do harm. Bossmomma rips the rest of his shadow-walker gear off him and he's wearing body armour under it. That's what stopped my blade.'

Colm hisses his breath out. 'And now Bossmomma knows for sure that she's been played for a fool.'

'You got it,' Sky says. 'Anyway, seeing him stripped, Slayer loyalty scars all the way up his arm, that sets me thinking about Peace Fairs and faked hangings! I figure maybe you guys aren't dead. That the offer thing was all faked too.

'I tell Bossmomma this. As I'm telling her the Slayer scowls, so now I'm sure. Bossmomma says I'm talking crazy. I kick and scream. To shut me up, Hekki agrees to take me up to the offer place. Only when we get there, there's no sign of anybody, just two sky lizards squabbling over some scraps of flesh under the big tree. But we chuck rocks until they clear off, take a closer look and spot two ropes dangling from the tree that have been cut, not ripped or torn like the others. Your Slayers were lazy, or in a hurry. Hekki scouts around and finds tracks heading further up the mountain where no Reaper ever goes, because the shadow-walker says their ancestors' ghosts haunt it. We followed them. The rest I guess you know.'

I let out a breath I hadn't known I was holding.

'We're glad you did!'

Hekki stops ahead of us. We've reached the far end of the ravine. She glares back at us, eyes wide in her painted face.

'What madness is this?'

We join her and stare down in the last dregs of dayshine. And madness is a good word for it. The ravine ends abruptly here, dropping away as sheer cliff. I'd say we're standing in the water-carved spout of a waterfall that's long run dry. Impressive, but not what has us all gasping. Way below us, the far side of a deep valley, a plateau lies hidden by the mountains around it. Across that plateau sprawl the ruins of an ancient city. Mostly the ruins are tumbled and overgrown, dragged down by countless years. Here and there though a few skeletons of weird, sail-like towers still reach for the sky. Built from some sort of woven glass or plastic, they fling the orange sunset back at us so that they seem on fire. Something wrong about them stands the hairs up on the back of my neck.

'Ever seen anything like this before?' I whisper to Colm.

He nods. 'Only in pictures. I reckon it's alien. Zhang. I mean, look at it. No humans built those towers.'

Zhang? Really? But Colm with his years of schooling seems sure. All I've heard are stories about how us humans fled our used-up Mother Earth and spread out into the galaxy, only to stumble across weird, crumbling ruins from an earlier star-wandering alien civilisation. The wordweavers always have some far-fetched theory about why the Zhang abandoned their world, and where they went. My favourite is the Zhang saw us humans coming, didn't like the look of us one bit and cleared off to a far-distant galaxy.

When we got here I was all for taking a quick glance and clearing the hell off. Now I stand like the rest, gazing in awe.

Hekki shifts uneasily beside me. 'What sort of place is this?'

Colm starts to explain. Sky interrupts him.

'Does anybody see the Slayer windjammer I winged?'

What with all the long shadows and the reflected glare, I can't see it anywhere. I ask her for her rifle's scope. She unclips it and hands it over. I sweep the ruins, pushing the zoom to max.

And find it. Landed. Still puking smoke.

'Gotcha. You hit it all right. And —'

I blink hard, make sure I'm seeing what I think I'm seeing. The small Slayer windjammer has landed in a cleared space among the rubble. Four much bigger freighters are lined up beyond it. Their loading ramps are down and loads of crates surround them. I figure these must be the ones Colm and I saw flying in.

'Let me see!' Sky says, snatching the scope back. Then, a few seconds later: 'Where's the base? There *has* to be another Slayer Facility here somewhere.' She sounds stricken.

'What's that?' I ask, squinting at a sort of low, blister-like construction. 'Behind the furthest windjammer.'

'Barracks dome,' Colm says. 'That's all.'

Whatever it is it's tiny compared to the massive domes we destroyed at the Slayer Facility. One glance shows me that it couldn't hold the hundreds of missing ident children.

'Maybe there *is* another Facility,' Sky says. 'Underground, like Bastion. Maybe that building's only the entrance.'

'Maybe,' I say, although I doubt it. 'I —'

Whatever I was saying, it sticks in my throat as I see something else. Something impossible. 'Sky, give me that scope. Quick!'

She scowls, but hands it back.

I rub my eyes, look again, magnified this time. It's still there. Battered. Fat. Scorch-marked hull blending into the ruins. Five times bigger than the biggest windjammer freighter. Hanging there in mid-air, rock steady, several metres above the ground!

I hand Sky's scope back and point. 'There.'

She searches, and stiffens visibly. 'What is that?'

'That,' Colm says, his voice hushed and awed, 'is a dropship.'

33
WRATH'S FINAL SECRET

Dropship. An orbit-to-surface-and-return shuttle. As soon as Colm says it I know he's right. Can't be anything else.

'But Wrath is off-limits,' I say.

My whole life, that's what I've been told. Dump worlds are prisons: no visitors allowed. After the Twist War, even the dumping stopped. We'd been locked down, left to rot.

Colm looks at me, his face thoughtful. 'We still are. And that's why we're seeing this all the way out here, not back at Prime.'

Sky lets out a small moan and staggers.

'What's the matter?' I say, putting my hand out to steady her.

Something close to despair slackens her lean and paint-daubed face. 'Tarn's gone,' she says. 'I'm too late. Aren't I?'

Confused, I pick up her scope and take another look through it at the Slayer transports and the crates around them. Suddenly, I get what my brother's on about. This *has* to be an illegal smuggling operation, where off-world goods are smuggled in and traded for Wrath stuff to be shipped out. Not just any Wrath stuff too – I'll bet most crates contain darkblende. One of the most valuable minerals in the galaxy, Murdo says. The root of all the evil being done here, that's what was secretly being mined in the Facility.

It's like Reapers start banging drums in my head. Minutes ago I was looking down a blaster barrel, sure I was dead. Now I'm staring down at Wrath's most devious secret laid bare.

That doesn't explain Sky's moan though. I look harder. And spot the cage among the crates. It's getting dark down there, but a flick of the scope to heat-see shows me red smudges inside.

I go cold all over. Each smudge will be a nublood child.

When I lower the scope, Sky meets my shocked gaze and swallows. 'They've shipped Tarn off-world. Haven't they?'

'Not just her,' Colm breathes. 'All the missing nublood kids.'

'We don't know that for sure,' I lie.

For the last six months Gemini has hunted for secret Facilities like the one we destroyed, but found none. Neither have they found any of the still-missing nublood kids. I feel gutted for Sky, but this spaceport *has* to be why. There are no Facilities to be found; the missing kids, Tarn included, are long gone from Wrath.

'Something's happening,' Colm says, all urgent.

By now the sun is behind the mountains surrounding this secret heart of the No-Zone, the ruins plunged deeper into twilight. Bright lights flicker on around the windjammers. I flip the scope back to day mode and see activity near the hovering dropship. Sitting on a sort of platform, a crate rises vertically up and disappears inside. Either a hatch closes behind it, or the platform merges with the hull. I can't tell which from here.

The dropship starts venting white gas. 'Is that steam?'

My brother snorts. 'Too low-tech. Drive coolant maybe. I'd say they're prepping to lift out of here.'

'You think we've spooked them? Our firefight maybe?'

'Must've. Still plenty of crates and cages not loaded.'

Hekki steps in front of us and blocks our view. 'A quick look, Sky said. You've had that. I say we go now.'

'She's lifting!' Colm calls out.

A fierce blue light blazes behind the Reaper girl.

I shove past. It's as if the dropship floats now in a pool of the bright blue light, which gets steadily brighter and whiter. I have to shield my eyes and watch through my fingers. Slowly at first, then faster and faster, the dropship rises higher. It's nose swings towards us. More blue lights flare from drive-pods at the back. It leaps forward, before pitching up to the vertical. To someone like me, who's only ever seen windjammers soaring along ridges, what happens next looks utterly impossible. One moment the dropship is a battered hull balanced on a blinding tail of drive-light, a blink later it's a white dot getting smaller as it shoots skywards towards orbit and – I'm guessing now – a rendezvous with its starship.

Colm yells something at me, but it's lost in a boom of thunder that makes us all jump. Hard on its heels comes an angry crackling sound, as if we're in the middle of a massive forest fire.

The sound of air being ripped apart.

The spaceport lights are killed. Darkness rushes in, and with it comes the distant cough of a steam winch being fired up. Oh great. That'll be Morana's sister sending her Slayers after us.

'Time to go,' I say, before Hekki says it for me.

We turn to leave.

Not Sky though. Nah. She stares down at the ruins as if she can drag her sister out of the gloom just by looking.

'Sky, c'mon. Stay and you'll only get yourself killed.'

'Leave me alone!' she growls, and shows no sign of moving.

But Hekki's had enough. She takes one of her blowpipe darts, moves in and jabs Sky, then catches her as she crumples.

I crouch, sling Sky over my shoulder and lift.

'There'll be hell to pay for this later.'

Colm curses. 'If we don't get moving, there won't be a later.'

We run as fast as we can back to the ravine's entrance, where three of Hekki's warriors have waited for us. As we arrive I hear the faint bellow of a steam winch going full throttle.

'They're launching,' I call out.

The roar cuts off. A Slayer windjammer will be on its way.

'I'll be back in a second,' Colm says.

With that he darts off into the gloom. I turn awkwardly, struggling with Sky's weight, to see him crouched over one of the dead Slayers, searching the body.

'Colm! Get back here. Let's get down the mountain!'

Hekki signals furiously. But before her Reapers can go and fetch him. he must find what he's looking for and comes running back without having to be dragged.

'Show you later,' he says, looking all pleased with himself.

Hekki has one of her warriors take over carrying Sky. We pick our way down the cleft and back on to the trail that wound its way up here. Slowgoing, with the dayshine fled. Too slow. Before we've descended very far the darkness tears apart as flares pop and the sky lights up with dazzling flashes. Livid orange blasts impact the trail below us. There's a massive *crack*, like the mountain's shattering. Geysers of dirt leap up into the air. I smell sulphur and a stink like welding makes. Some dwarf trailside trees near us burst into flames. Stones and other debris rain down to pelt us.

By the time I hit the dirt, the dark bulk of the armed Slayer transport is already banking into a turn to sweep around for a second firing pass. Fortunately this is no agile warjammer, it's a lumbering freighter. The turn will take time.

'Keep moving!' I yell. 'It can't follow us all the way down.'

'This way's faster!' Hekki shouts.

Taking me by surprise, she drags me off the left side of the ridge. One of her mates does the same for Colm. In the flareshine I glimpse a crazy steep slope, strewn with loose rocks. Next thing, she's striding down it, taking extra big steps, not bothered that rocks are sliding under her. Pulls me along after her too, yelling at me to do the same. I flail my arms, step high and somehow manage to stay on my feet. We pick up speed. Soon we're really travelling, getting lower every second. And the windjammer daren't follow us down because this side of the ridge is in the lee of the wind.

Colm and the other Reapers are right behind us.

Too busy watching where I stick my feet, I don't see the windjammer finish its turn, but I hear it open fire again. This time though the blasts impact nowhere near us.

We rush on down, a hurrying island of flesh in the midst of a sea of slipping, sliding, grinding stone.

I'm sure we must be out of blaster range when the next set of blasts crash into the slope way high above us. There's an explosion up there too, as if they've dropped a bomb. I don't even have to duck. I struggle to a halt, turn to jeer and whoop. More fool me. While we might be out of their blaster range, that doesn't mean they're done with trying to kill us. I hear an ominous rumble and the stones I'm standing on shift beneath my boots.

'Go left, go left!' Hekki yells, as the rumble becomes a roar.

They didn't miss. The whole scree-strewn slope is on the move. I throw myself left. Colm's a few metres below me, scrambling the same way. Only now he stumbles and falls. Without thinking, I change direction and slide down to help him. But he's trapped his ankle and can't get up. I try to pull him free. Can't. Rocks as big as our heads start crashing around us. I look upslope, glimpse a boiling avalanche of rock almost on us. All I can do is shove Colm down and throw myself across him.

The first rock slams into me. Another. And another . . .

34
BECOMING REAPERS

Colm holds me down while Sky sets my leg. Three agonising goes it takes to get it straight. After she's splinted it I guess I'm grateful. An aged Reaper, face on him like sun-cracked leather, gives me some leaves to chew on. Heart-shaped and mouldy, they taste as disgusting as they look, but take the edge off the pain.

They tell me to try and sleep. Yeah, right.

The others all made it clear of the rockslide. Hekki found us and dug us out with her bare hands. Colm walked away with cuts and bruises; I had to be carried down the mountain. We're back in one of their Reaper tree houses now. Outside it's a bright day, grey-bottomed clouds bulging up into a blue sky above the trees. Yet oddly I hear no thumping feet, no cries of children playing, none of the chopping or pounding I'd expect. What I *do* hear is a weird throbbing moan. More distant moans answer it.

I give up chasing sleep and sit up on the fur-covered shelf-bed. The old Reaper is gone. Colm looks up from a cleverbox, which must be what he scavved from the dead Slayers.

'How are you feeling?' he asks.

'Like dozens of bull fourhorns took turns trampling me.'

Huddled beneath one of the window holes, Sky sits head down, knees pulled up to her chin, the picture of hurt. No wonder. Her whole life since the camps has been about avenging Tarn or, after realising she might still be alive, fighting to save her. Only now she must know her sister's out of her reach.

'Sky, I'm sorry for you,' I say. 'I really am.'

She raises her head. Grits her teeth and nods. 'Yeah, me too.'

'You did everything you could,' Colm says. 'But –'

He hesitates as we both glare at him.

'But what?' Sky growls.

Colm takes a deep breath, and sighs it out. 'But,' he says, deliberately, 'I've been thinking. What we all saw up there is massive, and it could change everything. Okay, so the Slayers are shipping nubloods and darkblende off-world, and that's bad. Think what they'll be shipping *in* from off-world though. Technology. Weapons. Ammo. Armour. Did you ever wonder, Sky, why Slayer equipment is always so good? Now we know!'

'And what good does knowing do us?' Sky says.

'Nothing, while we sit here talking. But if we could get this news back to whatever's left of Gemini, maybe they could take out the spaceport. That would even things up a bit.'

I snort, can't help it.

'Is there anything left of Gemini? And even if Bossmomma lets us walk, we're still stuck in the No-Zone.'

He treats me to his fiercest frown. 'So what do *you* suggest? Stay here, hoping Bossmomma will protect us? We've had a reprieve, that's all. This new Morana wants us dead. She'll be back, and in force. Soon as you can walk, we need to get back to Murdo. Hopefully he's fixed his precious *Never Again*.'

I glance down at my splinted leg. 'Is that all?'

Colm opens his mouth, and shuts it again. Sky goes back to hunching over her knees. I squirm around until I'm as comfortable as I can be, and try to think. Okay, so Sky's opened Bossmomma's eyes to the cruel tricks Slayers have been playing on her clan, but being angry is one thing; facing up to Slayer firepower with spears as weapons is something else. I sigh and find myself listening to the weird throbbing sound again, which has never once let up.

'What the frag is that noise?' I say.

'Horns,' Sky mumbles. 'They blew them when Hekki went missing, to summon Reapers to go looking for her.'

'Why blow them now though?'

'How should I know?'

'Take a guess. You know these Reapers better than we do.'

She lifts her head and glares. 'If *I* was Bossmomma, and I'd been tricked into slaughtering loads of my clan's newborns for no good reason, I'd want vengeance. She's a warrior.'

'A summons to war then?'

Sky bares her teeth at me. 'Bound to be. I figure she'll gather all the warriors she can and hit that Slayer base.'

'Sounds good,' I say.

Colm shakes his head. 'It's *not* good.'

'Why not? You said yourself you wanted it shut down.'

'I *do*. But spears and axes against windjammers and pulse rifles? The Reapers won't stand a chance. They'll be slaughtered.'

'Don't be so sure,' I say. 'I've seen them fight.'

He doesn't answer, gets up and starts pacing around. Biting my tongue at the pain, I struggle up too and hobble over to sit beside Sky, sliding awkwardly down the clay wall. Almost risk putting an arm around her, but chicken out. At least she doesn't shrink away from me. We sit in silence, united in grief if nothing else. She's had her dream of saving Tarn ripped away; I've lost Rona.

'So what do we do?' she says, real hoarse. And leans closer, so her cold, bony shoulder rests against my arm.

I go for my arm around her. She doesn't seem to mind.

'Try to stay alive a bit longer,' I say. 'Failing that, take as many Slayers down with us as we can. How's that sound?'

Sky nods, then rests her head on my shoulder. 'Sounds good.'

Always the warrior, I knew she'd like that.

I pull her closer. She wriggles into me. My leg is killing me, but no way will I move, not wanting to disturb her. Sadly it's not long before a ladder thumps against the outside of the entrance. It creaks and shifts and a Reaper's painted face appears.

'We go now,' he orders, beckoning.

'Where?' Colm asks.

'Bossmomma,' the man says, as if this explains everything.

Being thrown over a Reaper's shoulder and carried down a rickety ladder was never going to be fun. With my broken leg it's torture. Luckily there's no climbing needed for Bossmomma's vast tree house. They stand us on a wooden platform, ropes rising from each corner, and haul us up using a block-and-tackle system. The platform rises to thump home and become a section of the floor. Sweet-smelling smoke stings my eyes and mutters

greet us. As we're helped off I look about. The hall is packed
with Reapers, all of them watching us. Some are pulling on long,
complicated-looking hookah things, and that's where all the
smoke comes from.

'Sit,' Bossmomma booms. 'Be welcome.'

A good start, I reckon. Nobody hisses *twains* at us anyway.

The Reaper leader sits cross-legged in front of one of the many
immense tree trunks that hold this place up. A carved wooden
canopy, painted silver and gold, sticks out over her. Hekki's
by her side, but I almost don't recognise her. She's dressed like
Bossmomma, beads and the rest hanging off her. Flanking both,
wearing the same ceremonial garb, are a dozen or so ancient Reaper
women, stick-thin and stony-faced. Behind these, the same number
of hard-faced warriors. Sky, Colm and me are made to sit on yak
furs in an open space left before them. I end up in the middle.

A long, stomach-churning silence follows.

We get thoroughly stared at. I try to look like I don't care.

Behind their time-hardened Reaper faces I glimpse them
wondering. And why not? Some will have seen Colm and me put
to death. Yet here we are alive, if not exactly kicking.

Bossmomma clears her throat and stands up, beads and skulls
rattling. She pulls off her fourhorn mask. No great improvement
on the looks front, but at least now she looks more like an old
woman and less like a devil. She hands it to Hekki, who puts it
carefully aside. Both fix bleak gazes on me. I can't help wishing
I had some leather to bite on, like when Sky set my leg.

'We've told our warriors and elders all you've told us,'
Bossmomma growls. 'But telling is one thing and seeing for
themselves is better. So it's good they can use their own eyes and

know I have spoken the truth – that you *are* alive, and not offered and dead like others would have us believe.'

Her watery eyes drift right, to look past my shoulder.

I follow her stare and there's the shadow-walker, spreadeagled against the chamber wall. His naked body is a mess of blood and gore, and his eyes have been put out. Spears stick out of his arms and legs, holding him upright. Won't be contradicting us then, I think savagely, until – unbelievably – I see he's still breathing.

Sky elbows me. I drag my eyes back to Bossmomma.

'Without a mask he wasn't so tough,' she says, sneering. 'He confessed. His shadow-talk was all lies, to control us.'

The other Reapers shift and mutter.

Hekki bares her teeth. 'Thanks to you, we are rid of him.'

'Good,' I say. 'We're, um, glad.'

I don't have to look to know my brother is wincing.

Bossmomma turns to face her clan elders. 'You are our oldest and wisest. With age comes the knowing of truths. I say if a man lies about one thing, he lies about many things. It is the way of men, and why we women lead. What do you say?'

They swap looks and nod. No kidding. They're all women.

'Slayer man here,' Bossmomma goes on, 'he had us believe twains like these are evil and would grow up to be monsters. But I see boys, not monsters! You heard my daughter – they spared her life. Why would monsters do that? It makes no sense.'

I try to look as least like a monster as I can.

Bossmomma spreads her arms wide to the elders.

'I say twains are *not* evil. Neither are our twain newborns, and never were! We've been made fools of. What do *you* say?'

Silence. One of the elders maybe blinks, but that's about it.

I start to feel dread. Finally the oldest-looking woman struggles to her feet. In a sagging face her bird-like eyes are still bright. She peers around at the other elders.

Her questioning look collects mainly nods. I breathe again.

'Bossmomma,' she says, her voice a dry rattle, 'our bodies are old and stiff, yet our minds still bend before the wind of truth. We see, we hear . . . and we believe you.'

Bossmomma grunts and looks satisfied.

Sky, Colm and me, we swap seriously relieved looks.

The Reapers take this last bit about seeing, hearing and believing and start chanting it loudly. Joy lights up their harsh faces. And why not? I've seen those sickening pots in the forest with the two sets of small bones in them. No more Reaper mothers will have to give up their babies. No wonder they're shouting about it.

Soon though the chanting changes. The Reapers at the back, her senior warriors at a guess, start calling for vengeance.

A second later most of the elders join them.

'Now we're talking!' I whisper. Sky nods, but Colm frowns.

Bossmomma lets them shout themselves hoarse, before raising a meaty fist and bellowing to be heard. She bares her teeth and points at the Slayer hanging from the wall. 'Men sent this trickster among us, and these men *will* pay!' she roars, eyes blazing. 'Our longspears will tear their flesh. We will stain the mountains red with their blood and the sky lizards will fight over their bodies. We will have our revenge. I am your Bossmomma and I swear this!'

More howls of approval and spear thumping.

Colm shakes his head. 'They don't know what they're up

against.' I think that's what he says. It's deafening in here.

At a nod from Bossmomma, Hekki holds her hands up and this quietens them down again. It's clear to me now that her say carries nearly as much weight as her mother's.

'There is much we don't yet fully understand,' Bossmomma booms. 'That will come with more telling, and can wait. But first we must give thanks . . .' She snaps her fingers loudly.

Scrawny Reaper kids scramble to hand out beakers, and wooden platters with sweet breads on them. One small brat staggers around the room, clutching a jug almost half as big as he is, and fills our beakers. Once everyone has a full beaker, Bossmomma intones something, none of which I follow. The elders chant whatever-she-said back at her while my long-empty stomach rumbles.

When their chanting stops, Bossmomma scoffs her bread and drains her beaker. Everybody follows her lead. The bread's almost pure salt, but no problem. The liquor, however, that's a killer. I choke it down and feel myself start to go blind.

The kids come back, clutching clay pots. Some are full of water, others with what looks like paint. White or blue or black.

'Take your shirts off,' Sky whispers.

'Do *what?*' I say.

'Strip!'

Next thing, she's tugging her stained and tattered jersey over her head. Her undershirt follows. And I can't help it – my eyes flick to the curve and swell of her breasts.

She sees, and I get scowled at like never before.

Hastily I struggle out of my jacket and pull my stinking shirt off.

'Now what?' Colm mutters, looking like a plucked chicken.

Sky's jaw clenches. 'You'll see.'

The Reaper kids with the water bowls step forward. They offer us rags and pumice stones. Sky thanks them, takes a stone and a rag and starts washing herself, wiping the old paint from her face. Colm and I trade shrugs. We give ourselves a quick scrub too.

Soon as we're done, the kids grab back the rags and stones and clear off. Hekki steps forward. The Reaper chanting, which has been going on the whole time, cuts off.

'Will you join us as clan brothers and sisters?' she asks.

Sky says yes, gives us the eye. We bleat our agreement too.

More saying and swearing follows. I yes my way through it, eyeing the bone-carved tools one kid has on his tray. They look fierce – a weird mix of chisel and sharp-toothed comb.

I'd ask Sky, only do I really want to know?

The boy holding the white paint pot hands it to Hekki. In turn, she hands it on to Sky and nods at me, with the hint of a grin. That throws me. I've only ever seen Reapers bare their teeth. Next thing I know, Sky's smearing white paint over my face. I only just get my eyes closed in time, and must pull one hell of a face because the Reapers roar with laughter.

But what goes around comes around. I get to do Sky's face, and give her a good splattering. I do Colm too, to save him from Sky's attentions. Next up is the eye stripe, done using two fingers dipped in grease mixed with black soot.

When it's my turn to do Sky's, I'm gentle and take more time than I need to. I'm about done with it when her green eyes open. Her hand flies up, finds mine and gives it a squeeze.

Just like that, I'm a lot less scared.

'The next bit hurts,' she warns.

'What *next* bit?'

'The bit that hurts. Whatever you do, don't cry out. Okay?'

I look at the bone tools, give my lip a worried chew, say nothing. And Sky's soon proved right – the next bit *does* hurt. The tools don't just look like chisels, they *are* chisels. Turns out – and Colm and I learn the hard way – this is how the Reapers do their swirling blue body tattoos. Only they're not tattoos like the little teardrop under Sky's left eye. Pin and ink isn't warrior enough. Instead they dip the bone-toothed tools in the blue muck, position them on us and smash them home using the wooden mallet. Each swirling blue line is a small trench in our skin, carved and filled. It fraggin' kills!

'What do they do to their enemies?' I gasp at Sky.

'Ask him, why don't you?' she grunts back, jerking her head towards the Slayer hanging off the wall.

The Reaper woman working on Sky turns her away from me. I grimace, horrified, seeing all the scrapes and bruises on her back, many so big I couldn't cover them with my spread hand. Some look fresh from the rockslide, others look older. Those must be from when she was held as a slave. Fists? Clubs? I shake my head. How Sky keeps going I don't know. I wish that she could heal as quick as me.

Thankfully the Reaper marks they give us are small. They don't take long and we all manage not to cry out.

I peer down at mine, swollen and still bleeding below my left collarbone. It's a spiral, the same as Colm's. Sky's is finer work, a delicate tracery of web. Which just goes to show, I think to myself, that these Reapers don't know her as well as I do.

Bossmomma's watched all this as keenly as the hungry sky lizards watched us back up at the place of the offer. Now we're all done, she gets up and lumbers forward. She has us display our marks to the room. There's lots of clapping and cheering.

I guess the three of us are Reapers of the white-face clan now.

35
THE WORM TURNS

A few hours and lots more telling later, the last Reaper elder has been lowered down on the platform and sent to spread Bossmomma's word around the gathered clans: that the shadow-walker has been found to be secretly spying for a rival tribe, that what he preached about twains being evil was a lie, and to tell every Reaper of fighting age to make ready for war.

I figure that's a fierce lot to swallow, when for years this shadow-walker has shouted the odds about how he and his shadow-magic were all that stood between the clans and destruction raining down. Hekki tells us we needn't worry. Bossmomma's mightiest warriors have gone with the elders, to stand behind them and scowl and finger their longspears. This way, Hekki says with a grin, her clanspeople will hear better and believe faster. And then there are the clan mothers, who've always hated the shadow-walker for pointing the finger of doom at their twain newborns. They won't argue; they'll be yelling to see his head on a pole.

'They'll believe what I tell 'em,' Bossmomma growls.

I twitch, and grind my teeth. The powerful get to shout the loudest. Do as I say, or die. It suits us now, but I hate it.

She goes to leave, so we all stand, Sky using a crutch, Colm giving me a helping hand. But she stops on the platform and peers at the two of us, almost sadly. 'Without your leg being splinted, there's no way could I tell you apart. You're so alike.'

Course we both shrug at the same time, as if to demonstrate.

Her stern mouth rearranges itself into something like a smile. 'Which of you must I thank for sparing my daughter's life?'

'Him,' Hekki says, pointing at me. 'Kyle.'

There's no point denying it, so I nod.

Bossmomma grunts. 'My daughter's eyes are strong indeed, to know which one of you she fought with. Kyle, before I leave I offer you a mother's thanks as well as a warrior's.'

Not knowing what to do or say, I make a little bow.

'My eyes are no stronger than yours, Bossmother,' Hekki says. 'I cut his face when we fought. Colm would still bear the scar. Only Kyle could heal it away so fast.' Behind her mother's back she shoots me a grim warning look.

Hoping surprise at her lie doesn't show on my face, I nod.

Bossmomma grunts as if satisfied. 'So you're the twain who's quick to heal. How long then before you can walk again?'

Truth is I've already sensed the first signs of healing – a creeping feeling, as if my leg bones are pulling themselves together. But these Reapers have only just decided we're not monsters. I don't want to shock them.

'A few more days.'

'He could probably walk on it already though,' Colm says.

I glare at him, shocked. Sky's head jerks around.

'Impress her,' Colm whispers.

He lets go of me and steps away. I'm forced to take my weight on my splinted leg or crumple to the floor. And it *hurts*, although nothing like as bad as it did before. Next thing I know, he's on his knees unwrapping the rag bindings holding my splints on.

'Ready?' he says, when he's nearly done.

'Yeah, well, we'll see won't we?' I say through my teeth.

Sky steps closer. I hang off her while Colm rips the splints off.

Dreading a snapping sound, I put weight on my leg again. More pain, enough to pull a grunt out of me, but my leg doesn't buckle. I even take a careful tottering step or three. Bossmomma looks stunned. Hekki mutters curses. Both saw how badly broken my leg was, with the bone ends sticking out.

'Impossible,' Bossmomma says.

'No. Neither is it evil,' Colm says quickly. 'Just different.'

The Reaper leader gives me a long, shrewd look.

'Or dangerous?'

'Depends whose side you're on,' Sky says.

Not something I'd have said, but Bossmomma lets out a huge rumbling laugh. 'A warrior's answer. I like that.' She nods. A Reaper working the ropes starts lowering her down. 'My daughter will look after you until I return.'

With that, she sinks out of sight.

I lower myself back to the floor to give my leg a rest, then look at Hekki. 'Why'd you say you cut me when we fought?'

'Didn't I?' She scowls. 'I thought I did.'

Next thing, she's snapping her fingers at one of the lurking Reaper brats. 'All this talk hurts my head, my new clan brothers and sister. This is a great day and we must celebrate it.'

The kid does the rounds again with the big liquor jug.

Me, I'd rather stick pins in my eyes than choke down more of the fierce Reaper hooch, but Hekki has a mad gleam in her eye. I've a feeling she won't take no for an answer.

'Revenge!' she shouts, and holds her beaker up.

'My sister Tarn, wherever she is,' Sky says, beaker raised, head tilted back like she's looking through the thatch above us.

'Freedom,' Colm says.

'Rona,' I say, a sob sneaking up on me.

We drink. Impressively, Hekki and Sky neck theirs with little more than pulled faces. When I try that, I end up wheezing and blinking tears away. Colm pours most of his down his front.

'Hekki,' he says, 'please listen. If your warriors attack that Slayer base it'll be a bloodbath. Your spears are no match for pulse rifles, composite armour and their flying machines. No matter how bravely you fight, you'll be slaughtered.'

She shrugs. 'We are not so easy slaughtered. And what would you have us do? Forget the Slayers have wronged us? Go back to living the way we were?' She spits into the dirt.

Colm goes to say something else. Sky beats him to it.

'Ignore him,' she snaps. 'I say we hit the base too. Give me a rifle, Hekki, and I'll be right beside you.'

The Reaper girl grins and snaps her fingers for another refill.

I groan, but say nothing. Nobody asks what I think.

A beaker or three later and the liquor tastes better, only I can't keep my eyes open. The sweet cloying smoke from the hookahs isn't helping either. I stretch out flat on my back.

Better down here. Can I stay here forever?

Blurry roof. Spreading branches holding up thatch. Spinning, spinning, spinning . . .

Somebody calls my name. They can go to hell. I need to sleep. Next thing I know, I'm soaking wet, spitting and spluttering. Sky is standing over me holding an empty leather bucket.

'What the hell?' I gasp, scrambling up.

Sky dumps the bucket. 'It's the only way I could wake you.'

I wipe my dripping face, only for my hand to come away grey and sticky with Reaper paint. About now I realise I'm standing without any pain, just some itching. I must be healed.

'How long have I been out?' I ask, appalled.

'A day and a half,' she says. 'We figured we'd let you sleep, and then we couldn't wake you. Colm reckons it's your nublood helping you heal faster. How's your leg feel?'

'Fine, I think.' I take some steps. 'Yeah, good.'

The two of us are alone in Bossmomma's tree house. Shadow-walker's gone too, just some bloody smears left on the wall.

Outside I hear shouting and wailing.

'Hey, where is everybody? And what's going on?'

Sky pulls a sour face. 'Your brother called it right. Bossmomma's Reapers attacked the Slayer spaceport. They got taken apart.'

I swallow. 'How bad?'

'Bad. They're still bringing the bodies down.'

The wailing outside. I limp to the window hole, even though I don't need to limp. In the distance, I glimpse Reaper warriors trailing into the village, bodies slung between them under poles, like we were. Closer, clumps of Reapers are gathered on their knees around what must be a son or daughter, father or mother.

Their desperate keening cuts through me.

'D'you think the Reapers will hand us over?'

Sky shakes her head impatiently, sending her dreads flying. 'No chance. Bossmomma's raging even more now. All she talks about is wringing Slayer necks. Look, we need you to do something.'

'We?' I say, suspiciously. 'And where's Colm?'

'Your brother's off with Bossmomma. He's got it all figured out.'

'Got *what* figured out?'

'How to beat the Slayers, what else?' She throws my old jacket at me. 'Where you're going, you'll be needing this.'

'Where am I going?' I say, pulling it on.

'Back to the *Never Again*,' she says. 'And you're taking Hekki.'

'What? Are you crazy?'

Sky doesn't so much as blink. 'Colm says Murdo's carrying crates of weapons. We need them, simple as that.'

'But the *Never Again* is our way out of here!' I splutter.

'It still can be. Think, Kyle. It's like Colm was saying – Morana's sister won't give up. She knows you're here. If they haven't hit us yet, it's only because they're light on numbers. Remember what we saw up there? It's a small garrison. Enough Slayers to defend the spaceport, not enough for offensive operations. That won't last. She'll have sent for reinforcements. Depending on how close their nearest base is, they could be here any time.'

'Right. We should get back to Murdo then.'

'Leaving Hekki and her Reapers to be slaughtered?'

I so nearly tell her that they're not my problem, but stop myself.

'And Murdo will just hand the guns over?' I say instead.

'We need them more than he does. Persuade him. If you don't, Hekki will. Look, Kyle, I'd go myself if I could. But I can't lead her back to the *Never Again*, and now your leg's healed you'll be three times as fast anyway. These Reapers didn't ask for what happened to them, no more than we did. The Slayers won't expect us to have guns. That'll give us an edge. Bring them, and Bossmomma swears she won't stop you if you still want out of the No-Zone.'

I hesitate. 'And you'd come with me?'

She grimaces. 'Come on, Hekki's waiting outside.'

At her nod, the Reaper guard lowers us down on the platform, ropes squealing through the pulleys. Hekki is there, back in her warrior gear, half a dozen other Reapers with her.

'What took you so long?' she snarls. 'Let's get moving.'

'Yeah, yeah, give us a second,' Sky says.

Wedging her crutch under her arm, she grabs my jacket with both hands and pulls me to her. I put my arms around her and hold her close, conscious of all the Reapers watching. Still, it's nice, even if I get no kiss and she pulls away seconds later.

She scowls and sticks her left hand out. We bump stumps.

'Haven't you forgotten something,' she says.

'What?' I say, suspiciously.

'Stay still.' She pulls a rag from her pouch, spits on it, and steps closer until we're eye to eye. And starts wiping my face.

Oh right. My Reaper face paint!

'I'll do it,' I protest, grabbing for the rag.

But she swats my hand and finishes the job, like I'm a child.

Hekki pretty much hauls me away now. Sky leans on her crutch, watching us.

'Make sure you come back,' she shouts.

I give her a wave. 'You make sure you're here when I do!'

36
BACK TO THE *NEVER AGAIN*

We're several hours on our way and my leg's holding up good, letting me set a fierce pace. I thought I'd struggle to keep up with Hekki's Reapers. If anything it's the other way around. When she calls a halt I hear mutters and get harsh looks from them.

That said, they're warriors. Harsh is what they do.

Ever since we passed out of their spirit lands they've been visibly edgy. Worried about running into other Reaper clans, I'm guessing. I haven't asked in case I get an answer I don't like. Hekki comes over. She squats down, pulls something from a pouch at her side and offers it to me. It's a munch-bug, shelled and salted.

'Thanks.' I force it down. Munch-bugs are well down my list of things to eat, but I'm hungry.

'They're best eaten still wriggling,' Hekki says.

'I'll take your word for it,' I say, watching how she moves, seeing how fresh she looks compared to her mates.

She frowns. 'What?'

I shrug. 'Your guys should quit smoking those hookahs. It's

not doing them any good. They look beat.'

Hekki glances at them, then back at me. 'You go too fast.'

'You kept up. How come?'

She goes to stand up. I grab her arm and stop her.

'How long have you known?' I ask.

'Let go of me,' she growls.

'You're nublood the same as me, aren't you?'

I let go. She takes a long, deep breath. 'How did you know?'

'That shoulder wound I gave you. It was bad, yet I see you a few days later and you're showing no sign of being hurt. What settled it was you lying about cutting my face. You wanted your mother to be *sure* it was me who spared you, the nublood who heals impossibly fast. If I'm not evil, neither are you, huh?'

Hekki's nostrils flare. She glances at her warriors, although I've been whispering so they can't have heard.

'Don't worry,' I say. 'I won't tell anyone. Only . . . how come you weren't left in the forest to die, like other twain newborns?'

Her head goes down.

'My mother is Bossmomma,' she says in a low voice. 'That doesn't mean she's a stranger to heartbreak. Three times she birthed twains and they were taken away. When my sister and I were born, she made a grim choice. I lived to be brought from the birthing shelter. My sister, Mikke, didn't.'

'I'm sorry,' I say. 'Shouldn't have asked.'

And I *am* sorry for her. For Bossmomma too, a mother forced by lies to make a terrible choice. But I also can't help feeling bitter and angry. Even out here in the No-Zone it's the same old story – one law for the grunts, another for their leaders.

'Never speak of this, Kyle,' Hekki says, fixing a brooding gaze back on me. 'It would bring great shame upon my mother when so many others lost both their newborns. Do you understand?'

'Sure.' I nod my head off.

She grunts and clears off back to her warriors.

A storm hits during the night, the rain and wind slowing us down. Later on it strengthens. Our firebrand torches fizzle out. Rushing clouds steal the moons. Hardly able to see our hands, let alone our way, we've no choice but to find shelter under some trees and wait it out. The Reapers have waterproof bag things made from stitched-together animal guts. They unroll these and wriggle into them so only their heads stick out. In the lightning flashes they look like big maggots. All I've got is my hooded jacket, so it's a miserable few hours for me. Fortunately the storm doesn't hang about. And now I see how tough these Reapers are. Only pureblood, but at Hekki's whistle they jump up, shake the water off themselves like hounds and hit the trail hard again. Sunrise sees us loping through a clammy, dripping landscape of wet and broken rock.

'How far?' Hekki asks, her breath misting.

I stop and peer towards the mist-shrouded top of this slope we're climbing. 'If it clears we'll see it from up there.'

An hour or so later the cloud has mostly lifted as we clamber up on to the col. Tree-lined river glitters a long way below us. As I stand there peering down, it's as if a cold hand clutches my guts. I can't see the *Never Again*. It's gone!

'Is that it?' Hekki says, pointing. 'Where the river bends?'

'Yeah, that's it all right,' I say, almost exploding with relief. Gom that I am – I was just looking in the wrong place.

Hekki and her warriors set off scrambling down. I call them

back and tell her that I'd better go on ahead. 'If my friends see Reapers coming they'll likely shoot first and ask questions later.'

She shakes her head. 'We go together then, just you and me.'

With that she sets off again down the rocky slope.

Cursing, I plunge after her. Her warriors follow, but at least they hang back. As we descend, our route happens to take us through the dip where we buried Rona. Already the copper-coloured grasses Colm and Fleur planted stand tall again, rustling in the breeze. You'd never know there was a grave here. I get a big lump in my throat and my eyes sting. It's heartbreaking, although I'm relieved to see no sign of the ground being disturbed by animals.

'What's the matter?' Hekki says.

I grit my teeth, and tell her how this is my mother's final resting place. 'Her name was Rona. She was a good woman.'

'A warrior like you?'

'A healer. She helped hurt and sick people.'

We're just the far side of the trees hiding the *Never Again*, stepping through scrub, when I hear metal clang on metal.

'That's close enough! Step out where I can see you!'

My heart races, but I know the voice.

'Fleur, it's me, Kyle.'

'Kyle!' I see movement in the shadow-swamped gloom under the trees. Moments later Fleur comes running towards us. She stops real fast as she sees Hekki and levels her pulse rifle.

I get in the way. 'Relax, Fleur. This is Hekki. She's a friend.'

Fleur glances past us. 'What the hell is this?'

I look over my shoulder. Hekki's warriors are watching from about fifty metres back, spears held ready, looking mean.

'Long story,' I say, hands spread in appeal. 'No need for the gun, they're on our side. I wouldn't have led them here otherwise.'

'What's going on?' Murdo calls from somewhere behind her.

Fleur shouts an explanation. There's a long, tense silence after that. I picture Murdo cursing and scrambling into his *Never Again*'s blaster turret. But in the end he calls out to Fleur to bring me in. 'Only Kyle. The Reapers stay where they are. Tell them if they take one step closer, I'll mow them down.'

Hekki glares at me.

'She comes too,' I say to Fleur.

Fleur scowls. 'Whatever. No weapons.'

Hekki hisses, clearly unhappy, and starts dumping them. Spear, blowpipe, knife, spike-thing, another knife, knotted cord.

It takes a while before she's done.

'That *all*?' I joke, impressed.

It isn't. Fleur gives Hekki a quick pat down and finds a vicious-looking bone needle hiding among her dreads.

'Oh yeah,' Hekki says, stony-faced.

'It's good to see you, Kyle,' Fleur says, fist out. But as we bump stumps, she gives me a searching look. 'Where's Colm?'

'He's fine. I'll tell you when we're all together.'

'Sounds good.' She weaves through the trees, guides us to an open hatch in the camo-shrouded lump that is the *Never Again*.

We're hardly off the ramp and inside when, with a flurry of beeps, Squint hurtles towards us and starts jumping up at me.

The look on poor Hekki's face . . . I fight back a laugh.

'Don't worry,' I tell her as I fend Squint off. 'He's just a work-bot. Like a big, friendly metal dog. He's pleased to see me, that's all.'

She mutters something and keeps her distance.

'Squint, standby mode,' I say. He hunkers down and settles.

Fleur sits cross-legged on a crate, rifle across her lap. Ness is at the front of the cargo-bay staring at Hekki like his eyes will pop. Murdo joins him now from the flight deck, a blaster in his hand. His gaze flicks from me to the Reaper girl. The hatch thumps closed behind us. He lowers the blaster, but doesn't holster it.

'What's with the Reapers, Kyle?'

Hekki bristles. 'We're here for the weapons.'

Shocked silence. Followed by everybody shouting at once.

It takes a while before I can get them all to shut up long enough for me to rattle through what's happened to Colm and me over the last few days. I leave out plenty, like Hekki turning out to be nublood too, and wrap up by telling them how the Reapers are our allies now, and facing an imminent Slayer attack.

'That's why we need the weapons.'

Murdo, Ness and Fleur look blown away. As soon as I draw breath, they're all firing questions. Dropship? Slayers? Here in the No-Zone? But Hekki's twitching and she's right. I can't risk the hours it will take to go through all this in detail.

'I'll tell you later,' I say. 'Right now, Slayer warjammers will be on their way, flying in reinforcements.'

The blood drains from Ness's face. 'That settles it. Murdo, we need to fire up the *Never Again* and get out of here.'

'What about Colm and Sky?' Fleur snaps at him.

'You give us the weapons,' Hekki growls.

I wave at them to cool it. 'So, Murdo, your jammer's fixed is it?' Three times I have to ask. He seems distracted.

'Another day or two and she'll fly,' he admits.

So that's a 'no' then. Good. I was counting on that.

I point at the two weapons crates.

'You like deals, don't you, Murdo? Well, we've got one for you. It's simple. We get the weapons and Squint to carry them. In return, Hekki's warriors will leave you be. It's hard to get stuff done while you're dodging spears.'

His face goes mottled. You'd think I'd asked for his liver. 'That's a threat not a deal. And those weapons are worth a fortune.'

'What's your neck worth?'

'No way. Forget it. I'll keep the weapons and take my chances.'

'We're not leaving without them,' Hekki says, real low.

'Oh yeah?' He shows her his blaster.

I'd kind of figured it'd go this way, so try a different angle.

'Gant said those weapons were for us, remember?'

I fish the necklace from my pocket, hold it up so the shine from the hold's glowtubes catches Gant's fake eye.

Murdo starts. 'Where'd you get that?'

'You told Gant we were making for the No-Zone. The Slayers caught her, made her talk and then killed her. That's how come Morana's sister got here so fast. She was already on our tail.'

Hekki stirs beside me. I frown at her to stay quiet.

Murdo takes the gemstone from me with a hand that's shaking, and stares at it for the longest time without saying anything.

'We'll put the guns to good use,' I say.

He looks through me. 'Fine. They're yours. Good luck to you.'

I glance at Hekki and she nods her approval.

'Okay. It's a deal. Thanks.'

Murdo grunts. 'You're *sure* you . . . saw a dropship?'

Surprised, I describe it – the scorched hull, its vertical climb-out. Then I ask him to come with us. 'Why not kill some Slayers, for Gant? We need all the fighters we can get.'

He gives himself a shake and grins, but it's clearly forced.

'Nah. I don't take sides.'

'You took sides when you fought for Gemini.'

'They paid me.'

'Not always they didn't.'

He shakes his head. 'Forget it, Kyle.'

'Don't suppose you'll wait for us?' I ask, my mouth dust-dry, conscious that not too long ago I was threatening him.

Murdo sneers. 'Soon as this jammer's fixed, I'm out of here.'

37
TRACKERS AND RATS

Murdo covers us from the blaster turret as we step off the lowered ramp and back outside. Squint trails along after us, the two weapons crates lashed securely to his back.

'Wish you'd stay and make sure he doesn't clear off,' I say.

Fleur shakes her head again. 'I'm coming with you. If Murdo decides he's out of here, I'd just end up shot in the back.'

I glance up at Murdo's face peering down at us from between the turret's blackened muzzles. 'He wouldn't.'

'Wouldn't he? I say we fight the Slayers first, then worry about getting out of here. Chances are we lose and die anyway.'

'That's a happy thought,' I say, watching as the loading ramp hisses up and locks closed behind us.

'Let's go,' Hekki says, hurrying back to her waiting warriors.

And so we turn our backs on the *Never Again* and start out on the long slog back the way we came. But we're not even halfway up our climb out of the valley when a Reaper hisses a warning. A heartbeat later we've all ducked into cover behind large boulders.

'What is it?' I whisper to Hekki.

'He says someone is following,' she whispers.

I peek over the rock, looking back the way we've come. Almost immediately I see two figures struggling up after us.

Amazed, I stand up. 'Changed your mind, huh?' I shout.

Murdo and Ness stop and pant up at us, their faces red and hot.

'Couldn't let you have all the fun, could I?' Murdo growls.

Fleur, Hekki and her warriors all emerge from their various hiding places as the two men climb up to our level.

'How far is this place we're headed?' Murdo says, pulling his daypack off. 'I hate this walking crap. It ain't natural.'

'A day's hike,' I tell him. 'It'll be good for you.'

'We should keep going,' Fleur says.

Murdo thrusts his pack at me, nearly knocking me off my feet.

'You heard her,' he says, and pushes past.

As he does, I glimpse a slender metal chain around his neck. Gant's false eye is tucked inside his shirt, next to his heart. And there was me thinking that Murdo didn't have a heart . . .

I grin, shoulder the pack and scramble up the slope after him.

More thunderstorms prowl the No-Zone's mountains, but we get lucky and they leave us alone. We slog along for the rest of that day, only with Ness and Murdo along we can't go anywhere near as quickly. Then Ness cramps up in the middle of the night. After that we let him ride on Squint for a while. To be fair to Murdo, he's fitter than he lets on and does his level best. Even so, the new dawn sees us with a good few klicks still to hike. Finally though, as the sun creeps ever higher, a familiar knife-edge ridge curves away ahead of us and I call a halt. This is where Colm and I first saw the smoke from Reaper firepits, although I don't see any now. A good sign? No sounds of fighting anyway. A few birds screech at each other, an unseen animal grunts down in the valley. That's about it.

'What are we waiting for?' Hekki asks me through a scowl.

By now I'm carrying Murdo's rifle too. I take a look through its scope. Leaves shimmer in a breeze. Nothing else moves.

'Wouldn't want to walk into a trap,' I say.

'Are we back in time?' Fleur asks.

But Hekki's had enough of my caution. Hands cupped together she lets out a shrill cry. In the distance, white-faced Reaper warriors rise up from cover beside the trail ahead and return her call. My stomach unclenches itself.

'We're in time. Come.' She lopes off towards them.

When we catch up with her she's listening intently to what one of these new warriors is saying. He's spitting words so fast I can't follow, but I see her Reaper face is worried.

'What's the deal?' Murdo asks her.

Hekki tells us Bossmomma's scouts have seen Slayers gathering at their base. 'And more windjammers flew in last night.'

'How many more?' I say.

The man hears me and holds up three fingers.

Murdo curses and spits. 'That's a shitload of Slayer troopers.'

'So?' Fleur says, showing us her teeth. 'More to kill.'

'Enough talk,' Hekki says. 'We go.'

More Reapers swarm up to us, staying well clear of Squint. Hekki has one of them carry Murdo's pack for me. She leads us along the ridgetop, then downslope through close-packed trees and giant sprawling ferns, until we pick up the start of one of the tunnel-like trails. Guarding this from above is another set of dried-out Reaper bodies, swinging in the breeze.

When Ness sees this he's so shocked he tumbles off Squint. Even Fleur looks a bit rattled.

'One way to say KEEP OUT,' she mutters.

The woods clinging to the slope start to thin out. Soon I spot my first tree house nestled among branches. Reaper kids appear and then dash on ahead of us, shrieking that we're back. Next thing, I see a distant Colm waving and beckoning. Sky's smaller figure limps into view beside him.

My heart leaps up into my throat and my legs decide they've still got some running left in them after all.

'You took your boggin' time,' Colm says, as I reach him. He's grinning as he says it and we bump stumps.

'Like to see you be faster,' I say.

I turn to Sky and am suddenly tongue-tied and awkward. She sighs, gives me a big mocking eye-roll and hugs me. Fiercely enough to make me forget Colm's watching and know that she means it. I hug her back as tightly. But when we pull apart I see pain and loss still lurking in her dark green eyes.

'You okay?' I ask her.

She shakes her head. 'Don't ask stupid questions. You?'

'Fine, I guess.' I shrug. 'Can't say I'm looking forward to taking on Morana's sister and her Slayer army though.'

'It'll be fine, I've got a plan,' Colm says.

I fake a moan. 'Oh great. Now I'm really scared.'

Sky frowns. 'Why'd you bring Murdo along? With him around, I'll have to be watching my back every second.'

'I didn't *bring* him,' I say. 'He's here because of Gant.'

Hekki, Murdo, Fleur and Ness arrive now. Colm greets them, seeming particularly delighted to see Ness.

Murdo and Sky swap tense glares, but that's all. For now.

'Hey, I don't suppose any of you goms remembered to bring my leg brace with you, did you?' she asks.

I cringe inside. How could I be so stupid? Only even as I despair, knowing there's no excuse good enough, I'm saved.

'In Kyle's pack, over there,' Fleur tells her. She points out the big Reaper who's carrying *her* pack.

'I'll get it,' I say quickly.

I rush over, grab the pack and rip it open.

And there it is, Sky's exo-leg. Oiled and shiny too, like somebody's given it some love. I could squeal, I'm so relieved.

I dart a pathetically grateful look at Fleur. She winks.

Behind me, Sky tells Colm loudly that she *knew* I wouldn't forget . . .

We're back in the Reapers' main hall as the light starts to leach out of the day. All the planning we can do is done. Bossmomma's warriors are in position, many armed with Gant's weapons. We've taught them how to use them, but I worry that when the fighting starts they'll drop the guns and reach for their blades.

All that's left is the waiting, always the worst bit.

Colm, our expert on Slayer tactics, is certain they'll hit us tonight. Outside it's drizzling rain from low dark clouds. Perfect cover. Rather than march here from their base, where Bossmomma's warriors could harry them every klick of the way, he reckons they'll do a night drop on to whatever open ground they can find near us. Using night-see goggles, they'll sneak up to launch a surprise attack an hour or so before the dawn, counting on us being asleep.

Only we won't be asleep – we'll be waiting for them.

Bossmomma stirs. She holds her charm up to the firelight, dangles it by its leather cord. 'Are you sure this will fool 'em?'

The charm looks like a carved and polished piece of tree resin with an eye symbol painted on it. But we know better now. Colm guessed. Ness opened one up and proved it.

'I'm sure,' Colm says, nodding.

He holds his battered cleverbox up so we can all see. It shows a cluster of bright dots at the centre. Most are green, a few are orange and there's a big red one. That's Bossmomma's charm.

She waves it around. The big red dot flickers.

That fake shadow-walker gave them out as wards against evil. Not every Reaper wore them, but most did. Inside each is a tracker. That's how those Slayers who took us from the offer place knew there was never a Reaper within five klicks of them.

Now we'll use these against them.

Hekki takes the charm and hangs it with the others. Most dangle from the beams, arranged so that on the cleverbox screen they give the impression of a Reaper gathering. The rest – and this is the bit I love – are tied to rats. I can't see them, but I hear them scuttling about in the shadows. This was Ness's idea, to make Colm's trick look more realistic. Most people still, a few shifting about.

Colm zooms in and points to some moving dots.

'Our little rat friends,' he says.

Bossmomma chuckles, low and hearty. 'Rats. Friends. Hah.'

With the coming of full darkness, drizzle turns to slamming-down rain. The clouds sink lower, clamping themselves to the treetops. It gets fierce chilly too. A ground mist rises to wind its way round the trunks of the trees. I feel real sorry for all the Reaper warriors hunkered down out there in their hiding places. Here in the hall not much is said. Bossmomma's gone off with Hekki to check on her warriors. Colm and Ness fool with the cleverbox. Murdo's flat on his back, sleeping maybe. Fleur sharpens her hunting knife, hissing a whetstone along the blade. I wish she'd give it a rest. The noise sets my teeth on edge.

Sky paces up and down, as if testing her leg brace is okay.

In the flickering firelight I check my pulse carbine yet again to give my shaking hands something to do. I worry about dying, being hurt so bad my nublood can't heal me. I imagine my life slipping away, and the cold, never-ending nothing of the long forever. Sky says if I *am* killed it's likely I won't know much about it. That would be good. But gom that I am, I picture some nasty slow deaths. A healer's son, I've got loads of material.

I end up sick to my stomach, wishing the Slayers would hurry up and attack us. I gaze at the dancing shadows and feel all hot and cold and shivery. In the end I say I need to take a piss, climb down the ladder and scuttle to the nearest bushes.

There I puke my guts up until I'm sore and ashamed.

When I drag myself back inside I get my wish. A breathless Hekki brings us the news we've been waiting for. Watchers on the ridges have seen dark shapes whining over them. These scattered what looked like massive leaves in their wake, which drifted down, with Slayer-sized seeds swinging beneath them.

Murdo gets up, yawns and stretches. 'Sounds like we're on.'

I've wanted to ask her this for ages and now might be my last chance. 'How come you're never scared?'

It's so dark, I sense more than see Sky raise her head.

'Who says I'm not scared?' she whispers.

I hesitate, enjoying her warm breath on my face, the feel of her fingers as they play with my hair.

'You don't look scared.'

'Says the man who can hardly see me.'

'Okay, but I can tell. And you don't sound scared.'

She sighs. 'To be scared, you have to care what happens to you. Guess I've forgotten how to.'

We're lying tangled up together in our firing pit, a hollow hacked into the topside of a branch that sticks out from one of the massive trees holding up the Reaper hall. From up here we overlook the hall's entrance platform. The window shutters are closed against the night chill, but a few slivers of light leak out. The smell of woodsmoke hangs in the air. Crafty, that. Look and sniff and picture a smouldering hearth with unsuspecting Reapers snoring and farting around it. That's what we want the Slayers to think.

See, Reapers don't fight at night. Everybody knows that.

When the Slayers storm the hall and find it empty, it's our job to cut them down when they come running back out. For now though we're just trying to stay warm and dry under my jacket, and are enjoying cuddling each other again.

'You should care what happens to you,' I say. 'I do.'

Sky rests her chin on my chest. 'Even after I ran out on you?'

I hesitate. 'Rona said she told you to go.'

For a while Sky doesn't answer. Then her chin digs in as she nods. 'She told me to get out while I still could.'

Not for the first time since we got here her body shudders against mine as she fights not to cough out loud. I run my fingers over her dreads, trying to comfort her. She pushes herself upright, pops something in her mouth and starts chewing on it.

The smell hits me. 'Sky, that's buzzweed!'

She lays her head back down on me. 'It's all I could get.'

'You don't want to chew that stuff. It'll mess —'

Her finger finds my lips and she shushes me. 'Not if you boil the stuff first. It makes it less nasty. Rona told me that too.'

I still don't like it, but a cough at the wrong time could soon get us both killed. And the weed does seem to be soothing her throat.

A gust of wind slams rain at us, tap-tapping at my jacket.

'Rona didn't tell you about me?' Sky says.

'What about you?' I say.

She takes a deep breath. Her fingers twine themselves tighter into my hair. 'Remember the day I dragged you to the captured Slayer transport and showed you where Tarn had tagged it? You pointed Ness's rad-sniffer at me and it went crazy.'

My mouth goes dry. 'I figured I wasn't using it right.'

Her fingers tighten in my hair. 'You were.'

I say nothing, wondering.

Sky lets out the breath she's been holding. Her voice is flat.

'See, after I hurt my leg, I couldn't work down the camp's pit. They stuck me in with the cripples and weaklings to run the crushing hammers. We mined and processed iron ore. Sometimes they'd ship stuff in from other mines if their hammers were down. I think my camp was the nearest to that Facility we destroyed and Rona reckoned I must've crushed a good few loads of darkblende in my time. Anyway, where we worked we got covered in dust. We wore rag masks. Still, we breathed loads of the stuff in. Not so bad for the nubloods, but for us pureblood scabs . . .'

She lets that hang in the air. And I'm no expert on rad poisoning, but I've heard horror stories. My brain pounds in my skull.

'How sick are you?' I croak.

'My lungs are bad, and it's started spreading to other bits of me. Rona told me I've maybe got a year or so.'

'Rona didn't know everything. Maybe she was wrong!'

Sky shushes me. 'Not so loud. Listen, Rona was amazing. She did everything she could, helped me manage the pain.'

And now I remember how often I'd run into Sky when I was visiting Rona. No wonder. They weren't just friends. All along Rona had been treating Sky behind my back.

'She should've told me!' I hiss, angrily. '*You* should.'

'I – we – didn't want you to worry. Even now I wish I hadn't told you. What good does it do, you knowing?'

Tears sting my eyes. I open my mouth, but close it again.

'Say something, Kyle.' She presses herself into me.

My arms are already around her, so I squeeze a bit harder.

'I'm crap with words.'

'So kiss me. I'm not dead yet, am I?'

We kiss. Shyly and awkwardly at first because it's been a long while, but soon more fiercely. I tease her head gently back and kiss her jaw, her neck, that little hollow at the base of her throat.

Sky tugs my shirt loose from my trousers and slides her cold hands up my sides, digging her nails in. I hesitate, then slide my hands down to the curve of her bottom and press her on to me.

Kyle! Sky!' My brother's whisper hisses out of the darkness.

We twitch and roll apart. I hear his boots scuffing their way along the branch towards us, very slowly and uncertainly.

'You want to kill him, or shall I?' Sky says.

He spots us, comes over and squats down. Water is running off his coat and I can just about make out his breath misting.

'The Slayers are on their way,' he tells us.

38
REVENGE SERVED COLD

'How long before the Slayers get here?' Sky whispers to Colm.

'Five minutes. Maybe ten. They're in no rush.'

I grab my brother's arm, wishing I could see his face more clearly. 'Be careful, Colm. Don't be a hero.'

He grunts like this is funny. 'I won't if you won't. Don't worry, Fleur's got my back.' He hesitates. 'Sky, you be careful too.'

'Will do.' Her voice is soft. 'Thanks, Colm.'

Doing it by touch, we take turns bumping stumps. And then my brother's off again, leaving only the mist of his breath behind.

'Here we go,' I say, sitting up and pulling my jacket on.

My voice seems to buzz in my head.

Sky shoves my pulse rifle at me, before rolling on to her belly and taking up her firing position. 'Don't waste time worrying, Kyle. Once the shooting starts it'll get easier. Trust me.'

I lie down beside her, rest the carbine's barrel on my rolled-up sleep bag and take a squint through its night-see scope. Only my heart's working so hard the green view jumps up and down.

I squeeze my eyes shut, take a breath and try to relax.

My thoughts flick back to the Facility raid. Back then I was a captive so didn't take part in any of the fighting. But one memory leads to another. Like how we saved Colm from dying by pumping some of my healing nublood into him.

Suddenly it's like a flare goes off in my head, lighting up stuff and making sense of it at last.

'Tarn!' I croak. 'Her blood. It would heal you, wouldn't it? Like mine healed Colm, back at the Facility.'

Sky's head lifts from her rifle's scope. 'I guess.'

'No, it would. For sure.'

'And a fat lot of good that does me now,' she says.

I could bite my tongue off. Tarn's gone, Wrath knows where, and won't be coming back. No wonder Sky was gutted at seeing the Slayer base and the dropship, the caged kids being shipped off-world. One look through her rifle's scope and she not only lost a sister, she saw her own death sentence.

I shiver just thinking about it. And now I hear a rustling sound.

Sky must hear it too. 'Here they come!' she hisses.

Through our carbines' night-see scopes we watch the Slayers advance through the Reaper camp. They move in stealthy little rushes, exactly like Gemini trained us to. Each fire-team takes turns to scuttle forward a few metres while another covers them. Their pulse rifles flick about, searching for threats. Squad leaders direct them with silent hand gestures. Their boots make almost no sound as the ground mist curls about their legs. With their rain-slick body armour and goggled faces they look like upright insects.

I was cold seconds ago, now I'm sweating.

They keep on coming. The nearest are soon right beneath us. I scan around, knowing Bossmomma's warriors are hiding out there in the darkness, but seeing none. I suddenly panic that I've not clicked my safety off. I think I did; I'm not sure though. My finger itches to curl itself round the trigger, but I stop myself. One twitch and I could fire too early and screw everything up.

'They packed them into those transports,' Sky whispers.

It's true. There are more Slayers than I'd have thought possible.

Normally the crude Reaper ladders are all drawn up at night, but we've left a few in place to tempt the Slayers. Turns out we didn't need to. Through my crosshairs I see a Slayer aim a stubby-looking weapon high in the air. It shoves back into his shoulder and I hear a slight *thunk*. Next thing, I glimpse a wire trailing down from a branch above the hall's entrance platform. The man leans his weight on the wire, then clips on to it. I watch, stunned, as holding lightly on with one hand, he rises into the air. There's no climbing involved. The wire just lifts him up silently and effortlessly until he's dangling level with the platform. I blink, amazed, as he swings on to the platform and unclips.

'See that?' I whisper to Sky.

'Off-world tech,' she whispers back.

More Slayer troopers clip on and rise up until at least thirty are crouched in the darkness on the platform, their weapons trained on the massive carved door. All over the camp the same is happening, with Slayers poised outside every tree house.

Sky leans over, puts her lips to my ear. 'Look!'

But I've already seen. Even in full body armour, her face hidden behind bulky night-see goggles, there's no mistaking Morana's sister. Where her soldiers sneaked and scuttled, she strides through the Reaper camp straight-backed, one arm in a black sling, head held high. A Slayer clips her on to the wire. And up she comes, stepping off light-footed on to the platform before the cable stops. After she unclips herself she takes her helmet off, tosses her mane of black hair and stands there, head cocked as if listening.

'What's the bitch waiting for?'

As Sky says this, the woman signals with a gloved hand.

Two Slayers attach something to the hall's bolted doors and dodge aside. There's a hiss, a flash and a bang. The same two Slayers haul the broken doors open, letting others charge inside. I hear the staccato thumps of rapid-fire and see the green flashes. It's as if a lightning storm prowls around inside the hall, a constant thumping and flickering as the unseen Slayers empty their pulse rifles into bundled-up sleepers. All through the camp it's the same story as Slayers kick their way past wicker shields, duck inside tree houses and go about their deadly business.

Soon though the shooting inside the hall falters and stops. A Slayer officer hurries back out, calls to the High Slayer. She ducks inside after him. They'll have discovered their victims are wood and straw and rags. Sky lets out a savage little chuckle.

'Wish I could see her face!'

And now, wherever Colm is, he shoves his thumb down.

Hell is unleashed. Ness's improvised rocket flares hiss up into the sky, to burst and chase the dark away with dazzling white light. There's a series of flashes and massive *whump, whump* sounds from inside the hall, like all Wrath's sky lizards flapping their leathery wings at once. The massive structure shudders. Flames and smoke erupt out of the open door. Spear-wielding Reaper warriors seem to boil up out of the misty ground below us. Others slide down ropes from their hiding places among the tree branches.

Sky opens fire on the Slayers still outside on the platform, sends vicious green flashes streaking downwards.

I quit gawping and jam my eye back to the carbine's scope. One Slayer is down. Others crouch, flames at their back, firing blindly in all directions.

I fix my crosshairs to one clawing her useless night-see goggles off. My first shot misses, but my second spins her and my third takes her square in the back. She flops down.

Sky yells at me to use rapid-fire.

I clamp my teeth and do as she says. Between us we spray hissing green rounds down at the platform. We scythe the rest of the Slayers down, cutting the legs from under them, slamming them into the wall, turning them into crumpled, smoking pieces of meat. They hardly get a shot off back at us. As we dump our empty mags and ram new ones home, the flares and skins full of liquor we bundled with the grenades do their work. The Reaper hall erupts in flame as the thatched roof catches fire. Even from up here I feel the heat licking at my face.

I kneel up and gaze around. Everywhere I look in the flickering light from the hall fire and the still-burning flares, I see fighting. Reapers swarm up ladders and hurl themselves at Slayers stumbling out from burning tree-house traps. Other Reapers drop on to them from above, or swing inside through windows.

The Slayers don't stand a chance.

A fierce joy courses through me and my lips peel themselves

back from my bared teeth. These bastard Slayers, with their swagger and their hard faces and their matt-black armour, they think they're so tough. Strutting around Wrath, keeping us all down.

'Yeah, kill 'em. Kill 'em all!' I roar, spit flying.

Reaper warriors swarm up the ladders below us, howling for blood. But even as they arrive on the platform an explosion tears through the wall their side of the burning door. The blast mows them down like a crop before a scythe. I just about have time to curse before Slayers pour out of the hole the explosion made and finish off the Reapers with bursts from their pulse rifles.

That shuts me up. I lie there, wide-eyed with disbelief.

Sky's more practical. She opens up on the Slayers again. Only now they're on to us. Straight away they return her fire, almost taking our heads off. Smaller branches fly to bits around us as pulse rounds rip through them, showering us with wet leaves and wood splinters. The big old limb we're lying on shudders.

Sky ducks and stays ducked.

I'm too stupid. I flinch but keep watching.

Morana's sister staggers from the blazing hall. The only Slayer not wearing a helmet, her hair is wild, her face red from burns or temper. Not strutting now, she crouches behind three of her troopers and screams orders into a hand-held comm. Loud thumps, whistles and shouts drag my eyes away to the open ground in the middle of the Reaper village. Every last bit of breath is ripped out of my lungs as I watch loads more Slayer fire-teams advancing out of the mist. Reinforcements, held back until now. Bossmomma's warriors see the threat behind them, turn and attack. But spears, knives and clubs are no match for pulse rifles in a straight fight, and these Slayers are battle-hardened killers. In a matter of seconds I see dozens of Reapers shot down. Their spears bounce off the Slayer's armour. And I taste bile, knowing we're screwed. How the frag did we think we could take Slayers on and win?

Everywhere I look I see Reaper warriors dying.

A branch shatters near my head, reminding me I'm still being shot at. I duck and look down to see one of the Slayers aiming a weird-looking gun up at us, the muzzle on it so fat I could stick my fist inside. I'm guessing this is what blew the hole in the wall. There's no time to warn Sky. I drop my rifle, grab her jacket and haul her back along the branch with me. There's a clang like metal pipes bashed together. Our branch takes a massive hit just behind us and a blistering wind lifts us and shoves us and dumps us on our arses further along it. Somehow I end up so I'm looking back. Our shallow firing pit is gone, nothing left but smoke, splinters and scorched heartwood. Glowing ash rains down.

Horrified, I turn to shove Sky towards the mighty trunk, hoping we might be able to climb behind it and take cover. But she's already up and scuttling away on her hands and knees.

Heart in mouth, I scramble after her.

The Slayer with the big gun thing is ahead of us both. There's another clang. Everything erupts in our faces, throwing Sky back into me, slamming us backwards. I flail about and find a handhold. Sky screams. Wood tears and splinters with a huge screech and the branch under us lurches sickeningly lower. Then sags lower again. Sky slides past me, back towards the guns of the waiting Slayers. I throw a hand out to her. She grabs it. For one despairing second we look each other in the eye.

Either the Slayer fires again, or the tree branch has simply taken too much punishment. It snaps clean off.

Falling. Stuff slashing at me. I hit something. Hard.

Dazed, I roll myself over and see rough-sawn planks. I'm stretched out full length on the platform, half buried in a mess of torn greenery. There's an agonised scream. Shouts. More shouts. Boots thumping. A pulse-rifle blast fizzes past over my head. I squirm around and glimpse Slayers scrambling over the fallen tree branch, firing as they come. Others lie crushed beneath it.

'Sky! Where are you?' I call out.

No answer.

I stare around wildly, but can't see her anywhere.

More rounds fizz past me. Desperately I try to tunnel deeper into the mess of broken tree and branches. Then, when I least expect it, I'm falling again. The wooden platform tips as the poles that hold it up give way under the impact and weight of the massive tree branch. Suddenly I'm sliding and flailing again. I slam into the rail around the edge, crunch through it. Tumble. Something else hard slams into me. This time it's the ground.

Branches, twigs and broken wood rain down on top of me. When this stops and I can look up again, I see the broken branch sitting there right over my head, so close I can touch it. It's still quivering, just propped up enough by snapped branches spreading off it to save me from being pulped.

And now a falling Slayer almost lands on me. Scares the crap out of me, and the fall doesn't do much for him. He kicks his legs and moans. My pulse carbine's gone. I figure I'll have his, except he won't let go. I pull harder. He's a big guy though and clings on.

I punch and kick him until he's persuaded.

Struggling clear of the tangled branches, I scuttle off into the darkness. Only there isn't much darkness to be had any more. The flares are long gone, but the hall and plenty of other tree huts are ablaze. Crackling flames leap skywards. All around me the sounds of battle and slaughter continue. The *tump-tump-tump* of pulse rifles on rapid-fire; the wild war cries of Reapers as they charge, only to choke off mid-howl; shouts and screams, wails and sobbing. Somehow I make it behind the nearest tree without being shot.

But I can't hide there for long. I imagine Sky scowling at me, all disappointed. Hissing the worst curses I know, I force my rubber legs to take me back into harm's way. To get to where the main fighting is I first have to get past the Slayers caught up in the wreckage of the collapsed platform. Some lie where they've fallen; others pick themselves up as I lurch towards them. One calls a warning and aims his rifle.

Too slow. I shoot him in the chest and he flies backwards, just as my borrowed pulse rifle clicks to empty. The forewarned Slayers take quick aim and open fire. Even though I duck, I'd be dead for sure if it weren't for the blur of metal and legs that is Squint. He hurtles out of the darkness, gets his big metal body in the way and takes several hits meant for me.

Next thing I know, Murdo and Fleur are beside me, blasting away until no Slayers are left standing.

Squint staggers, smoke pouring out of him, and collapses. I go to take a look at him, but Fleur grabs me.

'Where's Sky?'

'Somewhere under all this. I don't know.' I gesture helplessly at the jumble of broken wood and fallen tree branch.

'Over here!' Colm shouts.

My brother's on his knees off to our right. Blood streams down his face. He's pulling at something. Sky! One of her legs seems trapped under the fallen platform, but she's moving.

'We're coming!' I yell, shrill with relief.

Sky screams at us to leave her alone and fight the Slayers. I hesitate, torn. Pulse-rifle blasts whine overhead. A grenade goes off nearby. Its blast plucks at me.

'Well?' Fleur says, teeth bared.

'Sky's right,' I say. 'Let's go finish what we started.'

Murdo screws his face up and curses, but comes with us as we head back towards the sounds of battle. Fleur sees my pulse rifle's locked open and empty and tosses me a fresh magazine.

'Here. Make it count,' she says, grinning.

I've hardly slammed it home before more Slayers come at us.

Finally, all my combat training in the Deeps kicks in. Fleur and I work together as a fire-team. She shoots and covers me while I move. I keep Slayers' heads down while she moves. We're so much faster than the Slayers, we get right in among them. At this close range it's hard to miss. I glimpse Murdo doing his own thing off to our left and he's handy with that blaster of his.

Seconds later the Slayers are all dead or dying.

Grabbing a fresh mag off one of the bodies, I reload and clamber over the fallen tree branch – only to be stopped in my tracks. We're too late. The battle's over . . . and we've lost. The only Reapers I see are scattered on the ground. One lot of

Slayers are mopping up, treating each fallen body to a make-sure shot in the head. More advance towards us, led by that fraggin' Morana woman!

Dread squeezes my guts. I duck down.

Fleur has other ideas. A survivor of the ident camps and the horrors of the Facility, she snarls and opens rapid-fire on them. Knocks a good few down too before they start shooting back.

She's hit, and drops to her knees. 'Aw, shit. Kyle?'

I drag her back into cover. She lets out a pitiful moan.

Some primitive instinct possesses me now, launching me to my feet. Raging and cursing, I blaze away wildly at the Slayers, hoping only to take as many of them down with me as I can. And that's when I see the Reaper warriors loping silently out of the mist to fall on the advancing Slayers from behind. Way out in front, swinging a massive blood-drenched axe, is Bossmomma.

Seems she knew to keep some fighters in reserve too!

The Slayers turn to engage and get a few shots off that make Bossmomma stagger, but she butchers at least four with her axe before she goes down. And now her warriors crash in among them, stabbing, spearing and hacking. I quit firing, afraid I'll hit Reapers as more join the charge. There's hundreds of them, all howling at the top of their Reaper lungs. So many that the Slayers are a few black rocks swamped by a savage, tattooed sea.

I soon can't watch any more. It's all too nasty.

Afterwards, when the killing's done and the Reapers have started on the grisly business of hacking Slayer heads off to stick on spikes, Hekki brings us Morana's sister. The woman's face is burnt, her armour scuffed and battered. Blood oozes steadily out from between some of the plates, dark stains spreading across the dirt as she lies where she was dumped. Somehow she's still breathing.

Hekki, her painted warrior face spattered with Slayer blood, hands me back my old slug-thrower.

'This Slayer woman is yours for the killing.'

I check the gun. Still one round left.

'I'm – sorry for your loss.'

Bossmomma is dead. I helped carry her body back from where she'd fallen. A blaster shot had destroyed her throat.

'My mother died a warrior's death,' Hekki says. 'Her sorrows won't follow her through the long forever. Still . . . it's hard.'

'I know.' I sigh, thinking of Rona.

A Reaper calls out to Hekki. She grits her teeth at me and strides off, her warriors hurrying after her.

We're left looking down at the High Slayer.

Fleur's the first to say something, her voice raw. 'Make you a deal, Kyle. Finish fixing me up and I'll kill the bitch for you.'

I twitch guiltily and go back to dressing the shocking wound in her shoulder. She'll live, but I doubt even her nublood can save the arm. It's only hanging on by some burnt gristle.

'No more killing,' I say. 'Hasn't there been enough?'

'Kyle's right,' Sky says, surprising me.

I smile my thanks. More fool me.

'Why give her an easy death?' she says. 'Leave her to suffer.'

Colm, Sky, Murdo, Fleur and me, we're all hunkered down together out in the open, well away from the smouldering Reaper hall. All around us Reaper children wail while their elders fuss over the wounded and dying. Fragments of burnt straw and ash are still drifting down from the sky, like grey snow.

Poor Ness isn't with us. Colm says he stuck his head up when he shouldn't have. Other than losing him, Fleur's the worst hurt. Sky's got a bust wrist, but can't complain. Luckily it was her bad leg that was trapped, and the brace-thing saved it from being crushed again. A near miss from a Slayer grenade, Colm's wound is nothing serious, just a bleeder. As for Murdo, there's hardly a scratch on him. He's busy cleaning up my brother's forehead. I'll have to stitch it later and no way will he get away without a scar. A shame that. We'll be easy to tell apart in future.

I'm finishing tying off Fleur's bandage when Sky coughs and hands me her wad of boiled buzzweed.

'You don't need it?' I ask, my voice catching.

Sky shakes her head. 'I'll get by.'

I give it to Fleur. A few chews later, she sighs with relief.

Feeling suddenly drained, I sit back and wipe my bloody hands on my trousers. I close my eyes too, trying to shut out all the misery. But I can still hear the children sobbing for their dead mothers and fathers, the harsh crackle of the flames.

When will this end? I think to myself. *Will it ever end?*

That's when the dying Slayer woman whispers my name.

'Kyle.' It's like hearing dry leaves rustling in a breeze. 'Are you there? I want to tell you something.'

I open my eyes. 'Can't you just shut up and die?'

No such luck. She keeps whispering until I can't ignore her any more.

'Okay, okay, we're all listening,' I say.

She hisses that she'll only tell me, nobody else.

A blaster appears in Murdo's hand. He growls at me to shift

myself and he'll shut the woman up. 'Once and for all.'

I tell him to put the gun away and lean in. 'So tell me then.'

This is what Morana's sister has been waiting for. She catches me off-balance. One-handed, she pulls me down on top of her. Her head comes up, mouth gaping. I'm sure she's going for my throat, but it's only my ear she's after. She hisses into it.

Cursing, I break free at last. Her head thumps into the ground.

Murdo steps up with his blaster. No need. She's dead.

'What did she say?' Colm asks.

'Who cares?' Sky snarls.

'She wanted me to know her name. That's all,' I say, giving the body one last disgusted scowl.

'And?' Colm says.

'It dies with her,' I say. 'Why should she have the last word?'

39

BREAKING IN, BREAKING OUT

'Don't do this, Kyle,' Colm whispers. 'Stay. Fight with us.'

'That Slayer gear suits you,' I tell him.

Apart from the helmet in his hands, he's wearing the full matt-black uniform and body armour. We scavved loads after the battle, and managed to patch two undamaged outfits together. One for Murdo and one for my brother. They both look the part.

'Not funny,' he says. 'We need you. *I* need you.'

I shake my head. 'You don't *need* me.'

'This is madness!'

'As mad as you fighting on here?'

'Somebody has to fight on. If we don't, the Slayers win.'

He still looks confused and angry, even though we've been through this a million times already. But I won't get angry back at him. Not now. Not when this is the last time I'll ever see him.

'You're not making this any easier,' I say.

'Why should I? You'll end up dead, for nothing.'

'Nothing?' I make sure he sees my glance at Sky, where she's peering down at the Slayer space-port.

'That's not what I meant,' he says. 'And you know it.'

I bite my tongue. I just want to get on with this now before my nerve fails, or Colm talks me out of it.

Two months have gone by, long and harsh months full of suffering. We still argue about what might have been had Hekki led her surviving warriors up the mountain to attack the base. She'd called for it, only for her clan elders to urge caution. We paid the price soon afterwards. Even as they anointed Hekki their new Bossmomma, using the ash from her mother's still-smouldering funeral pyre, the Slayer transports hit us hard. Raining down bombs and incendiaries, they scattered us. Ever since that day, Hekki's led the clan in a return to their old hand-to-mouth nomadic life. On the move, with no tree houses, they're harder targets. We've been hiding out with them. The Slayers daren't come after us on foot, but they've based some warjammers here now. These soar the No-Zone's ridges day and night, hunting us from the air. It's been brutal.

But if the Slayers think they've won, they haven't.

We've gathered again and now we have a surprise for them.

Colm had it all worked out the moment he set eyes on the No-Zone. Remote. Mountainous. Surrounded by inaccessible jungle, with only one ridge route in and out for windjammers, controlled by wrecking chains. Plenty of water and fertile soil in the valleys for growing crops and grazing animals. A natural fortress. The perfect refuge for the shattered remains of the Gemini resistance to regroup in, and one day fight back from.

See, I'd given up on Gemini, but he hadn't.

It was the night after the battle when he first laid his vision out for us, all excited, eyes gleaming in the fireshine from old

Bossmomma's pyre. 'We take out the spaceport first. That's how the Slayers have been beating us, with off-world tech and weapons. Deny them that and we finally stand a chance. Then we seize control of those wrecking chains, so that only *our* windjammers –'

'Hang on. Who's this *we*?' I'd said. Fed up. Being awkward.

But he talked me round. Talked us all round.

A week or so after the bombing forced us to flee the camp, we'd stood and watched Murdo take off in his *Never Again*. With no steam winch he had to fire the set of self-launch rockets he'd been saving to get airborne again. Not willing to risk running into the Slayer warjammers patrolling the high ridges, he'd rigged the rockets so he could cut them early. His plan was to make for the gully we'd come in through, then relight the rockets to lift him over the arch and the wrecking cables. Hopefully he could then boost himself high enough to make it across the swamp. A long shot, even he said as much. Fleur, somehow still hanging on to her arm, went along with him. She's as crazy as Sky, that girl. I wasn't sure we'd ever see them again, but a month later they were back, having used Sky's trick of shadowing a Slayer transport in. By then we'd hacked out a place to set down on and camouflaged it. When the windjammer's ramp thumped down and those deadhead kids streamed out, hard-faced, armed to the teeth . . . that's when I started to believe. Maybe even to hope.

Turned out the deadheads stuck together after Gemini tore itself apart in the Deeps. Murdo tracked them down, and they'd follow Fleur to hell and back.

They brought grim news too though – of betrayal and slaughter out in the Barrenlands. Despite the doom moon coming and going without our capture, the Saviour's peace deal went ahead. The promised sanctuary was the trap we'd suspected. Slayer broadcasts are a looping boast of Gemini's total defeat.

Desperate times, but Colm said we can't let that stop us.

Hekki, out for revenge, didn't need too much convincing. Neither did Fleur's deadheads. Now, hidden among the rocks, our combined Reaper and deadhead army is waiting. Soon as Sky and me are out of the way, Colm will lead them in an attack to destroy the base and take over the No-Zone. He's with us now because he's my brother, and for a close-up recon.

Sky looks across at me. In the moonshine, I think I see her blink-and-you-miss-it smile.

'Is Colm still giving you a hard time?'

'It's what younger brothers do,' I say.

He scowls. 'You don't know you're older. And –'

Only now he swallows and has to look away quick. So do I.

Squint's here with us, hauling ammo boxes. He does a plaintive-sounding beep, scuttles over and nudges me. I squat down and give him one last hug for saving me. Weird thing is, since I welded him back together he hasn't deadlocked. Not once. Being shot up has somehow sorted him. Reaper kids have covered his body with cured hides and painted swirling blue warrior patterns all over him, so he looks different too. He's their big metal pet now.

Only a carry-bot when all's said and done, but I'll miss him.

'I can do this on my own,' Sky says, as I stand up.

'It's not *you* I'm worried about,' I say, forcing a smile. I glance up at the stars. 'Somebody's got to protect the people out there from you. Might as well be me. That's why I'm coming along.'

Murdo steps closer in his Slayer gear, a lopsided grin on his face. 'I still think I should come too. Bound to be opportunities out there for a man with all my skills.'

'You're too old,' I say. We've been through this already. His lived-in face could never pass for a nublood youth.

'No hard feelings, Murdo?' Sky says.

'Nah.' He shrugs. 'But cross me again and I'll kill you.'

She scowls at him.

'Enough talking. C'mon, Kyle, let's do this.'

I take a deep breath and nod. Colm curses, then startles me by giving me a hug I didn't expect. Ducking away before I can hug him back, he pulls on his helmet and snaps its visor down. Murdo winks and pulls his helmet on too. And I shiver as I go from standing with a brother and a friend to staring at Slayers. Even if these two hold fists out to be bumped.

Sky, with all her experience of sneaking into windjammer way stations from her freeriding days, leads us down. It's slow-going. We can't afford to trip wires, and even with Colm and Murdo in their Slayer get-up we don't want to run into a patrol. With so much to dread it's all I can do to stop my teeth from chattering. What's worse, I wonder, being caught or *not* being caught?

Eventually we're in among the alien ruins. In the moonshine, those still standing loom above us like impossible monsters. It's horribly creepy and I half expect something to pounce.

Ahead of us in the cleared area are four Slayer transports. The last one flew in the night before. Already unloaded, their crates are lined up. Among them is one cage.

Ready and waiting, we reckon, for a dropship to arrive.

It still blows my mind that the Slayers didn't shift this spaceport to a new location. But Colm called this. He grew up a Slayer so knows only too well how arrogant they are. They've got a good thing going on out here – why would they abandon it just because their tame Reapers rumbled the fake shadow-walker trick and lashed out? He reckons there's no way Morana's sister shared her sly reason for being in the No-Zone. All they probably know is that when she took her Slayer forces to sort out the Reapers, she never came back. Where we won a battle, they lost a firefight. They've shipped more troopers in and beefed up security. Otherwise it's business as usual down here.

For now anyway. Colm's attack will put an end to that.

As long as we don't screw up tonight.

What we're up to now is all Sky's idea, and Colm *hates* it. Not only will he lose me, but if we're caught it will frag any chance of their attack taking the base by surprise. Hekki's not fierce keen either. But Colm's my twin brother, and she owes me.

We're going after Tarn. Sky's not one for giving up either.

So here we are. And here – in the alien ruins – we split up. One last fist bump and we leave Colm shaking his head and crouched down in the cover of the ruins this side of the landing area. Sky and me, with Murdo as our fake Slayer escort, work our way around until we're on the far barracks side. My brother's too slight a Slayer for the next bit, so he lobs the stone to distract the guards. As soon as we hear its clatter, we scramble up and set off.

I pant like a dog. Doubts pound my head.

Will the guards be sufficiently distracted and assume we came from the dome? Will they see through Murdo's disguise? What if they call the dome to check what he has to say to them?

But somehow I keep putting one foot in front of the other.

I glance back at Murdo. He looks born to it, swaggering along behind us, Slayer-issue pulse rifle at the ready.

As we near the cage, a guard calls out a challenge.

Murdo answers in a bored voice. 'Hey, take it easy. I've got some more lousy twists for shipping out. Where do you want 'em?'

Sky and me, we stare at our feet.

'Where'd they come from?' the guard asks.

Murdo shrugs and makes up some crap for her about us doing cleaning in the dome that nobody else could stomach.

'Strange time of night to send 'em out.'

'You want me to take 'em back then? Your call.'

The Slayer grunts unhappily and has a short think. Next thing, she makes me jump by rasping her rifle's muzzle across the bars of the cage and snarling at the dark shapes huddled inside to 'get the hell away from the door'. Another guard flicks on a shiner mounted under his rifle's barrel. Dazzled and sleepy-looking kids blink into the light and drag themselves over to the far side.

He covers them. She unlocks the door and swings it open.

Murdo shoves Sky inside, hard enough to send her sprawling, and now his armoured hand beckons to me.

'What are you waiting for, twist? Get in there!'

Stiff-legged, every bit of me trembling, I lurch through the open door and into the cage. Murdo gives me a shove in the back to help me on my way, because that's what Slayers do.

The woman guard clangs the door shut behind me. The man kills his shiner. No search. Hardly a look. Because prisoners try to break out of cages, never *into* them.

Murdo stomps off into the darkness, making like he's returning to the dome. I watch him, but he doesn't look back.

And that's that. No looking back now for us neither . . .

The night drags by slowly. The next day too. We're given one small pot of water to fight over. Only there's no fighting. The kids in here look mean as hell, yet everybody gets a fair share. They've been stuck in this cage for days flying out to the No-Zone, so they're hollow-eyed and starving and doze most of the time. When we're asked which ident camp we're from we tell them Deepwater, a made-up name, and nobody questions it.

We curl up together and keep ourselves to ourselves. Sky gets some sleep, I think, but I'm too nervous. Another fat transport lands late in the day. It's quickly unloaded and more crates are lined up. Three more kids are thrown in with us.

'See that?' Sky whispers. 'They're in a hurry.'

I nod. It's not just the unloading: the Slayers seem restless.

'You think we'll go tonight?' I say.

'Looks like it. I could do with getting out of this cage.'

The new kids gawp dull-eyed at the alien ruins and must wonder why they've been brought here. I wish I could tell them, but we can't risk one panicking and shouting his gob off. Anyway, I figure they'll know soon enough.

As the sun sets, I take what may be my last look at Wrath.

The peaks around us remind me of my favourite mountains in the Barrenlands, where this mad journey of mine started. Floating round the peaks are loads of clouds. These catch the last of the dayshine and spin it into golden sheets lower down, with streaks of feathery red higher up. Sky lizards wheel and circle, shrieking at each other. Even as I watch, one by one they fold their wings and dive down out of sight. Could my queen lizard from the Deeps be among them? I'd like to think so. I keep watching until the sky turns purple higher up. If I look out of the side of my eyes, I can make out the first faint stars.

'Will you miss Colm?' Sky asks.

I look at her, surprised. 'Course. I miss him already.'

She scowls, but says nothing.

'Why wouldn't I?' I say. 'We got along. We worked on Squint together. And I could tell him stuff. I never had that when I was growing up. Told myself I wasn't jealous of other kids who had brothers or sisters, except I was. You know?'

'I know,' Sky says, in a small voice I've never heard before.

'You miss Tarn,' I say. 'She must miss you.'

Again she says nothing, but I feel her stiffen beside me.

'What's the matter? Are you okay?'

'I'm fine.' She sighs. 'You just don't know how lucky you are.'

'Me? You're joking?'

'You are,' she says. 'You found a brother *and* a friend.'

'When we find Tarn, you'll be friends again.'

Sky snorts. 'I don't think so.'

'Huh?' I say, or something clever and witty like that.

She takes a deep breath. 'Tarn hates me. She blames me for us ending up in the ident camp. And why not? It was my fault.'

I reach for her, but she's like wood in my arms.

'Oh, come on,' I whisper, confused. 'You told me what happened, remember? Your parents wouldn't hand you and your sister over, so the Slayers came and killed them and took you anyway. How can she think that's your fault?'

'Because I lied, Kyle. That's *not* what happened.'

As Sky says this, she lifts her head and looks me in the eye. I see how sad and drawn she looks, on the verge of tears even. Something I never thought I'd see.

'Whatever happened,' I say, 'you were only a child.'

'I was seven. I should've known better.'

Then, watching me the whole time from those green eyes of hers, Sky tells me why her sister hates her.

Two little ident sisters hidden by their parents. Nobody knowing there are two of them, because from birth their parents are careful to show one off at a time and keep the other hidden. As the girls get older, they take turns to play or work outside, to see and be seen. In the evenings, 'outside' girl would tell 'inside' girl everything she'd done. Because they looked so alike, nobody suspected. There were close calls, but it worked.

Only then came the awful day of the lambing, something neither girl had helped out at before. The girl who went first was so upset at having to drown newborn twin lambs she couldn't bring herself to warn her sister. The second sister was even more upset when she too was sent to drown another pair.

Sky shrugs. 'I just couldn't do it. Tried to, but I was weak. So I took a chance and hid them in a hole in a dead tree. Thought I could save the stupid little things. But I was seen by a kid called Marat. The bastard was smart enough to put three and three together. I begged him not to tell on me. He just laughed and dragged me back up the hill. Next thing, they're kicking in the door of our crappy little hut. They found Tarn and sent for the Slayers.'

By now I've a lump the size of a sky-lizard egg in my throat.

'My mistake ruined Tarn's life,' Sky says. She does a big shiver, like she's climbed out of a lake and is shaking water off.

Everything I think to say sounds dumb, so I say nothing. But I finally get my thick head around why Sky's in this cage. It's nothing to do with a last chance to heal herself. All along, Sky's just been trying to make amends for her childhood mistake. To save herself, she has to save Tarn. Something like that.

'Wanted to tell you, before –' She glances up.

I glance skyward too. 'Thanks. I guess.'

'Sorry you're here now?'

'No. I made my call and I'm glad I'm here. With you.'

I show her my left fist. She half-smiles and we bump stumps.

For a moment I'm tempted to be honest too and tell Sky why I'm really here. Only what good would that do? How often does anybody do anything for one reason alone?

Sure, I'm here because I am enough in love with Sky to risk my life trying to save hers. I'm also here because of what that Slayer woman, Morana's twin sister, wheezed into my ear.

I made that up about her telling me her name. She held off dying just so she could spit some last poison at me – that no matter how hard I fought or how far I ran, one day I'd be sold out again; that the Slayers would get me in the end.

And then there's the reason even Colm couldn't fault. If I'm gone from Wrath, I can't be used again. Without my nublood to save him, the Saviour's doomed. It's the one blow I can strike against his Slayer army that counts. If they end up squabbling over who'll succeed him, it might buy Gemini time to rebuild. Course, I could just blow my head off with the last round from my old slug-thrower, but . . . nah.

Or — and this nags at me — am I just running away?

Again.

Sky's cold hand takes mine and pulls me out of my thoughts. Next thing, there's a low moaning sound and a series of blindingly bright arc lights flick-flicker on around the landing area. Beside us startled kids suck air and struggle to their feet.

'Look,' Sky says. She points upwards.

High in the night sky a new star blossoms, red and angry-looking as it plunges down towards us. It's the dropship, tearing its fiery way through Wrath's upper atmosphere. Coming to take us away as cargo inside its metal belly, to who-knows-where.

'You know what?' I say. 'I've changed my mind.'

Sky makes a disgusted noise. 'Bit late for that, you big gom.'

Don't miss the final adventure,

COMING IN 2018

THE

LONG

FOREVER